A MESSAGE FROM THE STARS

Only the palest starshine filtered into Coconino's house when he struggled up from his sleeping mat. He climbed out onto the ledge in front of his door and rose stiffly to his feet.

Coconino sighed. Once Mother Earth had spoken to him with clarity, but lately it had become so hard to hear her voice. He stood at the lip of the ledge, looking up at the stars. What was it about stars? . . . He had dreamed . . . oh, yes, the stars had spoken to the Mother Earth, saying that they were coming . . .

With another great sigh, he dropped his head and rolled it around, feeling the stiffness in his neck. So they were coming again. It was inevitable, but it still created a strange aching in his chest. He had made such a terrible sacrifice to stop them the first time. He hoped the Mother Earth had a different defender to call on this time . . .

By Catherine Wells
Published by Ballantine Books:

THE EARTH IS ALL THAT LASTS
CHILDREN OF THE EARTH
THE EARTH SAVER

THE
EARTH
SAVER

Catherine Wells

A Del Rey Book

BALLANTINE BOOKS • NEW YORK

A Del Rey Book
Published by Ballantine Books

Copyright © 1993 by Catherine Wells Dimenstein

All rights reserved under International and Pan-American Copyright Conventions. Published in the United States of America by Ballantine Books, a division of Random House, Inc., New York, and simultaneously in Canada by Random House of Canada Limited, Toronto.

Library of Congress Catalog Card Number: 93-90186

ISBN 0-345-37464-9

Manufactured in the United States of America

First Edition: October 1993

PROLOGUE

The Legend of She Who Saves
And in the fullness of time the Mother Earth called to She
Who Saves, bidding her rest. So She Who Saves went down
to the Well, that place wherein the People had cast the fire-
shooters of the Others. There she descended to the bosom of
the Mother Earth and walked among the People no more.

So said the Legend of She Who Saves, of the hard and uncompromising woman who led the People for twenty-five years
after Coconino disappeared. But there were other stories whispered about her: that she and Coconino were lovers, that she
kept faith not with the Mother Earth but with her own grief, that
she descended into the Well to hasten the time when she and
Coconino would be together again.

They had lived some five hundred years after the Evacuation,
the mass withdrawal of humankind from a planet turned hostile,
a world intent on driving its careless, greedy offspring to
newer, more patient hosts. Only the People remained, inhabiting the ancient pueblo ruins of their ancestors; only the People,
and the Men-on-the-Mountain, who stayed in their lofty obser-
vatory to record the Earth's demise.

But the Earth did not die. Neither did she take her final vengeance on those who chose to stay. Instead, she forgave her
children. She spread her bounty once more before them and
offered them another chance to discover their place in the rhythm
and balance of her existence. The People heard her voice and
responded. Even the Men-on-the-Mountain had learned from
their mistakes and were more careful. Both groups survived.

Then the day came that the Others, the descendants of her
outcast children, came back from the stars to see how their

1

mother planet fared. They built a camp and sought out their cousins, *"but their touch was an abomination to the Mother Earth."*

So the Mother Earth raised up Coconino from among the People, and he conspired with the evil Lujan to send a message to the home world of the Others, saying that the Earth was filled with sickness, a place to be avoided. Then Coconino cast the Sky Ship of the Others from its orbit, marooning its crew, protecting the Mother Earth from reinfestation by thoughtless humans. But in so doing, he was caught in a time warp and flung generations into the future, to walk among the People in a later age.

The Others were wrathful and sought their vengeance on the People. Then She Who Saves intervened, leading the People to a new home that the Others agreed not to seek. There she kept the People safe from that day, until the day she departed from them.

It was a singular day indeed.

CHAPTER ONE

It was a fine tradition that he had brought back to the People, that a father should lay his child to rest in the Mother Earth. But as he trudged along the trail into the Canyon of the Speckled Quail, carrying his honored burden, Coconino felt that he had laid far too many such bundles to rest over the years. In his youth he had carried his wife, Hummingbird, to her rest, and in her time Ironwood Blossom as well. Then there had been the children: Peace, and Leaping Frog, and his stepchild, Leaf Song. Later he had shared the burdens of his son-in-law as they laid to rest all three of the young man's children, taken by fever. Too many tiny bundles; too many large ones.

But this bundle he carried now seemed the heaviest he had ever borne.

Behind him and around him the People chanted and danced the Dance of Grief. On either side rose the dusty canyon walls, and the sun shone coldly on the rocky ground. Soon farmers would come back to this canyon to plant their fields along the dry wash that would swell with spring runoff and water their crops. Then they would smile at one another and say, "It will be a good season for corn, for Teresa made fine *pika* bread, and now she watches over this canyon."

Teresa!

It was the child who had claimed Hummingbird's life, then given it back in her own. In her voice, in her face, in her unceasing joy, Teresa had been Hummingbird's reflection. She had been both trial and solace to Coconino, this daughter of his, and though he loved all his children, there was always something special about Teresa. When her spirit slipped away, it was as though a light had gone out in the world.

Coconino shifted the weight in his arms. It was a hard thing

3

to surrender a child to the bosom of the Mother Earth, but it was harder, he thought, to know that that child had children of her own. This was no babe he carried, no young girl, but a woman of twenty-eight summers. "She had a good life," the People said, "a full life: four children and a good husband." A husband, yes, whose duty this ought to have been. But Sees in the Distance was not there, and so the duty fell again to Coconino.

It is as well for me, Coconino thought as he looked down at her blanket-draped form. How could I bear to let another lay my Teresa to rest? Even her husband. I am afraid I would never really believe she was gone. It was that way once before: Though my youth has fled and my children's youth wanes, yet I have never been able to believe that my Witch Woman is dead. I did not lay her to rest.

Near his feet, a banded lizard scurried across the path, then paused to look back at him with mocking eye. *No, Coconino, you did not,* it chided him. *She did that herself.*

She was that stubborn, Coconino thought ruefully. And at times like this, when my heart aches so and I wonder if perhaps I have lived too long, I think I understand how she could have made such a choice. Yet I cannot believe what the legends say. I cannot believe that my Witch Woman surrendered her own life.

Surrendered? the lizard called after him as Coconino turned from the trail and began to search the canyon walls for an appropriate niche in which to lay his daughter. *No, I would not say that she surrendered it. I would not use the word "surrendered" at all.*

A clay pot went sailing across the room and smashed into the far wall. Swan gasped, startled as much by the waste as by the noise. A perfectly good clay pot, no doubt! She shook her head. The old woman was in another of her moods.

Phoenix sat brooding in a corner, long arms clasped around her knees, glaring at nothing. At fifty-five, she bore her years better than did most women of the People; though her face was lined and her hair more gray than black, her body was as hard and lean as ever. The pot had been well aimed and powerfully thrown. Swan threw her a reproachful glance, then gestured with the bowl in her hands. "I brought you some stew," she said conversationally, as though no outburst had occurred. "Good rabbit stew, with lots of sotol and onion and chili."

"I can cook my own meal!" Phoenix snapped. "I'm not an invalid!"

"You can, but you don't," Swan replied firmly. "And if you will not bother to take care of yourself, then you must suffer others to do it. Now, here." She plunked the bowl down on the crumbling adobe floor. "Eat or I will send Michael over to feed you with a spoon."

"I'd like to see him try," the older woman growled, but her tone was not truly angry. Only grumpy, Swan thought. *You are just a grumpy old woman whose moods are overindulged. But then, you are She Who Saves, and as Michael says, you have earned the right to be grumpy now and again.*

From outside came the shouts of children playing games along the steep, narrow path that connected the dwellings on this butte. It reminded Swan that her own children were waiting for her, though with Michael there, it was unlikely that they would miss her until it was time to eat. She turned back toward the low door. "Don't wait until the stew grows cold," she admonished as she pushed the hide covering aside and began to crawl out. "And if I don't smell food cooking in your house by evening, I will come back with both my babies and let them play on the floor here until I have cooked your dinner."

She heard another pot crash behind her.

"Good day, She Who Saves," Swan called back.

Inside her house Phoenix sat seething, her teeth gritted, her bony fists clenched. *My name is Phoenix!* she raged inwardly. *Why won't anyone call me Phoenix anymore?*

From the dirt floor came a voiceless reply. *I call you Phoenix.*

You would, Phoenix thought. *Now, you would.*

It seemed to her that the floor laughed.

For twenty-five years Phoenix had longed to hear the voice of the Mother Earth. It had been so clear to Coconino, to Nina, to Nakha-a, to others of the People. But Phoenix was not of the People; she had been born on the Mountain and had come here only when she was thirty and divorced and dispirited. The mysticism of the People had earned first her scorn and then her acceptance and lastly her envy. Finally, in the tumult of her parting from the Mountain, she had declared herself a Child of the Mother Earth.

Yet she had never known the communion that others took for granted. How often had she prayed for that word of affirmation, that assurance that the course she chose was the will of the Mother Earth! When she moved the tribe north to this colder valley, when she insisted on staying even though Nina and her followers had left—if only she could have heard the Mother Earth's voice then and known that she was doing the right thing. But though she listened to the call of birds and the gurgle of streams and the sighing of wind, never had she heard what others called the Voice of the Mother Earth.

Until now.

Now! Phoenix cast aside the fur from her shoulders and came to her feet, crouched in the low-ceilinged room. Now, when it was clear that the village would survive. Now that Michael had come, now that Sky Dancer had gone. Now that the path ahead seemed smooth and simple, *now* the Mother Earth had decided to speak to her. And what did she say?

Rest, child, the voice told her. *Your labor is over. It is time for you to come to my bosom. It is time to die.*

Tana had learned after so many years to screen out the background noise in Doc's transmissions, so his thought came clearly to her as they walked down the corridor of the Winthrop Institute for Dimensional Physics on Argo. *They come,* it said quite clearly in her mind. *I smell.* And in that way Montana Louise Winthrop-Rutgers knew that her board of directors was waiting for her.

She always preferred to have them waiting when she entered the holo-conference room, not because of the psychological implications of power it connoted but because it was one of the few areas of her life where Tana could indulge her natural impatience. The walk of 123 paces from her office to the conference room—and she knew, for she had counted those steps often enough—took her a full four minutes to accomplish. Her directors could jolly well be waiting for her when she arrived.

They turned a corner, she and her guardian Dalmatian, and there stood Delhi outside the conference room, waiting impatiently for her. Delhi Striker was also of Winthrop descent, though from a different branch of the family conjoined some three generations back. To look at the two women, however, no one would guess they were related. Delhi was tiny and dark, reflecting the strong bloodline of her mother's family, from whose ancient Terran home she had received her name. Tana, on the other hand, had inherited strong Scandinavian genes: honey-blond hair, fair skin, and a pair of gray eyes that could be as silent or as savage as a winter sky.

Delhi said nothing, but Tana could read her thoughts in her

angry dark eyes. We're waiting, they said. You are keeping us waiting.

Tana only smiled. Once she would have flared and sparked at such an attitude; now she could not afford the luxury of that emotional response. So she smiled as she approached her elder cousin, knowing that she had no need to defend her lack of haste, no reason to apologize to her directors for asking them to establish their holographic connections three full minutes before she arrived in the conference room. She could ask them to do it ten minutes ahead, or fifteen if she so desired. After all, she was the CEO of the Institute for Dimensional Physics, the oldest and most prestigious enterprise of the powerful Winthrop Dynasty.

"Conti is absent," Delhi told her, disapproval evident in her voice—but of whom? Tana wondered. Conti or me? Not that it matters.

"I'm sure we can conduct business without him," Tana replied amicably. "Shall we?"

The tiny woman turned and walked briskly into the room, a striking figure in her tailored navy-blue suit. It became her, this new fashion of skirts and jackets for women; at fifty-four, Delhi wore it better than many a young woman of twenty. But her hairstyle was a throwback to another century: long dark tresses were pulled back and wound in a knot at the nape of her neck. It did nothing to soften the stern expression of her face.

Angry, Doc thought at her as Tana paused in the doorway.

Yes, I know, Tana thought back. *She thinks this is her yard.*

Doc understood that. Though he had been Tana's companion since his birth eight years earlier, living in the house and rarely leaving her side, still the instinct was strong in the male Dalmatian to defend his territory for himself and his "pack." It was one of the reasons Tana needed him.

Now Tana made her own deliberate entrance. On three different planets directors in their holographic studios watched their CEO move confidently into the room, a well-groomed woman of thirty-seven with her hair cut in the latest style: short and bristling on the left side of her head, gathered in a long, flowing tail on the right. She did not, like many executives, project her image at one point two times its normal size; she had never felt the need for that psychological gimmick. Her own five feet, six inches seemed adequate to her. She dressed in the flowing garb that was traditional for the business community on Argo, but they were not the heavy, drapery-type robes of her ancestors that tended to mask the body. Rather, they were soft, supple robes of lightweight fabric that clung to her slender form, accenting every grace with which nature had endowed her. She had chosen shades of rose for this meeting to bring out the color in her complexion. As she approached the head of the conference table, Tana knew that she radiated health and high spirits. Had they not already known, no director would ever suspect that her joints were ravaged by the virus known as Gamaean palsy, making her stamina as fleeting as a rainbow.

Push my chair, Tana directed Doc, and the dog nudged her heavy chair away from the conference table for her. It moved easily, floating slightly above a superconductive mat so that it could respond to her slightest movement. Tana seated herself gracefully, a deliberate gesture honed by much practice, and surveyed her board with a level gaze.

They were Winthrops all, and here and there one could detect a horsey jaw that bespoke their ancestor Jacqueline Winthrop or a head of waving hair and a dazzling smile that witnessed to Clayton. The evidence was in their names, too: Marseille, Juneau, Dublin, Chattanooga. In the tradition begun over two hundred years before, each recalled a place on old Earth.

It was precisely because they were Winthrops that they could wield any power here, and only because every Winthrop company had a board of directors consisting of Winthrop descendants, that the Winthrop Dynasty existed as one of the six largest conglomerates in the civilized galaxy. In the early years of the Troaxian takeover, clever Zachery Zleboton had organized the holdings of his new wife and brother-in-law into a private, family-owned company. Because there was no public stock available, the Troaxian Cartel was unable to accomplish a hostile takeover of their extensive holdings, and because the true power in Troax was the cartel and not the government, they dared not break the corporate ethics of ownership on which their own legitimacy was based. The Troaxian government could invade Argo and Darius IV and other planets of the Centrallies, but neither they nor the cartel could breach the indomitable Winthrop-Zleboton family coalition.

Through the forty years of the Occupation the Troaxians tried unsuccessfully to force the Winthrops to surrender their holdings. With the collapse of the Troaxian empire, the backlash against the corporate structure of publicly owned companies again favored the Winthrop family's posture. While the new government passed strict laws to contain the power of corporations that sold their stock on the open market, those businesses which, like the Winthrops, were organized as family proprietorships were not restricted in size or in extent of commerce. They became the pillars of the new economy, establishing the model on which new businesses were established.

Doc settled himself at Tana's feet, his warm muzzle resting comfortably on her toes. He had long since ceased to be disconcerted by the fact that in this room he could see images of people he could not smell. He could smell the warp field that allowed the images to be relayed across light-years instantaneously, unrestricted by the time lags their ancestors had taken for granted, and so he gave a prolonged grunt of contentment and drifted off toward sleep.

"Cousins," Tana began. "By the magic of technology perfected in this place, we are once again gathered to discuss the business of the IDP. But let us never forget that that technology is only a means to our end. We do not create technology for technology's sake; we do not do it to turn a profit for the Winthrop Dynasty. We do it because two hundred years ago Chelsea and Cincinnati Winthrop and Zachery Zleboton wanted to know what happened to their parents. We do it, ladies and gentlemen, because we seek a safe and speedy way to return to Earth."

There were some who shifted uncomfortably in their chairs, for they did not like to be reminded of the altruistic but illegal nature of their mission. It was fine to extend the pursuit of dimensional physics for the sake of knowledge, to increase the accuracy of warp transportation so that vast distances could be crossed without aid of a spacecraft—so long as they did not lose money doing it. And if Tana wanted to think of Earth as the ultimate goal, that was fine, too, provided she could get Earth off the Transportation Guild's blacklist. At this point, however, Earth was still listed as a plague planet. Traffic with it was against the law.

But there were others who glowed with excitement at the notion. There was always a smattering of diehard Terraphiles among the Winthrop clan. When Tana had taken up the reigns of power at the IDP nine years earlier, they had been fascinated by what she revealed to them: a family history begun by Chelsea Winthrop during the Troaxian War, an accounting of the efforts to uncover the truth about the *Homeward Bound*, the absolute conviction that survivors could remain on a safe and habitable Earth. More conservative members of the board had been shocked by the illegal tactics used by their ancestors to obtain information, the shameless manipulation of the legal system to obtain Oswald Dillon's fortune, even as the Troaxians bore down on the Centrallies. To most, however—Tana could count five at this table—it had been evidence of the Winthrop-Zleboton industry and cunning, of their ability to make government and jurisprudence serve the ethics they were meant to serve. Suddenly their ancestors were not stodgy old family autocrats but young, daring, *driven* individuals who sacrificed much for the sacred bond of family.

The secret had been lost, buried during the war and ensuing occupation, closeted during the Restoration, passing out of mind as the IDP became notorious for its research and the more practical applications of its discoveries. It was Tana's father who had found the old records, but he could not believe his board of directors would espouse their content or the age-old mission of the IDP. For too many years the institute had been run as a research and development operation, concerned with generating new patents that would bring income and prestige to the Winthrop Dynasty. He did not attempt to enlighten his board.

To his daughter he left the choice, as he left the institute when he retired. For Tana, there had been no choice. Other arms of the Winthrop Dynasty made money; other arms generated prestige by their work in improving the quality of life throughout the colonized planets. The IDP had been established for one purpose, and to one purpose would it return.

With twinkling gray eyes she surveyed the faces of her directors, subordinating her excitement to her need to convey her authority. Unlike the heads of other companies, who owned their businesses and ruled as autocrats, Tana was subject to the will of the Dynasty as represented in this board of directors. Every energy she had now must be focused on projecting her confidence and charisma to retain control of these, her regulators. "Last week," she began, "several of you approached me about rumors surrounding the development of P-TUP—point-to-unknown-point warp transmission. As you know, I established that branch of research shortly after I joined the institute, and since that time our esteemed Dr. Rutgers has acquired no less than three VanKurtz Prizes for his work in the field. But it seems that there is word circulating that he has achieved a major breakthrough which will put P-TUP on our doorstep tomorrow."

And I know exactly who the source of the rumor is, Tana thought. But that is a moot point.

"Dr. Rutgers does not make a habit," she continued, "of publishing—or even announcing—until he has thoroughly tested. Is there something major in the wind? Yes. Dr. Rutgers is very excited about a theory he has, which, if proven correct, will make P-TUP a reality within the next five years." There was an audible gasp from her audience. At the other end of the long conference table Delhi started in her chair, a look of shock on her face.

"But I needn't tell you that testing is a long and tedious process," Tana went on. "When Dr. Rutgers is satisfied that his theory is correct, it will blaze through the scientific community like the Letini Nova. The development process will be implemented immediately, and I assure you we will charge forward to develop a prototype of the P-TUP system. But right now—" Tana gave a wry smile. "—you'll have to fly home as usual."

There was an easing of tension, a bit of laughter. P-TUP would be a great boon, but it was also a frightening change. Five years was a time frame they could live with. And apart from her opening speech, Tana had made no reference to going to Earth.

Tana leaned back in her chair and waited for the inevitable questions about second-quarter earnings. She wondered if they had any idea she was lying through her teeth.

Back in her office Tana settled into her comfortable chair and closed her eyes for a moment. The first time she'd ever had to address a meeting of the board of directors, she'd come back so exhausted that she had wobbled into the adjoining room and stretched out on a chaise longue there to sleep for an hour. Over the years she had learned to pace herself better, but, ah! how sweet it was just to sit here for a moment, eyes closed, and feel the tension drain gently from her muscles, feel the level of toxins in her bloodstream abate. Only a moment, though. Sleep would come too easily, and she had only begun her day. So she opened her eyes again and gazed about her office.

It was sparse and clean, with one or two sculptures that she changed from time to time, a free-form print in bold colors on one wall, and an evolving light display writhing and surging in the corner to her right. Her desktop was thin and clear, the other furniture was equally light in design, and the flooring was a facsimile of a woven straw mat. Only her chair was plush, upholstered in crushless corduroy of the deepest blue.

Tana sighed deeply and stretched her hands out in front of

her. Light from the pseudo-skylight glinted off her colorful ring, a band of platinum spun with gold in which were mounted seven tiny stones. Each stone was a pastel crystal: aqua, rose, amber, lavender, primrose, teal, peach. They were the seven crystals used in creating access to the fifth dimension, the warp field so crucial to intergalactic travel. The ring had been a wedding gift, and it nestled tightly against its companion, a simple band of platinum spun with gold.

Suddenly Doc lifted his head and gave a low growl in the direction of the door. "It's all right, Doc," Tana said aloud, although she reflexively thought the same message at him. "That will be Delhi, come to lecture me on the importance of patenting every step of the process."

Indeed, there was a perfunctory knock on the door, and the petite woman marched into Tana's office. "You might have told me Paul was this close," Delhi reprimanded.

Tana smiled, counted three, and replied, "I just did."

"I am the chief financial officer of this institute!" Delhi flared. "How can you expect me to make sound financial decisions if you withhold information about major research initiatives and potential patents?"

Tana continued to smile, for she genuinely respected Delhi, both for her abilities and for her integrity. But her gray eyes turned to steel as she reminded her elder cousin of the situation. "I do not expect you to make sound financial decisions," she corrected. "I expect you to make sound financial recommendations." The board of directors might vote on major issues concerning the institute—such as the annual budget or who the next CEO would be—but Tana made the working decisions. "And you sat in the board meeting fourteen years ago when I pitched this project," she reminded Delhi. "You know Paul has been accumulating VanKurtzes like lollipops. Did you think he wouldn't succeed?"

Delhi stalked closer, and Doc raised his head again. *Don't growl,* Tana instructed him firmly, glad that the implants in their two brains allowed them to communicate silently. *She is of our pack; she is no threat.* She could feel Doc's unhappiness, a nebulous wave of emotion swirling through her senses, but he lay back down at her feet.

"There is a great deal of difference," Delhi said tightly, "between devising a new method of expressing dimensional physics concepts and using that method to design a warp process which can be patented!"

Yes, Tana thought, you can't make money off Rutgersian ex-pression. And while you don't condone voyaging to a plague planet to look for survivors of a thwarted exploratory mission, you have no problem with selling the technology for others to do so.

But Tana said nothing, only smiled at her cousin with all the composure of an impenetrable fortress.

"When do you expect the first patent?" Delhi asked.

"When Paul tells me he's filing." Then, to soften her flip-pancy, she added in her most rational tone, "He's an old hand at this, Delhi. No one's more careful about protecting Paul's work than Paul."

It was true, and Delhi was somewhat mollified. "Just make sure he watches over the rest of his team," she grumbled. "The last thing we want is for unprotected information to leak out of his lab."

Oh, believe me, Tana thought fervently, the last thing I want is for any of this to leak. Not even to you.

Delhi held her unflappable CEO's gaze for a long moment. Finally she turned and started for the door. Halfway there she stopped and spun back. "Zim called me yesterday," she said. "He wanted to know which pocket the hole was in." Tana held her breath. "I told him the pocket with the fertilizer, and we expect great things to grow as a result." Then Delhi stalked out.

Tana exhaled carefully, thankful for Delhi's loyalty on that point. Zimbabwe Goetz was the reigning chief of the Winthrop Dynasty and a man of unequaled influence who had no board of directors to report to. More than once he had raised the issue of selling the institute, cutting it loose from the family conglom-erate to sink or swim on its own merits; more than once Tana, like her father before her, had convinced him that research had a vital stimulation value as well as being the source of new technology. Like the Interplanetary Museum of Art, it had to be underwritten for the health of the whole organization.

So far Delhi had supported Tana in that effort, as she had supported Tana's father. But should she ever throw her weight in the other direction, Tana knew her fragile research craft was all too likely to sink.

She touched a light on her desk, and a lyrical voice issued forth: "Four twenty-two," it announced. She had been with the board of directors for over an hour, answering questions, refut-ing objections, calmly laying all fears to rest. It was her forte, keeping everyone calm as she herself had to stay calm. The worst any of the rest of them could get was ulcers, but with her medical condition, a bout of panic or an angry outburst could land Tana in bed for days. So she exuded a calming influence in the boardroom, filling everyone with a sense of trust in her administration.

If only they knew, Tana thought. If only they knew . . . they would let the secret slip somehow. Probably not intentionally, but one of them would say something to someone, and the word would be out . . . And so I lied to them. I, who for years have lectured on the ethical responsibilities of scientists and engineers: I lied to them. Why? To preserve my ethics. Like my ancestors, Aunt Chelsea and Uncle Zachery, I have bent the letter of the law to uphold the spirit of it. Or so I believe.

Four twenty-two. It would take her twelve minutes to reach the lab: four thirty-four. By then the technicians would all be gone, leaving only Paul Rutgers and his assistant, Todd Chang. The timing was good. *Come, Doc,* she commanded. *We go to the lab.*

Dr. Paul Rutgers was not a handsome man by any means: At forty-three, he had a round, ruddy face, dark hair that was just long enough and just wavy enough to always look unkempt, and a forehead that extended to the crown of his head. But set in that ruddy face was a pair of the most startling blue eyes Tana had ever encountered. He glanced up as she came in. "Oh, there you are. How did it go with the board?"

His white lab coat hung open, revealing a dark plaid work shirt underneath, and from the bottom of his belled trousers protruded a pair of finely tooled but well-worn boots. Dr. Rutgers was a horseman and a fine one. Odd, thought Tana; the universe's finest minds were always so unassuming, whereas those who put on airs and decorated themselves mightily were nearly always made of rather ordinary stuff. It was a lesson her father had tried to drum into all three of his children. Tana had resisted it more than her brothers had; in the end, she had had to learn it painfully through her own bitter experience.

And so will my children, she thought ruefully. Lystra, at any rate. Dear God, it's like looking in a mirror . . .

"It went as I expected," Tana replied. "I told them there's something looming on the horizon but it needs extensive testing."

Paul stood up from the lab stool where he had been half-perched, banished a display from his slanted worktable with a wave of his hand, and turned to face her with his electric-blue eyes. "How long did you tell them?" he asked.

"Five years."

"Be careful," he warned with more irony than humor in his voice. "You might be right." Then he called into the next room. "Todd!"

Todd Chang appeared in the doorway, a rangy-looking young man of twenty-five with distinct Oriental features. His hairstyle was a masculine version of Tana's: shaved on the right side with jet-black locks gathered in a tail on the left. He had shown up with that cut only days after she had ventured to adopt it; recognizing the flattery of imitation, Tana tried not to smirk each time she saw it.

"Are we all set in there?" Paul asked.

"All set," Todd affirmed. "Hey, Chief, how did the big meeting go?"

"Fine, Todd," Tana responded. She tried to remember being that young: just out of graduate school, coming to work for her father here at the institute. Of course, she had not been troubled by a monumental crush on the CEO, something that Todd seemed to think no one but he knew about. No, she had only been troubled by a pair of electric-blue eyes and an infuriatingly unresponsive warp physicist who wouldn't, wouldn't, *wouldn't* ask her out no matter how many hints she threw in his direction.

"Jezebel," Paul called to the lab computer. "Security seal, code four." There was the *whoosh* and *whir* of hidden locks as the lab entrances were sealed, and a scanning beam sought and identified every animate and inanimate thing in the lab. In a moment it flashed a dazzling fountain of colored lights and announced that no anomalies had been detected. Paul Rutgers detested computers with no personality.

"How did Delhi react?" he asked, slipping an arm around Tana's shoulders and shepherding her into the next room. Doc padded quietly behind them.

"I think she was genuinely shocked that the pipe dream is coming to fruition," Tana replied. "She wants to know when you're going to patent."

"So do I," Paul muttered.

Tana ignored the remark. "She's probably at her desk right now compiling a list of the possible buyers for P-TUP. You know: the Darian Free Alliance, the Meta Zed Liberation Army, the Wasseli—"

"Oh, come on," he cajoled, giving her shoulders a quick squeeze. "You know very well she wouldn't knowingly sell to any of those radical groups, even if it were her decision—which it isn't.''

"Technically it's mine," Tana admitted, "but the board can make things very difficult for me if they feel I've acted outside the best interest of the family. And Delhi has three directors solidly in her pocket, plus two who waver back and forth between idealism and greed. Not to mention the fact that it wouldn't have to be sold directly to one of those groups for them to gain access to it. Once the secret is out, Paul, once the process is patented and published, who's to say we won't have another Scorpion on our hands?''

It had been toward the end of the twenty-ninth century, nearly eighty years earlier, that the IDP had perfected a viable long-distance warp transmitter. Able at last to screen out magnetic interference and keep time variables within reasonable boundaries, they had offered the known planets the capacity to send objects by warp transmission from a terminal on Argo to a terminal on DeBanes some ninety light-years distant. It nearly ruined the Transportation Guild, which was caught unawares with fleets of suddenly antiquated spacecraft. Fortunately, the initial cost was so exorbitant that there was a decade of grace for the transition to be made before long-distance warping became competitive with vessel-housed warp travel.

But before the economic situation had righted itself, another purpose had been found for the costly warp transportation. The Fenzali military had purchased the technology, and under the code name Scorpion they had used it to transport bombs into the nine major warp terminals of their ancient enemies, the Jaidu. Deprived of their major transportation centers, the Jaidu were crippled and in imminent danger of being overwhelmed and subjugated by the Fenzali, when the fledgling Pax Circumfra got involved.

Unlike its predecessor, the Galactic Alliance, or its inspiration, the United Nations of old Earth, the Pax Circumfra was not a voluntary organization that nations and planets could choose to obey or disobey. Born during the Restoration, out of the fear and debilitation of the Troaxian War and Occupation, the Pax was given tools with which to enforce its mandates. Once its members agreed on a thing—no mean feat for a body of some two thousand member governments—noncompliance meant that a nation would instantly be cut off from all contact with the rest of the colonized planets. Communications were cut, transportation forbidden, commerce halted. In these times no nation or planet was self-sufficient; a Pax embargo meant economic and political collapse.

The Fenzali argued passionately that the Jaidu had forced them to this action, that the bombs were only in retaliation for ongoing terrorism and economic blackmail, which was probably true. But the Pax Circumfra ruled that no sovereign power should profit from an act of aggression against another sovereign power. They were not interested in the petty whys and hows of this conflict, only that this sneak attack should not set an accepted precedent. The Fenzali were not allowed to enter Jaidu territory.

That did not, however, restore the lost lives of Jaidu citizens or repair the damage to their economy. When Tana first read the incident in her history book several decades later, she was filled with guilt for what her family's institute had done.

"We didn't tell them to use it for bombs!" her older brother, Wyoming, protested.

"We didn't tell them not to," she replied, tears streaming down ten-year-old cheeks.

"If people want to kill each other, they'll find a way," Wy grumbled.

"But we don't have to hand them the ax."

"Does that mean we shouldn't have axes?" he countered.

And so had begun Tana's lifelong struggle with the tension between science and ethics. Were those who created technology responsible for how it was used? Could they build safeguards? Should they leave the building of safeguards to others? Did they have a right to withhold technology from those who might abuse it? Did they have a duty to?

"Here you go, Chief," Todd greeted her, whisking an armchair out from an adjoining office as she entered the room with Paul. "Sit back and watch the show—Chamber Number Five."

Tana smiled at him and did her best to flow gracefully into the chair, although the fatigue of the meeting and the trip down from her office had robbed her of much of the strength she needed to keep her movements controlled. Was it pride to try to look unaffected by her illness? Or simply good politics?

A mesh of crystals lay glittering in the bottom of the warp chamber Todd indicated: the "traveling mat," they called it. It worked in concert with a revolutionary new warp transmitter, and their concepts constituted a major breakthrough in warp technology.

But the glittering mat and the nondescript chamber were no longer theory. The development process Tana had promised the board she would charge into had actually been going on for two years, and the items before her were a prototype that they were ready to test—today.

CHAPTER TWO

"What exactly are we doing today?" Tana asked Paul.

Paul was tossing a recording device from one hand to the other as though it were a ball of kite string. The jumbled-looking recorder did bear some resemblance to balled string, although it was a dull, nonreflecting gray, and the multiple fibers visible on its exterior were actually sensors that could detect and store enough information in a three-second time span to re-create its immediate surroundings down to the trace elements in the air. The recorders cost six thousand universal notes apiece, Tana knew, yet Paul tossed it back and forth absently, his mind as usual racing away on some other plane far, far from his occupied hands.

"We've tested the mat by sending it to another warp terminal," he told her, "and then seeing if we can yank it back using its own crystalline structure as the locater. It seems to work, but I can't guarantee that the very presence of the warp crystals in the other terminal isn't augmenting the process somehow. So today we're going to send it to a location where there is no receiver, then see if we can pull it back."

"And the recorder?" she asked, indicating the object with a slender finger.

"Todd!" Paul called, and without breaking rhythm lofted the device toward his assistant. The young man caught it deftly, activated the floater controls on it, then set it to levitating inside the warp terminal directly above the traveling mat. Boys! Tana thought.

"The recorder will verify that the mat actually arrived at the specified destination," Paul went on. "It will also record the effects of transporting to and from a location where there is no receiver. The process may do things to animal tissue that it won't do to the mat; the recorder will tell us that."

"And what is our specified destination?" Tana asked.

Paul grinned, an unabashed show of white teeth in his ruddy face. "I thought I'd check up on our kids," he told her, his blue eyes sparkling. Then he called to the computer, "Jezebel: execute test program rho twenty-three."

"Authorization?" the computer prompted.

Paul reached to a nearby keyboard and tapped out a sequence.

"Recognize Dr. Paul Rutgers, authorization code cross-matched to voice print," the computer acknowledged. Paul was scrupulous about security; not only was voice-print matching required for computer access, each person working in the lab had an individual security code. In addition, each program was person-specific; it would run only for authorized individuals. Though Paul had an entire team of twelve technicians, engineers, and physicists working on the project, for this program, Tana knew, only two people were authorized: Paul and Todd.

So young to be trusted with such potential power, Tana thought, watching Todd watching the control displays. Yet I was younger than that when my father trusted me. Younger, and with one very foolish and nearly fatal mistake to my credit . . .

Inside the warp transmitter colorful rainbow tubes now began to glow. At Tana's feet, Doc lifted his nose and tested the air. *Someone comes?* he asked.

No, Tana replied as the recorder and mat vanished simultaneously from their chamber. *A thing went. Be calm. It will come back soon.*

But Doc was not much impressed with things that came and went, only with people. He settled back down with a soft grunt and began to drowse.

Paul was watching his wrist chronometer, timing the recorder's absence. "Get ready to bring it home, Todd," he said after a moment. "On my mark."

Behind his console Todd sat poised. His face was as intent as Paul's, his every thought focused on the experiment. It was a trait that had recommended him highly when Paul had chosen only one assistant for the most clandestine part of his research. The other team members knew the nature of the project but only bits and pieces of the specifics. In the entire institute, only Paul and Todd knew it from beginning to end.

"Why Todd?" Tana had asked Paul once and only once.

"Because he's brilliant," Paul had replied. "Because he works like a fiend. Because he has exquisite taste in women."

Tana had punched him in the shoulder for that. "You could at least be jealous," she had chided.

Paul began counting now. "Three—two—*mark*." Instantly Todd began to manipulate controls on his console. "We haven't written a complete fetch program yet," Paul explained to Tana. "There are three variables we want to monitor because we got some odd readings on the earlier tests—"

"Got it, Paul!" Todd sang out. "Here she comes!" The tubes in the terminal glowed again as the recorder and the traveling mat reappeared. Todd let out a whoop of delight.

Tana's joy was tempered by the genuine excitement of the two men. Paul was grinning from ear to ear as he retrieved the recorder and carried it back to her like a child showing off a new toy. Was this really the stellar scientist and acknowledged genius in the field of dimensional physics, author of more landmark papers than any other warp physicist since Yuko himself, grinning like an idiot at the retrieval of a recorder? It was one of the things that had first drawn Tana to him: he was always so genuine, with never a trace of pretension or false dignity.

As he stood over her, Tana knew that at this moment it didn't matter to him that she was his wife and his CEO. It only mattered that she was someone he could share this secret with, this moment of achievement, this milestone in his life's work. "Now let's see where our traveler has really been," he said with a wink. There was a computer console near her chair; he attached the recorder to one of its ports. "Jezebel: access auxiliary port delta. Display visual data."

Above the console a holographic image appeared. There was a background of rolling hills and amber grass rippling in a gentle breeze. A stretch of fence could be seen cutting across the foreground, with two or three buff-colored *cherpura* birds perched on it. *Terra Firma*. Tana's heart always warmed at the sight of the Winthrop family estate.

Suddenly a pinto pony raced into view with a ten-year-old boy on its back

"Bareback, on Gypsy!" Tana exclaimed. "And no bridle, either! I'm going to kill that kid."

But Paul only laughed. "Aw, the boy's a natural," he said indulgently. "Besides, if your brother catches him doing that, you'll have to wait in line." Then, with characteristic preoccupation, he reverted to his experiment. "But look! We did it! We put an object on a planet eight light-years away *with no warp terminal to receive it.* And we got it back. We'll have to analyze the rest of the data, but obviously we've got at least a partial success.''

"Champagne?" Todd suggested hopefully.

Paul pointed a finger at him. "More work," he replied. "Start the analysis program, then get Mickey ready to go. If Jezebel gives us the all clear, we'll send our friend mouse for a little ride."

Tana rose from her chair, feeling better for having rested and wanting very much to share the joy of success with him. "It's wonderful, Paul," she whispered, sliding her arms around his neck and giving him the strongest hug she could manage.

He returned the hug, then settled comfortably with his hands locked behind the small of her back. "At this season we had to factor in the magnetic fields of not only Juno and Argo but of Juno's moon as well. It wasn't an idle choice to send it home; I needed to know we could control for that third magnetic influence."

"So it really was a simulation of a trip to Earth," she said.

"Well, not quite," he hedged. "Earth is a lot farther away— almost three hundred light-years. In warp travel the margin of error has always increased with distance. It takes only the tiniest error to warp your subject to a spot ten feet in the air—or ten feet underground. And then, what about foliage? Weather conditions? Suppose the subject arrived just as a bird was swooping through that particular piece of atmosphere?"

"But the recorder will eliminate those dangers, won't it?" Tana asked. "By warping a recorder to the target first, then yanking it back for a quick analysis, you can tell what the exact conditions of the target site are and how accurate your calculations were."

He sighed and released her. "True," he admitted, "but there are still things that could go wrong. The time variables get extremely touchy as the distance increases—it would be all too easy to have the recorder arrive weeks or even years after you sent it. It might even arrive *before* you sent it if the control algorithm overcompensated. It's scary business, Tana. Very scary business."

She couldn't help but grin at him. "Honey, Columbus getting in a wooden ship and sailing for the setting sun was scary business. By the time you're through testing this prototype, P-TUP will be a piece of cake."

He grimaced. "As long as it's not fruitcake. Todd, is that data coming in yet?"

Todd looked up from his console. "Yeah, and it looks good," he replied. But there was a reservation in his voice that had not been there before. He glanced up at Tana with thinly disguised concern in his dark eyes. "Hey, Chief," he ventured. "What did you mean about Earth?" His high, smooth forehead wrinkled slightly. "You can't go there, you know. It's a plague planet."

Tana felt her heart jump and knew that boded no good. So she took a quiet, deep breath and forced herself to relax. "It was reported as a plague planet two hundred sixteen years ago," she replied. "A lot can change in that amount of time."

"Two hundred sixteen years?" One heavy black eyebrow shot up. "You know that figure pretty precisely."

Tana gave him a wan smile. "Family fixation," she explained. "The report was made by a spacecraft called the *Homeward Bound*, which was lost with all hands. Including Captain Clayton Winthrop and Chief Medical Officer Jacqueline Winthrop."

Paul was leaning over Todd's shoulder now, reading the figures that scrambled across the console. They were curious figures, the three-dimensional notation called Rutgersi for which he had received his first VanKurtz Prize. "See, there's that point zero seven percent drop in body temperature we always see estimated," he told Todd. "I wonder what causes that. Projected fluid levels are excellent . . . You're right, Todd; these numbers look very good."

Then they were lost, the two of them, transported into their own world of fifth-dimensional physics, speaking a language in which Tana could only grasp a word here and there. It is justice, she thought, that two brilliant warp physicists should end the mystery of the *Homeward Bound*. Justice, because it was a brilliant warp physicist who began it. Were it not for the sabotage of First Officer Derek Lujan, perhaps Clayton and Jacqueline would have returned alive . . .

Clayton and Jacqueline. As she eased back into her chair, Tana's thoughts spun while Todd and Paul jabbered away over the results of the test. In surviving holographs, Clayton looked as sober and dignified as any military officer could be, but the family history recorded him as a dashing adventurer and an unmitigated Terraphile. But then, that part of the history had been written by his daughter, Chelsea, and didn't all girls see their fathers as dashing? Certainly Tana did. As Clayton had given up a life of security as a captain of a merchant vessel to lead the first return mission to Earth in five hundred years, so Monticello Winthrop had left his position at the institute to serve as a volunteer with the Pax Circumfra, the interglobal peace organization.

And then there was Jacqueline. She looked rather unforgiving in the old holos: stern mouth, long jaw, hair pulled back severely from her face. But the picture painted in the history was one of a compassionate and dedicated doctor, one who would keep patients alive by the sheer force of her iron will, a woman with a gruff exterior who loved without reservation: her husband, her children, her patients. Like Great-Aunt Juneau, Tana thought. She must have been a lot like Great-Aunt Juneau.

Tana had been thirteen when her father had first revealed the family history to her. It had surfaced in the care of a distant cousin, a direct descendent of Chelsea and Zachery Zleboton. This cousin had brought it to Monti at the annual Winthrop Roundup at *Terra Firma*, whispering in hushed tones that he was tired of the responsibility of it. There were things, he'd said, the public should never know about how the Winthrop family had come into its great wealth.

It had all been quite aboveboard, actually, under the laws of Argo at that time. In a legal dispute just before the Troaxian War, Chelsea and Cincinnati Winthrop, along with Zachery Zleboton, had succeeded in proving that the mission to Earth had been deliberately sabotaged by Derek Lujan at the direction of Oswald Dillon, a corporate magnate with a fortune in Terran art and artifacts. As heirs of crew members, the three had been awarded the total of Dillon's estate.

But the progress of their search for evidence, so carefully detailed in the family history, included obtaining illegal access to information. In modern times, with information being the coin of the realm and right of access a premium legal issue, the crime was tantamount to espionage. How the media would love to get their hands on that story! Tana thought. The impeccable Winthrop Dynasty, heroes of the Occupation and Restoration eras, archetypes of modern society, built on a court ruling forced by evidence the search for which had been fueled by illegal activities.

Why had her father ever given her the family history to read? ''Because you were thirteen and impossible,'' her mother, Charlotte, had told her. "He had to reach you somehow."

"Because you were so Winthrop," Monti had said. "Even at that age, so very, very Winthrop. I never worried what you would do with it."

The adolescent Tana had read the account avidly. Chelsea had become her heroine, and Chelsea's trials had become Tana's. Then, three years later, when Tana had been diagnosed with Gamaean palsy, Chelsea had become her strength. Chelsea would never give in to this pernicious disease. Chelsea would never let it keep her from doing what needed to be done. Chelsea would not resign herself to a placid life of inactivity, confined to a walking harness or a floater chair. And neither would Tana.

But would Chelsea, frustrated by years of struggle, discouraged by the very real limitations her disease put upon her, tired of being treated differently, have climbed a terrabaum tree one night and, nestled in the fork of a branch, swallowed an entire bottle of tranquilizers?

Maybe, Tana thought. Maybe she would have. But then, she would have sent her dog for help, just like I did. Because giving up is not the answer. It's never the answer. Not for a Winthrop.

"Tana?"

Startled, Tana looked up. Paul was still at the console with Todd, but he was looking back at her with a trace of concern in his blue eyes. "You okay?" he asked.

She flashed him a smile. "Fine," she assured him. "Just thinking. What's the verdict?"

"The test results are very encouraging," he told her. Did he ever say anything else when his experiments were a success? Paul never spoke in absolutes. There were no absolute successes; there were no absolute failures. "We're going to make a few adjustments, then we'll run it with the mouse. Do you want to stay for that?"

"Of course!" she exclaimed, then qualified it. "How long?"

"About twenty minutes to make these corrections," he guessed. Not enough time to get back to her office or even access her files from here and get anything accomplished.

"I'll just wait here," she told him. "Don't rush on my account, though."

Paul and Todd put their heads together once more, and Tana slipped back into her thoughts. The doctors hadn't held out much hope to Monti and Charlotte Winthrop that their daughter would ever lead a normal life. If the palsy were mild, Tana might remain ambulatory, but she would require daily therapy for the rest of her life. Even then, she would be subject to seizures. Studies at that time were inconclusive, but there was strong evidence that the seizures were triggered by stress, either physical or emotional. Victims had to avoid rigorous or prolonged physical activity, and they had to train themselves to stay calm. For high-energy, high-spirited Montana Winthrop, the future was bleak.

But they don't know, she had told herself. They don't really know what a person with Gamaean palsy can and can't do—it's too new a virus. And they don't know me. They don't know what I'm made of.

So she refused to believe their limitations until she tested them, each and every one. As a result, she had seizures with alarming frequency. They were dreadful things, beginning with a trembling of her limbs that became convulsions and always, always caused her to black out. Then it was days before she could get out of bed again, exercise her stiff joints, muster the strength to walk. Spurning harness and chair, she insisted on walking unaided. Then, month by month, lesson by painful lesson, she learned just where her limits were. *Her* limits, not those set by doctors or parents.

Getting her an aid dog had been brother Dak's idea. "Dogs can do lots of things for you," the ten-year-old insisted when she scoffed at the idea. "They can protect you from careless jostling, they can do a lot of your curiosity running, and if you have a seizure, they can get help. A dog will make you a lot more independent." Two days later Tana had her first aid dog, a female Dalmatian. The dog, Jasmine, had been raised and trained by her great-uncle Paris, who operated the family's animal husbandry enterprises. Along with this new companion came a headset that allowed Tana to communicate with an implant in Jasmine's brain. If the arrangement proved valuable, Tana would receive an implant as well.

Together Tana and Jas roamed *Terra Firma* first, then flew back and forth to Newamerica City, and finally challenged the board of regents for admission to the Omniversity as one of its select on-campus students. It took a year to overturn their initial ruling that her Gamaean palsy would preclude her full participation in on-campus life, but here as elsewhere Tana was determined to break new ground for people with her illness. Here, as in previous battles, she proved the naysayers wrong.

By the time she was twenty-one, her case was cited in numerous research papers as an example of just how active a person with Gamaean palsy could be. Doctors sent other patients to talk to her for inspiration. Tana always smiled and told them it was all in the attitude. You couldn't let the thing beat you. You couldn't let it win. But sitting in the terrabaum tree that night, watching the moon creep across the star-filled sky of Juno, Tana knew that she would never be well again. She would never be normal. She would always be relegated to a snail's pace, always wake to stiffened joints, always have to avoid situations that might make her angry or afraid. She would always be left behind while others were doing exciting things.

Paul and Todd were moving now, Paul to another bank of equipment, Todd to fetch their test mouse. Yet here I am, Tana thought. Here I am, present at one of the most exciting events in the history of space travel. And I helped make it happen. It was my vision, my desire, that set Paul along this track. I got my father to give him the assignment fourteen years ago, I've provided the conditions he needs to do this work, and I've seen that he is not thwarted by bureaucracy or politics or the machinations of competitors. I can't go mountain climbing or free soaring or even dancing until dawn, but my life has been rich and exciting beyond imagination.

"All set there, Todd?" Paul asked as Todd fussed with a wire cage on the traveling mat.

"All set, Paul," the young man replied. All of Paul's team called him by his first name; only in the boardroom was he known as Dr. Rutgers.

"Let's run from your program this time," Paul suggested. "You call it and I'll monitor the controls."

Todd drew himself up to his full five feet, nine inches—the tallest man in his family, he had told Tana once. With pride he called out the program, which was an exact duplicate of the file Paul had, keyed in his own authorization, and watched as mouse and mat disappeared from the terminal. No one had worked harder on this project than Todd; it was typical of Paul's intuitive people skills that he had thought to let Todd call his program.

And with all your sensitivity for people's feelings, Tana thought, why did it take you so long to catch on that I was crazy about you?

"Maybe he likes boys," her friend Jull had suggested.

"I thought of that," Tana had admitted. "But he's made reference to some girls he used to date and never to guys he used to date, so I don't think so.''

"Probably just wrapped up in his work," Jull had guessed.

"Probably," Tana had agreed. "I wish I could see him away from the institute sometime. Maybe something would click."

"Why don't you ask him out?" Jull had prodded.

"I don't do that anymore," Tana had reminded her tightly. "I've had too many guys say yes out of pity, and I hate that. It has to be the guy's idea or I don't want to go."

"So all you have to do is figure out how to give him the idea."

In the end it was Monti Winthrop who rescued his daughter. It was a Friday afternoon, and Tana, as usual, was down in the lab listening to Paul talk about the project when Monti came in on his way home. He lived on Juno and commuted to the institute on Argo by way of the warp terminals in the lab.

They welcomed him into their conversation, sharing the knotty problem of notation that Paul was currently struggling with. "I've been kicked by many a horse with less impact than inadequate notation is having on my work," Paul remarked.

"Do you ride, Paul?" Monti had asked in surprise.

"I did, growing up," he had replied. "There aren't any horses on Argo."

"Well, you should come out to the ranch sometime," Monti had said. "Winthrop stock has a fair reputation among horse folk."

"Oh, yes, sir, I know!" Paul had agreed enthusiastically, his round face glowing at the prospect. "But . . ." And there had been no artifice in his voice, only genuine deference. "That's your family retreat, and I don't want to impose—"

"Nonsense," Monti had cut him off. "Tana comes out every Saturday to ride—it's part of her therapy. Why don't you come along tomorrow?"

Still he had hesitated, looking back at Tana. "Would you mind?" he had asked.

Mind! "Not at all," she had managed to say when she could pry her tongue from the roof of her mouth.

"All right then," Paul had agreed with pleasure. "I'd like that." Dear Dad! Had he known at the time how desperately Tana wanted Paul to notice her? Or was it just that he genuinely liked Paul? She had never asked.

Now the rainbow tubes in the warp chamber were glowing

again, and mouse, cage, and mat reappeared. "Success!" Todd cried out.

"Preliminary success," Paul cautioned. "We'll monitor our friend Mickey for a few days before we make any sweeping statements." But as he crossed the room to where Tana sat, his smile was unreserved.

Tana laughed and reached out both hands for him to help her to her feet. "You, my dear," she said, "will *never* make any *sweeping* statements. But your maybe is worth a thousand other people's positive." She kissed him lightly. "You're the best."

A small cloud passed across his features. Why was that? "There are a lot of tests yet to be run, Tana," he reminded. "It's going to take time."

"Take all the time you need," she replied. "Heaven knows I'm going to need time myself to figure out how to protect this invention from abuse." She glanced at his wrist chrono. "Not quite six. I think I can reach Councilaire Varga about now. We have some legislation to discuss. I'll see you later."

For some reason he was reluctant to let go of her hands. "Do you want to catch supper in town?" he asked.

"No, no, Bertha's counting on us," she replied. "But if you can tear yourself away in about an hour, we can have a bite together."

"Call me," he said as she started for the door, with Doc padding half a step ahead of her, alert for any inconvenience, sniffing at the many scents of the people who roamed these premises.

Tana and Paul operated on *Terra Firma* time. It was currently some five hours behind New Sydney time, so that they came to work at nearly midday by the institute's work schedule and went home after ten. But it allowed them the luxury of having breakfast and supper with their children and enjoying the relaxed pace of Junoan evenings. It also allowed them to spend at least half of their working hours uninterrupted by the common distractions of intercom and intracom, people coming and going with a hundred concerns. Paul's research project was only one of fourteen currently being conducted by the institute, and it seemed sometimes as though each project manager thought her or his project deserved one hundred percent of the CEO's attention.

Tana turned a corner, and the walls spoke to her. "Tana, are you in for Zim?"

Tana heaved a great sigh. "Yes, Gerta," she told her secretary, a remarkably intuitive woman who screened Tana's calls and visitors better than the most complex computer program ever designed. "Tell him I'm on my way upstairs from the lab. I'll be in my office in five minutes."

There was a brief pause, and then the walls sounded again, but this time with a rich baritone. "Don't hurry on my account, Tana," said the bodiless voice of Zimbabwe Goetz. "I'm on my way out to a meeting of the President's Task Force on Indigenous Cultures. I just wanted to say congratulations."

Congratulations? "On what?"

"I hear you're projecting a completion date for P-TUP within the next five years. You really stuck this one out, kid."

Kid. He always called her kid. For a woman thirty-seven years old it was somehow demeaning. But Zim was of her father's generation; Tana sighed silently and tried to keep the irritation out of her voice. "Congratulations are a bit premature, Zim. And they should go to Paul, anyway. It's his baby."

"It takes two to make a baby," he reminded her. "You planted the seed; don't think I don't know that. You nurtured it. It's as much yours as his."

"Will be," she corrected. "Thanks, Zim."

"See you at the Roundup?" he asked.

"In the flesh," she promised. "How about you?"

"It's a little harder for me to come in person," he hedged. "We'll see. I have to go now, Tana. Give your dad my best when you talk to him."

"I will, Zim," she promised.

Gone, Doc told her. His hearing was acute enough to pick up the tiny noise of disconnection.

Glad, Tana thought back. Zim was a good person, but he had a different view of the institute's responsibility to the Dynasty than she did. He was also extremely astute. It would be difficult to keep P-TUP under wraps if he decided to scrutinize the situation. Fortunately, he was usually far too busy with the political areas of the Dynasty to bother much with the institute. Tana had proved her competence before she was appointed CEO in her father's place; as long as the appropriate reports were filed with acceptable numbers on them, he was not likely to interfere in her domain.

Doors to a glass lift slid open, and Tana and Doc stepped in. The walls were not truly glass; it was another of the illusions Argoan architecture was famous for. Except for the side with the door, the walls of the lift were actually image panels. When Doc pressed his nose against one and looked out at what appeared to be an open courtyard with verdant greenery twined around marble columns, he was actually seeing a recorded three-dimensional image. Twelve inches on the other side of his nose was the maintenance room, filled with a jumble of electronic and crystalline equipment that maintained the many systems in the building.

Tana was no longer charmed by the illusion. She leaned back against the wall and watched the reflected light from her ring playing across the doors. Thank God for Paul, she thought. Not just Paul the scientist but Paul the man who was her strength and her support in all of this. Without him . . .

Tana studied the rings on her finger and thought of the promise that went with each one. They had married for life, a custom widely practiced among her family but not his, yet it was Paul who would not hear of a short-term, renewable contract. When he had placed the simple band on her finger and had spoken the ancient vows of their religion, he had meant every word. No matter the course of her illness or either of their careers, they would travel the road together. Then later, when he had given her the other ring . . .

Tana curled her fingers into a fist. That was what had shadowed Paul's joy at the success of the tests, she realized. That was what had caused him to cling to her hands just a little longer. It was because of the promise he had made when he had slipped that ring on her finger fourteen years before. It was a promise that had begun to haunt him now that P-TUP was becoming a reality.

They had been standing just outside the paddock at *Terra Firma*, surrounded by wedding guests, watching her brother Dak and some of the hands put on a demonstration of equestrian skill. Paul had turned to her with that look of amused astonishment that had characterized his expression most of the day, as though he couldn't quite believe his good fortune. Then he'd taken her hand and slipped the ring on her finger while the others were cheering some feat by horse and rider; leaning close, he'd whispered intently in her ear. "A second ring and a second pledge," he had told her. "Some day I will put your feet on Earth. I swear I will."

And that promise frightens you now, doesn't it? she thought. More than it did the younger man who made it. It frightens me, too, sometimes, but I will hold you to it. When P-TUP is fully tested, I will not surrender my prerogative. I myself will fulfill Chelsea's dream. I myself will stand upon our forsaken mother world and find out what really happened to my ancestors.

CHAPTER THREE

Like an eagle in its aerie, Phoenix looked down from her mountain ledge and surveyed the village of her making. Twelve years, she thought. Twelve years since Nina took her followers and went south; twelve years since I refused to go along. One of us made a mistake, no doubt, but which one?

Well, it was beside the point now. It was over and done, and if there were ill consequences, there were good as well. They were a stubborn lot, those that stayed, and their struggle to survive and increase their numbers had made them clever and resilient. They still spoke with confidence of the day when Coconino would come again, but they did not wait for him to save them. In practical fashion, they had set about saving themselves.

Most of the adobe houses scattered around the butte on which she stood were occupied again. A new generation had begun to dominate the village, a generation that had never lived in the desert valley their elders still called the Valley of the People. They did not crave cotton goods or the baking heat of a summer that was eight months long. To them, the dramatic river canyon in which this island butte stood was home. Even the winter snow was their friend and not an alien.

Their influence was not always welcome to Phoenix. For years she had resisted the pressure to establish trade with the Camp of the Others. They did not know, these young ones, how dangerous the Others could be with their disrupter weapons and their knowledge of wars and murder. They had not seen, as Phoenix had, the bodies of their friends lying twisted and burned on the hillside. They could not conceive how terrible was the act she and Coconino had committed against the Others.

But if there was another generation in her village, there was another generation in the Camp of the Others as well. Hands that had never been raised in violence against the People now steered the plows; eyes that had never seen a planet other than Earth looked out on a rugged but verdant river valley that was their home. In Phoenix's mind, the Others were still a threat to the People and their way of life, but in the end she had had to admit that they were no more dangerous now than the biting cold of winter or the swirling floodwaters of spring. When Michael had come—Michael, who spoke fluently the language of the Others, which she herself now struggled to recall—Phoenix had reluctantly agreed to take a trading expedition south. Not that the Others had much to trade; they themselves often struggled to put up enough food for winter. But they did raise cotton, which their northern neighbors could not, and they had better tools. They also had medicines.

There was no medicine, though, to still the Mother Earth's voice.

Laughter drifted up to Phoenix, childish laughter from a group of scrappy children gathered around Michael. He sat outside his dried-mud-and-stone house, teaching them his native language, the one spoken by the Others and the Men-on-the-Mountain. There were shouts of delight as he teased one or the other or told outrageous, silly stories that used the words they were learning. There was never any lack of students when Michael sat down to teach. Michael made learning a joy.

Just then he turned, lifting his face up to the sky as he gestured to a circling hawk. Phoenix sucked in her breath as the light caught his features. His face had filled out some in the six years since he had first come to live with the People, taking on more mature contours as he passed from late adolescence into true manhood. But it was still the same face. It was Coconino's face.

What sweet agony there had been at the sight of that face when he had first arrived in the northern village, a strapping lad of eighteen, hungering to know if he could fit any better in his father's world than he had in his mother's. At first Phoenix had thought it was Coconino come back to her, that the love that had been swept away from her in a time warp was now cast up on the shores of her life once more. But Michael was not Coconino. He had neither the charisma nor the *moh-otay* with the Mother Earth that Coconino had had. More than that, he was himself—he was Michael. Phoenix never forgot that, except sometimes when the firelight played across the craggy features of his bronze face . . .

* * *

Phoenix watched them, squatting by the morning cook fire, whispering together. Michael shivered in the cool fall air, but he was too proud to don a shirt when the others on this trading expedition wore only their loincloths. Even Sky Dancer, his half sister, wore only a hunter's loincloth. I will have to tell her, Phoenix thought, that when she enters the Camp of the Others, she must wear a shirt. Their ways are not our ways.

And she worried as she watched the two young people hunched in earnest conversation. She worried because although Michael was dark of hair and coppery of skin, he was not truly of the People, not yet. When he looked at Sky Dancer, he looked with the eyes of a Man-on-the-Mountain, and he saw what a Man-on-the-Mountain saw when a woman wore no shirt. Oh, they called each other "my brother" and "my sister," but their eyes did not see what their lips tried to remind them was there. Instead, she saw the handsomest man in the village and the kindest, and he saw an exotic beauty such as could never be found on the Mountain.

For Sky Dancer was a beauty in a way that was unusual among the People. She was slender and lithe, which most women of the People were not when they reached nineteen. Her high cheekbones and finely sculpted nose gave an almost delicate quality to her face, whereas the faces of the People were generally bold and strong. But like Michael, Sky Dancer was of mixed blood. Her mother had been a woman of the Others, a woman she would now meet for the first time.

Suppressing a shiver, Phoenix turned away from them and looked down the hill toward the dirty little settlement that was the Camp of the Others. The clean, white geodesic domes were partially obscured by crude appendages of wood and leaves. There were drying racks for clothes and others for food; there were torn-up patches of earth that had been gardens; there were stacks of mesquite logs for smoking fires. They have learned much, Phoenix reflected, in the nineteen years since I brought Karen back here. But have they learned not to hate?

And Karen. A chill shot through Phoenix. Had Karen come to regret giving up her daughter to Phoenix? When she saw the girl now—saw the woman—how would she react? Would she beg Sky Dancer to stay there among the Others, beg for a chance to know the child she had rejected? And would Sky Dancer want to stay?

"Mother?"

Phoenix jumped, then turned to see Sky Dancer standing virtually at her elbow. It was not often the veteran huntress could be taken unawares.

"Everyone is ready," Sky Dancer told her. Phoenix glanced around to see that, indeed, the camp had been struck, and the five men who made up the rest of their party were standing and waiting. On their shoulders were bundles of furs and hides that they had brought to trade. Coral Snake, too, stood ready, his head held high, no trace of fear or anxiety on his lean, handsome face. To look at him, no one would know that the boy had been banished from the northern village, sent to the Others because he was no longer of the People.

Phoenix looked back at her foster daughter. "Wear a shirt," she said bluntly.

Sky Dancer looked nonplussed. "But no one else is in their finery, and the day will soon grow warm—"

"Wear a shirt!" Phoenix snapped. "Men of the Others are not accustomed to seeing women with no shirts; it will put evil thoughts in their heads."

Sky Dancer looked to Michael in distress. "Wear a shirt," he echoed more gently. "Your mother is right. They cannot help the thoughts that will come to them; it is what they have learned, and it cannot be easily unlearned."

There speaks the voice of experience, Phoenix thought cynically.

So Sky Dancer opened her blanket roll and extracted a leather shirt, which she slipped over her head. Her face was puckered in a pout, though, as she rolled her things deftly back into a compact bundle and slung it across her hip. "Now can we go?" she asked testily.

"Now we can go," Phoenix agreed, ignoring Sky Dancer's insolence and caring only that she had complied. The tasks before Phoenix were hard enough without quarreling pointlessly over things the girl could never understand. She must insure that her band would approach the camp with a full measure of caution but give no indication of hostility. She must explain Coral Snake's situation to the Others so they did not think he represented the People. She must trade these furs for something that the People needed, and she must watch helplessly as Sky Dancer sought out her birth mother . . .

In the end her courage had failed her. Having discharged the first and second duties, Phoenix had left the trading to Michael and Flint and had escaped from the Camp of the Others. As soon as she crested a hill so her companions could not see her, Phoenix fled up the creek toward the sanctuary she knew awaited. Crashing gracelessly through thickets of desert scrub that scratched at her mercilessly, she did not stop until she dropped exhausted before the Village of the Ancients, which still clung to its cliff face in the Valley of the People.

Why did you not call me then? she demanded of the Mother Earth. How much pain I could have been spared if you had only called me to you then. If I must leave the People anyway, why not then instead of now? They would be no worse off.

The answer swirled up from the dust at her feet. *Yes, they would,* it told her. *Besides, Sky Dancer still had need of you.*

She did not think so, Phoenix thought bitterly. Neither she nor Michael thought they had need of my advice. Children will choose their own course like a river, and there is no more chance of changing the one than the other. Yet I cannot help but wonder, if I had forbidden them to go . . .

Phoenix was seated on a fallen sycamore tree at the water's edge when the trading party came back up the creek from the southwest. She rose to greet them—and counted only four.

"Where are Sky Dancer and Michael?" she demanded, trying to quell her rising panic.

Flint looked uncomfortable. "Sky Dancer was very unhappy," he said. "Kah-ren was—a great disappointment to her, I think. She seemed no more interested in this grown daughter than she was in the babe. Perhaps it was because of that that she began to think of Nakha-a."

Nakha-a! The half brother Sky Dancer had not seen since she was twelve. Phoenix closed her eyes. "They went south, then," she whispered.

"Yes," he replied quietly. "She and Michael both. They went to find Nakha-a." Then, with a sensitivity peculiar to him, Flint turned away and left her, hiking up the bank from the stream toward the gentle slope on which the village of his childhood had stood.

Phoenix sat quivering, the blood pounding in her ears, her vision blurred by tears. She had promised herself that if they asked again, she would let them go, and perhaps she would have. But they had cheated her of any chance to play either devil or angel. They had made their own decision; they had gone. She wanted to race after them, to warn them of the danger

*they faced from their own feelings. She wanted to go with them,
to keep them company on this journey and protect them from
themselves. She wanted to abandon her companions, the northern village, everything except her daughter, her only daughter.*

*But she could not, and she knew it. She was She Who Saves,
the leader of the northern village. The People were in her care
and keeping until such time as Coconino returned to them. Damn
you, Coconino, she thought. Damn you for making me love you
and then leaving me here with this responsibility.*

*Finally she rose and, like Flint, turned her steps toward the
old village site. But she did not stop where he and the others
were spreading their blankets among the faint traces of previous
occupation. Instead, she passed beyond to the rock shelves and
ladders that led up the cliff face to the ancient cliff dwelling. In
the growing darkness she found her way to the chamber that had
once been hers. Here she had come to escape her old life on the
Mountain, to be near the People and yet not part of them. Here
Coconino had given her the medallion that she still wore, the
turquoise phoenix set in silver. From this stone house they had
set out on their last journey together, the journey to trick the
Others and destroy their spacecraft so that they could not return
to their home worlds and reveal that the Earth was once more
a sweet and habitable place.*

*Was it worth it, Coconino? she asked the empty chamber. Was
it worth the pain of our separation to keep more Others from
coming here? To delay them, rather, for that is all we have done.
One day they will come again, anyway. But perhaps you know.
In whatever future day to which the time warp carried you, perhaps you will see them come again.*

Phoenix stirred and looked down on her village once more.
The children with Michael were growing restless now; soon
their lessons would deteriorate into play. She had seen it happen
a hundred times before. He began by teaching them and ended
by wrestling with the older ones and tossing the little ones in
the air. His own son, Too Much Hair, was already climbing on
Michael's back; as Phoenix watched, Michael picked the four-
year-old up by the ankles and held him upside down over the
edge of the mountain, pretending he might drop the boy. The
children screamed and giggled hysterically.

It's a good thing, Phoenix thought, that Swan can't see him
doing that. What the child's mother doesn't know won't hurt
her.

But when my child was gone and I didn't know what was happening to her, I did not think so. And the next spring, when Michael returned alone, I thought I would die.

Michael felt a cold breeze brush the back of his neck; he looked up and saw Phoenix standing on a rock ledge farther up the butte. Surveying her territory, he thought, like a mountain lion or a hawk. Well, she had the right. It truly was her domain. They complained about her, the People who lived in this village: too hard, too cold, they said. But not one of them could fill her moccasins. "She Who Saves," they called her now. Once she had saved them from the wrath of the Others; now she saved them from the more mundane threats of privation, poor planning, and bickering.

And she would have saved us, Michael thought. She would have saved Sky Dancer and me from ourselves if we had only listened to her. She told us not to go alone looking for Nak-ha-a, and we pretended we didn't know what she meant. But I knew. Most likely Sky Dancer did, too. She didn't trust us alone together. She didn't trust us to walk in the Way of the People.

"Look at this!" Michael exclaimed, squatting over one of the stubby cacti that littered the landscape. Their seeding seemed intentional: not only were they prolific on this slope, but each one was carefully sheltered by a larger plant that shielded the six-inch plantlings from the scorching desert sun. "Do you know what these are?"

Sky Dancer peered over his shoulder and shrugged, her face set in hard lines. She always had a tough expression—in imitation of her stepmother, perhaps—but it had been worse since the meeting with Karen Reichert. Sky Dancer's birth mother had been extremely uncomfortable to see her daughter again and had terminated the interview at the first opportunity. The hurt in Sky Dancer's face had been painful to see.

"They look like small barrel cacti," Sky Dancer observed with disinterest. She had walled herself up inside with her disappointment.

"No, they're not barrels," Michael contradicted. "Look at the pattern of the spines. See how they're set in vertical ridges? These are saguaro, Sky Dancer. This whole hillside is bristling with tiny saguaro cacti!"

That startled her from her brooding. The People all knew what saguaro were: giant cacti reaching up to forty feet in height, with monstrous limbs jutting out like arms from a green trunk. They were one of the Things That Are No More, like the eagle and the wolf, Children of the Mother Earth whose existence had been blotted out in the Before Times. Only one was known to have survived; Coconino had found it and brought its seeds back to the People.

"Are you sure?" Sky Dancer asked Michael anxiously, squatting to look closer at the innocuous little sprout. It was no bigger around than her fist. "Because if these are truly saguaro—"

"They are, I swear they are!" Michael responded in excitement. "My mother has one—our father gave her some seeds before he left the Mountain, and she planted one. It was, oh, as tall as this when I left." His hand measured two feet from the ground. "But it was eighteen years old then. These look to be maybe six, seven years old at most."

"Seven years," Sky Dancer said softly. "It is seven years since my brother Nakha-a left the village. His mother carried saguaro seeds with her; they were a treasure which Coconino entrusted to the People."

"Then we're on the right trail," Michael said eagerly. "It means that Nina and Nakha-a must have come this way and planted these."

"Yes," Sky Dancer confirmed, looking down the slope toward a small creek that ran not far away. "Yes, this must be the right trail. They would stay close to the water when they traveled, as we have, and they would follow this rillito even farther to the southwest."

Michael grinned at his half sister. "I told you we could do it!" he said. "I knew we could find them, because you have it, too, when you trust yourself: the moh-ohtay, the communion of spirits. Communion with the Mother Earth."

She arched an eyebrow—such a finely sculpted eyebrow in such an exotically dark and beautiful face. "Of course I can hear the voice of the Mother Earth," she replied airily. "It is only that I don't know that is what I heard until much later."

He wanted to laugh at her, she was so serious. He wanted to laugh at her, to ruffle her hair, to cuff her playfully, to—to—

Michael turned away. "Let's keep going, then," he suggested suddenly. "There's plenty of daylight left—maybe they're just beyond that bend in the creek. Let's go see." He sprang to his feet and pelted down the hillside toward the water.

"Slow down!" she called after him. "You will put one of your big clumsy feet in a rabbit hole or on a scorpion, and I cannot carry you.''

Indeed, the idea of her carrying him was ludicrous. She was barely five foot five, and although strong, she was slender. He, on the other hand, was a full six feet with the well-muscled limbs of an athlete. A small, dressed-out mule deer she might handle, but Michael? He slowed his pace, and she soon caught up to him.

It was the third day of their journey. When the creek they had followed out of the Camp of the Others had bent back to the northeast, they had crossed a saddle in the mountains to pick up another stream that led them through this deep river valley. The autumn weather had been clear and invigorating, and had it not been for the hurt Sky Dancer nursed so silently, the trip would have been perfect. They had found plenty of small game for food, and even though the season was dry, there were edible plants enough along the river's edge. Sky Dancer was highly knowledgeable in plant life and woodcraft and other useful skills.

And she was so beautiful . . .

He glanced over his shoulder at her as they walked single file. Her long black hair was braided for the journey, and she wore a strip of leather binding her breasts for comfort. It would be better for me, Michael thought, if my Chosen Companion, Swan, were with us; there would be some acceptable vent for these feelings I cannot stem. But Swan would slow us down and interfere in our conversation. I do like Swan, she is a joy to me, but she is only fourteen and naive. Sky Dancer is so much wiser, so much more . . . interesting. There is a camaraderie between us that I have never felt with another human being. It will be all right. I will be strong.

I will be strong . . .

At midday the waters of the creek widened abruptly and became a lake. Sky Dancer's eyes grew wide, for it seemed to go on and on. ''Have you ever seen so much water?'' she asked Michael in hushed tones. ''This must be how the Valley of the People looked when the Survivors first took shelter there.''

Michael had heard the story of the Survivors several times since he had come to the People. It was the story of their earliest beginning, of a group of teenagers and children who survived the calamitous years after the Evacuation. In the Year That Summer Never Came, it rained continually and all the land flooded so that every place of shelter known to the children was washed away. Finally Alfonso, He Who Had Faith, climbed over the

*side of a cliff on a rope in a driving rainstorm and discovered
the Village of the Ancients, an old cliff dwelling nestled in the
limestone cave high upon the cliff wall.*

"This is only a lake, though," Michael replied as they skirted
the great body. *"Floodwaters would be much higher than this."*

"I have sat in my mother's house during a rainstorm," Sky
Dancer went on, still awed by the sight, *"and tried to imagine
myself as one of the Survivors. To be so tired, so cold and wet,
and have no hope of relief. To just go on and on in the rain with
no destination, wondering how long the little ones would survive. How grateful they must have been, how relieved to find
that shelter at the end of a treacherous rope."*

A wave of emotion washed through Michael as she spoke. He
had participated in the Dance of the Survivors just before they
had left; it had been a powerful experience for him. Even now
he could hear in his head the steady rhythm of the drums, the
massed voices of the People as they chanted the age-old story.
*"Long ago, at the beginning of the Time That Is, the People
stood on the edge of the world . . ."*

"How old do you think Alfonso was?" Michael asked suddenly. His grandfather had written a history of the People back
on the Mountain, piecing together records kept there with stories
of the People. He'd estimated Alfonso was only sixteen or seventeen at the time. Michael wondered if the People knew how
young their hero really was. Perhaps he could surprise the un-
shakable Sky Dancer.

But she shrugged. *"No older than we, I suppose. He was not
yet married."*

"Really?" Now it was Michael who was surprised. *"I thought
he was married to Ernestina."* She Who Also Had Faith.

"Not when they first came to the Village of the Ancients," Sky
Dancer corrected. *"None of the Survivors were married then;
they were all very young. There is a story about the first marriages of the People."*

"Tell it to me," he encouraged. The Stories of the People
were beautifully poetic, full of profound truths and subtle humor. And the story would keep Sky Dancer's mind off her birth
mother.

She took a moment to compose her thoughts, still watching
the huge lake sprawling on their left as they continued to walk
southeast. *"When the People first slept in the Village of the
Ancients, they had nothing,"* she began. *"No wood for fires, no
blankets or sleeping furs, and only the clothes they wore to keep*

them warm. Even those clothes they had were wet from the storm, and so although they were grateful to the Mother Earth for this shelter, they were still cold."

The autumn sun beat fiercely on Michael's back, yet in the pit of his stomach he could feel the misery of those wretched survivors.

"They huddled together for warmth, the older children rubbing the little ones with their hands to dry them. And Alfonso took Ernestina by the hand and led her into another chamber apart from the rest, and they were gone many hours.

"When they returned, Chico was angry. 'I know what you have done,' he said.

" 'I have made Ernestina my wife,' Alfonso replied. 'The Mother Earth gave her to me, and we consummated our marriage in this place which the Mother Earth provided.'

" 'It is not fair,' Chico cried. 'Why should the Mother Earth give you a wife, and not me?' For he, too, desired Ernestina."

Michael thought privately that the Mother Earth probably had precious little to do with Alfonso's decision, but he did not interrupt the story.

"Alfonso agreed that it was not fair for him to have a wife and for the other young men and women to be alone. So he gave them in marriage to each other: his sister Rosa to his friend Juan; Nina to Juan's brother, Carlos; Nina's sister Flora to Enrique; and Enrique's sister Celia to Estevan. Now Chico grew more angry than ever. 'You leave no one for me!' he cried. 'No one but Elena, who is my half sister.' "

Michael missed a step and nearly ran into a scraggly paloverde branch.

" 'Then you must wait until one of the children comes of age,' Alfonso told him; for Alfonso was angry with Chico, who had mocked him as he climbed over the cliff in the rain. And Alfonso allowed all the other marriages to be consummated, but to Chico he gave no wife."

"That's cruel," Michael muttered. His own sexuality had been an undeniable force for several years; he could not imagine being forced to live celibate while others indulged their passions in the close proximity of that cliff dwelling. Even in his own house, which shared only one wall with another house, he could often hear the gentle laughter and impassioned breathing of his neighbors. It never failed to kindle his own desire.

"And after some few days Alfonso also relented," Sky Dancer told him. *"He said to Chico, 'I have not been fair to you, as*

you said, but I cannot unmake the marriages that have been made. So I have spoken to the Mother Earth, and she says that you may take Elena as your wife, and it will not be an abomination.' '' Her voice was carefully noncommittal. ''And so Chico took Elena, and they had many children, and none were cursed.''

A knot tightened in Michael's stomach. In the clinical part of his mind he knew that the taboo against incest was rooted in the need to keep bloodlines fresh, that children of closely related parents had an increased possibility of receiving two of a defective gene, and that if the children were all healthy both mentally and physically, no harm had been done. But the emotional part of him was repulsed. Incest was wrong. It would be like him marrying his half sister Shelly on the Mountain.

Or Sky Dancer . . .

Suddenly Sky Dancer stopped walking, and her face paled. ''Oh, Michael,'' she whispered hoarsely. ''What do we do now?''

Michael followed her gaze, but it was a moment before he realized what had frightened her. Up ahead a small tributary stream emptied into the lake. If they were to go farther along this shore, they would have to cross the stream.

''Well, we could follow the stream,'' he suggested, ''but it seems to go up into the mountains. I would rather follow the lake, wouldn't you?''

''Yes, but how?'' she asked. ''The stream is so wide.'' It looked to be some twenty yards across. To Sky Dancer, who was familiar with creeks that dried to nothing each summer, it was enormous.

Michael laughed. ''Wide is nothing,'' he told her. ''Let's see how deep it is.'' Sprinting to the water's edge, he waded in. ''Not bad. See?'' he called back from the halfway point. ''Only up to my waist here, see? Come on!''

Tentatively Sky Dancer followed him in up to her knees. ''Are you sure it doesn't get deep?'' she asked anxiously.

He waded in farther, but the ground beneath him stayed level. ''It's fine,'' he assured her. ''There's hardly any current here where it runs into the lake.''

She ventured up to her thighs. ''Maybe if we went upstream some, it would be shallower,'' she suggested.

''And the current would be stronger,'' he pointed out. ''Come on, take my hand. I'll guide you across.''

With a grimace she pushed out farther into the water until she *could clasp his outstretched hand. What was only a little over waist-deep on him was chest-high for her. She was shivering, and it suddenly dawned on Michael that Sky Dancer probably could not swim. Where near her village was there water deep enough for such recreation?*

"I'll carry you," he offered then. "Here, put your arms around my neck.

Gratefully she slid up against him, letting him lift her off the mucky bottom. She was warm and slippery, and even in the cold water he could feel his flesh responding to her closeness. He set his face and steeled himself to the sensations as he stepped deliberately forward. There was fear in her grip as she clutched his shoulders, her legs wrapped tightly around his middle. He was glad the far bank was not far away now. "Relax," he soothed her. "We're almost there. Soon you'll have your feet on dry ground again—"

Suddenly the bottom gave way, and Michael found himself plunged beneath the waters. Sky Dancer squealed in fright as they bobbed back up, and she clamped down harder on his arms. "Let go!" he tried to shout at her. "Let go of my arms so I can swim!" But panic had taken hold of her; she struggled to keep her own face out of the water and so kept forcing his under.

A stealthy undertow sucked at them now, pulling them out into the lake. Michael fought his way to the surface. "Sky Dancer!" he shouted. "Sky Dancer, relax! Stop struggling! Let me swim!" Still she fettered him with her limbs, fingers digging into his flesh. Finally he gasped what breath he could and plunged to the bottom, feeling with his feet for solid ground. He found it, bent his knees, and launched them both back toward the surface. Another breath of air, and he plunged to the bottom again, this time directing his recoil toward the bank. Sky Dancer was weeping with terror as they came up the second time; he could hear her. "Breathe!" he shouted, gulped air, and went back under. The bottom didn't seem so far this time. "Breathe!" he shouted as they surfaced again, and he heard her gasp of air. One more jump— "Breathe!" But this time his head did not go under as he touched bottom. "There," he panted, beginning to wade toward the shore. "There, it's all right; we made it. Sky Dancer, let go. You have to let go of me, I can hardly breathe, let alone move. Relax, it's all right now."

Finally she began to loosen her grip, and he found movement easier. Still, by the time they staggered ashore, his limbs were trembling from exertion and from emotional release. They col-

*lapsed on the shore, both coughing from the lake water they had
swallowed. Sky Dancer was weeping softly.*

*"It's all right," he crooned when he had caught his breath.
"It's all right; you're safe. Only if that ever happens again, you
mustn't hang on to me so tight."*

"I'm sorry," she whimpered.

*"No, no, it's all right," he assured her, gathering her in his
arms. "Don't worry about it. It's over. There won't be a second
time."*

Still she trembled in his arms.

*He kissed the beads of water on her forehead and tasted the
salt of her sweat in them. "See? Now you are a Survivor, too,"
he teased gently. "You have survived the raging waters, just as
they did."*

"Hold me," she whispered. "Hold me till I stop shaking."

*"Of course," he agreed, and wrapped his arms more firmly
about her.*

"Tighter," she begged.

*Michael did not know how his arms could be any tighter
around her. So he stretched out his body full length on the sand
and pressed up against her, protecting her.*

Protecting her, he thought now. Someone should have protected her from me. God knows I never meant to do what I did,
but it was as though the trauma of the river crossing sprang the
latch on my carefully controlled feelings . . . and she did not
fight me. That was the worst of it. She was as eager as I to find
release for the burning desire that was in us.

Would that you had been there, She Who Saves, Michael
thought as he glanced back up at Phoenix. If you had only saved
us that one time, there would have been no others. There would
have been no offer from Nakha-a that we could stay in the southern village as husband and wife, just as Chico and Elena had
been, with special dispensation from the Mother Earth. There
would have been no agonizing choice for me to make.
There would have been no pain in her eyes when I told her that
I could not live that way, that I must return to this northern
village and my Chosen Companion. Then I would still have my
beloved sister and my Companion, and there would be no guilt
and no shame between us.

Up above him Phoenix could feel the pain and humiliation
emanating from Michael. Do you think I don't know? she asked

silently. Because I never speak of it, because I have never ranted and raved and condemned you for your actions, do you think I have no knowledge of them? I do, Michael. I know all that happened between you. But I will never reproach you with it; what would be the good of that? There is pain enough in this world. I have lost my desire to condemn you, or her, or anyone else in this sad tale.

For there is more to the story, Michael, than a tryst between you and Sky Dancer. More than you need ever know.

CHAPTER FOUR

Delhi Striker watched Tana carefully make her way through the reception area and disappear into her office. What had drawn the invalid out in the first place? Where had she been that she had to be there in person and not as a virtual presence? Delhi had worked with the younger woman long enough to know that a meeting like the one earlier had to have exhausted her. Why go creeping around the corridors so soon afterward?

Stepping back into her own office, Delhi crossed to her simulated window and looked out at an image of the carefully manicured grounds of the Institute for Dimensional Physics. The grounds actually looked just like this: a thick mat of rich green Terran grasses, clipped ornamental shrubs native to northern Caliente, and graceful soaring trees from a variety of worlds. But they couldn't be seen from Delhi's office; the executive offices were housed in the center of the institute, a paranoia of architecture dating back to the Troaxian Occupation nearly two centuries ago. The scene Delhi stared vacantly at, however, was genuine; the security guards strolling casually along the flagstone paths were actually patrolling the grounds at this moment.

Where had Tana been? The lab, of course. "Teeg," Delhi called out to the central computer. "Window program: Level Two."

Suddenly the verdant grounds disappeared, and instead Delhi was gazing out over the second-floor laboratory area. It was displayed from an elevated position, as though some giant had removed the upper floors of the building and allowed Delhi to look down into the various work areas. There was the crystal lab, where researchers grew mutant warp crystals to find those which would improve the functioning of spatial warping machinery. There was the solutions lab, where a team was working around the clock to test a variant electrolytic solution as a medium for suspending the warp crystals. Delhi smiled as she saw the busy figures in that lab; there would be a new patent out of that lab in less than six weeks, she was sure of it. Perhaps even two.

But one area of her simulation was hazy. The area of Paul Rutgers's lab was not a virtual representation. The walls and doors were there, but none of the equipment was clearly shown. Neither could any figures be seen moving about, though she knew very well Paul was there. Not that she expected anything else; Paul had run his laboratory in total secrecy for the past twelve years. Even Monticello Winthrop, before he retired, had been unable to see Paul's lab except by physically going there.

"Teeg. who is in Dr. Rutgers's lab?" Delhi asked peevishly.

"Dr. Rutgers and Todd Chang," the computer replied in mellow tones.

"Was Tana with them in the past hour?"

"Yes."

It was a small victory, however, that the computer would at least tell her their movements. It was also a dangerous one; at any time Tana could ask the computer who had been checking up on Paul and his work, and it would give her Delhi's name. Perhaps that was why Delhi continued to do it: to let Tana know she would not abdicate her executive responsibilities, or perhaps to establish a pattern so that her checking would not garner attention.

Delhi turned her back on the simulation and leaned against the windowsill, hands bracing her. Her long fingernails tapped irritably on the smooth surface and made a comforting clicking sound. Why would Tana drag herself down to the lab after a board of directors' meeting? To let Paul know how the meeting had gone? Not when a simple comm link would do. To confer with her husband on something? Again, a secured comm link would have been sufficient. And they were long past the days of running to each other's offices just to bask in a lover's radiant presence.

Was it something he wanted to show her, then? Something he was working on . . . But they could establish a virtual connection so that she saw everything as though she were present in the lab, just as Delhi had seen Level Two as though she were hovering above it. Why would she actually go to the lab?

To be in on some dramatic happening. To be part of an occasion, to share the excitement with her husband and team leader, to say "I was there."

What, though, was so exciting and dramatic that it called for her corporeal presence? Delhi frowned. What was it Tana had said at the meeting? "Dr. Rutgers is very excited about a theory he has which, if proven correct—" Was that what had happened today? Had he tested out his theory? "When Dr. Rutgers is satisfied that his theory is correct, it will blaze through the scientific community like the Letini Nova." Had there been starshine in the lab that afternoon? And if so, how long would it be before Tana deigned to tell her?

"Teeg," Delhi began slowly, "confidential inquiry: who on Dr. Rutgers's team has access to his current project?"

"Please define parameters of access," the computer requested.

Delhi's eyes flashed with impatience. "Posit Dr. Rutgers's access as ten; posit the janitor's access as one. Who has level nine access?"

"No one," the computer replied.

"Level eight?"

"No one."

Delhi muttered an oath in ancient Hindi. How could Paul Rutgers get the kind of work accomplished that he did and command the kind of loyalty from his team that he obviously commanded when he wouldn't let anyone else in on what he was really doing? "Teeg: how many people have access higher than level five?"

"Fourteen people," the computer replied promptly.

Fourteen! Feast or famine. Well, no doubt some of those fourteen had some inkling beyond what they'd been told as to how far along Paul was in his testing. Paul and Todd might write all their own computer programs for the testing, but someone had to supply the materials for the tests. Was he using crystals? If so, what kind? Was he using conventional suspension media, or was that why the solutions lab was working so diligently? Or was he using no materials at all, simply running computer simulations? Someone had to know.

"The development process will be implemented immediately," Tana had promised her directors, "and we will charge forward to develop a prototype—"

Suddenly Delhi gasped. "Teeg," she barked. "Are any of those fourteen people associated with construction?" It went without saying that Paul would have a crystologist or two on his team, and an electrochemist, maybe even a microelectrologist. But if he had a technician from the model shop in that elite fourteen—

"Negative," the computer replied.

Delhi slumped. It was an unkind suspicion to think that they were in the prototype phase of the project and had not told her. But somehow she was disappointed. Tana might think Delhi's only interest in all this was the financial standing of the institute, but Delhi wouldn't have stayed for this many years or worked this hard if she didn't enjoy the excitement of research. Working on the bleeding edge of technology, stunning the civilized worlds with their advances—it was a heady sensation, one in which Delhi reveled. The idea that the research was farther along than she had been told had both angered and elated her.

But there was no construction consultant in the upper levels of Paul's confidence. And on the periphery—

"Teeg," Delhi commanded. "How many persons associated with construction have access levels four or five to Dr. Rutgers's project?"

There was not an eye blink of hesitation before the computer responded.

"Twenty-seven."

Tana didn't apologize for having kept Lu Parnette at the office so late; when she and Paul had made the decision to run their lives on *Terra Firma* time, she had also made the decision not to apologize for whatever inconvenience it might cause her employees. She was sensitive to their schedules, of course, and if she wasn't, Gerta reminded her in a hurry. But the universe operated on a hundred different schedules: there were twenty time zones on Argo, as opposed to twenty-six on Juno and thirty on Darius IV. Of course, the hours on Argo were a hundred minutes long, as opposed to Juno's old-fashioned sixty-minute hours, so days on Argo were actually longer. On other worlds, other adjustments had been made to measure the planet's rotation, and only a computer could effectively translate the time differentials between them. Anyone who dealt with enterprises in other time zones on his own or distant planets expected to keep flexible working hours.

But Tana did welcome the lawyer warmly into her office, for she was always genuinely glad to see the woman. She'd hired Lu three years earlier, over the objections of her personnel manager and her chief legal adviser. "She doesn't fit the profile," they told her. "She's too timid. Besides, she's fifty-five and just beginning her career in law. How many years can she give us? She's a bad investment." But Tana had ignored them. Lu had a set of ethics akin to Tana's own and an intuitive sense of what Tana needed dug out of the law files. Coming late to the legal profession, she had no long-term career ambitions; she only wanted to do what she was good at for as many years as it pleased her and to be compensated at a level that reflected her value. Tana applauded the woman's courage and responded with a position and a salary that were appropriate. In return, she received a loyalty that was surpassed only by Doc's.

Doc liked Lu, too. *May I go to her?* he pleaded as the lawyer seated herself across from Tana. His tail thumped the floor loudly in his eagerness to greet his friend.

You may greet her, Tana allowed. *But don't be a pest.*

Doc bolted to Lu's chair and leaned against her knee. Lu laughed and reached down to scratch his floppy ears. "Hi, Doc, how are you?"

Nice, Doc radiated, his entire hindquarters wagging with pleasure.

Now lie down, Tana instructed.

Doc resisted a moment, then stretched out at Lu's feet. Lu turned her attention to her employer.

"What have you got on the blacklist?" Tana asked.

"I think we have a precedent we can use," Lu told her earnestly. "Teeg: show Tana this file." She keyed something in using a wristpad; like Paul, she did not trust a simple spoken code for her files. "As you know, for the past several years we've been going after the wording of the regulation—particularly the word 'traffic,' and here where it refers to the 'dangerous nature' of these planets. 'Traffic' is airtight—any transportation of persons or things to or from a blacklisted world is considered 'traffic' and is therefore illegal. And as for the 'dangerous nature,' your cousin Jordon is still in court on that one—he's taking the same tack that Zachery Zleboton did a hundred and seventy years ago, alleging that the dangerous nature of Earth has never been proven. There was no physical evidence, you know, beyond the disappearance of the *Homeward Bound.* The report which mentioned plague was an edited report, and all the original files were lost during the Troaxian Occupation."

Not quite, Tana thought. Chelsea's records still contained copies of the original logs of the *Homeward Bound*—copies obtained illegally.

"But it's not going well," Lu told her frankly. "It didn't work for Zachery, and Jordan doesn't seem to be doing any better. So I've come up with another idea. Earth is only one of seven planets listed in this regulation. One of these others was visited—legally—since being placed on the list."

Tana reviewed the list on her display. "Troax," she guessed.

"Exactly. When the Veritas Negra gas escaped its factory and poisoned the atmosphere, the flailing arms of the empire were the first to cut off their own home planet. In the final days before the Restoration, when it was clear their influence was doomed, the Troaxian managers on other worlds pressured the Transportation Guild to investigate conditions on Troax. The Guild refused, but the Omniversity requested permission to send a mechanical to Troax, as a 'research' project. They submitted a lengthy proposal on how they would retrieve data without risking contamination of the research vessel. The Guild accepted it, and they received a research waiver."

"Then we need to submit a proposal," Tana inferred, "for how we will prevent the spread of any possible contamination from Earth, should we venture there." She frowned. "Can we word the proposal to cover any method of travel? All Jordan's talked about is sending an unmanned ship, something that can launch a probe and relay messages. But that's talk. If we're going to put a proposal in writing, I want it to be . . . broad enough to cover . . . ." Her voice trailed off.

Lu looked her employer in the eye. "Human visitation," she supplied tactfully. Everyone connected with the IDP knew that P-TUP was in the wind, and everyone knew what Tana intended to do with it. But long ago Tana had cultivated the notion that she did not have to wait for P-TUP to launch an exploratory mission, once that was legal. It allowed her to proceed on a schedule that appeared inconsistent with her projections for Paul's project. On the surface, everyone bought it. Seeing the look in Lu's eye, however, Tana wondered how much the lawyer suspected.

Whatever it might have been, it remained unspoken. Lu smiled. "As a matter of fact, I have a draft ready for your perusal," she told Tana. "Teeg: mail this file—" And she keyed in another sequence. "—to Tana. Code to her voice with this password." Again her fingers tapped her wristpad, and the phrase "Treacherous Troaxians" appeared on the display. "Think you can remember that?" she asked.

"I'm not sure I can pronounce it," Tana observed dryly, "but I definitely won't forget it."

"Bear in mind," Lu added, "that the Guild knows we do business differently than the Omniversity; they know we deal with proprietary systems and must sometimes be a bit vague on exactly how we intend to accomplish a specific end. They also know that every major advance in their industry for the last hundred and fifty years has come out of this institute."

Tana liked Lu's style. "So you're saying I should call in some markers," she interpreted.

"Every one you've got."

"Let's do it." Tana ran her hand across the bristly side of her coiffure. "I'll look this over tonight and leave you a message; you can file for the waiver first thing in the morning. You say Jordan's not doing well with his case?"

Lu shook her head. "The Joint Court will rule next week, and it doesn't look good. The Guild has taken good care of humanity, and the court isn't about to force them to rescind a regulation that at worst isn't hurting the inhabited planets and at best is preventing the spread of a virulent plague. And if they rule against us, the Pax Circumfra won't even hear an appeal."

Tana's eyes clouded over as she considered a dangerous option to speed the process. Paul was ready to send a mechanical to Earth in a couple of weeks; even if Lu's method worked, it could take months before the waiver was granted, unless she had some leverage to force it through faster. But the only leverage she had—

"Lu, I'm going to give you a set of very old files," Tana said with decision. "They could bail Jordan out and force the court to rule in our favor; they could also put the Winthrop Dynasty in a very awkward position politically, maybe even legally. For that reason I don't want Jordan to have them—I know exactly what he'll do with them, and with how much finesse." She took a deep breath. "You, however, might find them useful in obtaining speedy attention when you apply for that waiver."

Lu's eyebrows went up. "Are these files legal?"

"You will know that better than I. And you will know how we can or cannot make use of them. I leave it to your discretion."

Recognizing the tone of dismissal in her CEO's voice, Lu rose, then hesitated. "You don't have to tell me this," she prefaced, "but do you have a particular deadline for this project?"

"I have a live line," Tana replied obliquely. "It was established two hundred and sixteen years ago, when the crew of the *Homeward Bound* was quite possibly marooned on Earth. Let us assume this is a rescue operation and proceed with appropriate speed.''

Delhi waved away the display on her computer terminal and tried another approach. ''Teeg: reference previous construction project. Has Dr. Rutgers requested anything similar within the past six months? Define similar as replication within twenty percent.'' If the computer couldn't tell her exactly what it was, perhaps it could give her some idea how long Paul had actually been testing it.

''Negative.''

''Same construct, increase time span to one year.''

''Affirmative. Dr. Rutgers requested construction which is similar within twenty percent to the project in question eight months ago, and another eleven months ago.''

Eleven months! By God, he'd been testing this thing for nearly a year! He ought to have published internally long before now—unless, of course, he was experiencing disastrous failures. Was that it? Was that what Tana was trying to keep covered up? Had her precious genius been going through company funds like water on what was now proving to be a snipe hunt?

I've got to know, Delhi thought vehemently. I've got to know if he's just throwing good money after bad, afraid to admit that he's latched on to a failure.

''Teeg,'' she barked. ''Give me the names of the fourteen people who have higher than level five access to Dr. Rutgers's project. Exclude Dr. Rutgers and Dr. Chang.'' There must be someone in that group who would know. There must be someone she could reach.

I warned you, Monti, she thought. I warned you not to turn the institute over to Tana. Not only was she too young, too inexperienced, but married to the chief physicist? Bad policy. Work and marriage shouldn't be mixed. And she was on a mission with this pet project of hers, this point-to-unknown-point warp transmission. An executive has to see the value of all projects and not hold one higher than the others.

But Monti, like Tana, had his weakness; only in his case it was not a project but his invalid daughter. Bringing her into the company, making her feel useful, that was one thing. But making it her sandbox, where she could play as she liked? And then turning the whole operation over to her?

You were better than that, my cousin, Delhi thought. You should have stayed with us another ten years, at least—then we wouldn't be in this situation. You would never have allowed a financial drain like this to continue with no results offered except the glib promise of a miracle within five years. Whatever "nobler purpose" called you into the service of the Pax Circumfra, it robbed the institute of the leadership it needs.

I cannot allow it to continue. CEO or not, I will break this web of secrecy your daughter has woven and have the truth out where it can be dealt with. We will keep all secrets from outsiders, but in the family *we will have truth*.

"Teeg," she commanded. "Give me a brief history and psychological profile on each of the twelve people left on the list."

A chime sounded, and Tana smiled in anticipation. "Teeg: is that my father?"

Gerta was gone for the day, and so the computer was screening calls for her. "Call from Monticello Winthrop coming through," it said. "Will you accept?"

"Yes!"

The holographic display area across from Tana's desk shimmered a moment; then suddenly she was looking at the inside of a suborbital commuting capsule, plushly appointed, with a classic masculine definition she could almost smell. There, on a sleek acceleration couch, sat Monticello Winthrop, his thick blond hair going gracefully white, his face gently lined, and his gray eyes sparkling as he looked back at her. It was a poor hologram, actually, by the standards Tana knew: bordering on transparent, with a fuzzing of detail that would earn her scorn and her ire in a conference-room setting. But it was only a commuter capsule holo, after all. Tana grinned, pleased to see even this poor representation. "Hi, Dad," she greeted.

"Hi, baby," he replied. He hardly ever called her that anymore, and never in front of other people. But she knew that they were alone; they had set up this call a week ago, timed to make good use of his corporeal travel time. "You look tired," he observed.

"It's the end of the day here," she reminded him, but she tried to sit up a little straighter and put some animation into her face and voice. "How are you?"

"I miss my instantaneous commuting," he complained goodnaturedly. "When are you and Paul going to perfect P-TUP so

I can get to these remote continents where they have no warp terminals to receive me?''

"When you're looking for undeveloped construction sites, Dad, that's part of the equation," she replied, deftly ignoring his question about P-TUP. "How's Mom?"

"Fine. Having lunch with Ambassador Tsorie today, I believe. He loves her, you know—one of the few staff people who can speak to him in that Doitchal dialect. Barbaric perversion of old German." Monti shuddered for effect.

Tana smiled, amused by the image of the sleek and sophisticated Charlotte Jensen-Winthrop, bedecked in trendy robes and glittering jewelry, sitting with a fossil of a man and croaking coarse, guttural words at him. And having every syllable as perfect as her hair.

"How did your meeting with Ambassador D'Agnus go yesterday?" Monti asked.

"She was extremely receptive to my line of thinking," Tana replied. "Enthusiastic, one might say. I have no doubt that she agrees with me in principle that we need laws now to cover future inventions. The question, of course, is, what will she do about it?"

Monti chuckled. "Oh, she'll do something, have no fear," he assured his daughter. "Once she has decided she believes in a thing and that it is worthy of her attention, she cannot rest until she has convinced everyone around her to believe the same way—or alienated them to the point of rejection. And as I told you, Ambassador D'Agnus moves in some of the most influential circles in the civilized worlds."

"Then it's a good start," she told him.

"But?"

Tana sighed, able to be more candid with her father than with anyone besides Paul. "It will never be enough," she said. "I've been working at this for the past seven years, and look how little progress I've made. No matter what I do, no matter how carefully I lay the groundwork for the coming of P-TUP, it will never be enough."

Monti's smile grew poignant as he gazed at his daughter. "That's your fate, Tana," he said softly. "Because you only undertake those tasks which can never be done perfectly by mortal beings. The possible doesn't challenge you, my little dynamo—only the impossible. So cherish the small victories as well as the large and know that in the arena you chose, no one shuts out the opponent."

Tana forced a smile. "Do you miss it?" she asked.

At that Monti laughed, a rich, round laugh that crinkled his eyes and deepened the creases around his mouth. "Tana, I never played in the same league you do, let alone the same arena."

"What do you mean?" she asked, laughing because his laughter was infectious. But she was puzzled by his remark.

"Oh, Tana," he sighed, but it was a sigh more of contentment than of resignation. "When I headed the institute, it was a business concern. A noble business concern, a 'contribution to humankind' business concern, but the object was to make it a credit to the Winthrop Dynasty—monetarily as well as prestigiously. But for you, young woman . . . For you it is a tool to achieve important goals. The goals of our ancestors. The goals of the human race. Goals that are part and parcel of Montana Winthrop. I thought I was good at what I did until I saw where you were going with it. You elevated the institute to another plateau. It made what I was doing look tawdry and commercial."

Tana shifted uncomfortably. "Dad, that's not true. People there still talk about your administration as the golden age."

"Oh, don't remind me," he laughed. "They still haven't caught on—maybe they never will. But I knew."

Tana was heartsick. "Dad—"

"And don't apologize," he directed in a tone that brooked no argument. "It's the best thing that ever happened to me. When I saw what you were doing, it inspired me. I wanted to do something like that with my life. But I couldn't do it at the institute; I'd already set a pattern for myself there, and it would have taken years to reshape it. I needed a new sandbox to play in, where I could build a new image."

"And has the Pax Circumfra been everything you wanted it to be?" she asked.

"Well—" He gave a rakish grin, the only strong Winthrop trait he bore. "I have to admit, trying to locate a new site for our headquarters when the Kovgorod lease expires in five years is not exactly my idea of a universe-phasing assignment. But on the whole, Tana, this is the place where mountains are moved and orbits altered, and if a person is truly concerned for the future of the human race, it's where you need to roll up your sleeves and get into the mud."

For a long moment Tana gazed at the image of her father and prayed fervently that the tone of his voice and the expression on his face were a true representation, not the product of a fuzzy transmission and her own desire. She wanted for him to be fulfilled in this new work he had chosen. She could not bear to think that she had forced him out of the institute, and with a sense of dissatisfaction for all that he had accomplished there. It had never been her intent to hurry his retirement or disturb his peace. It had never been her intent, really, to do anything but find something her restless soul wanted to do with itself.

It was just after her twenty-third birthday when Tana had approached her father. She was home on semester break, and they were eating breakfast together: Dak wolfing down biscuits and eggs with an appetite roused by three hours of chores already behind him; Charlotte carefully sectioning her rethfruit, the staple of her new diet; and Monti eating absently as he studied the morning news index scrolling past in the table beside his plate. Tana stole a covert glance at her father as she buttered a biscuit. "Dad, I was thinking I'd like to come and work with you at the institute."

Dak stopped chewing. Charlotte stopped cutting. Monti looked up from his index and cocked one bushy golden eyebrow. "Oh?" he responded quite calmly. And then, "And what do you think you could do for the institute?"

It was a fair question. Though Tana's grades were excellent, her studies had no apparent focus. She had begun as a warp physics major, determined to fulfill Chelsea's dream of finding a quick way to Earth, but in her second year she had realized that the tough technical courses that were such a struggle for her were a pleasure and passion for some of her classmates. If anyone made dramatic strides in the field, it would be they and not she.

So she had taken the next logical course: business. If she could not be the physicist who made the discovery, she would be the financier who made it possible. But she quickly grew disillusioned with her classmates' orientation to profit and her instructors' constant harangue about cost-effectiveness and cost feasibility. That was fine for building a better quark trap or manufacturing superwigets for the Coraxii. But she was going to Earth to solve a mystery two centuries old. What was cost?

In rebellion she had turned to a study of philosophy and ethics, which she enjoyed but which did nothing to achieve her goal. She grew despondent with her impotence and despaired of ever fulfilling Chelsea's dream. It was during this lowest of times that she had decided to surrender that struggle and all the others she had waged since the onset of her illness.

But there were in her too many things that would not bend to defeat, and around her too many people who would not let her succumb. Recovering, she pursued those courses which lifted her spirits and inspired her hope: art, music, drama, religion. The social sciences followed, and her degree was finally completed in human studies. But having acquired an appreciation for the process of learning and its profound effect on the human spirit, she did not want to stop there. Besides, she had not yet found her direction. Her graduate studies, then, were as diverse as her undergraduate ones had been. History, sociology, technocracy, management . . . and suddenly she knew. Beyond the shadow of a doubt, she knew where her future lay.

So when Monti asked her, in all honesty and with good cause, what she thought she could contribute to the institute, she replied confidently and without hesitation.

"Leadership."

Charlotte set her fork down loudly and threw a long-suffering look at her husband. Dak began to chew thoughtfully, eyes focused inward. And Monti . . . Monti turned off his news index, folded his hands on the table in front of him, and fixed his gaze on his only daughter. "Leadership," he repeated. "Well, heaven knows every company needs that. Do you feel you've learned leadership in your studies?"

"Of course not," she replied—haughtily, she had to admit afterward. "Leadership isn't something you learn from texts. A text might describe the need for it, or the effect of it, or even the characteristics of it, but no one can teach you how to be a leader. It's something you practice, it's something you can get better at, but not everyone has it. Not everyone has the gift."

"And you believe you have the gift," Monti deduced.

"Yes, I do," she replied frankly. "You have it. Dak has it, too, although he channels it in different ways." Dak looked up in surprise, being all of fifteen at the time. "But Wy doesn't, so it's probably better that he decided to teach instead of going into business." She took a careful breath to slow her pounding heart. It would not do to have an attack of the palsy now. "And I believe I have it."

There was silence; Tana knew her father was taking her seriously.

"Now, Tana," Charlotte began in her most patient tone, "you know that the stress levels of corporate management—"

"Can't be any worse than the stress levels in technical research or financial planning or, heaven knows, the performing arts," Tana interrupted. "My stress level is what I allow it to be, Mom. That's the bottom line." Then, remembering that her mother had good cause to worry, she added, "Even if I forget that sometimes."

Charlotte's eyes implored her husband to stop this insanity, but Monti was not looking at her. He was watching Tana, studying her face intently, seeing her now not as his daughter but as a potential employee. Tension tingled in Tana's spine; it was one thing to be assessed by her father for a job, it was another to be assessed by Monticello Winthrop, the CEO of one of the powerful Winthrop Dynasty's most prestigious companies. It took great concentration for her to keep calm under his level gaze, to remember that she really could do this. She really must.

"What type of position did you have in mind?" Monti asked finally.

"Anything that puts me in line for the CEO-ship when you retire."

A fork clattered to the floor—Charlotte's. Dak and his mother both reached for it, both feeling awkward and out of place in this conversation, but for different reasons. Monti's blue eyes never wavered from Tana's, but his mind was elsewhere, spinning at light speed as he considered all the possibilities, good and bad. At last he unfolded his hands and reached for his coffee cup. "All right. When you complete your master's—"

"I'll do that if you want me to, but I'd like to start work right away," Tana said quickly.

There was only the slightest hesitation as Monti brought the cup to his lips. "How many courses do you have left?"

"Nine hours," she replied. "I can do three next semester, three in intensive study, and co-op my job as an internship for the last three."

"You'll be exhausted!" Charlotte exploded. "You'll wind up in the hospital."

But Monti held up a hand and stopped her objection. "You start Monday," he told Tana. "You try taking one course, no more than three hours, next semester, and if it's too much, you come to me and we decide together whether you give up the job or the class. You're on a six-month probationary period, and your income from family assets goes into a trust fund for twelve months, just as it does for any other Winthrop who comes to work for me.''

Tana thrust out her hand. "Deal."

Monti clasped it firmly. "Deal," he echoed. Then a slow smile spread across his face, and he came around the table to hug her. "Welcome aboard, honey," he whispered.

It took Tana only six weeks to question the wisdom of her decision. As she followed Monti from meeting to meeting, tagging along as he inspected the labs and the design rooms, sat in on his discussions with his newly appointed CFO, Delhi Striker, she began to experience some of the same disillusionment she had known in college. The institute, she discovered, had lost its mission. They did not know that they were supposed to be finding a way to reach Earth.

As depression licked at her consciousness and stifled anger threatened to bring on an attack of the palsy, Tana knew she had to do something if she was going to continue there. So she marched into her father's office on the ninth floor and sat down across the desk from him.

"This institute is off the mark," she told him.

Monticello Winthrop leaned back in his chair, folded his hands in his lap, and waited.

For half an hour Tana lectured him on the history of the IDP, its purpose, and Chelsea's goal. She cited its achievements and its failures and how they had begun to take on a life apart from the mission to reach Earth. She told of the attitude she found pervading the institute, the commercialism, the negativism, the superficiality. "We have become like any other company," she lamented. "We have become mundane."

At which point there was a crisp rap on the door and Paul Rutgers walked in. "Excuse me, Mr. Winthrop," he began, "I need to talk to you."

Monti looked up from one pair of passionate eyes to another. "Join the fray," he invited, waving Paul to a chair.

"No, thank you, sir," Paul declined, seeming not to notice Tana's presence in the room. "I have a simple request, and then I'll go so you can think about it."

Uppity, Tana thought. She had met Paul Rutgers while touring the labs with her father and had thought him singularly unimpressive in light of the way Monti raved about his credentials and his merit. A relaxed, easygoing young postdoc who tended to work all the time Monti spoke to him. It surprised Tana to find him barging into her father's office without regard for decorum.

"Very well, Paul," Monti prompted.

"I'd like a different assignment."

Tana found her own anger suddenly defused by the unabashed Dr. Rutgers.

Both of Monti's bushy eyebrows flew up. More reaction than I got, Tana thought. But he remained calm. "Any particular reason?" he asked Paul.

"I feel I'm being wasted," Paul answered. "Refining existing warp systems—that's not what I should be doing. Lots of people can do that. This institute is known for pioneering research, for breakthrough technology. That's what I want to do. I want to broach new territory. I want to push the envelope."

There was a quirking around Monti's mouth that Tana recognized as an effort not to smile. Her father liked this young physicist; that was very evident. But he was still the CEO, the autocratic head of this Winthrop company. As he was still her father.

"Very well," Monti replied after a moment. "Let me think about it."

"Thank you, sir." That said, Paul Rutgers turned and left the room.

Tana sat staring after him, her mind a turmoil.

"Well!" Monti exclaimed when the door had shut. "What do you think we should do about our Dr. Rutgers?"

The turmoil snapped into focus, and Tana turned swiftly to her father. "Give him P-TUP," she said urgently.

"P-TUP?"

"Point-to-unknown-point warp transmission," Tana continued. "The reason this institute was created. He wants it, Dad. Give it to him."

Monti leaned forward, hands clasped on his desk now, a classic deal-cutting gleam in his eye. "Let's do this," he said shrewdly. "You want him to have this project? Fine. I'll consent to it. *If*—" He let the word hang heavily for a moment. "If *you* prepare a presentation for the board of directors justifying it. Now, we don't need their approval, but it will take a lot of heat off us later if we sell the project up front. So you justify it, justify Paul Rutgers being assigned. You and I can deal with each other on gut-level instinct, but if you're going to run this company, you've got to learn to work the board. Here's your chance. Here's your chance to put this institute on the path you think it should follow. You have ten days to prepare."

Landmarks. The chance interruption had changed everything. Tana went straight from her father's office to Paul's lab to lay the challenge before him and enlist his help in presenting it to the board. Paul had latched on to the project like a babe to its mother's breast, burying himself in reading material, churning out record cylinders of notes and ideas, spending sixteen and twenty hours a day at the institute. He met with Tana daily to fill her in so she could coordinate her presentation with his findings. She could not keep the hours that he did, nor could she understand all the technical aspects of his study, but he was, she discovered, very good at explaining things in terms others could understand—he made an excellent presenter. And somewhere in those hectic days before the board meeting she also discovered that his eyes were incredibly blue.

Now Tana shook her head and gave her father a wistful smile. "Dad, you did more good than you'll ever know at the institute. I couldn't do what I'm doing today if you hadn't done what you did before me."

"Oh, I don't know about that," he deferred.

"You hired Paul, didn't you?"

"That's true," he admitted. "And one other brilliant thing I did while I was there."

"What's that?"

"I hired you."

Delhi rose from her desk and headed for the door. She could see the light from Tana's office and knew the younger woman was still working, but it was nine o'clock, New Sydney time. Delhi decided she'd better use the warp terminal here in the institute and have Jedediah pick her up at the public transit station. If she wasted an hour flying home, he'd have gone to bed without her again.

Lights winked on in front of her as she entered the hall from the executive suites and headed toward the lift. In a moment, she knew, they would wink off again, sent back to their slumber by the computer that traced her path through the empty building. Somewhere below her second-shift workers were tending crystals and monitoring solutions and all the other things that could not be halted overnight.

One of them was a young man named Jarl, who hummed to himself as he went about his work in the model shop, relieved that he now knew how to pay back the twelve hundred universals he hadn't told his wife he'd borrowed from their savings account. And it was all in the best interests of the Winthrop Institute for Dimensional Physics.

CHAPTER FIVE

There was the comfortable pressure of Paul's arm around her, of Doc leaning up against her left leg, and then the unsettling of her stomach as Tana passed through the limbo of the fifth dimension to arrive in the warp terminal at *Terra Firma*. The chamber was not so small that they needed to crowd together so—it was fairly new and would accommodate up to four people—they just enjoyed crowding together. They had made this commute so often in this fashion that on those few occasions when Tana traveled alone, it felt very strange to warp through without being nestled in the crook of Paul's arm.

May I go? Doc asked impatiently, almost plaintively.

Go, Tana agreed with a smile, and the big Dalmatian bolted for the door of the terminal, out into the hangar that housed it. A barrage of information flooded Tana's mind as Doc identified the various smells in the large building: *Flivvers. Bailers. Dak. Food. Rain. Andy. Pinmice.*

"It must have rained today," Tana commented as she and her husband stepped out of the chamber and strolled, arms still about each other, toward the darkened doorway where the acrid smell of charging tanks and lubricants reached their less sensitive noses as well. Like Doc, Tana much preferred the horse and leather smell of the rustic riding stable across the yard. But when buyers came to see Winthrop stock, they expected the convenience of a warp terminal and perhaps a flivver ride; the hangar was as much a part of the ranching operation as the show ring.

Paul raised an eyebrow at her comment. "Rain? Are you sure?"

"Doc thinks it's rain, anyway," she told him. "Maybe Uncle Paris is adding things to the irrigation system in his garden again." Tana was seldom confused anymore by what Doc meant, but Doc could occasionally be wrong in his interpretation of various stimuli.

When Tana had gotten her first aid dog, Jasmine, at age seventeen, the onslaught on her mind of Jasmine's undefined thoughts had nearly overwhelmed her. Senses, emotions, desires, and impulses surged through the headpiece to her brain in a jumbled disarray, afflicting her with blinding headaches and a strange sense of vertigo. "You'll get used to it," Uncle Paris assured her. "You'll learn to sort out all the information, to disregard what is unimportant. Your brain will adjust. Give it a chance."

Fortunately, Jasmine was an experienced aid dog that responded immediately to Tana's attempts to communicate. Had the dog not proved her usefulness in those first few days, Tana doubted she would have stuck with the project longer than a week.

But just as she was about to give up, things began to sort themselves out. Tana learned to recognize thought images as opposed to sight images and to separate her own feelings from those being radiated by the dog. At some level Tana did not understand, her brain began to tune out the constant stream of background information and pick out only the more pertinent bits. The headaches stopped, the vertigo vanished, and out of the chaos came a form of communication that began to resemble conversation. Before the year was out Tana opted for the implant that made external headgear unnecessary.

Years later, as she was training Doc, Tana had experienced some of the same disorientation, but not to the extreme she had felt the first time. After all, *she* was well trained; it was only Doc that needed to learn. And with the higher intelligence Dak had engineered into the puppy, the communication between them was even more precise than it had been with Jasmine.

Doc ranged ahead now as she and Paul stepped out of the hangar, into the bright sunlight of a late summer day. Here on the grasslands of Juno the daylight would last for another four hours—plenty of time to enjoy the lingering warmth, to go for a ride or play a game of horseshoes, to enjoy a leisurely supper on the veranda. Then Tana could watch the sun settle slowly into the sea of rippling prairie grass, setting the sky aflame with reds and golds and indigos. One by one the stars would appear, winking into existence in the darkening sky, and the ever-present wind would finally fade away. When at last blackness enveloped *Terra Firma*, Tana could stand in the still, silent night beneath the jeweled canopy of the heavens and watch the great, amber globe of Juno's only moon rise in the east . . .

Tana sighed. If only she could stay awake that long. More likely she would be in bed before the kids, leaving Paul to work at his computer terminal until the small hours of the Junoan night, heedless of the glory spread just outside his window.

Hearing her sigh, he gave her a quick squeeze. "Tired?" he asked.

She smiled wanly. "No more than usual. I think I'll lie down for a bit before supper, though."

His hand wandered from her waist down to the fleshy curve of her hip and squeezed again. "Maybe I'll join you."

Tana stifled another sigh and wished doubly that her body did not succumb so easily to fatigue. During the workweek it seemed there was no good time for sex: In the morning her joints were too stiff, in the evening she was too tired, and in the middle of the day Paul was too absorbed in his work to tear himself away. Weekends were best, but it was a long time from Sunday to Saturday.

"Hi, Mom! Hi, Dad!" Derbe called from the yard in front of the dog runs, where he and his older sister, Lystra, were helping with the feeding chores. "Hey, Doc! Hi, Doc!"

Doc charged at the ten-year-old, bounding across the yard at incredible speed, eighty pounds of solid muscle. *Careful*, Tana warned him, and so the big dog skidded to a halt just short of his prospective playmate. But the boy was waiting; he had put down the food dispenser he was carrying and tackled the gleeful animal, sending them both sprawling. Over and over they tumbled on the well-packed dirt of the yard until both were covered in dust.

"Hey!" came a deep male voice from the stable. "Finish your chores first, laddie-my-boy, then you can play."

Enough, was Tana's silent command to Doc as her son extricated himself and struggled to his feet.

"I know, I know," Derbe called back to his uncle. "I was just saying hello." Then he picked up his dispenser and headed back to the runs.

Disappointment lanced through Tana's mind from Doc's. The dog turned hopefully toward Lystra, wondering if maybe she would play.

But Lystra was thirteen and above the indignity of rolling in the dirt with this or any other animal. "Doc, don't even think it," she snapped, holding her dispenser away from him so that in his enthusiasm he would not bump into it.

Tana sighed. So dour, so critical. Where was the little live wire she had been only two or three years ago? Where was the freckled face that always smiled, the eyes that shone at every antic of the puppies in the runs?

The same place mine were, Tana thought, when I was thirteen. They will come back. I keep telling myself, they will come back.

Grumpy, came Doc's interpretation. He turned and trotted toward the stable and his last hope for recreation.

Dakota Winthrop stepped out of the stable doorway into the sunlight, palming the oversized door shut behind him. "Hey, Doc," he greeted, squatting down to rub the dog's ears and scratched his broad Dalmatian chest. "How are you? Did you take good care of my sister today?"

Doc whined an answer, though Tana knew very well Doc didn't have a clue what Dak was asking him. He only heard the affectionate tone of voice and wanted to respond in some way. Dak rewarded him with a friendly slap on the side. No Winthrop raised on *Terra Firma* ever patted a dog on the head; head patting was an exercise of dominion, and they were all taught from early childhood to preserve an animal's pride.

Dak rose then and started across the yard toward Tana and Paul. He was a well-built man of thirty, over six feet tall, with broad shoulders and muscles accustomed to physical labor. His hair was a dark sandy color, cut to a length that did not blow too badly in the prairie wind. A strong cleft chin spoke plainly of his descent from Clayton and Cincinnati. All told, Tana thought, her ragamuffin little brother had become the handsomest man she knew, with the possible exception of her father. Sisterly affection might account for some of that perception, but there was no denying that when Dakota walked down the streets of Newamerica City, women turned to stare. His gait, his attitude, and his roguish Winthrop smile all drew attention wherever he went.

"How's work?" Dak greeted them as he approached.

Paul reached out to slap his brother-in-law's proffered palm. "Still having fun," he replied, grinning. There was a camaraderie between the two men that went back to their first meeting, before Paul and Tana were even dating. Then, Tana had been jealous of it; now, with Paul separated by distance and vocation from his own brothers, it warmed her heart to know that the bonding between those two was so strong. It especially pleased her since Dak had been living in their house for the past seven years.

"Got some time before supper?" Dak asked them. "I got my new steppe-horse stallion in. Why don't you come and have a look?"

Tana could feel the hesitation in her husband, the pull of two urges. "Oh, let's," she encouraged. "A visit to the stable always perks me up. Something about the smell, I think—that musty, pungent odor . . ."

"Reminds you of all those times rolling in the hay when you were a teenager," Dak said slyly.

"Hey!" She slapped his arm. "I never did that, and you know it."

"And when I reached puberty, guys were still talking about it," Dak commented dryly. "Come on—you've got to see this stallion; he came in from the Fabrian province today."

The cool, dank interior of the riding stable did indeed have an odor that was both soothing and energizing. Tana inhaled deeply to override the secondhand impressions she was getting from Doc. The smell was evocative of a carefree childhood, before she had contracted the Gamaean palsy, before that pernicious virus had bonded with the tissue of her large joints, making eradication impossible. It was evocative of the first time Paul had come out to go riding and all the longing she had felt for the unresponsive young physicist. She looked at him now in the dim interior, a man with more experience written in the contours of his face and more appreciation of his life for having lost a few battles along the way.

Paul let out a low, appreciative whistle as he saw the stallion, but Tana's eyes were on Paul as she silently echoed the sentiment. She was glad they had come to the stable.

"I thought steppe horses were small. He must be eighteen hands high!" Paul exclaimed as they drew near the stall where the shaggy dun-colored horse snorted and tossed his head, unaccustomed to being penned in. Doc trotted eagerly up to the stranger, sniffing and snuffing through the bars of the stall gate.

"Just over seventeen," Dak demurred. "Still, a full hand taller than any other steppe stock I've been able to locate. Certainly taller than the pintos I've been breeding. I put him in here for a day or two to let him calm down and to give us a chance to cut out the mares we want to breed him to."

"Pintos?" Paul asked.

Dak nodded. "I'm going for an animal that will do well in a harsh climate—coarse grasses and browse for fodder, extremes in temperature—but that is also surefooted and nimble. Crossing the pinto with the steppe horse should give me good building blocks. From there we'll do some genetic enhancement, but first I want to see what I get from natural-borns."

Tana hitched up the flowing skirts of her robes, wishing she had changed before coming into the stable, and stepped into the adjoining stall for a closer look at the animal's contours. The horse twitched nervously, but there was a bold gleam in his eye. Tana was sure she wouldn't like to be between him and the way out of his enclosure. "Are you still after the Polollian market?" she asked Dak.

"Horses are not a luxury there, they're a way of life," Dak replied, and Tana knew that was more important to him than the money a Polollian contract would bring. "You can't herd gaffoxen from vehicles—the gaff are singularly unimpressed, and you'll hurt them before you move them. But a gentle nudge from a horse will get them going in the right direction. This new cross should be hardy enough for the rather extreme heat and cold of the place and big enough for a gaffox to respect without losing much in the way of agility."

Tana nodded, reaching out carefully to stroke the shaggy coat of the big horse, to feel the sweaty warmth of him on her palm. "Do you have mares in season?" she asked, knowing that most of Dak's stock foaled in the spring, on schedule with the northern hemisphere's climate.

"I have some prepared," he replied. "I've been bargaining for this guy for a couple of months now, so I put some mares on an off schedule to accommodate him in case it came through."

"Will you put him out to pasture?" she wanted to know, "or bring them in?"

"We'll bring the mares in," Dak told her, "so we can monitor the mating conditions." He grinned wickedly. "Why? You want to watch?"

Tana blushed furiously because that was exactly what she was thinking. There was nothing more breathtaking than the sight of a fine stallion taking his mare; the effects of watching the coupling also livened her bedroom for several days following. But she was not about to admit that to her little brother.

"I thought maybe you'd invite Wanda out for the spectacle," she countered.

"Wanda," her brother replied frankly, "doesn't need the inspiration." Which was why, Tana supposed, Dak had been seeing the woman for five years with no hint of a marriage contract, long- or short-term.

"I don't understand," she had fumed to Paul one day, "what he sees in her. She hates the ranch—she won't ever come out here. She doesn't care about the science of genetics. *He* doesn't care about her career in fashion design, or the fast-living friends she keeps, or that pet rinatta of hers. What do they *talk* about when they're together?"

"I don't think they talk much," Paul had observed.

"Well, goodness, you can't build an entire relationship on sex," she had continued to fuss. "Five years; there must be *something* else between them. Why would he stay with her this long? And if there's something else between them, why don't they at least try a one-year marriage? I hear that's all the rage in her circle."

"Because he doesn't love her," Paul had replied bluntly, "and he's not stupid enough to marry for lust."

As Tana came out of the stall now, she was tempted to make a cutting remark about Wanda not coming to the Roundup again *this* year, but she thought better of it. It was Dak's life, after all. Besides, he took fiendish brotherly delight in offending her more prudish sensibilities at every opportunity. The less she made of her disapproval of Wanda and their relationship, the more likely Dak was to give up on it and find someone more suitable.

"I'm going to go change," she told Paul, "and stretch out for a little. Come up to the house when you're ready." His exploring hand as he gave her a quick kiss said he was already ready, but she knew he would linger in the stable with Dak, talking about the stallion and the ranch and, probably, Wanda. If Dak bothered to talk to anyone about Wanda. "Keep Doc with you, will you?"

Doc was perfectly content to stay behind in the delicious-smelling stable with the strange new horse. Although he was Tana's dog, all the members of her family were his pack, and he did not mind a few hours away from her. Tana, as well, enjoyed brief respites from his constant stream of thoughts. She could turn the implant off, of course, any time she chose by changing a setting on her biometer. But Doc seemed to find that experience disconcerting, so she seldom did it. Besides, recoding the tiny biometer chip embedded in her navel was a trivial task for which she had little patience.

Leaving the musky scent of the stable, Tana turned her careful steps toward an old house that stood just west of the paddock, its front partially screened by mature mocpin trees. There were actually five residences on *Terra Firma*, plus an assortment of guest bungalows for the relatives who drifted in and out. Most of the houses, however, were built closer to the creek that ran through the estate, away from the sights and smells of a working horse/dog ranch. Only two houses stood in close proximity to the kennels and stables. One was the old ranch-style house that had been on the property when Clayton and Jacqueline Winthrop had first purchased it over two centuries before. Tana's great-uncle Paris still lived there with his wife, Emily, although they had turned over the active running of the ranch to Dakota years before.

The other was this rambling two-story frame toward which Tana made her way. The main part was nearly as old as Paris's house, having been built by Chelsea Winthrop and Zachery Zleboton during the early years of the Troaxian War. It was made entirely of native materials, for Juno was one of the last of the planets to come under Troaxian sway, and they had been cut off from trade with Troaxian worlds during the time when the house was built. Tana's great-aunt Juneau had lived in it when Tana was a child, and rumors were rampant among the Winthrop clan younglings that it was full of hidden compartments and secret passages that were linked to resistance activities during the Occupation. But Paul and Tana had lived in it since she was pregnant with Derbe, and she had yet to find a single false wall or revolving bookcase.

By the time Tana made her way across the dust grid to the front door, Bertha was there holding it open for her. "Evening, Ms. Winthrop," she greeted. "Where's the doctor?" Tana was never sure if Bertha was truly impressed by Paul's title or if it was a private little joke with her that a man called "doctor" had less medical training than her son, who was the head wrangler for Winthrop Animal Husbandry. "Should have called it 'Winthrop Animal Husbandry Unlimited,' " Bertha would say again and again. " 'Wa-hu'!' "

"He's down at the stable looking at Dak's new stallion," Tana told her.

"Stallion?" Bertha snorted. "You mean he's going to breed foals the natural way for a change?" Bertha had a very low opinion of Dak's use of genetic engineering to advance selected traits in his stock.

Tana only smiled and passed by her housekeeper into the living room. It had taken only a few months to realize that the best way to deal with Bertha was not to take up an issue with her. Any issue. "I'm going to rest for a while before supper," Tana called over her shoulder. "Buzz me if there's anything critical." Then she slid into the ornamental chair lift and let it spiral her up to the second floor, knowing that the house could burn down around her ears and Bertha would not think it was important enough to disturb Tana's rest.

On the way to her bedroom Tana passed by her children's rooms. They had finished their chores, and Derbe was now sprawled on the floor of his room following a learning trail through a holo on the aquatic life of Dvorik. Giant fimfazores swam across the room with odd-looking crustaceans clinging to their tendrils. As she watched, Derbe stopped the action and zeroed in on a crescent-shaped aperture near a fimfazore's eye. "Luke: what is that?" he asked the computer.

"This opening, known as an eye pouch," the computer began, "is actually a sensory organ similar to a tongue. The fimfazore 'tastes' the water which passes through this orifice—"

Tana shook her head and continued down the hall, pleased that Derbe took nearly as much interest in his studies as he did in the horses and dogs. At times she hoped Derbe would go into the ranching business with Dak someday, but at other times she hoped he would follow Paul's footsteps into a more academic career. She gave a sigh. Whatever made him happy, that was what the boy would do.

The next door was Lystra's, and it was tightly shut. Tana hesitated, then stopped and knocked.

"What do you want?" came the muffled voice from inside.

"A hug," Tana called back. There was the sound of feet hitting the floor, and then the door slid open and Lystra stood in front of her. She was nearly as tall as Tana now, with the same slender build, but her hair was dark like Paul's. It was long and straight. Isn't everyone's, Tana wondered, when they're thirteen?

"Hi, Mom," she said, throwing her arms obediently around Tana's neck and giving her a quick squeeze.

Tana hugged her back and, looking over her shoulder into the room, was dismayed by the incredible clutter it contained. "Good grief, your room is worse than Derbe's!" she observed.

"Oh, Mom!" Lystra detached herself and stomped back into the center of her domain. "If I'd known you were going to start on my room, I wouldn't have opened the door."

Tana wanted to snap that she was still the girl's mother and the door would be opened any time she requested. But she thought better of it and said instead, "What are you up to?"

"I've got all my homework done," Lystra defended.

"That isn't what I asked," Tana replied with tried patience. "I just asked what you were up to."

"Reading," Lystra replied, flinging herself back onto the mounded covers of her bed. She picked up a book folder and snapped it on; Tana could see the sparkle of the words appearing on the leaves of the folder.

"What book?" she asked.

"A mystery," Lystra replied. "A Truly Tolnie mystery."

Not great works of literature, Tana thought, but innocuous fare. At least the girl read. Derbe rarely ventured out of his holographic learning files. "If you like mysteries," Tana said, "I should give you the family history to read. The early years are full of mysteries and adventures."

"Yeah, yeah, Zachery escaping the Troaxian invasion, Chelsea looking for a missing letter," Lystra chanted deprecatingly. "I know the story, Mom."

Tana was more than a little nettled. At thirteen, she had found the family history the most exciting piece of reading in existence, and it had changed the course of her entire life. "The whole thing is quite intriguing," she encouraged.

"Yeah, well, let me finish Truly Tolnie first," Lystra replied. "Then maybe I'll look at it."

Maybe? *Maybe!?* Tana felt her mood deteriorating rapidly. "Don't show so much enthusiasm," she snapped, and knew it was time to leave. Palming the door shut on her irksome daughter, she stared back down the hallway toward her own room.

The master suite was part of an addition to the house made only fifty years before. Dressers and wardrobes were all built into the walls, and even the bed seemed to be nestled in an uplifting of the floor. Tana slipped out of her shoes and kicked them in the general direction of the maidslot, which would suck them up, clean them, and store them in one of the wardrobes. Her robes quickly followed, and then with some difficulty she peeled off her shirt and panties and sent them along. The soft purr of the bath motor beckoned.

Touching a control on the wall, Tana watched as a section of the floor rolled away to reveal a steaming tub. She descended slowly into the bubbling water, feeling its warmth penetrate her ravaged joints, stepping up her circulation and carrying off the noxious by-products of the Gamaean palsy that inhibited her movements and, in large doses, could set her muscles to spasming violently. Inching her way carefully into its depths, she lowered herself until she sat comfortably on one of the shelves with the frothing liquid up to her neck.

Tension drained from her body like water from a sieve, leaving her feeling limp and luxurious. At the very edges of her consciousness she could sense Doc's continued excitement about the new horse, but he was so far away and she so accustomed to his transmissions that it did not intrude on her languor. Should have hit the scent button, she thought drowsily, her mind clouding rapidly. But she hadn't the ambition to call out to the computer. I wonder what Chelsea would have thought of this opulence, she mused, a woman who built a ranch up from nothing and hung on to it through a war . . . Her life was so different from mine, and yet I feel as though we are soul mates. Both trying to do the impossible, like dad said; both struggling to prove the naysayers wrong. I wonder if she argued with her niece, Verde, the way I find myself bickering with Lystra. I wonder if she loved soaking in a hot bath at the end of the day.

I wonder if she ever watched the horses mating . . .

Drifting on the edge of sleep, it was not difficult for her to imagine Chelsea squatting at the edge of the tub, her graying hair caught back in a clasp at the nape of her neck, her worn denim trousers tight on a body kept fit by hard work. She wore a long-sleeved shirt, open at the neck, and her deeply tanned skin showed the creases of age, but she was still a strong and vital woman. "Of course I watched the horses," Chelsea told her. "That was my livelihood in the making, those foals. It was a matter of great concern to me."

And afterward? Tana wondered. All those times when Zachery was still on Argo and you were here alone, what did you do?

"Hated it," Chelsea said bluntly. "Not the feeling, just not having him here. I always hated not having him here. I could almost bless the Troaxians for driving him off Argo so he had to stay with me."

Was he ever there when the horses mated? Tana wanted to know.

Chelsea gave a low, throaty laugh that sounded remarkably

like Dak's. "Oh, yes, he knew when the horses came into season, and he knew it was to his advantage to be around when they did."

Tana felt flushed at the thought of her unmarried ancestors indulging their passions in a darkened boudoir or even an empty stall in the stable. Is it more exciting when you aren't married? she wondered. I never considered having a sexual relationship while I was single, not even with Paul, not even when we were engaged. It was a decision I made, to follow the letter of my religion on that point, but I've always wondered—is it more exciting to make love to someone you haven't promised your life to?

"Not particularly," Chelsea replied. "And it wasn't as though we hadn't made . . . some kind of promise. Just not a promise of marriage."

Had Dak made some kind of promise to Wanda? Paul didn't seem to think so. But maybe Paul was wrong.

Did you always love Zachery, Chelsea? Did you always *know* you loved him?

A nostalgic smile tugged at Chelsea's mouth. "Always."

Then why didn't you marry him sooner?

"Stupidity, mostly," Chelsea admitted. "I got smarter as I got older. Damn lucky for me."

Tana winced at the flagrant use of profanity. It was, of course, the way Chelsea talked, but Tana still hated to think of her heroine that way.

"Hell, woman," Chelsea chided, "don't be so touchy."

You sound like Dak. Does ranching always make people so . . . tough?

"I don't know about Dak," Chelsea replied, "but I learned to be this tough from my mother. I don't know where she learned it. But I'll tell you one thing." Tears glistened in tough Chelsea's eyes. "If there was any way to survive on Earth, my mother found it. Even if she lost my dad, which had to happen when his medication ran out, she would have kept on living, out of sheer spite for Derek Lujan." The name of the saboteur aboard the *Homeward Bound* was bitter in her mouth. "And I would have proved it, too, after the Restoration; I'd have hired a ship and proved it if the Transportation Guild hadn't slapped that damned regulation on the books while the Troaxians were in power."

I'll take care of the regulation, Tana promised. Even if I have to give Jordan those files and compromise the entire Winthrop Dynasty, I will find a way to bring the Survivors home.

"You can't bring my mother home," Chelsea said sadly, and a tear escaped to trickle down one lined cheek. "But find her anyway, Tana. Find her and tell her that I tried till the very end. Even after Zachery passed away, I never gave up. I never gave up."

Neither will I.

"I know you won't. We are much alike, you and I." Chelsea grinned. "Even if you are a clean-mouthed, chaste, religious sort of a bitch." She stood up. "Well, stoke up the fire, sweetie; your husband's on his way."

Tana could feel Doc's enthusiasm pressing gently on her consciousness now; he and Paul had run all the way up to the house from the stable, and Doc was ecstatic. Then, from just outside the house, she could hear the sound of Paul's voice as he greeted Bertha and stomped his boots on the dust grid.

Did you like marriage? Tana asked as the image of Chelsea began to slip away.

"Definitely. One man, one woman, one life, one commitment—I recommend it highly."

Would you tell Dakota?

"Dakota doesn't need to be told." Chelsea laughed. "Hell, woman, he's only thirty! How old was Paul when you met?"

Twenty-eight.

"My father was thirty-three when he married. My mother was thirty-eight! You were lucky, Tana. You found the right man early, and you were smart enough to marry him."

Tana smiled dreamily. I know.

"Let him know you know," Chelsea advised. She winked broadly. "Take him with you to watch the horses."

Then she was gone, and Paul was opening the door. "Ah! You're soaking," he observed.

"Mm, I was almost asleep, too." Tana stirred languidly, feeling a blessed suppleness in her joints. "Bring me a towel, will you."

"Sure." He touched a wall panel, and a drawer slid out with an assortment of thick towels. "So what did you think of Dak's stallion?"

"I think," Tana said, climbing slowly out of the tub and coming dripping across the floor to him, "that if I were a mare, I wouldn't want to hear about artificial insemination." Then she pressed her wet body up hard against her man.

* * *

From the adjoining mud dwelling Coconino could hear the sounds of his stepson and daughter-in-law making love. He smiled to himself, thinking of his own youth with Hummingbird and with Ironwood Blossom. But he moved to the other side of his adobe chamber, where the sounds were less obvious. For though he thought with fond nostalgia of those distant days with his young brides, it was Jumping Moon with whom he had spent his most recent years, and it was she whom he missed now. The Mother Earth had called her over a year ago, but it still seemed to Coconino as though at any moment she might come through the door with a bundle of wood for the fire or a basket of corn she had been grinding in the sun.

I should take another wife, he thought. But who is there left in this northern village? So many have gone to the south to join the People there—and that is good. It is a rich place, full of the bounty of the Mother Earth, and the Way of the People there is loving. But here in the north, only the young and the old are left. The old ones, like me, are too set in their ways to move, and the young ones are too devoted to them to leave them alone. We should all go. I should tell them at the end of the summer that the time has come to leave this place and we should all pack our belongings and journey to the south. I would only have to say it and they would all go; the old ones still think I am a god.

But I have spent my whole life convincing them to do things because they are good to do and not because Coconino says so. I will not change now. I will not even go to the south myself and give them an opportunity to follow me like a quail chick follows its mother. It must be their own decision. So I will stay. Alone.

Of course, there was Sleeps in the Sun, who was a widow of some forty summers, but she tended to talk ceaselessly of nothing; Coconino could not imagine living in the same house with her. Tender Dove had been a possibility, but before Coconino was ready to consider taking a new wife, Tender Dove had decided to move with her two sons to the southern village. It was a good choice, and Coconino did not begrudge her.

Now the only single women left in the northern village were the maidens, those nubile young things whose parents watched with growing concern the dwindling number of young males in the north. No doubt any one of them would be thrilled if the great Coconino should bring his gifts to their door, but Coconino did not want a young wife. After Ironwood Blossom had died of a rattlesnake bite nearly eighteen years ago, Coconino had ended his year of mourning by taking a young bride called Feather Seed. She was in her fifteenth summer, a lively, laughing girl, but Coconino soon discovered that the frivolous nature he had found so endearing in Hummingbird when he was a young man of twenty was tiresome at forty-three. Worse, the child—for so she seemed to Coconino, who had daughters older than she—held the old, ridiculous notion that he was a god of some sort. If that had irritated him when the Magic Place That Bends Time first coughed him up in This Time, he found it even more obnoxious in a generation that had seen him toil and strain, err and bleed, like all the other men and women of the People.

So at the end of a year and a half, when Feather Seed delivered herself of a healthy son, Coconino smiled and patted her on the head and told her he had made arrangements for her to go and be the wife of a young hunter called Black Ram. Eyes had grown wide in the village at this dismissal of a wife lawfully taken, but Coconino had quickly assured them that this was not a practice for all the People to follow, only Coconino. There was some advantage, after all, to being thought a god. And as for Feather Seed, she had had her heart set on Black Ram before the great Coconino had called at her mother's house, so she was perfectly happy to make the change. Coconino had blessed her with his child, and now she had the young man she truly loved to help her raise it.

After that Coconino had resolved to live alone. But he was still robust and vigorous, and celibacy did not suit him. Beyond that, he was lonely; he had not been without a companion since his youth, and the emptiness of his house only echoed the emptiness of his life. So he cast his eye about the village and found it resting on Jumping Moon.

She was a widow of thirty-five years, with four children still at home. There was nothing much of beauty in her face, but there was kindness and wisdom. He tried striking up conversations with her and found her an intelligent and forthright woman, not the least bit awed by his exalted status. She was comfortable with him, and he with her, and so he brought a gift of a bighorn kid to her door and offered it.

At first Jumping Moon had looked surprised, then sad. "I will get Sunflower for you," she had said, referring to her fourteen-year-old daughter.

"No, no!" he had exclaimed hastily. "This gift is not for her.

I have no desire for a bride who will giggle and blush and disturb my peace with petty weeping. It is you I seek, Jumping Moon.''

That had surprised her even more. "But I am old and fat!'' she had protested. "And I was never a beauty.''

"Neither was Ironwood Blossom,'' Coconino had reminded her. "But she was all the wife a man could ask for. I want a sensible woman, Jumping Moon, a woman who will tell me to roll over if I am snoring or to close my mouth if I am making a fool of myself. I want a woman who knows where to put her hands and will not be shocked at where I put mine. I want a companion for my days as well as my nights, someone I can grow old with.''

Jumping Moon had studied him carefully, for she had never thought to marry again after her husband had died. She had certainly never thought to marry such an infamous character as Coconino! But new ideas did not frighten her, only made her stop and think. Finally her eyes had misted a little and she had sighed. "It would be good not to be alone,'' she had admitted.

So they had entered into a union with no illusions. It had taken them some months to adjust, for both were possessed of habits that, after so many years, they were uninclined to change. Yet they always found compromises, for they were always frank with each other and willing to listen to the other's point of view. What began as a convenient arrangement grew in fifteen years to be a warm and comfortable relationship. When in the autumn before last Coconino found her dozing in the sun outside their house and tried to waken her, only to discover that she would never waken again, his grief was not the boundless despair that had marked the passing of his previous wives. But it was a deep sadness.

And he missed her now. He missed her pragmatism and her presence. He missed the familiar way she would touch him. And he missed her warm and welcoming arms when he crawled into his sleeping furs at night.

The sounds from the next house had stopped; Coconino wondered how long he should wait before he went next door to see if his stepson wanted to go hunting with him. They could take the young man's two sons and teach them how to hunt rabbits with a throwing club.

If I keep myself busy, Coconino thought, I will not need to take another wife. For in truth, I do not relish going through all that again—calling her by the wrong name, teaching her not to rearrange my weapons, wondering if she minds all the time I spend telling stories to the children. It is not an easy thing to make two lives fit together that way. I cannot think of a woman I know for whom I would truly want to make that kind of sacrifice again. Except one.

Coconino fingered the turquoise phoenix that hung around his neck.

And she has been dead for seven generations.

Paul finished fastening his shirt, then helped Tana with the waist hook on her robes. "These are more fun to take off than to put on," he told her.

Tana giggled, put her arms around his neck, and rested against him for a moment. "Everyone likes to uncover a mystery."

His hold on her tightened. "Like the mystery of the *Homeward Bound*?"

There was fear in his voice—well masked, well controlled, but Tana knew the sound of it. It was the fear he'd tried to keep from her during her first pregnancy: What if her body really couldn't take the strain of childbearing? It was the fear in his eyes when it was time to put Jasmine down: What if the pain of separation from her aid dog triggered a violent seizure? Only now the unvoiced fear was, What if I transport you to Earth and something goes wrong?

"We're very close, aren't we?" she asked softly.

"We could be closer if you'd let me publish," he replied. "Even internally. The more minds working on this project, the faster it will go."

It was a dodge, and she knew it. "The more people who know about it, the sooner it will leak, and the sooner it will be abused."

"Tana." He drew back just enough to look into her eyes. "It's going to leak. Sooner or later word is going to get out. Sooner or later we will publish and we will patent, and then what?"

"Then we'll own it," she replied with more edge than she had intended. "And we'll control it."

"For how long?"

She sighed. "Long enough to finish getting some safeguards in place. Paul, you know I've been working with legislators and leaders on a dozen worlds. Using the privacy issue as a base, we're starting to get local laws into effect which will cover the use of P-TUP when it breaks on the scene. And with Ambassador D'Angus of the Pax Circumfra on our side now, there are things that can be done on an interglobal level to minimize the military danger, cushion the economic blow to industries like the Transportation Guild. There are so many ramifications to this project, Paul. I just want all the bases covered before we go public.''

"So do I," he agreed. "But Tana, we'll never get them all. In the final analysis, we can't be responsible for what twisted minds will do with a tool we mean only for good.''

She gave him a wry smile, for they'd had this conversation so many times before, and she really didn't want to have it again now. "Like giving money to a beggar?" she asked. "We can't be responsible if he spends it on stimulants instead of food.''

"Something like that.'' He hugged her again, wrapping himself protectively around her. "Tana.'' His cheek nestled in her honey-colored hair. "Don't make the trip to Earth yourself.''

There. He'd said it. Tears sprang to Tana's eyes. "Paul, I'm going to go.'' *Paul, I'm going to have this baby. Paul, I'm going to take Jas to the infirmary myself.* "I've spent too much of my life working toward this goal. It would be like you inventing P-TUP and letting someone else test it. Or Dak developing this new breed of horses and then not being there the first time they were shown. It's my child, Paul. I've carried it for years. Let me give it birth.''

He gave a ragged sigh, and she knew how close to tears he was himself. "I know,'' he said. "But you don't go until I say it's ready. Absolutely, perfectly, flawlessly ready.''

She laughed into his chest. "Don't worry; I haven't been suicidal in a number of years.'' She squeezed her arms more tightly around his neck. "Besides, how can I rescue any survivors if I'm in trouble myself?''

Jarl looked at the trace he'd picked up when he'd talked his way into Dr. Rutgers's lab with Mercrutia. She hadn't seen him lift it, of course—she'd been busy checking the security codes on the other equipment, making sure nothing had been tampered with. "All secure,'' she'd announced, and he'd stood there smiling with his hand in his pocket, the trace locked inside a memory capsule. Then she'd sauntered out behind him, never suspecting that her talkative companion had been lifting traces while he conversed animatedly about the previous night's windleball game.

But looking at this clip, he was disappointed. It was just a kid on a horse, running through an open field. How could that be important? Still, if it had been in the equipment in Dr. Rutgers's lab, it must have some significance. He'd show it to Ms. Striker, anyway.

Maybe Dr. Rutgers was just showing someone a holo of his son, Jarl thought. Maybe that was all this was.

If so, then there *certainly* wouldn't be any harm in passing it along to Ms. Striker.

CHAPTER SIX

Phoenix stopped on the ledge in front of Michael's house, toying unconsciously with the turquoise medallion that hung from her neck. The air was pleasantly warm, for it was the Moon of Cactus Flowers, and even here in the high country the kiss of summer was upon the land. From within she could hear Swan's light giggle and Michael's deeper playful laugh in a bantering exchange. Phoenix coughed once and wondered if she should come back later, but the response from inside was quick. "My door is open," called Swan, although there followed a muted instruction to her lover.

Ducking low, Phoenix entered the adobe chamber in the hillside. Ages ago a powerful river had eroded this shelf in its bank, then dwindled to nothing, leaving the shallow cave that provided ceiling and floor to a dozen houses. The ancient Sinagua had first divided the cave with walls of dried brick, but it was only twenty-five years ago that the People had reinhabited this place, shoring up its crumbling walls and stamping out paths between this group of homes and similar clusters scattered around the freestanding butte.

"Good afternoon, She Who Saves," Swan said politely, sending a well-placed elbow back toward Michael, who lounged on the floor directly behind where she sat. "Would you like some food?"

"No, but perhaps a drink of water," Phoenix replied, kneeling on the floor, facing the couple.

Swan's eyebrows flew up, and her highly expressive face registered surprise. Phoenix asked for nothing from anyone as far as the younger woman knew; she had established herself as a provider and a giver of gifts, not as a gracious recipient. So

Swan jumped to fetch anything the old woman was inclined to accept from her hand, even if it was only a cool drink of water.

Phoenix had Michael's attention now, too. He sat up and looked across at her with dark, questioning eyes. In the dim light of the adobe chamber the shadows on his face masked any trace of his Mountain heritage, making him the very image of Coconino.

"What is on your mind?" he asked—far too direct a question for one of the People. Ah, you and I are too much alike, Michael, Phoenix thought. We will always betray our upbringing in that other culture, where life is longer but more hectic, where machines remove people from the voice of the Mother Earth.

"I need a piece of paper," she responded with kindred frankness. "Do you have any?"

"Paper?" His surprise was clear. Across the room, Swan paused as she filled a clay bowl for Phoenix; the word was foreign to her, having no equivalent in the language of the People.

"Yes, paper," Phoenix replied impatiently, knowing he had traded for some on his last journey to the Camp of the Others. Like his grandfather, he intended to make a written record of some of the stories of the People. "I want to write something down."

There was a short pause; then Michael rose to his knees and crawled to the shelf that served as a storage area in the rear of the house. He rummaged around through a large woven basket and, after a moment, came back with a sheet of heavy, crude papyrus that resembled parchment more than paper. "It's not very good quality," he apologized. "They were experimenting with a new paper-making process using some of the river reeds. I got the rejects for almost nothing."

"It will do," she told him, taking the stiff sheet from him. "And do you have ink?"

He returned to the basket and produced a small pot with a leather cover. "Mix some water with it," he told her. "It stores better dry, so I don't wet it till I'm ready to use it."

"I'll bring it back," she promised as she tucked the pot inside her leather shirt.

Swan handed her the bowl of water now. "Thank you," Phoenix said, and drank deeply.

"Why do you need paper?" Michael asked finally.

"I need to write a letter," she told him, handing the bowl

back to Swan. Then she added casually, in that other language, "A sort of last will and testament."

Shock froze Michael's face. "What?!"

She was afraid his reaction would be that. "I'm not immortal," she growled, and wondered if she should have said anything. But she had to eventually. "And when I'm gone," she went on, "I want to leave a message behind for Coconino. He will show up some day, you know. Nina foretold it, and she was not wrong about much. So when he gets here, I want him to know what happened. That I took up the service of the Mother Earth. That I saw his children grow to adulthood. I want him to know . . ." Her voice trailed off. "That I have heard the voice of the Mother Earth," she finished.

For a moment there was silence. Then, "You have?" Michael asked with more longing than disbelief. He, too, coveted that communion that his father was said to have had and that his half brother, Nakha-a, was famous for. "What does she say?"

Phoenix let out a breath she didn't realize she had been holding. "That it is time to die."

Michael sprang up in consternation, as though he could forbid such a thing through a physical confrontation. "No!" he cried. "What do you mean? Are you sick? What are you saying?"

Towering over her like that, seeking to stop the inevitable course of events, he was so like his father that Phoenix wanted to weep. Instead she climbed wearily to her feet, bent over as he was in the low-ceilinged room. "No, I am not sick," she said quietly. "And I do not know why she has given me this word. But it is as clear as the cry of a hawk, Michael, or the bleating of a bighorn. The Mother Earth is calling me to her, and I am too old and too battle-worn to resist any longer. She is right, after all. It is time."

"No!" he protested, but she turned away from him toward the door.

"Thank you for the water, Swan," she said, and ducked back outside.

Once on the ledge, she straightened up and breathed deeply of the blossom-scented air. How she loved this time of year! It was at this season that she and Coconino had first come to this canyon as he searched for the one-horned antelope they called Tala. They had been the first humans in some five centuries to lay eyes on the stone houses baking in the canyon walls. How insufferably proud Coconino had been at that discovery! How young and strong and enticingly masculine . . .

Phoenix closed her eyes and tried to shut out the vision of him. For a number of years it had faded from her mind, so that she thought of him only rarely. But with Michael's return all the old emotions had flooded back to her. It seemed that each season she missed Coconino more acutely. She found herself having imaginary conversations with him, sharing stories about his children, laughing about his grandchildren . . . But the tears always followed. Because when Coconino came out of the time warp that had snatched him away from her, he would still be the twenty-year-old youth he had been then.

I don't want youth anymore, Phoenix had to admit. I thought you were young for me then, Coconino, for I was ten years older. Now I am fifty-five, and I appreciate the wisdom and comparative serenity bought with a lifetime of experience. I do not envy the young their simple vision of the world or their hormone-driven exploits.

But I remember. Mother Earth, do I remember! The closeness of Coconino, the smell of him, the rush of desire when his eyes rested on me. I can well understand how Sky Dancer could have succumbed to Michael's captivating smile, to the strangeness of him, and to the depth of her own longing.

Perhaps, Phoenix thought as she started down the trail toward her own house, I could even have accepted a union between them. They are only half brother and sister, after all, and ancient history tells of other such unions. Isis and Osiris, who established the Egyptian culture. Abraham and Sarah, who founded the nation of Israel. Even the People have their story of Chico and Elena, though that couple is not highly revered. But the precedent is there. I could have declared it acceptable and forced the Council to concur. I could have done that for them.

But I never had the chance. The decision was out of my hands.

Phoenix waited three months after Michael's return from the south, until the crops were in and the People were caught up in the bustling activity of summer. Then she packed her traveling gear, took up her bow, and struck off to find the southern village. Perhaps she could talk Sky Dancer into coming home again; perhaps it was still too soon. But one way or the other, Phoenix had to make the journey. She had to see Sky Dancer again.

The trail Michael had left on his return was faint, but she was tracker enough to follow it back to its source. Through mountain passes, along rivers dried to almost nothing in the summer heat, across a sea of grass she traveled until she came upon cultivated fields at the foot of a range of mountains.

The woman who looked up from her hoe was familiar, but the sun was in Phoenix's eyes and she could not tell at first who it was. It was obvious, however, that the woman recognized her, for she gave a short gasp and dropped her implement. "She Who Saves!" the woman cried. Then, to Phoenix's amazement, the woman turned and ran across the field to where other farmers were at work.

They had formed a tight knot when Phoenix approached them, and their faces were filled with apprehension. "Good day, my brothers and sisters," Phoenix said solemnly, feeling somehow that her unexpected arrival should not cause quite such a commotion. "Mended Wing, is it not? And Muddy Hands? How fare the People in this place?"

"We have fared well, She Who Saves," replied Muddy Hands, but behind him there was a hiss. "We have," he repeated stubbornly, "although we have done better in past seasons than we do in this one."

"Why? What is the trouble?" Phoenix asked.

There was an uncomfortable pause. "Nakha-a is sick," Muddy Hands said finally. "Night and day the People implore the Mother Earth for his recovery, but he grows no better. We fear she will take him from us."

"She is angry," growled one of the women, whom Phoenix recognized as a daughter of Loves the Dust, although she could not tell which one. They had been mere children when Nina's band had left the northern village.

"Why is she angry?" Phoenix asked, feeling the hostility radiating from that young woman and others around her.

"You have come a long way, She Who Saves," Muddy Hands interrupted. "No doubt you have come to see your daughter. Come with me. I will take you to her."

Phoenix suppressed a shiver as she turned and followed Muddy Hands away from the cluster of people in the field. There had been some bitterness when she and Nina had split the tribe eight years earlier, but Michael had said nothing of any lingering resentment. Rather, he had spoken of how warmly he and Sky Dancer had been greeted, of how ecstatic Nakha-a had been at his reunion not only with his sister but with the brother he had felt only as a tugging at his consciousness. They had held each other by the shoulders and searched, each in the other's face, for some reflection of their common parentage. There was little *enough, for Nakha-a resembled his mother more strongly than his father, and Michael bore upon his features the stamp of mixed blood. Still they commented on eyes that tilted the same way, a smile that showed the same even white teeth.*

Why, then, was there this discomfiture at her arrival? "I have had news of your village from Michael," Phoenix began, and wondered that the man with her flinched. "He says that this is a rich place to live, with good fields and plenty of game in the mountains. He says that the People are happy here."

"The Mother Earth has been good to us here," Muddy Hands conceded. "We tried another place, a river valley farther north, but Nakha-a told us it was not the place we should stay. Many of us questioned him, for he was only a boy then, but his mother trusted, and we all followed. I am glad we did, for this is a good place. Better, I think, than the Valley of the People where I grew up. Since then we have come to trust in all that Nakha-a says. We are very fearful, She Who Saves, that we might lose him now. He is as wise as the Mother ever was, and he is yet a youth of twenty summers."

Phoenix nodded, knowing what a tribute it was to compare the lad to the woman who had led the People when Phoenix first had come to them. "That is what Michael says," she agreed.

Suddenly Muddy Hands stopped. "It would be better if you did not mention that name," he said. "It is not held with honor in our village."

Phoenix was shocked into silence. She continued to follow Muddy Hands through the fields and up into a wooded river valley until they came at last to the summer camp of the People. Gloom hung over the clearing in which stood the dozens of wicki-ups that were their habitation.

All activity stopped as she followed Muddy Hands into the village. Eyes watched not with curiosity but almost with fear as she passed one brush dwelling after another. Finally a woman with graying hair came out of one and stood before them.

"Witch Woman," she said quietly.

"Nina."

Time had not been kind to Nina. Although she was younger than Phoenix by thirteen years, her face was deeply lined and her oversized nose stood out like a hawk's beak. Worst of all, there was no lightness in her eyes, no trace of the warmth of contentment that Phoenix had known in her when she bore Coconino's child. Instead, Nina had become pinched and hard, *her eyes a glistening black as she surveyed this intruder in her domain.*

"You have come to see your daughter," Nina said, as though that were a revelation of the gift of prophecy she no longer possessed and not a deduction of simple logic. I'm sorry, Phoenix thought. I'm sorry the Mother Earth took away your gift of prophecy. But perhaps it was never yours. You never had it until you conceived Nakha-a from Coconino's seed. Perhaps it was always the child inside you, near you, that let you hear her voice so clearly. But I am sorry. You never had much in life outside that.

"Yes, I have come to see Sky Dancer," Phoenix replied. "But I hear that your son is ill. I would like to see him, too. Perhaps the knowledge I have from the Mountain will be of some help."

Nina stiffened, and her mouth puckered as though she had eaten a green chokecherry. But after a moment she relaxed. "You will see your daughter first," Nina dictated. "Then perhaps you will visit my son."

Perhaps? Phoenix thought incredulously. I half raised the boy! Taught him to hunt, gave him his first bow . . . But she said nothing and simply followed Nina's gesture to enter the nearby wickiup.

It was a moment before her eyes adjusted to the darkness. "Mother?" came a tearful voice.

Phoenix knelt beside the form lying on a hide in the pungent-smelling wickiup. "Sky Dancer, are you all right? What is it? What's happened?"

"Oh, Mother, I'm so glad you're here!" Sky Dancer sobbed, clutching her mother in a desperate embrace.

As Phoenix held the trembling form tightly against her, it was obvious what the problem was. Sky Dancer was pregnant. Her womb was swollen to impossible proportions for her tiny frame, ripe with a child due to make its appearance any day. Michael's child. It explained so much.

For several long moments Phoenix could do nothing but hold her daughter and weep with her. Weep for her loneliness, weep for her fear. Weep for the condemnation she must be suffering from the People of the village.

"Is this why you wouldn't come back with Michael?" Phoenix asked hoarsely when she was able to speak.

"Michael doesn't know, and you mustn't tell him," Sky Dancer sobbed. "Promise me you won't ever tell him! It would kill him. He was so ashamed the way it was."

Phoenix stroked her daughter's hair and tried to soothe her. "No, we won't ever tell him," she whispered. "He doesn't need to know."

"I never believed it could happen to us," Sky Dancer whimpered. "And then when it did, I was so glad. I thought nothing in life could be so wonderful as loving Michael. But we tried to stop it. When we reached the village here, we said we wouldn't anymore. We said we would live as brother and sister again. But I couldn't go back to the way it was." Her words tumbled out, a pent-up flow of emotion released by the safety of her mother's arms. "Nakha-a knew. He knew even though we didn't say anything. He told me he could make it all right with the people of the village, but he couldn't make it all right for Michael. Michael just couldn't live with it. He's a good man, Mother, he really is, and you mustn't blame him for any of this."

"Hush," Phoenix crooned, "hush, little one. I am the last person to cast stones."

"Oh, but Mother!" Sky Dancer cried, pulling away and imploring her mother with terror-filled eyes. "You must do something; you must! Nakha-a is sick, he's dreadfully sick and they say he might die, and they say it's because of the baby. They think the Mother Earth is angry because of what Michael and I did, and she's going to punish them by taking Nakha-a away, and, oh, Mother—! They want to kill my baby!"

Fear lanced through Phoenix like a knife. "They what?"

"They say that my baby is an abomination, and that's why the Mother Earth is making Nakha-a so sick. But it's not true, it can't be true. The Mother Earth wouldn't punish Nakha-a for what Michael and I did. And it's not the baby's fault, he didn't do anything. If she would punish anyone, it would be Michael and me."

"Don't worry," Phoenix said firmly. "No one is going to hurt you, and no one is going to hurt your baby. I promise you that."

Rash promise! Phoenix thought now as she trudged along the trail toward her house with her single sheet of paper clutched in one hand. Oh, Coconino, if only you had been there—but what could you have done that was any more than what I did? Only kept me company, matched your steps to mine through the coming trials. What I would give, Coconino, to have you match strides with me once again! But that is not to be. The Mother Earth was gracious to bless me with a child—your child, though another woman was her mother. I must be content with that. I must be content with that.

Reaching her home, Phoenix ducked through the doorway and headed straight for the water jar. She mixed the ink carefully, pared a quill into an acceptable pen, and then sat poised in the fading light. What would she write? What could she say to her absent love that would give him comfort, that would convey to him all the joys of the life she had known among the People and none of the sorrows? She would tell him of the children, of course: Sky Dancer, Nakha-a, Michael. She would tell him that though she had never known conjugal pleasure with him, still she had his child. He would know how much that meant to her.

But she would tell him nothing of the cost . . .

Phoenix found Nakha-a lying on a bed of fir boughs covered by a soft hide. He was sweating out of proportion to the heat of the day yet shivering despite a light cotton blanket drawn over him, and the rasping of his breath was frightening to hear.

"It's some kind of respiratory infection," she told Nina. "A bad one. How long has he been like this?"

"He began coughing just after the new moon," Nina replied, bathing her son's forehead with a damp cloth. The young man's wife was absent; she had small children and had been told by the village Healer that she must keep them away from the sick man. "In three days he had to take to his bed. Now he does nothing but sleep; I can hardly get any food into him."

The young man opened his eyes at the sound of the unfamiliar voice. "Phoenix?"

"Hush, my son, don't speak," Nina urged. "Yes, Phoenix has come to us. She will take Sky Dancer away, and then you will get better."

"No!" Nakha-a protested weakly, but it took no more than a hand on his chest to restrain him. "Do not take her, Phoenix," he rasped. "She must stay here."

"She won't go anywhere till her child is born," Phoenix hedged.

Suddenly Nakha-a was seized with a violent fit of coughing. Nina clutched her son, holding his spasming body as Phoenix watched helplessly until finally, finally it passed and Nakha-a fell back exhausted.

"He needs medicine," Phoenix said urgently to Nina. "They have medicines on the Mountain that can help."

"He has medicine," Nina hissed. *"Pepper Woman has brought every herb she has to fight the coughing sickness. It is the Mother Earth's anger that must be appeased. As soon as the child is born, as soon as the abomination is destroyed—"*

"No!" Phoenix gritted. *"His sickness has nothing to do with the child! It is—"* How could she explain bacteria and viruses to this primitive woman? *"It is an evil kachina which has entered his lungs, and we must get medicine to chase it away. There is medicine on the Mountain. I will go there to get it. You are so far south here, it cannot be many days journey to the west. I can make it in time to save him, Nina, I know I can."*

Nina's mouth twisted in a bitter expression that was a mockery of the smile Phoenix remembered. *"She Who Saves again, Witch Woman?"* she sneered.

"Only promise me you will not hurt Sky Dancer while I am gone."

Nina drew back. *"She is like a daughter to me,"* she protested. *"I nursed her at my breast. I will do nothing to harm her."*

"But you would kill her child."

"The child is an abomination!" Nina spit. *"Got on her by her own brother, cursed be his name! It cannot be allowed to live!"*

"The child has nothing to do with this!" Phoenix insisted. *"You must do nothing—nothing!—to harm it until I return!"*

"You are wrong, Witch Woman," Nina scoffed. *"You were wrong to keep so many of the People in the north, and you are wrong now. Go for the medicine if you like, but nothing will help my son until the child dies!"*

"Your gift of prophecy has dried up like your womb!" Phoenix said. *"The Mother Earth does not tell you such filth, only your own bitterness."*

"At least my womb bore fruit before it dried!" Nina shot back. *"And I am not so deaf to the Mother Earth's voice—"*

"Stop." The mere whisper of Nakha-a's voice put an end to their argument. *"Phoenix, go. To the west . . . find the old Black Path. Six days . . . till the babe . . ."* He hadn't the strength to continue.

But it was enough for Phoenix. As she had trusted his mother's judgment so many years ago, now she trusted the son. She had six days to get to the Mountain and bring back medicine, perhaps even a doctor. Six days to save Sky Dancer's child . . .

It took her only four days to get there. Heading due west

across the grasslands, she skirted a mountain range and found the remains of a highway snaking through the desert. It led her to the Dead City from which she knew her way to the Mountain. As the sun set on that fourth day, she labored up the smooth, winding road to the artificial lights of the settlement where she had been born.

They were waiting for her, warned by an electronic monitoring system installed after Derek Lujan had sabotaged the last of their aircraft. "The Infirmary," she croaked to the man carrying a disrupter rifle. "I need to see a doctor."

"Are you hurt?" he asked cautiously, the rifle not aimed at her but resting lightly in his hands. Though she had left her weapons in the southern village, her primitive dress and bedraggled appearance had the small group on edge.

"Just thirsty," she gasped, coming farther into the light. Her long black hair was braided, and she had not bothered to don a shirt. "Anyone got a cold beer on him?"

"My God, it's Debbie McKay," the man realized. "Terry! Run and get Dick. Luis, bring up a pedal car; she's exhausted. We'll get you to the Infirmary, Ms. McKay. Just take it easy."

"Phoenix," she panted. "My name is Phoenix. And it's not me that needs the doctor . . ."

But no one was listening. Shouts echoed across the mountain installation, and moments later she was in the front seat of a pedal car cruising past the ancient observatories to a low building that served as their medical facility. Someone pushed a glass of water into her hand, and she drank it gratefully. She was glad it was not beer; her remark had been facetious, for she had not touched alcohol in so long, she did not know what it would do to her system anymore. Especially when she had run for four days straight.

A blond woman met them as her husky escorts walked Phoenix into the Infirmary. "What's going on?" she asked. "Who—?"

"Krista!" Phoenix exclaimed as she recognized Michael's mother. She was nearly forty now, heavier than she had been as a teenager, but the shining blond hair and the clear, sweet face were unmistakable. "Krista, thank God. Pack a bag, woman. We have to get right back; there's no time to lose."

Krista stared at her a moment. "Debbie McKay," she said finally. "Well. Sit down."

Phoenix was perplexed by this reception, but as her escort faded away, she felt a certain weakness in her knees and sank into the chair Krista indicated. Krista found another chair and set it where she could face her visitor. For a moment she just looked at Phoenix. Then, "How is Michael?" she asked dispassionately.

Still Phoenix did not understand. "Fine," she answered. "Thriving. But his half brother is dying. It's some kind of respiratory infection, I don't know what. You have to come with me. The village is east of here."

"Ms. McKay, you know we don't interfere in the life of the primitive village," Krista interrupted. "We can't go running out there every time there's an injury or an illness—they wouldn't want us to. That's always been their policy, and ours. We sent—" Her voice caught suddenly; she cleared it and continued. "We sent teachers in the old days, but now they don't even want those. Now, if you require medical care while you're here—"

"Damn your sanctimonious policies!" Phoenix said, cutting her off. "There's a boy dying out there. Coconino's other son. Coconino, you remember him? The man whose child you bore?"

Sparks flashed in Krista's blue eyes. "That was long ago," she replied evenly. "I was very young and very romantic. I have a little different view of primitives these days. I also have different responsibilities. I'm the administrator of this facility, and I can tell you that our medicines are in short supply. We have been providing some to Camp Crusoe in exchange for the medical expertise Dr. Winthrop rendered in the past. And now that we no longer have air power, it's extremely difficult for us to get to the manufacturing facilities where we used to make a variety of medications. We've brought what we could back here to the mountain, but—"

"I don't want to hear your problems!" Phoenix snapped, slapping her hand on a nearby cart. "All I want is a ten-day course of antibiotics, maybe a small oxygen tank—"

"Out of the question," Krista said, rising abruptly.

"Damn your blue eyes!" Phoenix flared, leaping to her feet. "If we don't save this boy, they're going to kill Michael's son!"

Krista blanched and reached for the chair she had just vacated. "His son?" She wavered dangerously, and Phoenix reached out a hand to steady the younger woman.

"It gets worse," she told Krista gently. "The girl who's having the baby is Michael's half sister."

A cry escaped Krista as her hand flew to her mouth.

"He didn't know," Phoenix lied. "He didn't know until it was too late. Then he gave her up. Before he knew she was pregnant,

he gave her up and went back to the northern village. Now she's all alone. She's all alone, having Michael's baby, and if Nakha-a dies, the People will kill Michael's son as soon as it's born.''

Krista sank into the chair, tears sliding down her face. ''And Michael's not there.''

''No. Nakha-a's village is due east of here, and Michael is in the north.''

Krista's head dropped forward, and her shoulders shook slightly. Then she took a deep breath and straightened up. ''How long will it take us to get there?'' she asked, her voice calm and steady once more.

''Half a day by truck,'' Phoenix estimated. ''The old roads are in bad shape, so we'll have to wait for morning, much as I hate to. But Nakha-a said we have six days, and it's only been four. That will give us a day and a half to spare.''

Krista rose more slowly this time. ''I'll talk to Rex Fisher about a truck—he's the new administrator here, and he owes me a favor. I'm sorry I can't offer you the hospitality of my home, but you may sleep here in the Infirmary if you like. There's food in the health techs' lounge. I'll pick you up first thing in the morning.''

Phoenix remembered the relief with which she'd climbed into the Infirmary bed, knowing that Krista would accompany her on her mission to save both Nakha-a and Sky Dancer's baby. She had thought when the young doctor had walked out of the room that night that she had secured Krista's full cooperation.

She had been wrong.

A tear blotched the fresh paper in Phoenix's hand. Taking a braid of her own graying hair, Phoenix blotted the moisture carefully, then blew on the paper to dry it. What would Coconino think if he saw tear stains on this letter when it finally came into his hands?

He would think that I loved him to the very end, Phoenix knew. And he would be right. But his heart will be heavy with his own grief; I must not add mine to it. I must write a letter that will lift his spirit and tell him I am at peace with my destiny. After all, had I not the privilege of learning from him to serve the Mother Earth? Did I not serve her children, and his, as faithfully as I could? Let him know those things when his feet walk once more upon the Paths of the People. Let him know that, finally, I heard her voice and obeyed it.

She dipped her quill in the ink pot and began to scratch on the stiff paper, and because she had never written in the language of the People, she found herself using the language of the Mountain, which Coconino could read as well. "I am Phoenix," she wrote, "sister-brother of Coconino: He Who Was and Will Be Again. At his coming, give these words to him . . ."

CHAPTER SEVEN

"Stop!" Tana called as the news headlines scrolled past. The letters shimmered in the air over her desk; holographic display was more conducive to moving images than stationary text. "Teeg: show me this," she commanded as she poked her finger through Monique D'Agnus's name.

At her feet Doc grunted and stretched, unperturbed by the low level of excitement his mistress was exuding.

The image of a familiar commentator appeared in the display, an ageless woman with striking Oriental features. It was a composite, Tana knew, generated and voiced by a sophisticated computer, but the program was a good one, and the script for this commentator was usually well written. "Yesterday, in an address to the Camera Prima on her native Bati, Pax Circumfra Ambassador Monique D'Agnus surprised legislators with a scathing attack on what she called 'uninvited intrusion.' "

A phrase I gave her, Tana thought.

The commentator's image shrank to one-sixteenth the display size and looked on with rapt attention as a holo of the ambassador addressing the Camera took over the bulk of the display. "Those who believe," D'Agnus said in fluid and forceful English—translated from Italian, no doubt, by another computer program and reissued in a perfect replication of the ambassador's voice, "that they may bypass customs checkpoints to conduct their business—no matter how legitimate that business may be—and suffer no ill consequences are gravely mistaken." The Camera faded away as the image of the ambassador grew to full size, and Tana could see the forthright glint in her eye. She had an incredible personal magnetism, this Monique D'Agnus; Tana had felt it in their meeting several weeks earlier.

"I tell you," D'Agnus asserted, "that uninvited intrusion

into the lawful domain of another government is nothing less than invasion and piracy. Whether through the use of slipper ships, private warp terminals—''

Or means yet to be discovered, Tana urged silently.

''—or any conveyance available now or in the future—''

Close enough.

''—the transportation of persons or objects into domains or premises, without the knowledge of the authority holders of that domain or premises, constitutes invasion.'' There was a brief reaction shot of some legislators looking very offended; the display identified them as being from the mercantile province of Cor. ''It is an invasion of privacy; it is the usurpation of authority. Furthermore, the transaction of business under these conditions should be branded as illegal and subjected to the same criminal code as smuggling, *whether or not any goods change hands.*''

Excellent! Tana thought. Hammer it home: It's the *concept* of uninvited intrusion that is offensive, not just the monetary damage.

''To enter a place—even a public place—without the knowledge of the authority holder is invasion, and to take away anything—even the information provided by your own senses—is theft. When it occurs between nations, it is piracy.''

Tana's eyebrows arched. The ambassador was certainly pulling no punches! Her father had been right, as usual: D'Agnus was a good person to have on one's side.

The news article continued with reactions from prominent Batian citizens, but Tana clicked it off, her mind humming on another topic. ''Teeg: get me Jordan Zleboton.''

''Jordan is not available at this time,'' the computer replied promptly and politely. ''Would you like to leave a message?''

''Yes,'' Tana said. ''Tell him—''

Suddenly, at her feet, Doc began to growl, and waves of warning pounded against Tana. *Delhi*, he thought at her. *Angry. Hostile. Aggressive—*

Caught by surprise, Tana hardly had time to abort the message when Delhi stormed through the door. Doc came up snarling, barking at the intruder, so that Delhi stopped short and nailed him with an uncompromising stare.

Tana's heart pounded. No, she thought, feeling the first rush of toxins that the Gamaean virus was releasing into her bloodstream. No, I cannot respond to her with anger. I must stay calm. I must assume a relaxed posture. "Doc," she snapped at her aid dog, "quiet."

Hostile, his thoughts kept blaring at her, but Tana thought back, *No. She is no threat. Be calm. Lie down. Do not bark.*

Doc responded by softening his protests to a low growl far back in his throat and backing up half a pace, but he would not lie down. Tana repeated her mental command, but he resisted stubbornly.

Delhi still glared at the big Dalmatian, but she did not come farther into the room while he was growling. Instead she commanded tightly, "Send that animal out of the room—or have you lost control of him completely?"

Tana was taken aback by both the command and the comment. Her first instinct was to tell Delhi which of them she would banish from the office, but from long training she held that back. Instead she took time to wipe the news index from her display and arrange herself more comfortably in her chair. She felt it mold to her shape, took a deep breath, and exhaled slowly; only then did she speak. "You know I won't do that, Delhi," she said calmly. "I need Doc. He's my emotional barometer. Without his audible feedback, I would undoubtedly let myself be irritated by your attitude."

"*My* attitude!" Delhi shrieked, and took two steps toward Tana in spite of the dog. "After what you've done, you have the nerve to sit there and lecture me about *my* attitude?"

Doc flattened his ears and bared his teeth again, erupting in another spate of barking. This time Tana turned all her thoughts ferociously on the dog until he backed down, coming reluctantly to sit by her chair, head submissively bowed. But he didn't like it.

Tana gave herself and the dog several moments to calm down before turning back to Delhi. Her nerves felt jangled, her joints were weak, and she knew she had narrowly missed raising her toxin levels to a point where they brought on a seizure. The hostility in Delhi had roused Doc to a pitch he seldom reached, and her words had stirred an abiding apprehension in Tana. The woman was clearly angrier than Tana had seen her in a long time, perhaps ever. What did she know? Or at least suspect?

"Now," Tana said with an affability designed to distract her cousin. "Why don't you sit down and tell me what it is that's got you in such a dither."

But Delhi was not about to have her ire diffused by either Tana's unruffled tone or her patronizing words. Ignoring the invitation to sit, she strode forward and leaned on Tana's desk. "You sat there and told the board of directors that P-TUP was five years off," she accused. "Now I find out that not only has Paul had three prototypes built, but he's been playing with the same one for the past eleven months. Eleven months, Tana! And to top it all off, there's this." She turned toward the display area of Tana's desk. "Teeg: show my file Incident Five."

Suddenly in the air where she gazed was the image of Derbe riding bareback on Gypsy. Tana felt her cheeks burn as she realized that someone in Paul's organization had stolen the recording, stolen the results of their recent test and turned them over to Delhi. Theft—or, more accurately, espionage—within her own company. Within Paul's elite team. Someone they trusted, someone had betrayed them—

Paul will know, she assured herself, forcing her heart rate back down. Paul will know, and Paul will deal with it. I need only deal with Delhi. I need only keep control of her until we are ready . . .

". . . by the angle of the sun's rays Teeg dates this piece as three weeks ago at eleven forty-six Junoan Time Zone Four," Delhi was saying, "the equivalent of five fifty-two here. Teeg confirms that both you and Paul were in the lab at that time, that none of the standard commuting terminals had been activated. These are not home holos, Tana, these are test results, and there is no receiving terminal in that pasture. This is a successful test of P-TUP."

There was no point denying it. A small smile quirked Tana's mouth. "I said *within* five years," she pointed out. "Not necessarily at the end of five years."

Delhi slammed her hands on the desktop, furious. "Damn it, Tana, why weren't the early phases of this published internally?" she demanded. "Paul is obviously using technology here which other avenues of research could benefit from. And they could assist—"

"Too risky," Tana replied quickly and smoothly. "We can't afford to have this leak outside the institute yet, so the fewer people who know about it, the better. We've a long way to go with it, and I don't want to invite attention and industrial espionage. That's what will happen, you know, if it gets in the wind that we're close to perfecting P-TUP."

"We've got to start the patent process!" Delhi snapped. "An undocumented discovery is an invitation to disaster. My God, what if someone on a research team decides to resign from the institute and go over to—''

"No one who knows anything is going anywhere," Tana told her sharply. "There are precious few of them, and they're happy. Happy! They're thrilled; they love Paul." And one of them has betrayed him. "Besides, even if they didn't, I've got ironclad contracts." She took a slow breath and decreased the intensity in her voice. "Nor is the project undocumented, not really. All the forms are filled out, all the statements written; Paul has seen to that. But I've called a Code Forty-two on them, do you understand me? Code Forty-two. I will not have another Andreas fiasco on our hands."

Delhi drew back with a short laugh. "An Andreas fiasco?" It was the only incident in the IDP's history in which they had published erroneous findings. An overzealous crystologist had claimed the discovery of an eighth crystal that would augment the power and distance of warp transmission, but upon publication, a pair of graduate students had proved that the "new" crystal was simply a mutant form of a previously known crystal. The embarrassment to the institute and the reflection on its reputation had taken decades to fade. "Paul Rutgers doesn't create fiascoes, my dear," Delhi told her. "We both know that."

Tana let the air hang silent a moment, conceding the point while not withdrawing from her stand. "Then let's wait till Paul is ready to publish," she suggested after a beat. Delhi clearly did not trust her judgment, but it was likely that she still had respect for Paul's.

"And when will that be?"

Tana did some quick calculations in her head. She wanted to stall Delhi as long as possible without having to simply pull rank and say "My way"—that was a poor method of leadership. So . . . The actual publishing process would take six to eight months; the conferences her father was arranging for her with more Pax Circumfra envoys couldn't be accomplished any sooner than . . .

"Eight to twelve months," she replied, knowing that would be cutting it fine. But they could stall as they went along if that was necessary, claiming this or that defect.

"Hrmm," Delhi grunted, and Tana could see the numbers whirring in her mind as well. How soon before we can announce publicly. What events to tie into for maximum publicity. Which buyers would be most interested in this product, and what their strategic time frames were. "All right, then," she said finally. "Code Forty-two, another eight months—"

"Eight to twelve," Tana corrected.

"—and I'll destroy this file." She waved the replay out of existence. "Because you're right; it shouldn't exist outside the lab. But you may as well keep me apprised of your progress every step of the way, for as you can see, I will find out anyway. And if you continue to deny me the information I need to do my job effectively, I will take the matter directly to the board of directors."

A minor threat, Tana thought wickedly. I control the board, and you know it. The real threat is that you'll go to Zim. And for that I must be prepared.

Paul Rutgers slammed his hand against the wall of his office, an outburst of frustration he could not contain. Out in the lab, Todd Chang looked up in surprise from the experiment he was setting up; there was a question on his face, but he did not inquire. Whatever Paul was talking about with "the Chief," if they wanted him to know, they'd tell him.

"Chapter and verse," Paul swore tightly, betraying his upbringing in the fundamentalist culture of New Texas. "No one has access to that data except Todd and me."

"She didn't have data, Paul," Tana pointed out. "All she had was a piece of the holographic recording. But she dated it and ran cross-checks against our movements. Not something someone on the outside could do but plenty disconcerting nonetheless."

"Still," he said, "even the holograph . . ." He strode to the door. "Todd, come here a minute." When the lanky youth came to the doorway, he asked, "Is there any way someone could have gotten a piece of the recording we made from Test Eighty-three a couple weeks ago?"

Todd's eyes grew round. "Jesus, no!" he exclaimed; then, growing flustered, "I mean, gee. I mean—" His face grew crimson, for he was acquainted with Tana's bias against profanity and was normally flawless in his respect of it. "Sorry, Chief," he finished lamely.

But Tana waved it off. She was far too concerned with the recording even to be amused by the young man's consternation at having offended the one woman he wanted most in the universe to please. "Todd, someone got a clip of Derbe riding

Gypsy from that test we did and funneled it to Delhi Striker. We have to find the hole and plug it.''

"It wasn't me!'' Todd squawked.

Paul looked genuinely shocked. "Of course it wasn't you!'' he exclaimed, for the idea had never occurred to him. "That's not the question. The question is, who was it and how did he or she do it?''

"I drained the 'corder, Paul,'' Todd told him adamantly. "I secured the data, including the holo, in our files and then wiped the 'corder. Unless . . .''

"What?'' Paul prompted.

"Did we run it through the display on Workstation D the first time?''

Paul searched mentally. "I think we did. We just played that little clip on D, then funneled all the results to your workstation.''

Todd looked a little ashen. "It might have left a trace in the port. No data, just the video trace. Enough to make a decent copy. Geez, I'm sorry, Paul. I didn't think—''

Tana laid a hand on his arm. "It's all right,'' she said softly. "Paul didn't think of it, either. If Delhi hadn't set someone to searching the lab, no one would have stumbled onto it.''

"New procedure,'' Paul said simply. "After every test we wipe all the equipment, whether we've used it or not. If she's set someone in our own ranks to spy on us, they'll be around searching our electronic wastebaskets again.''

"Good idea,'' Tana encouraged. "And see if you can find a way to track down who it was. Delhi may have the person too well protected for me to do much, but I want to know who it is, anyway.'' She could feel Todd relax a little, though the air of guilt still hung strongly about him. She smiled brightly and changed the topic.

"Now. How about today's tests?'' She knew they'd had trouble the week before with an inconsistency in the time-stabilizing algorithm they were using. A mouse they had sent to Juno hadn't arrived until several hours after it had left the institute. It was unharmed, of course, but P-TUP needed pinpoint accuracy not only in warping space but in preventing the backlash warping of time that had plagued the early years of fifth-dimensional travel. Paul and Todd had worked thirty-six hours straight until they had found the anomaly and corrected it. The balance of the week had been spent repeating earlier tests, making sure the adjusted algorithm worked properly. Today's scheduled tests were the last in the series that would prove that they had corrected the error.

But at the mention of them, the two men exchanged an unhappy look.

"What happened?" Tana asked anxiously. Spatial control without time control was useless to her.

"Nothing," Paul said quietly.

"Nothing?"

"That's right, nothing. We put the polyzig on the traveling mat and ran the program, and nothing happened."

Tana could not help feeling a certain relief. Nonfunctioning equipment might be easily explained as a power interruption; at least they had not lost another test animal or had one materialize inside a rock.

"It's got to be in the altphase deconnector," Todd said with more frustration than certainty. "It's that new twenty-six ninety, I know it is. When you're working with time-stabilizing algorithms, the old k-fifteen is more reliable."

"But a k-fifteen doesn't have the capacity," Paul argued. "When you use a thirty-eighty-two, you need the multidimensional—"

"Well, you boys figure it out," Tana interrupted, rising from her chair. Doc rose as well and padded toward the door. "I'm going back to my office." They sounded more embarrassed than distressed about the problem, which meant it was probably minor. And when they started talking numbers and acronyms, it was time for Tana to find something else to do.

"It'll only take a couple of hours," Paul assured her. "Even if we have to replace the whole twelve-twenty—"

"No need to rush," she told him. "If the test doesn't go up for another week or even two, it won't matter much in the scope of things."

"The test will go up tonight," Paul told her with simple confidence. "Do you want us to buzz you?"

But Tana shook her head. "I'm going to be tied up later. You can fill me in at home tonight or tomorrow morning." She gave his arm a gentle squeeze and wished suddenly that she could just rest in his arms for a moment or two, feel his strength and support flowing into her weary body. The idea of Delhi having members of Paul's own team spying on him had pushed Tana to her very limits. But she and Paul had established an unspoken policy early in their relationship of not indulging in intimate contact while at work. Though they were often more relaxed in front of Todd than others, it still seemed unprofessional. So Tana only smiled and let her fingers trail across his arm as she dropped her hand. Then she smiled a farewell at Todd and left the room.

The two men watched her go; the upper half of the office walls were transparent so that Paul could survey his domain from his desk. Doc led by half a step, knowing from their silent communication exactly where Tana was going. She slid smoothly through the lab with a careful, almost gliding motion that disguised the fact that each step was an effort for her.

"Ms. Striker really tore into her, didn't she?" Todd guessed.

"Most likely."

"Why don't you tell her to go home?" Todd asked. "She's so tired."

"She doesn't want to go home," Paul replied. "If she went home, she'd just sit there and chafe because she wanted to be here, doing things. I learned that long ago. She knows how to pace herself, Todd, and if she pushes too hard, Doc will let her know. We just have to trust her judgment and his warnings."

Tana and Doc disappeared through the lab door. Still the two men watched after her.

Suddenly Todd turned to his mentor. "Send me through first," he said bluntly. "Don't send her to Earth until you let me go and check it out."

Paul gave a great sigh. "I can't, Todd. I can check the system every which way, I can do the warp with equipment and animals, but she has to be the first person. Anything else would be a breach of faith. Besides." He forced a smile. "I need you on this end."

"But Paul, her illness—"

"Hasn't made a difference in short jumps and shouldn't in long ones," Paul finished. "But I intend to warp her to Juno and back a few times, just as trials. Don't worry. I'm quite as concerned for her safety as you are."

Todd flushed. "I didn't mean—"

"You meant well, and I appreciate it," Paul told him. "And I appreciate your bringing it up, and making suggestions, and making me accountable. We need always to test each other, to look for the holes . . ." His voice trailed off.

"To plug the leaks," Todd said, completing the thought. "Geez, I'm sorry, Paul. Maybe we should wipe all the equipment before we fix the altphase deconnector."

"Good idea," Paul agreed heartily, with a fatherly slap on the back for his young protégé. "Let's get started."

"It's not fair," Jordan Zleboton accused, shaking a holographic finger at Tana.

Tana was back at her desk, still feeling shaky from the physical and emotional exertions of her day. It was now nearly midnight in New Sydney, where the institute was located, but for Tana it was midafternoon and she was feeling the need for a brief respite before her scheduled call to Katya Bazarov, an economic forecaster on the faculty of the Omniversity. She did not need Jordan waving a finger in her face.

Leaning back in her chair, Tana tried to see something humorous in the man's patronizing tone.

"You've given Lu Parnette something you didn't give me," Jordan went on. "You're undermining my case, Tana."

"Why, Jordan," she replied sweetly, "Lu is filing routine papers. What could that have to do with your case before the Joint Court?"

"Routine, my ass!" Jordan harrumphed, abandoning his patronizing attitude. "A research waiver for a trip to Earth? They should have laughed her right out of the Guild halls, but you know what's happened, Tana? There were some very nervous Guild officials calling the Joint Court justices, and the next thing I know, my case is postponed. Now there's a buzz coming out of the Guild rumor mill that Parnette has some kind of ace up her sleeve and the Guild is going to grant us that waiver."

Good! Tana thought triumphantly.

"So I want to know," Jordan persisted, "what kind of club you gave her that's causing such a fuss."

Tana was careful not to smile, even in the slightest. Lu had told her up front just what she intended to do with Chelsea's pirated files and how things were apt to shake down. Without ever showing more than small pieces of the files, she intended to convince Guild bureaucrats that the Dynasty had stumbled across proof positive that the Terran plague was a hoax. Thus armed, Jordan not only would win his case but would make the Guild look foolish for having blacklisted the planet in the first place—and given Jordan's penchant for the dramatic, the case would be etched across all the news indexes in the galaxy. However, the IDP did not want to cause the Guild such embarrassment, Lu would contend. Thus, they proposed that a research waiver be granted so that the institute could make its investigation on a very low key while Jordan's case was put on hold. If Earth was contaminated, the regulation was still in place; if it was not, the Guild could gracefully withdraw Earth from the blacklist in light of "new evidence" that it had authorized and Jordan's case would quietly go away.

The plan hinged on scaring the Guild bureaucrats into believing Jordan could win and convincing them that they would save face by granting the waiver instead. Apparently the ploy had worked, for here was Jordan wheedling and conniving to find out why Lu was getting results while he was getting none.

"None of your business, Jordan," Tana replied smoothly, glad that none of Jordan's sources in the Guild had tipped him off. "What does it matter as long as the job gets done?"

"It makes me look like a flaming idiot!" he squawked, no longer trying to cajole her. Tana thought his reference a wonderful, evocative image. She could just see her high-powered cousin with his expensive robes going up like a torch, a stupefied look on his face. "I have a lot of years in with this organization, and I don't appreciate being made to take a backseat to your pet attorney!"

"Jordan, I have a new assignment for you," Tana said suddenly.

His face froze in shock. Clearly, he was not through haranguing her yet, using whatever ploy would work to squeeze the information out of her, but that was immaterial to Tana. It was she who would use Jordan, not the other way around. "I suppose you want me to assist Ms. Parnette in this little exercise," he groused.

"Oh, no, I'm sure she can handle it all by herself," Tana replied affably. "No, I need your expertise on some contracts I want drawn up. I want you to hire a spacecraft with full warp capabilities. And a launching staff."

There was a moment of stunned silence. Then, "You're serious!" he gasped. "You're not going to wait for P-TUP, are you? You're going to use the research waiver to take a ship to Earth!"

"Not really," she admitted, for Jordan would carry out the deception better if he knew exactly what she was up to. "The waiver Lu applied for has a five-year span, and I believe we can act within that frame. But I don't want the Guild or anyone else to know I intend to use a radical new technology to make the trip. I want them to think we're going to warp an uncrewed vessel, possibly with some proprietary systems on it, but by basically conventional means. I want you to fool them.''

Jordan paused as the possibilities began to race through his mind. ''What about the case before the Joint Court?'' he asked.

''Fight to win,'' she instructed, knowing Lu's plan to have that case postponed but wanting pressure on from both sides. ''I'd still rather have that restriction lifted. But fight with what you've got, Jordan. I can't give you anything more. And in the meantime move ahead with this charade. Don't give anyone reason to suspect that we plan to make our research excursion by any means other than vessel-housed warp travel. All right?''

''You're the boss,'' he replied, and the lack of sarcasm in his voice was a credit to his acting ability. But he loved a performance, and this charade smacked of high theatrics to him; Tana knew he would play it to the hilt.

''Let me know how you do,'' she said, and signed off.

Jordan's image had barely faded when the computer spoke gently again. ''There is a call pending from Wolfgang Montag of Transuniversal Shipping.''

Tana hesitated, wondering what the freight baron wanted. Like most of the major transplanetary shippers, his company used freight terminals that had been designed and perfected by the IDP, but the patent for the current model had been sold off five years ago.

It took her only a heartbeat to decide how to handle the call but somewhat longer to exercise her strategy. She shifted the lighting in her office to something more austere, then she commanded Doc to sit at attention beside her. Besides his striking coloring, Doc was possessed of a breathtaking physique. Seen from straight on, his chest was massive and his head regal. People who had never seen a live Dalmatian were always stunned by the sight of him. Tana used that now as she used the lighting and the oversized furniture to create an impression of hauteur and immovability.

Montag's image materialized in the space across the room, seated at a great desk. He was a tall man with slick, artificially dark hair—at least in the holo. Tana strongly suspected that his image was augmented. It would be interesting sometime to meet him in person and see if he wasn't really five-foot-nine and overweight. Rumor had it he never actually left his house but went to all social and business functions by holo.

He rose immediately, an impressive figure in his crisp robes with their stiffened, winglike shoulders. "Tana!" he sang out merrily.

"Mr. Montag," she replied formally, staying seated.

There was only the slightest hesitation as he adjusted his style and tried again. "Good to see you," he said warmly, but with a bit more reserve, coming around his desk. The colorful robes swirled around his knees, and his pantaloons were tucked into tight caloosa-skin boots.

Tana only inclined her head cordially and stayed seated.

Seeing that she was determined in her stance, Montag chuckled to himself and leaned back against his desk. "How's business?" he asked.

Tana let the question hang for a moment, smiling pleasantly. "We're a research institution, Mr. Montag; we don't do business."

At that he let out a guffaw and shook his head. "Tana, Tana, Tana, you always were slicker than buckyballs. But you're in the business of research, so let's not pretend otherwise, all right?" A cold glitter flashed through his eyes, and he reminded Tana of a snake. "So how is the business of research?"

"Pursuing its inevitable course," she replied. "What can I do for you today, Mr. Montag?"

He crossed his arms across his chest. "Right to the point, just like your paterfamilias. Well, let's see. I'm interested in a patent today."

"Got a million of 'em," Tana said glibly. "Which one are you interested in?"

"I'm interested," he said slowly, "in one you haven't filed yet."

"If it hasn't been filed, it's not a patent."

Montag gave another laugh, and Tana knew he was straining to keep his patience. "I'm interested," he continued, "in one that's going to come out of your institute in the next five years."

Tana betrayed no flicker of surprise, for she had seen this coming from the moment he had said the word "patent." She had known when she had given her forecast to the board of directors that it was inevitable that the news would leak; it was the very reason she had told them five years instead of two. This contact was one she had been expecting, although not from Transuniversal, and that still puzzled her. Transuniversal was not in the habit of acquiring patents. Normally they acquired equipment.

"Now, Mr. Montag," she said evenly, "you know I can't talk to you about something that doesn't exist."

His image advanced across the room and Doc gave a low warning growl. Montag stopped and looked at the dog. "Interesting tactic," he muttered. Then he leaned forward across Tana's desk, being careful not to ruin the illusion by having his image pass through the furniture. "Look, Ms. Winthrop-Rutgers," he pronounced, "let's not play verbal games."

"You began it," she pointed out.

"Then I will end it," he said flatly, and Tana felt sure he was privately glad to drop the facade of warm friendliness and get down to the nitty-gritty of whatever deal he wanted to cut. "You're working on a project called P-TUP: point-to-unknown-point warp transport."

"It's the reason the institute was founded; the concept goes back centuries."

"But you're close. You're very close."

"What makes you think so?"

His laugh was low and unpleasant. "Even if the wind didn't whisper in my ear, it's not too hard to figure out," he told her. "Dr. Paul Rutgers has a track record for a certain number of papers and patents each year. He's been off the mark for three years. I'm not inclined to believe he's spending his time unproductively."

"Absolutely not," Tana agreed. "However, my idea of productivity may be very different from yours."

"Not as much as you'd like to think." Montag straightened up. "But all speculation aside, let me put my offer very plainly. I want an option on that patent. Whenever it's available."

Tana wanted to tell him that she'd sooner give an option to a pirrarah, that vicious birdlike carnivore that still inhabited the open grasslands of her native Juno. Instead she gave him a cat-like smile. "I'll mention it to our CFO."

"Who'll do exactly what you tell her," Montag said, aware only of the power of a Winthrop CEO and not of the internal conflict at the institute. "I'll option it now; I don't care if it takes five years or even ten to produce it. I'll wait. In the meantime I'm willing to put forward a good deal of money for the opportunity to negotiate that sale. Say, half a million universals. That would keep your research going for a while."

Half a million! The man was deadly serious, then, if he was willing to pay that price for the option, outside the price of the actual patent. Why? Tana wondered. Is he bailing out of the shipping business and going into manufacturing? Does he have some scheme going with the Transportation Guild? He is one of their more notorious members.

"It's far too early to talk options," she replied smoothly. "When the time comes, I'll be delighted to consider your offer with the others."

Now it was Montag's turn to smile, and not kindly. He flicked the folds of his robes and brushed at a sleeve. "Oh, no, my dear," he said. "This is a limited-time offer, to be considered now, before you have any others. Before the wind whispers in anyone else's ear. This offer is good until midnight, four-one, Argoan Standard. Then it disappears like a holocon, with no trace of its existence." He crossed back behind his own desk. "Good day, Ms. Winthrop."

With that, Wolfgang Montag himself disappeared.

For the next half hour Tana did not move from her chair. Doc grew tired and stretched out on the floor, dozing peacefully. But although she appeared tranquil, Tana's mind was racing at light speed.

Why in the universe did Wolfgang Montag want P-TUP? For profit or power, of course. But did he plan to develop it or simply resell the technology? Was he a front for another buyer? If so, who? And why would the offer disappear at the end of sixty days?

Finally she put a call in to the institute's Information Resources Center. "Doreen," she told the head investigator, "I want a full workup on Wolfgang Montag of Transuniversal Shipping. His business interests, his personal interests, his association with political or other activist groups, his financial condition—anything that might tell me why he wants to do business with the institute, and why in the next sixty days."

"We're on it," Doreen replied immediately. "We'll have the public information in a couple of days, root around for the real juicy stuff—say, two weeks?"

"Feed it to me as you get it," Tana instructed. "I need to know where he's coming from on a deal he's proposed."

"We'll update daily, then," Doreen agreed. "Call for the file 'Wolfpack'—I'll code access for your voice only."

"Done."

Tana had barely disconnected when a chime sounded. "Audio call from Todd Chang."

Todd? "I'll take it," Tana called out. An audio call? Where was he calling from? "Todd? What is it?"

There was thinly concealed excitement in Todd's voice. "Guess where I am!"

Tana was puzzled. "Not at work, I gather."

"No, actually I'm at Aunt Shelby's," Todd admitted with a snicker. Aunt Shelby's was a resort planet in the next system, a place where college students took their semester breaks and retirees went to gamble away their life savings. "Once we fixed the altphase deconnector, the test with the polyzig went so well, we decided to accelerate the schedule."

Tana sat bolt upright in her chair.

"Paul gave me a company voucher and told me to pick up a case of callimray. Then he warped me to the polo field at Harrigan's—via P-TUP."

CHAPTER EIGHT

Tana gasped as the image materialized over Paul's workstation. "Is that it?" she breathed. "Is that Earth?"

"Must be," Paul murmured, as fascinated as she by the holographic scene before them.

They had warped a recording device to the coordinates Chelsea's old files gave as the landing site of the shuttle, but high in the atmosphere, where it would not be detected by casual observation. It had brought back this aerial view of what appeared to be a settlement established by the crew of the *Homeward Bound*. The village was composed in part of geodesic domes such as the lost ship had carried with it, scattered around the hulk of the grounded shuttle. There were other structures, too—crude buildings of native materials—and plantings made to shade or beautify the dwellings. Cultivated fields stretched on both sides of a river that ran through the settlement, and tiny clusters of buildings indicated that outposts or annexes had been established.

"Can we put it in the VR room?" Tana asked eagerly.

Paul shook his head. "Not yet. We really need more data, preferably from numerous perspectives, before we can create the VR environment."

"Do it."

Paul threw a look at Todd, who was reviewing nonvisual data that streamed across his workstation from the recorder. Todd grinned like a fool on parade. "Told you."

"We usually like to review all the data from the first transmission," Paul told his wife, "before we send out any more equipment."

"Just do it," she repeated, her rapt attention on the holo. "Look! What's that moving?"

"Some kind of vehicle," Todd responded, reading from his display. "Slow-moving, with a self-contained power source of some kind. Most likely a storage battery."

"Old Clayton Winthrop was right," Tana sighed. "It's green and it's growing, and the people survived. The people survived."

"We don't know that," Paul cautioned as he picked up a fresh recorder and attached a propulsion unit. "These might be descendants of the crew; they might be survivors of the Evacuation inhabiting the crew's quarters; they might even be survivors of some other lost expedition. There were one hundred forty-three vessels unaccounted for, you know, in the past seven hundred years."

"But none of the others was near Earth."

"None of them was *supposed* to be. Tana, when a ship goes through a spatial warp and doesn't come out on our instruments, there's no telling where it landed. Or when."

"But that's the shuttle of the *Homeward Bound*, right?" she insisted.

Paul punched up data on his display. "Yes, it matches the specs. So do the domes. We'll need more precise readings to verify age and composition, but odds run high that that's what it is."

Todd joined them and relieved Paul of the recorder. "This is great!" he exclaimed, still grinning, and took the instrument to Chamber Five, where the finding mat was lying on the floor. A short tripod with a hook jutted up from the mat; the first recorder had been attached to it for the aerial survey.

"Clear the tripod," Paul instructed now. "Let's try to put this 'corder on solid ground and let it fly from there."

"Should we send Mickey along?" Todd suggested.

Paul shook his head. "One step at a time. Let's send a sampler along with this 'corder. The readings *look* good—breathable air, bearable pressure, standard gravity—but I don't want to transport any living creature there until we've verified there are no contaminants either to harm it or for it to carry back. Program the 'corder, will you, Todd. Three slow circles around the colony, varying heights from forty to sixty feet. I don't want anyone to spot this intruder. Heaven only knows what they'd think." He inserted his hands in a pair of programming gloves and began to manipulate data on his display. "I'm going to set the target for the back side of a hill above the settlement, away from the cultivated area."

"Got it," Todd replied, returning to his workstation and slipping into a similar pair of gloves.

The gloves were another invention of the institute. Though gloves had been used for centuries to input and manipulate data, when Paul had developed his complex notation to express fifth-dimensional equations, they had become essential. He himself had not designed these programming gloves, but a member of his research team had done so in response to his need. He used them deftly, each twitch and flick of his fingers translating into either a mathematical expression or an instruction to the computer that completed the programming. At his station, Todd worked in conjunction with his mentor, adjusting his program to fit the site Paul had selected as a destination.

Tana moved restlessly in her chair, unable to maintain the quiescence that would preserve her strength. Seeing Earth, watching the recording of the quaint village and spreading farmlands, she chafed to be there, to smell the scents of that foreign vegetation, to feel the brush of the wind on her cheeks. She thought of asking Paul to add the audio to the holo, but she didn't want to interrupt his work. Time enough for that when they moved into the VR room.

The virtual reality, or VR, room was the largest area in the institute, a circular space a hundred feet in diameter. Complex equipment translated data into visual, auditory, and olfactory stimuli. In addition, when a person donned a special VR suit and entered the room, electrical impulses from the suit provided the illusion of tactile contact with the objects projected there. The VR room at the institute was even more sophisticated than most: it would replicate not only temperature and humidity but even air currents and gusts of wind.

Doc had caught Tana's excitement; he pranced and paced in the lab, sniffing at all the equipment until Tana called him to heel. Then, sitting obediently at her side, he began to whine softly.

Quiet, Tana reprimanded.

Want to go, came his response.

Wait.

Why?

Yes, why? she wondered. "Paul, how long will this take?"

He looked up in surprise. "To get the data? Forty minutes, maybe. If all goes smoothly."

"I'm going to put the suit on."

"Tana!" he objected as she launched herself too quickly from the chair and tottered dangerously, stiff joints reluctant to adjust for her overexertion.

"It'll take me a while. I just can't sit here, Paul. I'll put the suit on and meet you back here."

"And you're going to just waltz around the halls dressed in a VR suit?" He snorted. "Isn't that inviting Delhi's interest?"

Tana stopped and considered the wisdom of it. "All right. Can I work from your office, though?" she asked. "I don't want to miss anything."

"Be my guest," he replied, and almost instantly he was absorbed in his work again.

It was nearly three hours before the three of them stood in the observation area off the VR room, Paul and Todd monitoring controls and Tana dressed in the VR suit. It was skintight—not very flattering, Tana felt, for despite her daily exercising, her belly retained a rounded shape it hadn't had before the kids were born. "That's the way women are *supposed* to be shaped," Paul told her when she fretted over it. "Not in this century," she always replied. It didn't bother Paul, of course, that she bulged a little where she didn't want to, and the only other person present was Todd. Dear Todd! A glance at him told her he was trying his very best *not* to look at her, a sure sign that he didn't want to be caught ogling the Chief. Is there anything more flattering, she wondered, than to know that a younger man still finds you attractive?

In the large viewport they could see the interior of the VR room as though they were looking through a window into the environment being created there. Paul had chosen a section at the very edge of the village to portray. A woman worked, sweating, in a garden plot beside a log cabin in the foreground, while toward the end of the room a teenage boy chopped wood with a long-handled ax. Near him were several raised cages in which small, plump birds fluttered and scratched. A penned area contained several quadrupeds that looked like some sort of goat. In the background were the images of other buildings, some of them domed, others of wooden construction like the cabin.

Paul handed Tana an earpiece, which she slipped into her left ear. "Now, I'm going to run it in actual mode first," he told her, "so don't expect anyone to respond to your presence."

"Ghost mode?" she asked.

"No, you'll be able to feel all the objects," he assured her, "and touch the people. No point in wearing the suit if you're going to pass right through them."

Tana nodded. "Good. Are we ready, then?"

Paul smiled and gestured broadly. "Earth awaits you."

"Come on, Doc," Tana called, and headed for the door into Wonderland.

There was a soft *whoosh* as the door sealed behind her and the room readjusted its environment to reflect the recorded data. For a moment Tana closed her eyes and stood stock still, waiting for the sensations from the suit to filter through her, to let her mind adjust to the virtual experience.

"It's warm!" she exclaimed.

Paul's voice in her ear: "Seventy-eight degrees Fahrenheit in the shade, reaching into the high eighties in zones where the sun has been heating the ground. By the relative position of Sol, the natives would call it spring—definitely a desert climate."

"It does feel dry," Tana agreed, concentrating on the feel of radiant heat striking her skin. "Hot and dry. Remind me to tan before I come." A few pills would darken her skin enough to prevent damage by the sun's radiation.

Doc was sampling the air in discerning sniffs. *Sweet,* he told her. *Flowers.* Tana could smell them, too, though not as strongly. *People. Animals. Dirt.* And what Tana could not smell herself she could hear: the gentle scratch, scratch of the woman digging in her garden, the buzzing and clicking of insects, the constant background chatter of birds. Something bleated; something else cooed; the *chink* of the distant ax in the wood sounded rhythmically.

"There's no wind!" Tana noted with surprise. The only agrarian setting she knew well was her native Juno, where the wind blew across the prairie every daylight hour.

"It comes and goes," Paul told her. "Never very strong, at least not when we recorded this. We'll send a couple of 'corders back and let them monitor conditions over a few days, see what fluctuations occur. Move into the scene a little, will you?"

Opening her eyes, Tana found herself squinting against the brightness around her. "I'll need eye filters," she commented.

"And a hat," Paul replied. "Look at them; they're all wearing hats." There was a brief pause, then, "To retain body moisture, Todd says, as well as shade the eyes and face. He's probably right."

A loam smell reached Tana, and she turned her attention to the gardener. She was an older woman, sixty or better, her dark hair shot with gray and her skin showing the effects of numerous years in the heat and dryness of the place. Tana studied her face as she knelt in the dirt, pulling weeds and loosening the ground around green seedlings. It was a Caucasian face, although there was a flatness to the features that was not normally associated with Caucasian characteristics. "Paul, can we get a genetic trace on these people?"

"Not without tissue samples," he replied. "After two hundred thirty years, the genes ought to be so intermingled, nothing can be established from skeletal patterning. Even tissue samples might turn up nothing conclusive."

"Then we'll just ask them," Tana said softly. "We'll just ask them who their ancestors were."

Tana knelt beside the woman, the flexible flooring of the VR room creating the illusion that her knees had sunk into the cultivated dirt. Doc sniffed curiously at the gardener's image, for although he could smell a people scent, it did not seem to come from this spot. Tana smiled as his nose pierced the woman's hip. Since Doc wore no suit, he did not have the tactile input that let him "feel" when he bumped into something; without that or distinct degrees of odor, he could not tell when he reached too far. *Step back*, she instructed him, not wanting the illusion spoiled.

Not real, Doc thought at her petulantly.

No, not real, she agreed. *Like shadows*.

Doc harrumphed as though to clear his nostrils of false information and trotted off to investigate the birds in their coop.

But Tana reached out to touch the woman before her. The woman did not respond, and Tana had to anticipate her moves carefully so as not to suffer an unkind pressure as the suit reflected the gardener twisting this way and that, reaching for weeds, lifting an arm to brush the sweat from her brow. Tana touched the hat. "Straw," she reported. "But very coarse straw."

"Real straw," Paul responded in her ear. "Not manufactured."

Real straw. Woven by hand, with the smell of dust and vegetation still clinging to it. Straw, most likely, that had supported grain heads, bent under the weight of ripe seeds that were harvested and ground to feed the people of this place. Tana wondered what flavor the food had there, if it tasted different from the refined, processed foods they produced in the civilized worlds.

"*Rawf!*"

Tana caught the sudden startlement from her dog and looked

up to see what had happened. Doc was sitting back, staring at the boy cutting wood, an air of caution and question emanating from him. "What happened?" she asked.

"A wood chip went sailing right through him," Paul chuckled. "He saw it coming and couldn't figure out why it didn't hit him."

Shadows, Tana thought again at the surprised animal. *Don't be alarmed. They will not hurt us.* But a sense of unease lingered in the dog. Tana rose stiffly to her feet and went to join him.

The boy chopping wood was lean and muscular. Not as muscular as Dak, Tana thought, but part of that was simply his youth. He looked to be fourteen or fifteen. His skin was darker than the gardener's, although whether from natural pigmentation or from excessive exposure to the UV radiation she could not tell. His hair was a rich, curling dark brown, which made Tana think he might carry the genetic coding of Delhi's ancestors or perhaps that of one of the Semitic peoples. As the ax flew through the air, his body moved with a strength and economy of motion that said he did this task often.

Next Tana crossed to the coop and stooped down to examine the fluffy, fat birds inside. "What are they?" she asked.

"The computer can't decide," Paul told her. "Most likely some species of quail, but they have probably been crossbred with a larger bird, perhaps a grouse or even a chicken."

"I've seen pictures of quail," Tana replied. "They don't look anything like this. And I've heard of chickens, but I don't really know what they look like. They were a domestic bird, weren't they?"

"I think they still exist on Darius IV," Paul said. "They're used for egg producers, although they could be a meat source as well. I don't recall offhand."

Tana shivered at the thought of eating an egg.

"What about the quadrupeds?" she asked, continuing to that pen. "They look like goats."

"Sheep, actually," Paul replied.

"With horns like that?" Tana could not get through the split-rail fence to examine them more closely and was not sure she wanted to: the fat, curling horns looked wicked.

"A variety of sheep," Paul amended. "They may have made genetic adjustments to the conditions, but that doesn't seem likely in so short a time span as seven hundred years. You might ask your brother about that. Or they could be crossbreeds, like the quail. I think there used to be a wild sheep of some sort on

Earth; let me check the computer.'' A moment later his voice returned. ''Yes, there was something called a bighorn sheep, and it was indigenous to this part of North America. As a matter of fact, these creatures seem to be more bighorn than domestic sheep.''

''Domestic food sources were virtually nonexistent at the time of the Evacuation,'' Tana recalled. ''Maybe these villagers have had to catch and tame wild animals to provide a ready supply of meat.'' Noticing the swollen udders on the ewes, she added, ''And milk products.''

One of the sheep brushed up against the fence near Tana, and she reached out to stroke its shaggy coat. ''What's their clothing made of?'' she asked Paul. ''This fur feels as if it would make excellent textiles.''

''We can't tell that from the data,'' Paul responded. ''High percentage of probability that it's a vegetable fiber rather than animal, but we can't say for certain.''

''I'll need clothes like these,'' Tana murmured, going back to study the articles the youth was wearing. Loose trousers, a blousing shirt, a straw hat—

''My hair!'' she said suddenly, one hand flying to the short, bristling side of her coiffure. ''I don't suppose they've seen a style like this one. If I'm to blend in, I'll have to wind the long side around the short side and pin it.''

''Unless you want to announce you're from offplanet,'' he agreed, ''and see what kind of panic you can start first thing.''

She ignored the remark, caught up again in the strangeness of the Terran's life-style. ''Paul, look at these shoes!'' she exclaimed.

''Mm. Sandals,'' Paul grunted. ''Appropriate for the climate.''

''But they look like they're made of rope!''

''Leather, I think,'' Paul contradicted.

''The straps, yes, but the soles!''

There was a brief pause as Paul ran checks on the item in question. ''You could be right,'' he agreed finally. ''Again, we can't tell conclusively from our data, but the appearance is of a woven fiber rather than a smooth piece of hide. Why do you suppose they don't use leather?''

''Let me ask him,'' Tana suggested.

''He won't answer,'' Paul reminded her.

''I know, but let me ask him anyway. Switch me into projectual mode. I want to talk to him.''

She heard Paul's sigh, but she knew he was making the adjustments in the program. In projectual mode, the computer projected how objects in the room would react to the presence of the person in the VR suit. In a moment the boy stopped chopping wood and looked up at Tana in amazement.

"Hello," Tana said.

"Who are you?" the boy demanded in surprise.

"My name is Tana Winthrop," she responded. "What's yours?"

"I don't have one," the image replied, for there was no data in the computer to generate an accurate response.

"Then I shall give you one," she said. "Your name is Abel." Somehow the Biblical name for the first farmer born seemed appropriate.

"What are you doing here?" Abel pursued.

"Looking at your farm. Can you tell me about it?"

"I can tell you a little," Abel hedged. "It's an average-sized farm compared to others in the area. We grow grains, legumes, and vegetables like our neighbors. We keep a few animals, too; not everyone does that."

Tana sighed inwardly and wished someone would create a program that made people in projectual mode speak like real people instead of like computers trying to cram accumulated data into topical groupings.

"There's a streambed over there," the boy continued, pointing to his right. "Just a little one that only has water during the rainy season. It feeds into a larger river which runs through our village. We have irrigation ditches running from the small stream to our fields, which is why we are able to raise crops in this arid climate."

Irritation flicked at Tana's consciousness, and Doc whined beside her. "Do you manage to keep your family fed?" she asked Abel. "You look healthy."

"I'm quite healthy," Abel replied. "Most of the inhabitants here are healthy, although some are very old and show signs of weakening. There are also a lot of children, who all seem to be healthy, but then, the unhealthy ones might not come outdoors. This is a pleasant day, but our climate can be quite harsh in the summer."

Did a fifteen-year-old boy ever speak in such precise phrases, build such perfect paragraphs in his speech? Tana felt a suppressed anger. "Do you like it here?"

The image hesitated. "I can't answer that," it told her.

"Do you have parents?" Tana persisted. "Brothers and sisters? How long has your family farmed this land? Do you remember coming to this place?" The questions tumbled out one after another. "Who are your ancestors? Will the shuttle in the village still fly?"

"Tana!" Paul reprimanded.

"Turn it off, Paul, just turn it off."

Instantly the farm disappeared around her, and Tana stood in a large, empty room. Doc barked his annoyance once; then the door opened and Paul came in.

Tana made her way slowly to him, feeling a slight trembling in her arms and legs. Paul's reproving face did not help her mood. "It won't satisfy," she told him bluntly.

His eyes softened a bit. "Did you really expect it would?"

"No." She looked up at him, at the round, ruddy face and the dazzling blue eyes. "Did you?"

For a long moment he held her gaze, quite capable of being at least as stubborn as she. Finally he wrapped his arms around her, and she knew he could feel the quaking of her body, which would probably take the best part of an hour for her to control. "If you get this worked up," he began, "over a simulation—"

"Because a simulation can't answer my questions!" she cried in frustration; then she clung to him even tighter because the outburst had sent a surge of toxins flooding through her already poisoned system. "Paul, it's been twenty-four years since I first read Chelsea's version of the fate of the *Homeward Bound.* Now we're so close, and I . . ." Her voice trailed off, and she stood quietly with her head on his chest, trying to will the toxins out of her bloodstream, to keep her irritated muscle tissue from spasming.

I must stay calm. I must be calm—but, oh, how I want answers to my questions!

"Go home," he said softly. "Let us finish analyzing the data. I promised you once I would put your feet on Earth, and I will. But we have to do it right, Tana. And you have to keep yourself under control until we're ready. I won't send you unless you are at your maximum physical condition."

"That's fair," she whispered. "That's fair." Reluctantly she separated herself from him, from his strength. "Come on, Doc." Carefully, slowly, she wobbled her way to the door.

Delhi recognized the code phrase that appeared in her display's message sector. She stored her confidential file but

kept the high-security environment as she took the call.
"Yes, Jarl."

"We got another order from Dr. Rutgers's lab," the young
man told her. "It's a duplicate of a device we built for him
earlier—at least, my part's a duplicate. The fiber we're to make
it from comes from somewhere in the institute, and I don't know
what it's made of."

"Can you speculate?" she asked.

"Could be . . . I know this sounds crazy, but there's a rainbow sheen to it, and the colors are like the colors of warp crystals. I have a friend in crystology; you want me to ask him if he
knows anything about it?"

"Yes," Delhi agreed. "But be discreet. Don't let him know
it's important to you. And *don't* mention my name."

The image of the young man withered a bit on her display. "I
wouldn't!" he protested weakly.

"Good. Let me know what you find out." Delhi cut the call
off abruptly.

On the other end Jarl stared dumbly at his empty display for
a moment. Who did she think he was, treating him like that?

A slinker, said a voice inside him. *A dirty slinker, spying on
your coworkers.*

But I'm not, he protested to himself. This is company business, and she's the number-two person in the company, the CFO.
Dr. Rutgers ought to be telling her this stuff himself. I shouldn't
have to do this.

Maybe he has a reason, the voice nagged. *Maybe she's got
some kind of scheme going, and she's using you to hurt the
institute.*

Nonsense, Jarl thought, dismissing the idea. There's no more
upstanding person than Ms. Striker. Whatever's going on, it's
in-house politics, that's what it is. And politics is for the big
players, not little guys like me. I'll just do what they tell me to,
tell them what they ask, and let them fight it out between themselves.

That's all a second-shift nontech like me can do, isn't it?

Tana puzzled over the snowy white field in the frozen hologram. The temperature readings Paul had given her were not
consistent with snow—it was downright hot at the target site. So
what was this white stuff? "Teeg: identify the white substance
in this picture," she directed the computer.

"The white substance is known as cotton," the smooth voice

of the computer told her. "It is a fibrous seed pod from which textiles are made."

"And is that a field of cotton, then?" Tana probed.

"Yes."

"Elaborate." She hated one-word answers.

"The field of plants is in bloom, exposing the white fibers inside the seed pod. The fibers can be harvested, 'carded' or combed, and spun into thread. The thread can be woven into textiles for the construction of garments and bedclothes as well as put to many industrial uses. Cotton is grown on Tricyrus and on the southern continent of Darius IV. As a natural fiber, cotton is preferred—"

"Enough." Tana let the holo roll on until one or two figures came into the scope. "Teeg: enlarge the human figures in this." The images sprang to eighteen inches, and Tana thought of transferring them onto the conference projector, which would make them full size, but she refrained. They were captured from such a long distance, enlarging them further would only show up the flaws in the picture quality. "Teeg: could the clothing on these people be made of cotton?"

"That would be consistent with the data in this report."

Tana studied the two figures, who were striding across a rough dirt track. They were dressed similarly to Abel, except that instead of a straw hat, one had a straw basket balanced on his head. The second figure was a young woman who carried a digging implement. Do they dig by hand? Tana thought. They have machines that work the fields; why would they dig by hand?

"Teeg: how old are the machines in other parts of this report?" Tana asked.

"The materials from which the machines are made range from two hundred to three hundred years old," the computer replied. "The time at which they were arranged in these configurations is unknown."

They have no manufacturing, then, Tana realized. Not of plasmers or other building materials. No refining of metals, either, at least not on a large enough scale to make farm machinery. Then how have they kept these machines going? "Teeg: are the machines made from pieces of equipment which were originally aboard the *Homeward Bound*?"

"There is not enough information to speculate."

Tana frowned. There had to be a way to ask. "Teeg: given the mass of all the manufactured materials recorded at the settlement, could all of those materials have come from equipment and supplies on the *Homeward Bound*?''

''Negative.''

There! That proved something, then. They had either manufactured some of the things themselves or found local resources, perhaps a native population.

''Teeg: given the conditions which exist in this report—and the high ingenuity and intelligence of the crew of the *Homeward Bound*—and the absence of contraceptives after the first six months following their arrival on Earth—could the base population provided by the crew have given rise to the number of persons now inhabiting the settlement?''

''It is possible that the numbers could be achieved,'' the computer agreed. ''However, there is a high probability that inbreeding would have affected the genetic makeup of succeeding generations in a way which is not consistent with the data in this report.''

Then there *had* to have been a native population when the crew landed! ''Teeg: is there any evidence that there are population centers other than this settlement?''

''Roads leading out of the settlement do appear to have been traveled frequently. While it is possible that the traffic has been for hunting and gathering, the heavy use of some roads would indicate that they lead to an area of high interest for the settlers. Areas of interest would include population centers, food supplies, recreational areas—''

The computer went on, but Tana was distracted. Recreational areas! What kind of recreational areas might these people have? Not resort hotels, certainly! Nor amphitheaters, nor domed ballparks, nor museums—natural wonders, maybe. But their entire world is a natural wonder to me! What would they consider a wonder?

Resort hotels, and amphitheaters, and domed ballparks!

Do they remember at all? she wondered. Did the crew pass on to their children the story of how things were on other worlds? Do these people even know that they came from the stars? Do they know the names of other star systems, of the colonized planets? Or will it all be astounding to them when I arrive to reestablish contact? What will they ask for first? Medicine? Knowledge? Entertainment?

On the floor at her feet, Doc raised his head, listening. *Delhi comes*, he warned her. Quickly Tana waved away the report. It was doubtful Delhi could have identified the scene as Earth, but she would undoubtedly have asked.

Delhi strolled casually into the office. "Good afternoon, Tana." Her voice was easy, and she smiled charmingly. That alone was enough to make Tana suspicious.

"Good afternoon, Delhi," Tana replied, tossing down the light pen with which she had been manipulating the file.

"You're looking well," Delhi commented. "I understand you went home early last week. Nothing serious, I hope."

"No, just let myself get frustrated by something," Tana replied. She wondered if anyone had told Delhi they'd been using the VR Room.

"The testing's not going well, then?"

Ah. A fishing expedition. "Well enough," Tana hedged. "Just not as quickly as I'd hoped." It was true, after all. It was also what she wanted Delhi to believe.

Delhi moved to a chair near the desk and sat down. "What is it exactly that they're testing?"

For a split second Tana considered how much to divulge and what the consequences would be. Then, without missing a beat, she told Delhi, "It's a retrieval aid Paul is experimenting with. We call it a traveling mat. It's a mesh woven with warp crystals in it; crystals, not in a solution to create a warp field but in a configuration which *attracts* a warp field. Knowing the general coordinates from which you want to retrieve an object, the traveling mat focuses the target from the other end, allowing pinpoint accuracy."

Delhi's eyebrows shot up. "You mean he's using a warp device to *retrieve* objects rather than send them?"

"Both," Tana told her. "In his inimitable fashion, he decided the hardest part of the equation was not how to transport someone *to* an unknown point but how to get them back afterward, with no sending unit on that end. So he tackled that part first."

Delhi chuckled and shook her head. "That's our Paul."

Tana smiled, too, and wondered why Delhi chose to be so hard-nosed and confrontational so much of the time. Sitting and chatting like this, she was such a pleasant person to be with. "Are you coming to Roundup?" Tana asked.

At that Delhi sighed regretfully. "I don't think so, dear," she said, and Tana almost flinched at the patronizing tone. "I would love to see all my Winthrop relatives, but with third-quarter reports coming up . . ."

Tana smiled and refused to take the bait.

"So Paul is retrieving objects with his—what did you call it? Traveling mat?"

"Yes, we've picked up mechanicals from Juno several times," Tana conceded, remembering that Delhi had seen the holo of Derbe on horseback. "Of course, the transport of animate objects like animals is more complex. It, ah, presents new challenges."

"The source of your recent frustration?" Delhi guessed. "Well, transportation of inert cargo is still a major accomplishment. I assume Paul will patent the traveling mat, anyway, while he works the bugs out of the rest of the process."

Tana kept the smile on her face. "I don't think so."

Anger flashed in Delhi's dark eyes. "And why not?"

"Because the instant a patent is filed, the Omniversity and half a dozen commercial research programs will be on it like a pirrarah on a corkberry. Once the concept of the traveling mat is made public, everyone will be trying to develop their own version, throwing the Transportation Guild into a panic, causing the same kind of damage the arrival of long-distance warp caused. I won't be responsible for that, Delhi."

"And you think stalling around another year or even two is going to help?" Delhi flared.

"I think waiting until we can patent the *whole* process, including the transport of human beings, will buy us the time we need to cushion the blow. It will also assure our dominance at the bargaining table when we go to sell the patent, since no one else will even be close to developing a competing product."

That halted Delhi's objections temporarily. But a wicked gleam flickered through the older woman's eyes. "And when will you make your journey to Earth?"

Tana's own gray eyes narrowed in response. "Why, my dear cousin, you know that such a trip is illegal. Earth is still on the Transportation Guild's blacklist."

"And the research waiver Lu Parnette has applied for?"

Tana could not resist testing Delhi's network of information. "Has it come through yet?" she asked, knowing only she and Lu and one high-level Guild official knew it had been approved. It was signed and sealed in his files and Lu's but would not be registered for anther month. More time to cloud issues.

"Not to my knowledge," Delhi admitted.

There was some pleasure, at least, in knowing she was still one step ahead. Her smile was sardonic now. "Too bad. I thought perhaps your spies had more current information than I do."

Delhi ignored the jibe. "That is your ultimate destination, isn't it?"

"That was the reason this institute was founded."

"Tell me," Delhi said, rising from the chair in preparation to leave. "Once you accomplish this goal, then what? What do you do next? What does the institute do next?"

Tana shrugged and grinned. "I don't know. Maybe we'll tackle universal peace."

"There are some contagious microbes," Paul admitted, "but nothing we don't run into in the air here or on Juno. It seems Chelsea and Zachery were right—no plague."

They were in his office off the lab, reviewing the last of the reports generated from data brought back from Earth. A thrill shot up Tana's spine. "When can I go?" she asked.

Paul took her hand and studied the ring with its seven pale crystals. A ring and a promise. "Jaria is out gathering appropriate clothing for you. She thinks it's for a costume party." He caressed her hand with its slender fingers, kissed it gently, clasped it protectively between his own broad palms, and finally looked into her gray eyes with his startling blue ones. A promise was a promise. "Tomorrow."

Tomorrow! Tears sprang to her eyes. Tomorrow, tomorrow, tomorrow— "Thank you," she whispered.

At their feet, Doc heaved a great, noisy sigh, and they burst out laughing. "Is that a commentary?" Paul asked.

Doc lifted his head and looked at them expectantly. *What? Nothing,* Tana told him. *We're nervous, and you made us laugh. Good?*

Very good.

At that Doc settled back down, stretching out on his side on the cool floor.

Tomorrow.

"Let's go home early tonight," Paul suggested.

"Not home, out," she replied. "If I sit at home, I'll only worry about it and get my toxin levels up. Let's go out somewhere and do something to keep both our minds off it."

"Where do you want to go?"

"I don't know. The Museum?" The Interplanetary Museum of Art had been in the Winthrop family for two centuries; Paul and Tana had gone there on one of their first dates. The artwork and artifacts in the Earth Room never failed to move them.

"I don't think the Museum is open this late," he pointed out. "It may be midday on Juno, but it's nearly ten o'clock here. And speaking of the time—" He glanced out the door of the office to where Todd was working in the lab. "Todd! Have you picked up the zig yet?"

"Two minutes and counting!" Todd called back.

Tomorrow it would be Tana they would be waiting to retrieve. Paul squeezed his wife's hand. "Come on," he said. "Let's see how our timed pickup works on the polyzig." But his eyes said, I've done this for you. There are so many puzzles I could have solved, but this is the one I chose. I chose it because of you. Now I am both proud and afraid.

Tana slipped herself into the crook of his arm. I know you're afraid. But nothing will happen to me; believe that. Trust in the God we have trusted in all along. He will be with me even when you are not.

They had not reached the door to the lab when the computer chimed. "Dr. Rutgers, a message from Jaria M'hai," it announced.

"Go ahead," Paul instructed, waiting.

The image of a slender-faced black woman appeared on his display. "Paul, I got the costume for your wife, and if you didn't have such terrible taste in clothes, I'd reprimand you for sending your staff out to take care of your personal business. But tell the Chief I came to her rescue and a very lovely pair of khaki trousers and a stunning olive-green blouse are waiting with her secretary. And I'll be in late tomorrow, thank you very much." Paul grinned, knowing full well that the diligent woman would be in her office long before dawn.

"Oh, and Paul . . ." An uneasy quality crept into Jaria's voice. "I don't know if this is important, but Ms. Striker stopped me when I dropped off the clothes. She looked—well, the way she always looks, sort of angry and suspicious—and she asked about the clothes. What they were for, why did you send me— just nosy things." An impish gleam came into Jaria's eye. "I told her you were planning a surprise costume party for her birthday and I'd get her a costume to come as a Shimbalian Shapechanger." Tana winced at the insult. "Anyway, if I've created a problem for you, I'm sorry. If I've created a problem for *her*, I expect a bonus in my next check. See you tomorrow."

Both Paul and Tana gazed at the empty display for a long moment after the image of Jaria had vanished. Finally Paul spoke. "Want to bet that Delhi is down here tomorrow morning when we come in, asking about the clothes?"

"No bets," Tana said softly. They were still another moment; then Tana called out, "Teeg: has Delhi gone home yet?"

"Negative," came the reply.

"Has Gerta?"

"Negative."

"Connect me with Gerta." Almost instantly the round, motherly face of Tana's secretary appeared on the display. "Yes, Tana?"

"Jaria left a package for me, Gerta. Please send it down by chute." The chute was a small cargo-warping system used to transport equipment and other objects from place to place within the institute and other Winthrop enterprises. "And if Delhi asks, you still have it and I'm not planning to pick it up until tomorrow noon. All right?"

"Done," the woman replied.

"What are you up to?" Paul asked suspiciously.

"Paul, you've got to send me tonight."

There was a long pause. "Tana, you need to be rested," he tried to object.

"I won't sleep knowing she'll be here tomorrow trying to find out what we're up to. As a matter of fact, my anxiety level will probably shoot up and put me in a worse state. Send me now, before I have time to get angry about her meddling."

She could see his inward struggle and knew she had won even before he did. "All right," he said finally. "I'll send you, but only for a trial run. Two hours."

"Six."

"Tana, you can't stay awake that long!"

"Four, then."

"Three," he compromised.

"Done." She headed for the door. "I'll get changed. Put together the equipment I'll need—I'll have to do without the tanning medication."

"That's all right; it's nearly dark at the target site," he replied, following her out and making for his workstation. "You won't need UV protection this trip."

Todd was just retrieving the polyzig from Chamber Five; overhearing their last remarks, he looked a question at Paul.

"Check that zig's biometer right now," Paul told him brusquely. "Unless it's showing any anomalies, Tana's going out in thirty minutes."

CHAPTER NINE

Phoenix heard them coming along the path, although they walked softly in the manner of the People and did not speak as they neared her dwelling. But she had grown accustomed to listening to the sounds of the village from within her house, identifying individuals by their voices and their steps, guessing at activities from the sounds they made. Besides, the Mother Earth whispered to her now.

Your Council is coming.

Yes, Phoenix thought, inspecting her knife blade carefully before sheathing it. My Council and Michael. Undoubtedly he went running to his uncle after I left him with the strange tale that the Mother Earth calls me. I wonder what Flint thought. That I wouldn't know the voice of the Mother Earth if I heard it? That I am up to some sort of trick? Or has she spoken to him, too, and told him that it is true?

Phoenix tucked a bone funnel into the mouth of her gourd canteen and crawled to where a large water jar stood in the corner of the room. She tilted the jar carefully, for it was very full, and filled the canteen. One or two? she wondered. One. They would be traveling along creeks most of the way. She could refill this one often.

Shadows flickered in the room; several pairs of legs blocked the sun that was coming through her low, open doorway. "Come in, Michael," she called. "Come in, Flint, and Gray Fox, and Three Squirrels, and Talia, and Sun on My Back."

One by one they ducked through the opening and came to sit on the hard dirt floor. She ignored them as she gently worked the wooden stopper into the neck of the gourd. As it drew moisture from the contents of the canteen, the stopper would swell and seal tightly. She added the canteen to the strip of leather that

131

would be her traveling belt. It already held her pouch of necessities: flint and stone for starting a fire, a few leather thongs, a cake of dried food. Before she left, she would slip her knife onto it as well, though for the time being she wore that implement on the thong that secured her leather breechclout. After twenty-five years the useful blade seemed as much a part of her as her right hand.

Gray Fox cleared his throat. He was the oldest of the Council members, having served the Mother and Two Moons before he sat on Phoenix's Council. "Thank you for welcoming us, She Who Saves," he began formally.

"My Council is always welcome." Phoenix laid aside the traveling belt and pulled a large basket from the storage shelf at the back of the house. Sorting through the contents, she continued to ignore her guests.

"Forgive the intrusion," the old man continued, "but we heard a strange thing which concerned us deeply, and we came to inquire. But perhaps we have come at a bad time."

"This is not a bad time," she replied, pulling winter leggings and shirts out of the basket and tossing them carelessly aside.

Even after so many years the old man was accustomed to her impolite behavior. She should have given them her attention, asked after their families, commented on the crops or the hunting, *something*. Yet the impossible woman said nothing, leaving it entirely up to him to come gracefully to the point. "You seem to be preparing for a journey," he tried again.

"I am."

At that the Council members exchanged glances of relief. "That is good," Gray Fox encouraged. "Michael came to us with a strange tale; you spoke to him of hearing the Mother Earth call you, and he was afraid you meant she called you to rest. But we see that she has called you on a journey." Michael looked daggers at the old man, for he knew Phoenix had not been speaking of a journey. "We are pleased to see you planning such an undertaking. Where will you go this time? To the Camp of the Others to trade? Or perhaps hunting the Great Antelope of the eastern prairie?"

"Neither," she told him bluntly. "I am going to the Well."

Now the Council was more puzzled than ever. The Well was a lake cupped in the top of a hill near the old Valley of the People. It was actually a huge sinkhole filled and refreshed by underground springs. The sides were steep and required expert climbing skill or a sturdy rope to descend to the water level.

"The Well!" Flint spoke up. "I have not been there since I was a boy. Not since we threw the fireshooters of the Others into it to keep them from harming any more of the People."

Ah, yes! The fireshooters. Knowing that the Others, upon learning that they were marooned, were likely to take out their anger on the peaceful People, Coconino had instructed a band of young hunters to steal as many of the disrupter-style weapons as they could and destroy them. They had succeeded in stealing several cases from a supply dome. Flint had been with the group that had thrown the weapons into the deep, mucky-bottomed lake from which there was no hope of recovery. But five young hunters had lost their lives in the effort, burned down as they tried to explain to the Others that they only wanted to insure that no one was harmed. One of the five was Falling Star, the husband of Talia and the son of Gray Fox. Those two shifted uncomfortably now as Flint recalled the tragic time.

"What will you do at the Well?" Gray Fox prodded.

"The will of the Mother Earth," Phoenix replied. "I will take you along, my Council, and as many of the People as wish to come and witness. For Michael was not mistaken. The Mother Earth is calling me to her, and I must go. I will descend beneath the waters of the Well and not return."

"No!" Talia exclaimed. She was a comely matron of thirty years and bore in her face a strong resemblance to her mother, Two Moons. "You cannot leave us. If the Mother Earth calls you, she will choose the time and the place. It is not for you to decide."

"I have not decided!" Phoenix snapped. "And I am not particularly happy to go, but her voice is clear, Talia, and I cannot ignore it. If she told you to cross a river, would you wait for her to roll stepping-stones into the water?"

They were silent then, not knowing how to respond.

Phoenix picked up a square of leather and handed it to Michael. "Here. Keep this for me."

"What is it?" he asked.

"A letter to Coconino. Give it to him when he finally gets here."

Anger filled Michael's dark eyes. Abruptly he threw the parcel on the floor in front of her. "Give it to him yourself."

"I won't be here."

"You've waited for him all your life," he challenged. "Wait a little longer."

A knot tightened in Phoenix's throat. "I wish I could. If only you knew how I wish I could! But I must wait for him in the bosom of the Mother Earth. He will come to me there eventually. There will be a day when we will be together again."

Finally Phoenix found what she was looking for in the large basket. It was her ribbon shirt, the last article of cotton clothing she owned. The smocklike garment was an unbleached white with colorful strips of cloth sewn to it along the sleeves and yoke, leaving the ends dangling like a fringe from shoulder and cuff. She wore it only for ceremonial occasions; she would wear it as she went to the Well.

"I wish to leave in the morning," she told her Council. "Those of you who will come should go home and gather your things. Tell the People; give them this short time to prepare. I have dragged my feet long enough in this matter; it is best I go quickly now."

Still the Council sat, casting uneasy glances at each other. How could they speak to her in this matter? What could they say? Did she expect something of them, a plea, a farewell? Finally Talia rose and started for the door. When had She Who Saves ever really wanted their advice, anyway? Sun on My Back followed, then Three Squirrels and Gray Fox, and finally Flint. None of them had truly liked the Witch Woman, but they had respected her. After all, Coconino had called her his sister-brother and loved her better. Beyond that, she was a strong woman in her own right, passionate in her protection of the People, tireless in her efforts on their behalf. Her absence would be keenly felt.

Only Michael stayed behind in the dim adobe chamber. Phoenix could feel his glowering anger as she calmly folded up the ribbon shirt and laid it with her traveling belt. If I look at your face, she thought, I will see Coconino there. I will see his anger when he thought I was wrong, when he thought I was being stubborn and stupid. But I'm not wrong this time, Michael. The voice is clear. It is time to leave this place behind.

"I never took you for a coward," he said harshly.

Phoenix put the lid back on the wicker basket of clothing and returned it to the shelf. There was nothing else in it she would need for this journey.

"There's a word for it on the Mountain," he pressed angrily, "but not in the language of the People. The People don't have such a word. The concept is so alien to them, they don't even recognize it when it confronts them. It's 'suicide.' " He snarled the word at her, his voice full of contempt. "Do you hear me,

Phoenix? *Suicide!* It's not grand and it's not glorious; it's cowardly and despicable.''

"When you get back, Michael," Phoenix said mildly, "see that my things are given to someone who needs them. There's not much—I've given most of it away already." She picked up a small clay bowl. "That is, what I haven't broken.''

Michael sprang to a crouched position and fairly launched himself at her, grabbing her sinewy arm in a telling grip. "How can you do this?" he demanded. "How can you abandon these people when they need you? How can you be so selfish, so caught up in your own pain, that you can't see what it will do to them? I know it hurts that Sky Dancer won't come back! It hurts me, too. I know it hurts that Coconino is not here with you, but there are many widowed men and women among the People, and there will be many more. *They* don't give up!''

"I never gave up!" Phoenix flared. "After Coconino disappeared, don't you think I wanted to? I didn't want this life! I didn't want the responsibility. But he stuck me with it. He changed me, and I couldn't change back. This has nothing to do with Coconino or Sky Dancer. I'm not opting out on life, Michael; you know me better than that. I'm too stubborn for that. But I hear—" She broke off. Not having heard the voice of the Mother Earth, he could not understand or accept that explanation. She would have to explain it in other terms.

"Michael, have you ever made a decision you didn't want to make and then you felt—at peace? Not that it was a relief just to have the struggling done but that what you chose to do—was *right*. Even though it didn't make any kind of logical sense, it was the right thing to do. Did you ever?''

Slowly his grip on her arm lessened. Phoenix could read his thoughts as clearly as if he had spoken.

"When you left Sky Dancer," she said gently, "in the southern village. When you came back here to Swan and your son— you felt it, didn't you? It wasn't something you wanted to do. It was painful, and it seemed like desertion and cowardice—but it was the right thing to do, wasn't it?''

He sat back and lowered his eyes. "It was the right thing to do," he whispered.

"That's what going to the Well is for me," she told him. "I'm not looking forward to it. Truth be known, I'm pretty well terrified. I'm too stubborn to surrender my life. I don't submit that easily, but the depths of the Well beckon to me as though they were a portal to . . . to peace. And it may seem that I am abandoning the People, but Michael, it is the best thing for them. I took them through tough times, but they need someone else now, and no one else will take over while I'm still here."

"It doesn't mean you have to die!" he cried in anguish.

Ah, Michael, do you care so much for a hard, bitter old woman like me? No. I have been your crutch, that is all. I have been not only your mentor but your one remaining link to your past. Now you will lose that, Michael, and you are afraid.

"The Mother Earth calls me," she repeated. "I must go."

"But why this ceremony and this . . . glorification?" he protested. "Why not just go hunting one day and not come back?"

"Because the People would never believe I was gone," she told him. "They would wait for me as they do for Coconino. I don't want that. No, they have to witness my passing, Michael, and they have to feel a conclusion to this era. Time for a fresh start."

"And why the Well?" He was grasping for protests now. "Some of these people are old, and you're asking them to make a journey of two or three days just to watch you drown yourself!"

Why the Well, indeed? A wave of nostalgia swept over Phoenix. In her mind he was always there, lounging on the bank, stretching his muscular body as he woke from sleep. Or up on the rim, his arms outstretched in invocation to the Mother Earth . . . "When I first came to the village of the People," she told Michael, "your father and I were as wary of each other as two stags, stamping and snorting and bellowing challenges. He told me I couldn't hold up for a trip to the Red Rock Country to look for Tala; I told him I could. So he decided to test me. We set off one morning to run from the village to the Well." It was a distance of over ten miles.

"And you passed his test as a hare passes a tortoise," Michael guessed.

Phoenix laughed roundly. "I failed miserably," she remembered. "I didn't make it five miles before I had to stop and walk, and by the time we reached the Well, I could hardly move. And then—" She chuckled. "—I had to climb down into that pit to get to the water." Michael's eyebrows flew up, for though he had never been to the Well, he had heard much of it from his uncle. By all accounts, the sides dropped fifty feet nearly straight down. "Oh, Coconino offered to bring water up for me," Phoenix continued, "but I wanted to swim. I was hot and tired, and I couldn't think of anything I wanted more than to jump into that lake. So he helped me climb down. It wasn't until we climbed back out and headed for home that he told me the creek was just over the hill, out of sight."

Michael looked confused. "Why . . . ?"

"It was a joke," she explained. "A hunter's joke: to run me cross-country and let me think the only water and shade were at the bottom of the Well." Phoenix gave a sharp laugh. "The truth is, the creek is so close by that water from the Well actually spills out into it from an opening below the surface—and the hill that hides the creek is so steep, there would have been plenty of shade. But because I couldn't see the creek, I assumed the Well was my only option. Coconino thought it was a great joke."

"I'm surprised you didn't kill him on the spot," Michael observed dryly.

But Phoenix shook her head. "That journey did something to me. To us. It broke down the walls of suspicion between us. He said I surprised him because I finished the trip at all. And I—I guess the sheer exertion took some of the fight out of me. Knocked my pride down a peg or two as well. Also, that trick, that was something they did to all the young boys—sort of an initiation rite. When he played the trick on me, it was as though he began the process of making me of the People." A knot formed in Phoenix's throat again. "It was there, on the rim of the Well, that he gave me the name Phoenix. I didn't know until later that the People considered it a name of great power and respect because it came from the Before Times." She touched the turquoise phoenix pendant that hung from her neck. "I only knew it said so much about me, about who I was." Tenderly she caressed the stone pendant with her thumb and forefinger. "Now it's time to give the name back. No one uses it anymore, anyway—except you. And truth be known, Michael, I've grown weary of rising up from ashes."

Sitting across from her in the cool, damp adobe room, Michael felt his heart burning within him. There were so few times when she let anyone see her like this: tired, vulnerable. He ached for her pain, for the great burden she had borne—by choice—for so many years. But he did not want to let her go. "And what shall we tell Sky Dancer?" he asked softly. "How shall we tell her that her mother answered a call from the Mother Earth and descended into the Well?"

Suddenly all tenderness and approachability disappeared from the intrepid leader. Her defensive walls slammed into place, and she withdrew from him as surely as if she had left the room.

"You will tell her nothing," she replied coldly. "You will not go to the southern village with the news—no one will go there. She has made a decision, and we will respect it. If some day she returns here, then you can tell her: tell her that at last I heard the voice of the Mother Earth—she will rejoice for me. Tell her that in the end I was wise enough to listen."

Phoenix got to her feet, crouched over in the low-ceilinged room. "You'd better get ready. I expect you to come with me tomorrow," she directed Michael. "I'm going out to the fields to check on the crops one last time. And to visit some old friends." Then she went out the door, leaving Michael alone in the sun-baked house.

Outside, Phoenix paused to stretch her limbs, to rid herself of the stiffness caused less by the increasing number of her years than by the tension of her encounter with the Council and Michael. Michael! He must never go back to the southern village and learn what had transpired there. No one from this village must ever go to bring back the news. Somehow, before she left, she would have to ensure that.

Phoenix started down the trail toward First Canyon, where the corn had come up thickly for a change. Was it five years already since she and Krista had coaxed that rickety old truck over the broken highway to the southern village? Yes, five years next month. The sun had been ferocious, as it always was in July, without a hint of rain clouds to bring a cooling shower. They had broken down twice, but Phoenix had not entirely forgotten her skill with vehicles, and she was able to patch a leaky hose and connect a loose wire and keep them going, going, going over the brushy remains of the highway to the dry lakebed the People referred to as a sea of grass. They cut straight across it through vegetation well over the height of the windshield, taking their bearings from the tops of the mountains where the People lived.

"Don't try this when you go back," Phoenix advised Krista. "Stick to the old roadbeds so you don't get lost. And drive in the early morning or the early evening so this monster won't overheat. And whatever you do, don't try to get out and walk. You won't last ten miles in this heat."

"Why don't you just come back with me?" Krista asked.

Phoenix shook her head. "This is Coconino's grandchild and, though not biologically, mine as well. I will not leave it."

It was nearly dark when they bounced to a halt at the base of

*the mountains. The forest grew thick just ahead; they could take
the truck no farther. The fields they had come across to reach
this brief tableland were deserted, and though Phoenix called
out repeatedly, no one stepped from the trees to offer to guide
them.*

"That's all right, it's simple," she told Krista. "We just find
the stream and follow it up to the village. It won't be hard to
find the stream; we'll be able to hear it."

"I'm not going in the dark," Krista said flatly.

"Don't you have a torch in this truck?" Phoenix asked.

"Torch or not, I'm not going into those woods in the dark,"
Krista told her.

"There's no bogeyman, I promise you," Phoenix cajoled.
"And no animals stupid enough to hunt humans. Come on. I'll
take care of you."

"I'm not going in the dark," Krista repeated. "If I trip over
a root or a stone and twist an ankle, how am I going to get up
there and help your precious Nakha-a?"

"I'll carry you on my back!" Phoenix flared. "We'll make
it."

"And if I break a bone, who's going to drive me back to the
Mountain? You?"

*Phoenix paused and drew a great breath of the balmy night
air.*

"Your mystic said you had six days, didn't he?" Krista continued. "Then there's one left. We can wait till morning."

*But mystics can be wrong! Phoenix wanted to scream. Be-
sides, he said I had six days to save the baby, not six days to
save him. If he dies before we arrive, there may be nothing I
can do . . .*

*Krista climbed back into the cab of the truck and rolled up its
cracked windows against the mosquitoes. Phoenix called out a
few more times, then gave up and crawled into the back, swat-
ting at the pesky insects. Nakha-a had promised her six days.
She must rely on his gift to preserve both him and the baby until
dawn.*

*At first light she roused Krista, and they started into the woods
to find the stream. It was harder than Phoenix had thought, for
in midsummer, before the rainy season began, there was very
little water flowing in it. Yet they managed to locate it in less
than half an hour and begin their upward trek.*

"I've been telling myself I need to get more exercise," Krista *observed as she panted along behind Phoenix. "But somehow I didn't have this in mind."*

Phoenix did not respond; she was too worried about what they would find when they reached the village. She adjusted the backpack with Krista's medical supplies and trudged onward.

Because Krista needed to stop and rest so often, the going was slow. It made Phoenix uneasy that they passed no one coming down on their way to tend the fields; Nakha-a must be much worse if the People neglected their fields to chant and pray to the Mother Earth for his recovery. Or perhaps they were making their way down to the fields by other paths and avoiding the two noisy women who climbed upward.

Finally, at midmorning, a young woman met them. She carried an infant in a sling, and though she looked familiar, Phoenix could not call up her name.

"I am Tender Corn," she greeted them, "the wife of Nakha-a. He said you would be coming this way, so I came to lead you."

"How is he?" Phoenix asked anxiously.

The young woman looked tired, and her eyes were red and puffy. "They keep me from him," she replied, "so that my children will not be touched by his sickness. I got the message about you from Changing Hare, who spoke to him two days ago. Nina is with him constantly, but she will only say that he struggles with some great evil and that he grows weary." Tears sprang unwanted to her eyes. "I do not know what that means."

"It means," Phoenix said gently, putting an arm around the young woman as they started back up the trail, "that Nina fears what she does not understand. I have brought a Witch Woman with me who understands the way of sicknesses and can cure them. You will have your husband back, Tender Corn." But privately Phoenix wondered if she was encouraging false hope in the young mother. Had she not promised Sky Dancer the same thing just before Dreams of Hawks had died?

When Phoenix explained to Krista who their guide was, Krista asked Phoenix to translate as she asked the girl some questions. How long had Nakha-a been sick? How quickly had the disease come on? What had he eaten? Had he drunk from any standing water source? Did anyone else in the village have similar symptoms? Phoenix was impressed as the young doctor prodded and probed, trying to narrow down the range of illnesses that could cause Nakha-a's condition.

Finally they reached the clearing in which stood the wickiups *of the People. Confronted with the brush houses, Krista seemed suddenly hesitant. She paused to stare at one and at the old woman squatting in front of it. All around her were the cautious, subdued faces of the People. Children ran naked; men clustered around an open fire, speaking in hushed tones; women gathered in twos and threes to scrape hides or shell mesquite beans. Phoenix tried to recall the alienness of such a village when she had first arrived. She could not.*

"Do they live like this . . . in winter, too?" Krista asked.

"The wickiups are warm," Phoenix assured her.

"But the smoke . . ."

"Goes out the smoke hole for the most part. And keeps the insects out of the thatch. Most of the People, as you can see, are very healthy."

"Is it true," Krista ventured, "that they eat lizards and—"

"For God's sake, woman, they've survived for centuries!" Phoenix snapped. "Their general living conditions are fine. They just don't have strong enough medicines for pneumonia!"

Anger sparked in Krista's eyes. "Is that your diagnosis?"

Phoenix gave an exasperated sigh. "No, it's the only Greek word I know. Come on, Hippocrates, your patient is over here."

It was warm and stuffy in the dusty-smelling wickiup, and Phoenix longed for the coolness of her adobe house in the island canyon. Why couldn't you have stayed with us? she wondered as she gazed at the pallid young man on his woven mat. Why did she have to take you so far away from me in the north? If there had been no place for Michael and Sky Dancer to journey, if there had been no temptation of being alone together for so long . . . But she shook her head. Too many "if onlys." They did no one any good.

Krista knelt beside her patient, checking his pulse, his skin temperature, his eyes. Nakha-a made no movement or sound. "Ask how long he's been comatose," she directed Phoenix.

Phoenix turned to Nina, who knelt near the wall, watching them both with suspicious eyes. "How long has Nakha-a been sleeping?" she asked.

"Since you left," Nina replied. "Sometimes he wakes for a few moments, but soon he slips away again."

Phoenix translated that to Krista, who had her stethoscope out and was listening to Nakha-a's labored breathing.

"Well, I don't think it's tuberculosis," Krista decided. "That was my greatest fear. And if it's valley fever, it's the most severe case I've ever seen. Most likely you are right; most likely it is

pneumonia.'' She pulled a small metal cylinder from the pack that Phoenix had toted. *"I'll put him on oxygen. Tell that woman over there what I'm doing; I don't want a knife in my back. She looks like she'd stab me first and ask questions later. Then I'm going to give him a megadose of antibiotics, intravenously. The pump I use looks dangerous, so tell her about that, too. Then—''*

Suddenly a scream pierced the air from outside the wickiup. *"Sky Dancer!"* Phoenix cried, and bolted from the dwelling.

She found her foster daughter far advanced in her labor. *"It will be over by midafternoon,"* the midwife in attendance told her. *"She will be delivered of this evil, and then the Mother Earth will cease to trouble her.''*

"Out!" Phoenix roared at the woman. *"Out of this dwelling, this instant! The child is not evil, and I will not have you say such a thing in my daughter's hearing!"* The startled midwife gathered her things and scuttled out the door, remembering well the wrath of She Who Saves.

Sky Dancer struggled to reach her mother. Phoenix seized her child and held her close, cradling the girl's head against her chest. *"It's all right,"* she crooned. *"I won't let them hurt you or the baby. I've brought Michael's mother back with me. She is a Witch Woman of great power. She will save Nakha-a and your baby. Everything is going to be all right.''*

After that Phoenix would allow no one else into the wickiup, fearful that they would do the child harm when it was born. She had assisted at Sky Dancer's birth, and that had been a difficult one, indeed; she would deliver this child alone if need be. But in a few hours time Krista appeared.

"How is he?" Phoenix asked.

"Still comatose," Krista replied. *"It's a severe infection, no doubt of that, but he's young and strong. The oxygen has eased his breathing; he should be all right. We'll know better by morning.''*

"The child's not going to wait that long," Phoenix advised her.

Krista did a quick examination of the expectant mother. *"You're right,"* she agreed. *"She's in the final stages of labor. This child is in a hurry to see daylight.''*

Sky Dancer was gazing openmouthed at the doctor. *"You are beautiful,"* she breathed.

Krista did not understand what she said, but she smiled at

the young woman. When Phoenix translated, Krista said, "And you are pregnant."

At that Sky Dancer laughed, for she knew a little of the Mountain language. "You have Michael's sense of humor," she said in her own language, then struggled with Krista's. "I glad we meet. I know you to save my brother Nakha-a—and my baby. We be safe now."

But as the young woman began panting with the onset of another contraction, Krista knit her brows. "I wish I had her confidence," she told Phoenix. "Nakha-a's recovery will depend largely on his own recuperative powers. And as for the baby—" She lowered her voice. "It might be healthy enough, but those people out there, Ms. McKay. I don't know what they will do."

"What? What is it?" Sky Dancer demanded, seeing Krista's face. "What do you whisper?"

"She says she is worried about the People," Phoenix told her honestly. "So am I. I am going to speak to them. I will not be gone long."

Indeed, it did not take Phoenix long at all to realize she had no influence among these people. They had rejected her authority when they had chosen to follow Nina south; they were not about to give credence to her words when Nakha-a lay ill and Nina had laid the blame squarely at the feet of the unborn child. Though she argued vehemently that the child had not asked for its parentage, though she promised and promised that Nakha-a would live, they seemed determined; a child of incest was an abomination, and it must die. Even if it were born without deformity—which they did not believe—they would destroy it to preserve the Way of the People, the way that said brother must not mate with sister, or uncle with niece, or parent with child. Recollections of the story of Chico and Elena did not help; this was not the First Years, and they were not Survivors. The fiend Michael had come from the Mountain and trespassed against the Way of the People.

Finally Phoenix gave up and went back to be with her daughter. She could only hope that once the child was born, the natural passivity of the People would stay their hand until it could be seen that Nakha-a would recover.

The boy was born late in the afternoon, and Phoenix begged the Mother Earth not to let him cry, hoping that the People would not know for several hours that he had arrived. But the child had his own mind and wailed loudly. Sky Dancer wept with joy, for he was healthy and whole, a perfect child without mark or blemish. Krista examined him and pronounced him fit, but her diagnosis was made with professional detachment. This is your grandchild, too, Phoenix thought. Or hasn't that hit home to you yet?

A murmur of voices from outside drew Phoenix to the door. A knot of people had collected there, Nina among them. Phoenix reached for her bow, nocked an arrow, but left the weapon slack as she ducked outside to face them.

"The child is born," Nina said bluntly.

"Let the People rejoice," Phoenix replied. "It is a healthy boy, with no deformity, no mark of the Mother Earth's displeasure on him. How is Nakha-a?"

"He sleeps," Nine replied. "His breathing is easier, but he does not wake."

"He will," Phoenix promised.

"Are you a prophetess?" Nina sneered.

"I am a Witch Woman!" Phoenix flared. "And I tell you the magic I brought from the Mountain will make Nakha-a live. His illness has nothing to do with the child; it never did." In the background the baby boy continued to voice his displeasure at having to exit his watery domain.

A heavyset man moved forward. Phoenix recognized him: Many Waters, who had served on the Council of the Mother. Immediately her hands sprang up, bow drawn, arrow aimed squarely at him. "Do you offer your congratulations, Many Waters?" she asked.

"Give us the child," he said quietly.

"I think not."

No one moved. They did not doubt for a moment that Phoenix would release the shaft if anyone tried to approach.

"And how long will you stand there?" Many Waters asked. "Until sunset? Through the night?"

"Until Nakha-a wakes," Phoenix replied, "and tells you all what fools you are being." If they did not believe her, perhaps they would believe the young man himself.

"You only make it harder on your daughter by leaving the child with her," Nina told her. "Let us take it away now and be done with it."

Phoenix could not bring herself to shift the focus of the arrow to her old friend. She could not bring herself even to look at the woman who had been a second mother to Sky Dancer. How could she have become so twisted? "You will not take this child,

Nina,'' she replied. *"No one will take this child from his mother."*

"The Mother Earth will," Nina promised. *"If you do not surrender it, the Mother Earth herself will take it away."* Then she turned her back on Phoenix and returned to her son's wick-iup.

The others drifted away then, too, knowing the standoff was apt to take hours. Phoenix watched them go, then eased off the tension on her bow and crouched down in the doorway. *"They're gone,"* she announced.

The child's cries had settled down to whimpers. Sky Dancer cradled it tenderly, her face streaked with tears. *"But they will come back, won't they?"*

"I'm afraid so."

"It doesn't matter anymore if Nakha-a lives, does it?" Sky Dancer realized. *"They have decided, and they won't change their minds. Nina won't back down. She won't wait for Nakha-a to get better and put her in her place; she'll make sure she gets her way before that. She has changed, Mother. She is not the woman she used to be."* Her voice was filled with sorrow.

"Rest, child," Phoenix soothed. *"Nina will not hurt your baby. I will see to that."*

"But you will not always be here," Sky Dancer said bitterly. *"You cannot walk by his side day and night as he grows up here. What kind of life will he have, scorned by all the People? Remember how it was with Coral Snake, how we taunted him because he was the son of Lu-jan. It will be like that for my child, only worse. What can we do? What can any of us do for him?"*

"We will take him back north with us," Phoenix decided. *"No one will know—"*

"I can't go back north!" Sky Dancer wailed. *"Michael will be there. Michael must never know. He must never know or it will kill him! Mother, please,"* she pleaded. *"Think of something. Save my baby."*

A noise from outside sent Phoenix flying back to the doorway to crouch there, bow drawn. Many Waters was back with two or three strong men. Each was armed.

"We have run out of options," she called softly to the other two women. *"It seems they are prepared to kill me to get to the child."*

"No!" Sky Dancer shrieked. *"No, you cannot let that happen."*

"I'm not going to!" Phoenix snapped. *"I have a healthy sense

of self-preservation. Krista,'' she said, switching to the language of the Mountain. *"Krista, do you have a strong sedative in your medical supplies?"*

"Of course," Krista replied.

"Can you give the baby enough to make it look dead?"

There was a pregnant pause. *"Look dead?"* Sky Dancer echoed in her own language to make sure she understood correctly.

"Yes, medicine to make the child look dead. Krista, can you do it?"

"Most likely."

"Then do it now."

But Sky Dancer was reluctantly to surrender the child for such treatment. *"And then what? They may want to cut his throat to be sure."*

"I'll bury him," Phoenix replied.

"What?"

"It's all right," Krista reassured the terrified mother. *"It can be done. If we put the child in a box—or a basket—so that there is air for it to breathe. We can bury it, then come back later to dig it up."*

Sky Dancer made her mind up quickly, for she was her mother's daughter. *"Then do it,"* she said, handing over the infant.

"Tell me when it's done," Phoenix said. *"I'm going to stall them."* She relaxed her bow and stood up outside. *"Men of the People,"* she called. *"For whom are your weapons?"*

"For whoever opposes the will of the Mother Earth," Many Waters replied.

"And what is the will of the Mother Earth that you think is being opposed?"

"The child must die, She Who Saves," Many Waters told her. *"It is an abomination. It must be destroyed."*

"Then let the Mother Earth destroy it," Phoenix challenged. *"Did Nina not say she would?"*

"Give me the child, then," he came back, *"and I will take it to the top of this mountain and leave it for the Mother Earth to deal with."*

That would have been another way, Phoenix thought. Let him take the child, then come for it when he was gone. If I could track him. If I could trust him.

From inside came Sky Dancer's piercing wail, and she knew the decision was behind her. Phoenix dropped her bow and darted back inside.

"I told her to scream," Krista said. She was packing up her medical supplies.

"Good," Phoenix dropped to her knees beside the young mother and added her own wails to the commotion. Carefully she took the little boy from Krista. She felt for a pulse; she listened for breathing. For a moment fear seized her and she wondered if perhaps Krista had done her job too well, but there was no time for such doubts now. The ruse had to be played out.

Phoenix looked down into her sobbing daughter's face. "You know I cannot bring your baby back to this village again."

Sky Dancer nodded, and the tears that flooded down her cheeks were real. "Just save him, Mother," she whispered. "Just save Michael's child."

Phoenix turned to Krista. "How many hours till this wears off?"

"Ten or twelve," Krista replied. "Ms. McKay—Phoenix— what are you going to do with the child when it wakes?"

"I'll pretend to leave tonight, after the burial," Phoenix told her. "Tomorrow morning let the People escort you back down the mountain to your truck. Take your time. Then head north along this ridge of mountains; I'll meet you there. If you get to the end of it and haven't seen me, stop and wait."

There was a heavy pause. "And then?" Krista asked.

"You must take him back to the Mountain with you. There's no place for him among the People; his life would be miserable. Take him back where he'll have a chance to grow up."

Krista had finished loading her pack. "No," she said simply.

Phoenix's heart stopped. "What?"

"I said no," Krista repeated. "I've done what I can for this baby; the rest is up to you. I won't take it back with me."

"For God's sake, woman, this is your grandchild!" Phoenix exploded. "Don't you care what kind of life he has?"

"Listen, Ms. McKay!" Krista snapped back. "I raised one primitive child, and that was plenty. I had my heart broken a hundred times by the way people treated him because of what his father did! But he was my son, and I loved him, and I stuck by him, and I fought for him, and I made sure he knew he was loved. And do you know what happened, Ms. McKay?" Krista's eyes were hard with pain. "He left. He walked away from the mountain and the life I helped to carve for him there. He went back to his father's people, and I—" Suddenly her voice broke. "I will probably never see him again. Well, that's enough for one lifetime, thank you very much. Whatever you do with this *child, this darling, dark-haired boy, you must do by yourself. I'm going to give my other patient one more dose of antibiotics and leave the rest with his mother; then I'm starting back while there's still light to drive."* With that, Krista crawled out of the wickiup and walked away.

Phoenix sat stunned, looking down at the tiny infant who lay deathly still in her arms. She could go through with the charade—of course, she must go through with it. But once she had recovered the buried infant and revived it, then what? Krista and her truck would be long gone. Even if Phoenix dared to take the boy back north with her, that was a journey of several weeks, and she had no milk to feed it. How could it possibly survive?

"She Who Saves." The voice from the doorway startled Phoenix, for the name was a mockery. She turned to see Nina crouched in the doorway, her face an enigmatic mass of shadows.

Have you won in spite of my ingenuity? she wondered. *In this contest you have made between us, will death make you the victor, after all?*

CHAPTER TEN

Tana experienced a moment of vertigo and then a faint lurching as a slightly heavier gravity dragged on her slender body. And there she was, standing on a hillside in the fading light, gazing out over the bristly, ragged-looking vegetation of the Sonoran desert. Earth. She was on Earth.

Earth! It seemed unreal.

Explore?! Doc fairly demanded.

Yes, Tana thought, and he was off in an instant, nose to the ground, his transmissions bombarding her: *Strange! Creatures. New. Exciting. Curious. Insects. This one. That one. Another. Another. New, new, new, new—*

Tana had to pull back from the onslaught of scent and sound that reached her through Doc. She took several deep breaths of her own, concentrating on what her own senses told her, to mitigate the rapid-fire input from the dog. There was a heavy scent of pollen in the air, mingled with dust. The creaking of crickets pervaded the area, along with chirpings and buzzings she could not identify. A breeze stirred her hair, rustled her loose clothing, and felt cool against her exposed skin. The temperature was not as warm as it had been in the VR room, but it was nearly nightfall now. Tana was glad for the long sleeves and full pants.

Then she opened her eyes again and looked around. I am here! her heart sang. Here, on the home world of the human race. Here, where history was first recorded on the walls of caves, here, where the god I worship first spoke to his people, here, where the first crude attempts at spaceflight were launched. This is the world of Copernicus and Einstein and Yuko, of Alexander and Caesar and Snahchi. This is the world Clayton Winthrop left Argo to find; this is the world Chelsea spent her life trying to reach. And I am here.

Chelsea, I am here.

As she stepped off the traveling mat, she still could not grasp the reality of it. Turning around slowly, she might have been in a VR room for all her senses told her. Like a child, she knelt and touched the stiff, dry grass, the hard, chalky dirt to make sure it was real. She rubbed her fingers through the gritty dust and then brushed them together to reassure herself that this was soil, indeed, and not some trick of a holographic sensory duplicating system. But the sky was so impossibly clear and the horizon shimmered, given an aura of artificiality by the waves of heat rising up from the baking desert.

Paul had set her down on the back side of the hill, out of sight of the village and its outlying cottages. Her eyes were drawn to the west, where the sky was ablaze with dramatic golds and roses and indigos as the sun sank behind low, wooded mountains. Mountains always impressed Tana; raised on the prairie, she found their towering presence awesome and the boldness of their contours inspiring. She watched them until she was in danger of losing the daylight entirely. Then she called Doc and adjusted the tiny recorder concealed as a piece of jewelry hanging from her neck. *Remember this place,* she directed the dog as she rolled up the traveling mat and tucked it into a large pocket sewn in her trousers. It would be easier for Paul to pick her up in three hours if she came back to approximately the same location. Doc sniffed the ground carefully and assured her that he would remember, then the two of them headed over the hill.

It was difficult to pick her way through the shrubby vegetation that scratched at her trousers and threatened to trip her halting feet. *Doc! Find a path for me,* she commanded. Immediately the dog took the lead, winding this way and that to choose the least treacherous route for her. All the same, Tana was glad when she crested the hill and saw a dirt track just down the slope that led in the general direction of the village.

It seemed terribly far away to her, though it was less than a mile. It would take her an hour, she was sure, just to get to the cluster of buildings; and then how long would she have before she must begin her slow journey back to this place?

I run for you? Doc asked.

No, she replied. *I must go there myself.* But she hesitated, looking up the road in the other direction. There was a small installation less than a quarter of a mile in that direction. In the brilliant beams of the setting sun the main building seemed to glow with golden fire, and the dark timbers of the outbuildings stood out starkly.

Suddenly, Doc gave a low warning growl.

What is it? Tana asked.

They were still on the hillock looking over the road. *Someone comes,* Doc told her.

Tana's heart thudded. *Where?* she asked, straining to see movement on the road.

There, Doc responded, eyes riveted in the direction of the settlement. The dying light cast deceptive shadows, but in a moment Tana saw him, too: a tall figure trudging steadily up the dirt track from the village. His walk was a weary one, but it still covered the ground at a rate that Tana envied. In a few moments he would be at the foot of this hillock. Her heart pounded with excitement, but she felt no anxiety about this meeting. The virus would lie quiet in her joints.

Doc stood poised, ears cocked, muscles tense, watching the man's approach. *I chase him away?* he asked, growling low in his throat again.

No, Tana told him firmly. *I want to meet this man.*

Friend? Doc asked suspiciously.

We shall see.

Carefully they made their way down to the dirt track to wait for him.

Tana could tell the moment the walker spotted them: his pace slowed and his approach became more cautious. About ten feet away from them he stopped.

"Good evening," Tana called out. Conversations picked up by the recorders had shown the local dialect to be similar to Tana's native speech, another indication that these were descendants of the *Homeward Bound*'s crew. Communication should be relatively easy.

"Evening," the man called back. He had a curious drawl to his voice that made his speech almost musical; but there was caution even in that simple word.

Afraid, Doc informed her triumphantly.

Of you, no doubt, Tana replied. Even when he was quiescent, Doc could be intimidating for his sheer size, and at the moment he was on full alert, radiating power and dominance.

"Are you coming back from the settlement?" Tana asked.

His clothes were sweat- and dirt-stained from a day of hard labor. In the fields? In some kind of factory?

"Just dropped off a tractor at the equipment bay," he told her. "Headed for home now."

"There?" Tana asked, pointing with delight toward the farm. What luck to meet a resident from this nearer location!

But the man did not answer. He only stared at Doc.

"Doc, lie down," Tana commanded, and the Dalmatian immediately dropped at her feet. But he never took his eyes off the man. "It's all right, he won't hurt you as long as you don't threaten me."

Still the man stared at Doc. *Afraid,* Doc informed her. *Confused. Worried.*

"I'm Tana Winthrop," Tana continued. "This is Doc."

"Tame, is he?" the man asked. His voice was even, almost nonchalant, but his bearing did not change.

"He listens to me," Tana replied.

"That's not a coyote," the man said finally. "And I've never seen a wolf, but I don't think they're that color."

Tana laughed. "No, he's a Dalmatian. It's just a breed of dog. I guess you don't have that breed here."

Now the man lifted his eyes to meet hers. "Just a breed of dog?" he echoed. "That's like saying, just a kind of dinosaur."

Confusion swept through Tana, and then dismay. "Oh, no," she sighed. "You don't have dogs here, do you?"

"No, ma'am," he replied. "They don't have them on the Mountain, either. To the best of my knowledge, there haven't been dogs here for seven hundred years."

"Oh." Tana shifted uncomfortably, then forced a smile. "I'm not from around here."

Now he studied her more critically. "Winthrop, you say?"

"Tana Winthrop."

"That name . . . has some meaning for us," he said carefully.

Hope flooded through Tana. "Are you descended from the crew of the *Homeward Bound*?" she blurted.

"That I am," he replied. "Mike and Terry Johanneson, mech techs. I'm Nathan."

Tears sprang to Tana's eyes. "And I," she said, "am descended from Clayton and Jacqueline Winthrop."

For a long moment they stood silent as the sun slipped behind the western mountains. "Well," Nathan said finally. "You've come a long way then."

"A very long way."

He sighed heavily. "Say-ayka-pee always said you would.

Even when folks in Camp Crusoe gave up believing, Say-ayka-pee said you'd be back.''

"And now you can go home."

At that Nathan gave a short laugh. He pointed to the farm. "That's home," he said. "And you're right, it is time to go there. If I'm late for supper, my boys will have eaten everything in sight." And with that he started up the road again.

Tana was stunned. "Wait!" she cried as he came abreast of her. Doc came to his feet with a snarl.

Nathan stopped dead in his tracks.

Lie down! Tana commanded silently, and Doc obeyed. "I'm sorry," she apologized. "He won't hurt you, really. I just—I have so many questions."

Nathan tore his eyes away from the dog long enough to look at her. "Yes, I suppose you do," he said quietly. Then he seemed to come to a decision. "Well, come along then," he invited. "There's always room for one more at the supper table."

Tana moved to walk on his left, so that Doc would be on the far side of her. "I need to know what happened," she said. "To the *Homeward Bound.* How you were stranded here."

"Coconino happened," he replied.

"What?" She was struggling to keep pace with him. "I'm sorry, can you slow down a little? I can't walk very well. I have an affliction of the joints."

"Arthritis?" he guessed, slacking his pace immediately.

"Something like that." She didn't want to waste time on ex-planations. "Please tell me. What happened to my ancestors? What happened to Clayton and Jacqueline?"

So he told her, how Clayton had disappeared with a small aircraft over the desert; how Jacqueline had laid the blame squarely at Derek Lujan's feet; how the primitive Coconino had tricked them all, only to be snatched away in a time warp along with Lujan. It was an incredible story; but no more incredible, Tana thought, than her own. As they approached the farmyard she asked, "Do you believe me? That I am Jacqueline's descen-dant? That I have come here across light years to find the lost crew of the *Homeward Bound*?"

He paused to consider that. "If the stories they tell about old Doc Winthrop are true," he said, "it would be like her children to find us."

"You don't seem very excited about it," she commented.

There was something like amusement in his eyes as he looked down at her, the darkness pooling around them. "Miz Winthrop, I see you wear a fancy set of rings.'' Tana fingered her wedding band reflexively. ''I'll assume that whatever metal they're made of is precious on your world. You know what's precious here? Tempered steel, for plows. Extrudable copper, for wire. If a person here came across a diamond, he'd only care how to make a tool out of it. We have a different set of standards than you. Am I excited about your coming? No. As a matter of fact, Miz Winthrop, it makes me sad. It makes me very sad.''

Tana's jaw dropped. She was about to voice a protest when a child burst out of the farmhouse and raced across the yard toward them. ''Grandpa, Grandpa! Grandma says quit lollygagging and wash up for supper, we're *hungry*.''

And then the little girl stopped, her eyes fastened on Doc's glistening coat. Doc's tail wagged in anticipation; he liked children. ''What's *that*?'' the girl demanded in astonishment.

Nathan whisked her up in his powerful arms. ''Why, that's a piebald coyote,'' he lied smoothly. ''You know, sometimes an albino one mates with a dark one and the pups come out spotted.''

''It's too *big* to be a coyote,'' the girl protested.

''Well, maybe he's got a little wolf in him,'' Nathan admitted.

''Or puma,'' the girl agreed.

He set her down. ''Run tell your grandma we've got a guest for dinner.'' And when she had gone, he turned to Tana. ''Can you get him to stay out of sight? Shanna might buy that tale, but I doubt anyone else would.''

Nathan's house was an anomaly for the settlement, constructed of sun-dried brick. ''Damnfool neighbors of mine have been living here for two centuries,'' Nathan observed as they stepped out into the cool evening air, ''and they still keep making their homes out of wood. Wood is a poor insulator, it burns, it gets infested with termites, and it's a whole lot of work to strip and split. Adobe is cool in the summer, it holds the heat better in the winter, it shapes into neat squares, and you don't have to go up into the mountains to get it.'' He snorted, stopping under a canopy of sticks that sheltered the doorway to retrieve a lantern. ''And they think the primitives are slow learners.''

There had been much talk over the supper table of the primitives, or the People, as Nathan's family called them. Nathan's particular friend, Say-ayka-pee, was quoted often by the three strapping boys he and his wife Marjean had raised, and even Matt's wife Lonissa spoke of the beautiful pottery Say-ayka-

pee's daughter made. The mountain settlement was spoken of
less, though Matt and Hjal had both gone there for some advanced schooling, and young Tory expected to go in the fall.
But Tana suspected that was because of the ruse Nathan had
constructed, and the deft manner in which he steered the conversation at the table.

"Tell them you're from the Mountain," he had instructed her
before they entered the dwelling. "And don't say your name is
Winthrop. Use . . . Wind-drop. Tell them a primitive gave you
that name; they'll believe that and they won't be able to place
you in a family. Tell them your truck overheated and as soon as
it's cooled off you'll go back to it."

Before she could protest he opened the heavy timber door and
stepped inside. After that it was more politic to play along than
to argue with him.

And during the meal he had kept conversation turned deftly
away from Tana herself and kept it on the history of Camp
Crusoe, as they called the settlement. It was a simple, "Marjean, the woman's tired, let her be." Or, "Miz Wind-drop is
thinking of writing a history. Hjal, why don't you tell her
about . . ." And once the storytelling began, the time flew
until Tana felt the slight vibration of her chronometer alerting
her that it was time to start back.

Now, as Nathan lighted her way back with the awkward looking lantern, her head still reeled with the magic and the beauty
of his storytelling. The boys were good at it, but when Nathan
spoke, it was like listening to an epic poem. Oral history, she
thought. What we have lost by surrendering that tradition! "Was
there really a—what did you call it? A celux something? Tala.
Was there really such a creature?"

"Of course!" Nathan seemed surprised that she should question it. "That's how Coconino defeated the Sky Ship—he got
his friend Tala to fire a stream of electricity into the control
panel of the *Homeward Bound*."

It seemed so preposterous—but who am I to speak of preposterous? she thought. I, who show up claiming to be from a place
several hundred light years distant, in the company of a tame
"piebald coyote."

As if on cue, Doc materialized out of the shadows. Tana
greeted him with praise and petting while he danced and
squirmed around her feet, rubbing against her legs and smack-
ing his whiplike tail painfully into her shins. When she had
calmed him down somewhat, she and Nathan began walking

along the dirt track back toward her rendezvous point. The lantern was a poor one—or, rather, its power source was very weak—and the brilliant display of stars overhead seemed to grant more illumination to their journey.

"So," Nathan asked, "did you get what you came for?"

"Oh, yes," she replied fervently. "It will take me days to assimilate everything you've told me tonight, but yes, you've answered so many questions."

"And raised a few more," he guessed.

"More than a few!" She laughed. "I'm fascinated by this primitive culture you keep referring to. I'd love to meet your Say-ayka-pee."

Nathan smiled sadly in the moonlight. "He doesn't come to Camp Crusoe if he can avoid it. He says it's like a callus on the Mother Earth; he can't feel her presence here."

"How did you get to know him so well?" Tana asked.

"I lived with him when I was a boy," Nathan explained. "He invited me to come and learn the Way of the People, and my father was a wise enough man to let me go. I spent a year and a half with them; then Say-ayka-pee made me come home. He said I had been a student long enough; it was time for me to return to the Others and be a Teacher."

"And have you been?" Tana asked frankly.

"We've made some progress in the past thirty years," he admitted. "I haven't been alone. A number of young men have gone to the southern village; our medic has gone, too. She went down there to see if she could improve their health practices and discovered they knew more about natural medicines than she did. She wrote a letter to the administrator of the Infirmary on the Mountain telling him a six-month stay with the primitives ought to be a required part of the health tech curriculum. I don't think the idea was favorably received."

"Maybe I should go there," Tana laughed. "Perhaps they can do something about my condition that doctors on the civilized planets can't." Then she caught herself. "I'm sorry," she apologized. "I didn't mean to imply that Earth isn't civilized."

"It's all right," Nathan assured her. "I've read about the so-called civilized planets. I'm not impressed. And I don't mean to imply, Miz Winthrop, that the People are miracle workers, that everything they do is right and everything we do is wrong. But—" He hesitated, and Tana wondered that the man whose storytelling had been so fluid and so poetic should struggle for words now. "There is so much of value in their culture, in the

way they see life and the role of humankind in it. I would hate
to see that destroyed."

Tana stopped and looked up at him. "Is there a danger of
that?" she asked.

The lantern flickered as its meager power source began to run
out. Shadow deepened the lines in Nathan's weather-worn face
as he looked down at her. "You'll have to tell me that," he
answered.

"What do you mean?"

"When you go back, Miz Winthrop," he said, "what will
you tell the people who are waiting for you?"

Tana's heart crashed against her ribs as she realized what he
meant. "I will tell them what you told me," she replied.

"And how long will it be before they want to come and investigate themselves?"

A heartbeat, she knew. When they find out there are people
here, and clay pots, and curiosities— "Is that why you wanted
me to masquerade as someone from the Mountain?"

"Please, Miz Winthrop," he whispered, "don't let anyone
else come. We may not have all the knowledge that you have
and all the fancy computers and other technology, and you may
have a thousand ways to make our lives easier and longer, but
please—keep your gifts. We have carved out our place here, and
we are learning, as the People have learned, how to strike a
balance with the Mother Earth. If any more of you come, it will
disrupt our fragile harmony. Coconino knew that two hundred
years ago. Please, Miz Winthrop. My people are not wise
enough yet to have learned from his lesson." The lantern died,
and they stood on a hillside lit only by starlight. "Be wise enough
to learn it for them."

CHAPTER ELEVEN

Todd had obviously opened a few champagne bottles before. The cork yielded to the gentle pressure of his thumbs with a soft pop and dropped onto the floor of the veranda without ceremony. "You've had practice at that," Paul accused as he peeled the seal from a bottle of callimray for Tana.

They had been reviewing the data Tana had brought back from Camp Crusoe stored in her recorder necklace, when Paul had suddenly decided they were all working too hard and needed an afternoon off. So the three of them had retired to *Terra Firma* for an impromptu celebration, complete with the champagne Todd had inquired wistfully about. The children were at their studies, the hands were at their chores, and Bertha, having laid the table on the veranda with more food than they could eat in a week, had headed for the bungalow she shared with her son to catch up on her favorite holosoap.

"I worked my way through the Omniversity as a waiter," Todd told them, filling two champagne flutes with a flourish.

"Liar," Paul replied. "You had a full scholarship. I've read your file."

Todd grinned. "All right, I spent one intersession as a bellboy at the Riser on Aunt Shelby's," he admitted. "I delivered complimentary champagne to the rooms and made fantastic tips, which I proceeded to gamble away in the casino. My grandmother yanked me out of there in a hurry."

"I take it she disapproved of your gambling," Tana observed, sipping at her callimray.

"I'll say," Todd agreed, handing an effervescing flute to Paul. "She told me anyone stupid enough to split kings deserved to be stuck in a laboratory for the rest of his life, and I might just as well go back to school."

"A toast!" Paul cried. "To P-TUP and the successful journey to—" He made a great show of looking over his shoulder to make sure no one was listening. "—you know where!" Tana recognized in his exuberant antics an ocean of relief at her safe return.

"So said," Todd and Tana chimed, and they all clinked glasses.

Tana herself, however, was having difficulty getting into the mood of the celebration. "To Chelsea and Zachery," she proposed, "and the solution of the mystery of the *Homeward Bound.*"

"So, said."

The fragrance of cut hay reached Tana from the near west hay field, where one of the hands was putting up the first cutting of the season against the long, snowy winter. It reminded her of the hillside where she had left Nathan standing, his very stance in the starlight seeming to plead with her: *Keep our secret.*

"To Grandmother," Todd put in, "without whose sound advice I might still be popping corks at Aunt Shelby's!"

They all laughed merrily at that, and Tana thought again how lucky she was to have men like this in her life. Oh, there were plenty of women within her sphere of activity as well, but somehow the men were more entertaining. A hormonal reaction, she supposed.

Paul turned to the heavily laden table behind them and surveyed the meats and breads and concoctions Bertha had prepared for them. "Come on, Todd, dig in," he invited. "There's enough here to feed a flock of pirrarahs. Look at this: corkberries, melons, five—no, six different cold cuts, homemade bread and asorbas—"

"What, no caviar?" Todd asked, peering over his shoulder. "Paul, next time let's send Tana to old Russia and see if any sturgeon survived."

The smile slipped suddenly from Tana's face. Paul noticed. "What is it?" he asked.

She forced the smile back. "Nothing," she lied. "This isn't the time to talk about it. Hand me a plate, will you."

But Todd's jesting remark had troubled her. It was indicative of the way they had approached this adventure, the way everyone else would receive the news that Earth was not only habitable but inhabited. They thought only of what they could get from Earth. For Tana, it had been the answers to a centuries-old mystery and vindication for her ancestors. For some, like the Interglobal Association of Terraphiles, it would be the story of Earth's near demise and subsequent resurgence. For others, like her distant cousin Lourdes, who was the current curator of the Interplanetary Museum of Art, it would be the art and artifacts that could yet be gleaned from Earth's ruins. Interest among the scholastic community would be monumental, interest among the general public would run high as well, but it would all be based on one thing: what Earth could provide to them.

And what, Tana thought, can we provide to Earth? What can we offer her citizens that is of equal value to what they give us?

And do they really want it?

That was the question that truly troubled her. She had assumed that the descendants of the *Homeward Bound*'s crew would want to be found. She had assumed they would be overjoyed to have contact with other planets again, would want to come *home*. Vaporhead, she thought. They *are* home. Why would they want to come to strange worlds like ours, where everything is unfamiliar?

At least we can share with them, another part of her argued. Think of what we can provide: tools, medicines, education, opportunities. Climate-controlled housing and crystal-powered transportation. Investment income. Art. They can't truly want to remain isolated, can they?

Nathan's request had set her back on her heels. He was like any good farmer; it was the closeness to the land he didn't want to lose. She understood that; having been raised here in the country on Juno, she understood wanting always to be aware of one's relationship to the land. The balance of the ecosystem, the place of one being in the scope of the universe. Yet it was possible to sense that, to know it, in other places and other professions without adopting an isolationist attitude. Wasn't she proof? Wasn't Paul?

And yet she had been so quick to break all barriers to reach Earth because it served *her* purposes. Was that what Nathan really feared: that Earth would become a pawn in the machinations of centillions of other beings? Did they all feel like that, the Crusoans? Did most of them feel like that? Or was Nathan one man, afraid of change, trying to preserve a way of life that he found satisfactory, while others in his community would disagree? And if he was just one man, was he right?

Paul's hand on her shoulder brought Tana back. "Are you going to put some of that food on your plate, or are you just going to stare at it?"

"Sorry," she apologized. "It's just that I don't know what to make of Nathan and his attitude."

"Well, you've got three months to think about it," he reminded her. "We can't possibly announce that we've been to Earth for at least that long—otherwise the charade of having hired a ship won't hold up."

"I know." Tana sighed. "It's just that—"

"Am I too late?" a voice boomed from the doorway. They looked up to see Dak running a comb through his hair and brushing a last drop of moisture from his freshly washed face. "Someone told me there was a celebration going on here."

Paul picked up the champagne bottle with a questioning look, to which Dak nodded as he sauntered out onto the veranda. "Don't tell me," Tana teased, "that I have spies in my own household."

"Naw," he assured her. "You know me, I can hear the pop of a champagne cork at a quarter mile." He took the flute of vintage bubbly Paul handed him. "Besides, I ran into Bertha on her way back to her house, and she muttered something about maybe the festivities would give you an appetite for a change."

"There's nothing wrong with my appetite," Tana groused, lifted temporarily from her depression by Dak's buoyant presence. "Just because I don't want to be Bertha's size doesn't mean I don't enjoy my food." And to prove it she added another slice of mock ham to her plate.

"Well, what are we celebrating?" Dak asked, lifting his champagne flute. "P-TUP in general or Tana's recent journey in particular?" Alone of all Tana's family, Dak knew the nature and extent of their testing. The onus of keeping it secret did not seem to bother him in the least, and it was good for her and Paul both to have someone they could talk to about the project, someone who was not as closely involved as they were.

"All of the above," Todd replied. "As well as the wisdom of my grandmother, the fulfillment of dreams, and anything else you'd care to name."

"Summer help," Dak replied instantly. "Andy hired a couple of students on intersession—that's why the boss man gets to take a break in the middle of the day and drink champagne."

"So said!" Tana agreed heartily. Perhaps if Dak did not work for four weeks straight before going into town to blow off steam, he'd have time to discover that there were women available who would treat him better than Wanda did.

"Say, Dak," Paul said around a mouthful of roast marpet,

"I wanted to ask you. Have you ever heard of an animal called a celux?"

"There are several varieties of celux," Dak replied. "From Searg, I believe—you know, where they have all the six-legged creatures. Celuxes are quadrupeds, though—just vestigial wings instead of another set of limbs. Some varieties are raised domestically as a meat source. Why?"

"Were they ever exported to Earth?" Tana asked, picking up Paul's line of thought. Tana had been perfectly willing to accept Nathan's story of the time warp that had caught Lujan and the primitive, but Paul and Todd were both skeptical. They didn't know what kind of animal could interfere with the functioning of a warp terminal, even one as archaic as the *Homeward Bound*'s.

"As meat, sure," Dak agreed. "Before the Evacuation they'd import anything edible or even close."

"But were there any live ones?" Tana pursued. She had meant to access the computer before Paul had distracted them all with the suggestion of a celebration. It was more fun to access Dak, anyway.

He shrugged. "In a zoo, maybe. Or some enterprising rancher might have brought them in to raise, although that would have been frightfully expensive. Why?" He regarded his sister seriously. "Did you see one?"

Tana laughed. "No. I wouldn't know what one was if it jumped up and bit me."

"You can't miss 'em," Dak assured her. "Their horns twist together in a single spike on the crown of the head. They look like unicorns."

Tana, Paul, and Todd exchanged a look.

"You *did* see one!" Dak exclaimed.

"No, but I heard about one," Tana told him. "Dak, can they give off electrical charges, like eels or tzimori?"

"Absolutely," he replied. "It's channeled through their horns. I've seen holograms of a couple of bucks fighting over does—very impressive. They can actually shoot charges at each other. You can see the sparks arcing through the air."

"Then the story could be true," Todd breathed. "If an animal like that let loose a charge in a warp terminal, it undoubtedly would have played havoc with the transmission. With antiquated equipment and programs like that, they might very well have landed two hundred years in the future. They could have landed two planets away, as well."

"Who?" Dak asked.

They filled him in on some of the stories Tana had brought back from Earth, including the bizarre tale of the primitive youth and his celux who had thwarted Derek Lujan and sealed the fate of the *Homeward Bound*. Dak was intrigued. "Coca . . . what did you call him?"

"Coconino, I think," Tana said. "I'd have to look it up; we left all the files sealed at work."

"And this is a Stone Age culture that lives off the land— hunter-gatherers?"

She nodded.

"Do you suppose I could sell them a few horses?"

Tana punched him in the arm. "Don't you do it, too!" she accused. "It seems all anyone thinks about is what this discovery can do for *them*. Tell me, what's it going to do for the Crusoans? What's it going to do for the Mountain dwellers? And what's it going to do for that primitive culture?"

As usual, Dak did not seem much impressed by such weighty philosophical questions. "Humanity doesn't have a very good track record for the way it brings technology to less advanced cultures," he admitted. "But we haven't had any to practice on for a while. Maybe we'll do it better this time."

"I don't think it's a matter for us to decide," Paul put in. "This is something the Pax Circumfra should struggle with. Is Earth a sovereign planet? Does it need a central government to handle commerce and communications? Those decisions are way over our heads."

"But why should they be made by the Pax Circumfra, either?" Tana argued. "Earth isn't even represented in the Pax. Why should it dictate what happens to them?"

"Why should you?" Paul challenged.

"I don't want to," Tana told him. "But I opened the door to this world, and now I've been put in the position of deciding when and how to tell the rest of humanity about it. The way I handle the news directly affects the natives of Earth. I have the responsibility, not because I want it but because *I opened the door*. What do I do now?"

"Tana, sooner or later the word is going to get out," Paul pointed out. "Once we announce P-TUP, be that in two years or two decades, someone is going to be curious enough about Earth to go there. Maybe what we need to do is tell the Crusoans so they can prepare for the inevitable invasion."

Tana sighed deeply. "Maybe you're right," she agreed. "It

should be their decision, anyway, not mine. At any rate, I have to go back there. I have to go back and talk to Nathan again and to others in Camp Crusoe. I need to know how they feel about it."

But Paul was alarmed at the prospect. "Tana, it doesn't have to be you!" he protested. "You've done what you needed to do on Earth. Let someone else do the negotiating."

"Who?" she asked.

"Your father," Paul suggested. "That's his line of work."

But Tana shook her head. "To involve him is tantamount to involving the Pax Circumfra. I'm the only logical choice, Paul. I'm the only *ethical* choice. I'm going back to Earth."

It was a strange, almost bereft feeling to walk along the dirt track without Doc, but Tana had determined not to betray her offworld origins to any other Crusoans until she knew more about them, so she had left the dog behind. Paul had been adamantly opposed to that. "Tana, in primitive conditions like those you need Doc more than ever!" he protested.

"I'll be fine with Nathan," she assured him. "Give me thirty-six hours."

"Six!" he snapped.

"Thirty-six. Paul, it takes time to get from one place to another, especially at the rate I walk. Even with thirty-six hours I can't get to the Mountain on this trip, or one of the primitive villages. Give me time to meet the Crusoans, at least."

"Twelve hours," he compromised.

"There's no point in me warping back and forth a number of times," she argued. "Marjean was disappointed I wouldn't stay the night last time; I'm sure there will be no problem finding a bed there. Thirty-six hours, two Terran days and a night. I have to talk to them, Paul. I have to know how they feel."

"You can't push yourself for twelve and sixteen hours at a time under those conditions," he warned her. "You'll have a seizure, and how can I retrieve you if you're lying unconscious with a traveling mat rolled up in your pocket? Be reasonable, Tana!"

"I need two days at least," she insisted. "I'll be careful, I promise. I'll check my biometer regularly, and at the first sign of tremors I'll back out of wherever I am and go rest. I promise."

Paul wavered, but he was not quite through objecting. "How

are you going to explain your absence from the institute for two days?'' he asked. "You know Delhi will be all over that.''

"I'm going offplanet on business,'' Tana replied smoothly. "I may stop and visit with some old Omniversity friends while I'm there. What's curious about that?''

"For someone so concerned with ethics,'' Paul grumbled, "you lie like a fiend.''

"If I weren't spied on in my own organization, I wouldn't have to!'' Tana snapped, and felt the surge of toxins in her bloodstream warning her not to continue in that vein. "Paul, it's the husband in you objecting to this, not the scientist. There's nothing dangerous about it.''

For a moment he continued to scowl at her, but then he put his arms around her and drew her close to him. "Do you think the husband in me won't win out over the scientist every time?'' he asked, his cheek nestled in the softness of her honey-blond hair.

"I know it will,'' she replied. "But although the husband in you worries about my welfare, it also loves me enough to let me do what I have to do. Like have babies. And travel to Earth.''

At last he had surrendered. Leaving Doc at *Terra Firma*, Tana had had Paul warp her to a site much nearer Nathan's adobe house than the first drop. Now she approached the ramshackle roof extension, which they called a ramada, in the cool and radiant splendor of a summer dawn.

Several birds in a shade tree by the house announced her arrival, and the front door swung open while she was still several yards away. "Well, look who's here!'' Marjean called in delight. "Nathan, you were right; look who's here!''

Tana smiled in surprise. "Am I expected?'' she asked.

Nathan appeared in the doorway behind his wife. "I knew you'd be back,'' he said quietly. "Just a matter of when.''

"Well, come on in; I'm just starting breakfast,'' Marjean invited. "It'll be ready in half an hour. The others are doing chores, but you can keep Shanna and me company in the kitchen while—''

"I think maybe Miz Wind-drop would like to see the farm,'' Nathan interrupted.

"Please called me Tana,'' she hastened. "And yes, I would. I understand you do things somewhat differently than we do on the Mountain.''

Marjean's disappointment was evident. "But if I could prevail upon your hospitality,'' Tana added quickly, ''I need a place to stay this evening. Could you find a bed for me here?''

''Why, of course!'' Marjean exclaimed, pleased once more at the prospect of company. '' *'Mi casa, su casa,'* as the primitives say.''

''It means 'My house is your house,' '' Nathan translated as they walked around the adobe structure to the rear, where pens made of native materials were interspersed with metal machinery and a few fruit trees were covered with what appeared to be synthetic netting. Human voices and the sound of the animal grunts and bleats came from the open door of an adobe outbuilding.

''What's that on the trees?'' Tana asked.

''Netting, to keep the birds away from the peaches,'' Nathan replied. ''I've got a bumper crop coming along this year, and I don't intend to surrender any more than I have to.''

''But what's the netting made of?''

He shrugged. ''Don Mahitsu found it in one of the Dead Cities,'' he explained. ''One of those outstanding products from the Before Times—excuse me, from pre-Evacuation days—that lasts forever when it's buried in the ground but deteriorates in two or three seasons when it's exposed to the sun. I figured the Mother Earth wouldn't be too offended if I used some on my fruit trees and helped degrade it.''

Nondegradable substances, Tana thought. It was an issue again for humanity. A colony on the moon Dhirga had been systematically launching its nondegradable waste into the gas giant that it circled, until a massive explosion on a departing cargo vessel had spread contaminants throughout the atmosphere. The ecology was critically upset, and most of the population had died before they could be evacuated. A hue and cry had gone up in the aftermath: Wasn't it enough that we killed our ancestral planet with our carelessness? Must we now destroy our new habitations as well?

Only this planet wasn't destroyed, Tana thought, looking around her. It is very much alive, and its people—or Nathan, at least—have grown more conscious of their responsibility for it.

But what an odd way of speaking! The Mother Earth wouldn't be offended?

''And these machines,'' she continued, tapping one complicated-looking object that appeared to have numerous moving parts. ''How do you make these?''

''There's a foundry near the Mountain,'' Nathan told her. ''At least, we call it a foundry. Basically they scavenge metal from the Dead Cities and melt it down to reuse. They've been able to maintain capabilities on the Mountain to machine the salvaged metal; consequently, they have about five times the number of working vehicles that we do.''

''So their technology is more advanced than yours,'' Tana concluded.

''In some ways,'' Nathan hedged. ''But we've had to be more inventive than they have. See that chimney on the end of my house?'' He pointed up at the tall structure that soared some fifty feet into the air. ''That's part of an air-cooling system designed by Claire Ryan—uses the principles of evaporation and cold air sinking. She put the Mountain dwellers to shame on that one; they have all kinds of electrical gadgets we don't, but they can't afford to waste their precious batteries cooling their houses.''

Tana smiled at him. ''Do I detect something of a rivalry here?''

A smirk stole across Nathan's face, and she thought it became him much better than the brooding look he had worn for most of her first visit. This was a man accustomed to seeing the humor in life. She wished her presence were more of a joy to him.

''You know, when Lujan showed up here,'' he told her, ''he managed to get one of our computers to run for a little while. You should have heard the Exec! We had a working computer, which the Mountain hadn't had in a hundred and fifty years! The only problem was—'' He gave her a lopsided grin. ''—no one knew what to do with it, except Lujan. And he was too far gone to take direction from anyone.''

''How long ago was that?'' Tana asked.

Nathan rubbed his chin. ''Oh, forty years, I guess. I was just a boy, ten years old. He scared the daylights out of me.''

''What happened to him?''

A curious look passed over Nathan's features, as though a veil were dropping to obscure the truth. ''The Mother Earth claimed her revenge,'' he said obliquely.

It was the second time he had skimmed warily over Lujan's fate, alluding to violence without revealing its nature. Tana's curiosity was piqued, but she did not want to press Nathan too much just yet. She intended to ask much of him before her thirty-six hours was up. ''Can you spend some time with me today?'' she asked.

''Doing what?'' he asked suspiciously.

"I'd like to meet some of the other residents of Camp Crusoe," she explained. "I want to know how they feel about . . . being found."

Nathan's eyes sparked dangerously. "It's not something you can put to a vote! The minute you tell them you're from offworld, there's no choice to be made anymore."

"I'm aware of that," Tana responded calmly, accustomed to such flares of temper from her staff. "I don't intend to tell them who I am—or, more aptly, where I'm from. My inquiries will be discreet. But I need to know, Nathan. I need to know how they feel."

"So you can make a decision." There was accusation in his tone.

Tana sighed, feeling she had just had this discussion with Paul. "I didn't expect to be a gatekeeper when I came here. Maybe that was naive of me, but now I'm in this situation, and you've asked me to withhold information from people on my world. I'm not sure I *can* do that, but if I can, I need to know if I *should*."

For a long moment Nathan studied her, as though weighing— what? she wondered. My logic? My intentions? My wisdom? Does he wonder if I am another Lujan, come to exploit the primitives, including the Crusoans? Does he wonder if he can do anything about it?

Finally Nathan nodded. "All right, I'll take you around, in-troduce you to some other folks. You'll find," he promised, "that people don't all agree with me."

Now it was Tana's turn to smile. "I run an organization of fourteen hundred people," she replied. "They don't all agree with me, either; it doesn't mean my way isn't right."

They stopped first at another adobe house. Winded from the long walk, which took them over an hour, Tana was relieved to see the soaring chimney that meant this house was cooled. Al-ready the day was growing warm, and it promised to get much hotter. "Hello, Claire, Eddie—anyone home?" Nathan sang out as they approached.

In a moment the heavy plank door swung open. "Nathan!" cried a young woman in short trousers and a sleeveless shirt. "Come in! Did you walk the whole way? You must be parched. Let me get you some lemonade."

The lemonade sounded wonderful to Tana. This time she was better prepared; Paul had retrieved samples of the local water supply for analysis, and Tana was now equipped with a supply of pills that would neutralize the effects of its native microbes.

Inside the house Tana was shocked to see the large common room cluttered with what could only be described as gadgets. Tools lay about in profusion, with bits and scraps of raw materials heaped in boxes and baskets everywhere. "Claire, this is Tana Wind-drop," Nathan introduced as Claire came back in from the kitchen with two tall glasses of a pale liquid that swam with translucent bits. "She's visiting me from the Mountain—from West Flats, actually. I brought her by to see some of your inventions."

"Oh, there's nothing here they can't make on the Mountain," Claire told her, handing them each a glass. She was a long-limbed woman with hair that was something between blond and brown twisted into a knot on top of her head. "I've got a small refrigerator working—feel that nice cold glass?—but it won't make ice. That's my project for this summer, Nathan; I'm going to build an ice maker." Her wide smile and bright eyes belied her humility, however. Claire was proud of her refrigerator.

"Boy, that hits the spot!" Nathan exclaimed when he had downed half the concoction in his glass. Tana sipped at hers carefully and found it quite bitter, with a strong aftertaste. It was not what they called lemonade back on Juno, but then, she suspected this was made from real lemons.

"Claire, show Tana your idea for a water-powered generator," Nathan urged.

Again the young woman's face fairly glowed. "Oh, it's not very sophisticated," she demurred, shuffling through a stack of papers on a table in the corner. "More like a water wheel than a turbine, but then, the Verde isn't a very big river. Still, it would generate some electricity during rainy seasons, which is when our solar power lags a bit. The problem, of course, is the materials for construction . . ."

For the next hour Claire showed them project after project, design after design, from a new kind of hinge to plans for connecting all the houses in Camp Crusoe with communication lines. "It all comes down to wire," Claire lamented. "We need tons and tons of copper wire, but copper is so scarce. Funny, isn't it? This used to be a copper-mining region. Now we have to excavate ruins in search of ancient copper tubing or maybe even a storehouse of wire. I keep going out on digs, hoping we'll find a storehouse full of copper wire."

Tana was astounded by the woman's energy and ingenuity.

How Paul would eat this up! she thought. I can hear him now, getting into the physics of these things, making suggestions, posing questions—just a couple of inventors talking shop. "Or better yet," Tana said in joking fashion, "maybe a ship will show up from some distant planet with a whole load of wire. Or optical fiber. Or crystals, or whatever they're using nowadays."

Claire's face lit like the fiery orb climbing higher and higher outside. "Wouldn't that be outstanding?" she enthused. "Just imagine how far technology must have advanced since our ancestors landed here! They probably have power sources we haven't even dreamed of. Tools that make lasers and sonic wrenches look like stone hammers. I'll tell you, Tana, I hope I live to see the day. I really hope I live to see the day."

"If a ship came here from some other planet," Nathan put in, "we wouldn't have to worry about inventing anything. They'd have done it all for us. We'd just press a button and order it. That is, if we could pay for it." He grinned a hollow grin. "You'd be out of a job, Claire."

"Not me," she disputed. "I'd be on the first ship out of here, off to whatever kind of school they have to learn everything I can. Then I'd invent engines to power planets instead of ice makers. People like my dad would have trouble," she admitted. "At this point he'd probably even turn down a prosthetic arm because he wouldn't want to learn how to use it at seventy-nine. But not me, Nathan. I wouldn't have any trouble jumping into that other kind of life. My dreams are big enough."

"I would never question the bigness of your dreams." Nathan grinned. "Or your heart. Which is why I was wondering if we could borrow your pedal car so I can show Tana around a bit more. She has arthritis and can't walk too much."

"By all means!" Claire agreed, jumping up from her place. "I've got new gearing in it; it shifts like butter now. All the way up to twenty-five gears!"

"So that's the other side," Tana commented as they bounced away from Claire's adobe house in the borrowed vehicle. It looked to Tana like a tubular frame on a four-wheeled platform, shaded by a wicker roof on poles. There were two sets of pedals, one for the driver and another for the passenger, but Nathan had instructed her to rest her feet off to one side; he could propel the car quite successfully alone.

"That's one of them," Nathan agreed, upshifting with no appreciable change in effort. "Claire's a survivor—no matter where you put her, she'll adapt and she'll keep on inventing wonderful new things. It's just the way her mind works. I'll take you to see old Doc Hanson next—she's another one who'd be quick to welcome contact with other worlds. Medicines, you know. She's lost too many patients who wouldn't have been lost if she'd had proper medicines. And the injuries—Claire's father lost an arm before Claire was born. Accident with an old disrupter-style weapon took it right off. I suppose you could regenerate something like that on your world.''

"We could synthesize it," Tana hedged.

"And Harry Tsorks's little girl, who died of diabetes," Nathan continued. "They manufacture small quantities of insulin near the Mountain, but it's perishable; transporting it from the Mountain here—hell, you can probably cure diabetes now, can't you? Replace the pancreas? Grow a new one?"

"I've never even heard of diabetes," Tana admitted. "But then, you've never heard of Gamaean palsy, have you?"

"Which is my point," Nathan replied. "I get this terrible feeling we'd be trading one set of evils for another." He sighed as he made the last gear shift and settled into a steady rhythm of pedaling over the dusty road. "Maybe that's my problem; maybe I prefer known evils to unknown ones. But Tana—" He lifted his straw hat and wiped an arm across a brow creased by sun and age. "I've read about the days when a person could be stabbed repeatedly while a dozen people watched and no one tried to interfere—that kind of atrocity can't happen here. Even if it were a total stranger, even if it were someone we didn't *like*, not a soul in this community would stand idly by while that happened! We need each other, and we *know* we need each other. Some people are still not too sure we need the primitives, but *I* know. I know how much we can learn from them. There's a—a harmony here, a balance. If people start to come from outside, it will throw off the balance. That's the long and the short of it: it will throw off the balance."

Tana was silent a moment. Then, "Maybe your balance isn't as fragile as you think," she ventured.

Nathan sighed. "Maybe not. Come on, Doc should be in the Infirmary; that's right in the center of town, near the old shuttle."

By the afternoon of the next day Nathan had bounced Tana over the dusty roads to visit half a dozen different families. Each had a different reaction to her subtle remarks about renewed contact with other planets. Lupe Johnson didn't see any point unless they could control the rainfall on his land. Liv Martin wanted treatment for her aging mother, who was showing signs of Alzheimer's disease. Young Timmy Johanneson, Nathan's great-nephew, wanted to be a starship pilot and fly the first mission back to Argo; his older brother, Sayed, was more concerned with getting to the Mountain to study medicine. Their sister, Tass, wanted to explore the ruins of Earth's previous cultures, feeling there was more to be learned from their own past than from the advances made on distant planets. "Why should we let them come here and have all the fun of discovering what we've got?" she joked.

"If a ship landed here tomorrow, would you send it away?" Tana asked her.

Tass shrugged her shoulders. "No," she admitted. "Even assuming I could—which I can't—no. What happens, happens, and we'll make the best of it. I'm just not going to lose a lot of sleep over it."

"Would you leave here?" Tana asked Timmy.

"In a minute," he replied. "Not forever, of course. Well, maybe forever. It depends on what I found out there."

"Sayed?"

The older youth shrugged. "If I had to, to get the schooling I needed. But I'd want to come back. Even if they sent other doctors here, I'd want to come back. No one else could understand us the way someone who was raised here can. A doctor has to understand his patients."

Tana smiled. "I think Jacqueline Winthrop would be proud of you."

They chatted on then about Jacqueline and the original crew, about how life in Camp Crusoe had evolved, about the gradual intermingling of the three cultures in the region. Tana was delighted by the young people's comments and perceptions. She was disappointed when Nathan rose from his chair and announced it was time to go. "There's one more person I'd like you to meet," he told Tana, "and then it's quite a drive back to our place."

He turned the pedal car down the twisting dirt track that ran along the river toward the southwest. "You know, when I was a boy," he said, "nearly everyone still lived in town and drove out to their fields on a tractor or a harvester—whatever machine they needed that day. But in the past twenty-five, thirty years more and more young couples have chosen to build homes out in the country. I don't know why. Someone did it, and then others thought that was a good way to do things. We've started to spread out, away from each other, as though—well, as though we weren't frightened to be here. Maybe it was when we finally believed Lujan wasn't going to show up again. I know my mother barred the door every night for years after he disappeared. It wasn't till I—'' Nathan stopped abruptly and amended his sentence. ''It wasn't until she had assurances from someone she trusted that the man was dead that she stopped throwing that wooden crossbar into its hooks before she went to bed.''

''*Is* he dead?'' Tana asked.

''Oh, yes, he's dead,'' Nathan replied with certainty.

''Did you kill him?''

Nathan looked genuinely startled. ''Me? Lord, no! I was just a boy at the time.''

''But you know who did.''

He was a moment in answering. ''Yes, I know who did.''

''Who?'' A list of suspects was whizzing through Tana's mind. Doc Hanson? Not likely. Claire's father, the one who had lost an arm? He didn't seem capable of it, either.

Again Nathan hesitated to answer. ''How do people where you come from view it when one man takes the life of another?'' he asked.

''They call it murder,'' she said quickly—too quickly, she realized. That would not encourage Nathan to divulge his secret.

''Always?'' he persisted. ''Is there no legal execution of criminals?''

Tana was sure Derek Lujan had not been executed. Not by the Crusoans, anyway. ''On some planets,'' she responded. ''Not mine.''

''And you disapprove of it,'' Nathan guessed.

Tana was caught now. She knew Nathan was trying to justify Lujan's killer, but one thing she would never shy away from was the tenets of her faith. ''I'm a member of a very old religious sect,'' she replied honestly. ''We believe one death thousands of years ago changed the punitive nature of the law and replaced it with a more forgiving ethic. We believe each man is our brother, each woman our sister, and how could we demand the life of even one?''

''And if a man broke into your house,'' Nathan said, ''and threatened your children, would you kill him?''

Now it was Tana who hesitated. ''If there were no other way to stop him, yes,'' Tana admitted. ''I'm not sure that's the righteous thing to do, but it's what I would do. I know that about myself.''

Nathan nodded, having found the bridge he needed into her ethic. ''Lujan stalked a man who only wanted to be left alone,'' Nathan told her. ''He tried to kill the man's pregnant wife and young child. The only way to stop him was to kill him.''

''You must have admired this man very much,'' Tana observed. ''Otherwise you wouldn't go to such lengths to justify his behavior to me.''

''I'm afraid that people coming back from the stars won't understand,'' Nathan confided. ''It would be so easy to misunderstand. So easy to call him a savage, and that's not what he is. He is perhaps the most deeply moral person I know.''

''Let me guess,'' Tana said. ''It must be your Coconino, the one who destroyed the *Homeward Bound.* The one who came through the time warp with Lujan.''

Nathan nodded.

''Is he still alive?'' she wanted to know.

''Alive?'' A wry smile twisted Nathan's face. ''Coconino will live forever. To the People, he is a god whose return they awaited for two hundred years. To the Mountain dwellers, he's a thief who stole their chance to regain the stars. To the Crusoans, he's the nagging reminder that maybe—just maybe—the People are right and it really is the Earth who is in control here. Is Coconino alive?'' He nodded. ''Very much so.'' Then he added, ''And may he always be.''

They had reached the far end of the settlement now, and Nathan parked the pedal car in the shade of a wooden cabin. It was small in comparison to the other houses Tana had seen, perhaps sixteen feet square. ''I saw her chopping cotton this morning,'' Nathan said as he climbed off the seat, ''but since her heart attack two years ago, her son makes her come in from the fields at noon. I doubt she's inside, but—'' He rapped on the front door. ''Mrs. Mason?'' When there was no response, he led Tana around the cabin toward the back.

As they rounded the corner, Tana gasped. ''What is it?'' Nathan asked, concern in his voice. She had told him about the danger of seizures brought on by anxiety or anger.

But Tana waved him off. ''Nothing,'' she assured him. ''Just a moment of déjà vu.''

Before her spread the farmyard she had visited in the VR room. There was no young man chopping wood near the outbuildings now, but the pens were there, the quail and the sheep, and in front of them was the large garden plot and the elderly, intense gardener. She wore the same straw hat, had the same flattened, work-worn face. Plants that had been mere seedlings now rose to her shoulders as she knelt and hacked at their roots with a cultivator.

"Mrs. Mason," Nathan called out.

She looked up with bright dark eyes. In the space of a heart-beat she surveyed them, took them in, weighed them, considered their motives, and reached a decision. "Nathan," she acknowledged. "You'll have to come here if you want to talk to me; I'm working."

"She's always working," Nathan muttered under his breath. Tana sensed disapproval in his tone and perhaps a little fear. What was there to fear in this elderly gardener? Carefully they picked their way between rows of zucchini to reach the woman.

"Must be nice having three boys to do all your work, Nathan," she commented. "Gives you time to go touring the countryside with pretty girls during the height of the growing season."

Nathan opened his mouth to protest, realized the futility of it, and closed it again. He was a grown man with grandchildren, but this woman treated him like a schoolboy. "Miz Wind-drop is interested in the early days of Camp Crusoe," he told the old woman in a controlled voice. "Particularly an old acquaintance of yours: Derek Lujan."

Mrs. Mason stopped and looked sharply at Nathan, then at Tana. "Until yesterday I'd have said that one was best forgotten," she said. "Here, Nathan; if you're going to stand in my garden, you might as well be useful. Pull back these vines for me; see if there are any small squash underneath. I want two for supper, and they taste better if you don't let them balloon up like watermelons."

Nathan gave a resigned shake of his head and began to inspect the vines she indicated.

"You, too, Miz *Wind-drop*," she said, stressing the name. She indicated a patch of vines climbing four and five feet into the air on wooden stakes. "I presume you can tell a red tomato from a green one. Take that basket there and fill it up. No sense letting them go to vinegar on the vine."

"Now, Mrs. Mason," Nathan protested gently, "Tana can't do much labor; she has arthritis."

That seemed to surprise the older woman. She stopped to consider Tana. "How old are you, thirty-two, thirty-three?"

"Thirty-seven," Tana replied. "It's all right; I can pick to-matoes. I just can't pick very fast."

The gardener snorted. "Huh. I'm sixty-eight; I'm in better shape than you are."

Tana smiled. "I'm sure you are."

Mrs. Mason went back to her cultivating. "Wind-drop. Interesting name."

A cold tingle crept up Tana's spine. "I wasn't born Wind-drop," she said truthfully. "But my name was a rather common one, so . . ."

"Sounds a bit like Winthrop, doesn't it?" Mrs. Mason continued.

Tana's heart pounded, but she forced herself to relax. "So I've been told."

Mrs. Mason chuckled to herself as though there were something funny in that. "So, Miz Wind-drop, you want to know about Derek Lujan." She wiped a sleeve across her sweaty brow. "Handsomest man I ever saw. Well built—thick, gorgeous wavy hair—fine, pointed chin and such blue eyes . . . He was my worst nightmare."

"Puma got him," Nathan put in. "Took out an eye, scarred up his face and chest—"

"It had nothing to do with the puma!" Mrs. Mason snapped. "If anything, he was less dangerous after that because he looked like what he was: a monster. It was before, it was before when he was so handsome and so seductive—I wasn't the only girl in this village who looked at him with greedy eyes when he first showed up. Even in his madness there was an allure to him—can't tell you how many times I was tempted. But it was always too frightening, and I was always . . . too rigid. Still, he managed to seduce us, anyway, didn't he, Nathan? Not our bodies but our minds. We knew he had the secrets of the old machines locked in his head. We knew that if we could just tap it, his mind would give us wealth beyond imagining. Wealth of knowledge. Wealth of comfort. Oh, yes, we knew that if Derek Lujan just weren't *crazy*, he would be the best thing that ever happened to us."

Mrs. Mason was moving steadily down the row with her cultivating. Tana left the vines she was picking from to get a little closer to the redoubtable woman.

"I'll tell you what I think," the gardener continued. "I think his being *crazy* was the best thing that ever happened to us. Derek Lujan was an infection, and he would have destroyed us all. He came from a time and a place where deceit was commonplace and treading on your neighbor to elevate yourself was a way of life. And he was not alone. There were five headed back with him when the ship crashed. And your ancestors, Nathan, were in league with him; you know that—only Lujan betrayed them and left them behind, just as he left poor Karen Reichert. No doubt there were others who never did confess.''

Mrs. Mason had reached the end of her row and stood up. ''No matter how much knowledge was in that head of his,'' she proclaimed, ''if we had not distrusted him because of his madness, he would have led us astray once more. We have become gullible, trusting fools—capons, as they used to say, emasculated and fattened for roasting.'' She looked Tana straight in the eye as she took the basket of vegetables from her. ''My life in this place has not been easy, Miz *Winthrop*, but the only true evil I have ever encountered was in Derek Lujan. I don't care to encounter it again.''

With that she turned and went into the cabin.

Nathan and Tana rode in silence as the blazing ball of the sun sank in front of them. Finally they reached the rendezvous point, and Nathan brought the car to a gentle stop. Tana glanced at her wrist chrono: fifteen minutes to spare. For a moment they just sat.

''Does everyone know?'' Tana asked finally.

''Who you are? I doubt it,'' he replied. ''Some have guessed. We're not all the fools Tav Mason makes us out to be.''

''Tav?''

''Tavaria. Only don't ever call her that to her face. She was past thirty when she finally landed a husband; she thinks there's more respect in using her married name. Hell, if I called Marjean 'Mrs. Johanneson,' she'd think I'd been sipping Uncle Park's moonshine. But Tav is unique, and I've learned to respect people's choices.'' He glanced over at his sober passenger. ''She is, incidentally, the driving force on the Exec and the closest thing we have to a leader. If you wanted an official opinion . . .''

But Tana shook her head. ''She's too bitter a person to be making decisions for other people.''

''She is that,'' Nathan agreed. ''I almost didn't take you to see her even though she supports my position, because she can be so abrasive. And she was in rare form today.''

''She's frightened,'' Tana observed.

''So am I.''

Tana studied her host for a moment. He was younger than her father, maybe fifty, and he had spent his entire life as a laborer, yet there was something about him that reminded her of Monticello Winthrop. A sense of justice. A willingness to acknowledge the validity of an opposing viewpoint. "You should lead these people," she told Nathan.

An embarrassed smile broke across his face. "No, no, not me," he said. "I have no craving for power."

"That's why you should lead them."

Still he shook his head. "Too much responsibility comes with it. Say-ayka-pee showed me that. All the weight that's been put on that man's shoulders—no thanks. My family is weight enough."

She put a hand on one of his shoulders; it was hard with muscle. "But your family has only strengthened you," she replied. "They'll help you bear the weight. Mine does." Paul and Dak and Monti—where would she be without them?

A solitary ocotillo marked the rendezvous point. Nathan had explained to her that the sticklike plant dropped its leaves in the parching heat to preserve moisture, then sprouted new ones after every rain. Nathan was like that, harboring his moisture, biding his time until a situation arose that prompted him to action, as her coming had done. There was no doubt in her mind after talking with the Crusoans that Nathan was well liked and well respected by his peers; he simply had none of the trappings by which leaders were normally known. "No, you're right," she said finally. "You don't need to assume any position of authority here. You're already the best kind of authority these people could have."

She glanced at her wrist chrono—only three minutes left. Suddenly she was anxious to be home, anxious to see Paul again. She knew full well that he had been warping recorders in and out every couple of hours to monitor her progress through the settlement, but she had missed him. She had missed sharing with him her experiences and her perceptions these past two days. Maybe she would clear her calendar for another half day when she got back just so they could sit together in his office and discuss it all. "Say good-bye to Marjean for me," she told Nathan as she climbed out of the ungainly vehicle and fished in her trouser leg pocket for the traveling mat.

Nathan climbed out as well, but he stayed beside the vehicle, leaning on one of the roof poles, his sandaled foot resting on one of the tubes. "Stay at least ten feet away," she cautioned as she spread the mat on the spot she had marked with small stones. "The warp field should only balloon out four or five feet at most, but better safe than sorry." She positioned herself on the rainbow mesh.

Nathan watched her. "How will you keep our existence quiet?" he asked.

Tana felt a flush of annoyance. "What makes you think I've decided to do that?"

"I think you decided before you came," he told her evenly. "You were only playing devil's advocate here, prodding people to say what you wanted to hear. You do it very well, by the way."

Tana's annoyance increased. "You're mistaken," she told Nathan. "I haven't made up my mind yet. There are other settlements on this planet I need to visit. I haven't been to the Mountain; I haven't seen the People."

His brow darkened. "Don't go there," he told her flatly.

"Why? Are you afraid of what they'll say?"

"The Mountain dwellers will spot you in a minute," he said, "and you'll have lost your options. Besides, I'll tell you straight out, they'll do anything to regain contact with the stars. They're still weeping over the loss of their computers and their flight capabilities, and they haven't weighed the cost of getting them back. And the People—just leave the People alone. They won't welcome any suggestion of contact with the Sisters of the Mother Earth."

This high-handedness was new in Nathan, and it irritated Tana. She felt the level of toxin in her bloodstream rising. I need Doc, she realized suddenly. I'm tired, and I'm losing track of my emotions. Doc wouldn't let them sneak up on me; he'd be growling and sending me messages when the tension started to rise.

Tana forced herself to take a deep breath and relax. "You don't know my situation," she told Nathan serenely. "I may not be able to do what you ask. I may only be able to control how contact is made, and to do that effectively, I think I need to visit more than one location."

They locked eyes, and Tana struggled to keep her gaze powerful without any anger driving it. Finally Nathan shrugged. "I've done what I can. As Say-ayka-pee would say, even Coconino can only *ask* for rain."

Tana glanced once more at her wrist chrono; it was a minute past the appointed time. Paul was late. She straightened herself on the mat, preparing for the quivering feeling she associated with warp travel. She closed her eyes, took a deep breath, and waited.

And waited.

And waited . . .

"Something wrong?" Nathan asked.

"He's late, that's all," Tana replied. She took another deep breath, trying to stem the rising tide of toxins. This was the most extended trip made yet with P-TUP; maybe the passage of time had required a few last-minute adjustments.

The minutes ticked by.

Nathan shifted uncomfortably, coming around to the front of the pedal car. "You don't suppose we missed it, do you?"

"No, we were on time," she replied, feeling her heart begin to thud. "Besides, if I'd been late, Paul would have sent someone after me. He didn't want me to stay this long; he certainly wouldn't stand for my being late." She felt a stiffness creeping into her hips and knees, an achy sort of feeling. "Maybe I looked at my chrono wrong. I keep about six different times on it: Argo, Juno, Pax, Darius—" She checked the chrono again. "No, this is it. Unless the warping did something to disturb it— but no, it shouldn't affect the chrono. It didn't before." She was babbling, and she knew it. "It's just—it's just taking—"

Too long! she wanted to scream. Paul would never be this late. Something's happened to Paul—no, no, Todd would be there. Todd and Jaria; they'd brought her in to share the shifts while Tana was out on this mission. Even if Paul were delayed— even if Delhi had cornered him and—no, no, he wouldn't stand for Delhi interfering when it was time to pick her up. Paul would be there, and Todd, both of them, and—

—and she knew very well the dangers of working with bleeding edge technology. There was the day they'd lost the zig—an equipment failure, one they couldn't predict. Of course they'd fixed that problem. They'd fixed it, it was fine, it had all been tested—

Tana's fingers began to tremble.

"Are you all right?" Nathan asked, his voice edged with worry.

"Yes, I'm all right!" she flared and recanted immediately. "No, I'm not. It could be—there's always the chance, you know—and—"

Suddenly Tana looked at her hands and saw they were shaking. "Oh, no," she whispered. She couldn't let this happen, not now. She had to be calm, had to slow her heart rate—

"What is it?" Nathan asked in alarm.

Now her arms were beginning to shake, and her legs. "I— I—" she stammered, but her jaw trembled too violently for her to be articulate. It was too late now to reverse the effect, and she knew it. She'd let it get away from her. The parasitic virus in her joints was in full revolt, pumping more and more toxins into her bloodstream, which carried them to her limbs, to her chest, to her brain— Paul, help me! her fogging mind cried out. Paul, get me out of here! Doc, get Paul, get Paul for me. Doc, hurry, please— Paul, I need you! Paul, Paul, Paul, Paul—

CHAPTER TWELVE

Only the palest starshine filtered into Coconino's house through the uncovered doorway when he gave up and struggled up from his sleeping mat. Crawling across the smooth adobe floor, he climbed out onto the ledge in front of his door and rose stiffly to his feet. The canyon lay like a cleft of deeper darkness in the night, but it was a darkness he did not fear. It was a familiar place, his home for twice the number of seasons he had lived in the Valley of the People.

Why, then, did he dream so much lately of that other home? And why, after so many years and such a full life, had he begun to dream again of her . . . ?

Coconino stood on the ledge and waited for his bladder to perform the duty it had wakened him to discharge. Were it not for that persistent urging, he might still be sleeping, or not, but it frustrated him these days that what his body woke him from sleep to do, it then did not hasten to accomplish. Ah, in my heart I am still the impatient, headstrong youth, he thought. Only my experience has taught me to consider things more carefully before acting—and my body gives me little choice.

Only what was I dreaming before it wakened me?

Above him the stars glittered in the summer sky, a brilliant spray of cold fire against the warm black canvas. It had something to do with stars, he thought. Friendly stars. Sad stars. Or was it me who was sad? It has slipped away from me already. I only remember that she was there . . .

My Witch Woman. I have dreamed of her more in the past season than in the past twenty seasons combined. Sometimes she is young and vigorous with long black hair, just as I left her; other times she is older, like me, with graying braids, and she moves more slowly. But she always has that same strength of spirit, that indomitable pride that made her who she was: Phoenix, the bird that rose from the ashes of its nest.

Finally his reluctant bladder responded to the permission it had been given. Coconino heard the sound of his urine as it streamed over the ledge and onto the steep wall of the canyon. It was not the powerful stream of a young man, but it was steady—at this point that was all he asked. He smiled a little as he remembered the games he and his friends had played as boys: who could make his stream go farthest, who could hit a particular rock. Even in those foolish games Coconino had always had to be the best. He always had to be the best at everything he did. He was Coconino, the son of a Man-on-the-Mountain by his Chosen Companion, Two Moons, who was high in the Council of the Mother. Coconino, who spoke the language of the Men-on-the-Mountain. Coconino, who understood the magic of books. Coconino, who was favored by the Mother Earth.

Coconino sighed. Once the Mother Earth had spoken to him with such clarity. But then, when she took him from his Witch Woman, it became so hard to hear her voice.

Because I did not like what she was saying, Coconino thought. Because I preferred the sound of my self-righteous anger. Because I did not want to know that the deeds of a twenty-year-old youth were not the culmination of a life's work but only the beginning.

The stream dribbled away to nothing, but Coconino continued to stand on the ledge, looking up at the stars. What was it about the stars . . . ? He had dreamed . . . oh, yes, that they had spoken to the Mother Earth. The stars had spoken again to the Mother Earth, saying that they were coming . . . they were coming . . .

With another great sigh Coconino dropped his head and rolled it around on his neck, feeling the stiffness in it. So they were coming again. It was inevitable, after all, and he had known that for a long time. Still, it created a strange aching in his chest. He had made such a terrible sacrifice to stop them the first time.

Coconino crouched down and eased himself back through the low doorway into his house. He hoped the Mother Earth had a different defender to call on this time.

"Doc!" Tana called. "Doc, where are you? Doc, come! We have to get on the shuttle." They had to get on the shuttle; it was leaving. Where was Doc? Why didn't he come when she called? "Doc?"

I can't leave him, Tana thought in panic. But I have to leave him. It's time, I'm going to miss the shuttle, and I'll be stuck here on Earth. Paul is in the shuttle, and it's leaving— She tried to run toward the bulky white craft squatting in the center of the village, but it was like slogging through swamp water. Her limbs wouldn't respond, they wouldn't move fast enough—*"Paul! Paul, wait for me!"* She had to get to the shuttle, had to get there before it was too late—

Suddenly someone blocked her way—Nathan. *"What's your hurry?"* he drawled, catching her arms. He was tall, taller than Paul, and she felt tiny beside him.

"I have to get to the shuttle!" Tana cried. *"I have to get to the shuttle, it's leaving, and I can't find Doc—"*

"Whoa! Hold on, there, little lady," Nathan said, holding her back. *"No need to rush; that shuttle's not going anywhere. Look."*

Tana looked at the shuttle then and saw that the cargo bay door was open and there were crates inside. Crates and crates of vegetables, and sacks of grain, and boxes of tools. There was grass growing up around the vehicle's base, and scrubby desert broom, and tall gray weeds that had roasted and died in the desert sun. *"It won't fly!"* she cried as she realized the vehicle was as dead as the weeds. *"How will I get back?"*

"You won't get back," said a gruff woman's voice, and a slight figure moved out of the shadows toward her. *"None of us will get back. We're stuck here—Lujan saw to that."* There was terrible venom in the woman's quiet tone. *"Well, he hasn't defeated us. We'll survive, by God. We'll build houses and raise crops, and we'll survive."*

The woman's face became clearer as she approached. *"Jacqueline!"* Tana exclaimed. *"Jacqueline, you're alive!"*

"Of course I'm alive," the woman grumped. *"It's Clayton who's dead. It's Clayton who will never go home."*

"But I can't stay here," Tana protested. *"I have children—"*

"So do I!" Jacqueline snapped. *"Mine got along fine without me."*

"But yours were older," Tana countered. *"Mine are young; they're not in secondary school yet."*

"Cincinnati never grew up," Jacqueline replied. *"He had the mental faculties of a nine-year-old. He was a child till the day he died."*

"But Paul," Tana persisted. *"I have to get back to Paul.*

Paul's waiting for me. I can't stay here without him; I'm no good without him. I have to be with Paul—''

"No one asked if we like being here,"Jacqueline told her. "No one asked if this was any good for us. We're just here, we're stuck, and that's it. Clayton's gone. The kids are gone. The ship is gone. There's no way back.''

"But there is,'' Tana said suddenly. "There is a way back; it's the way I came. There's P-TUP. Paul will come for us. He'll just step in the transport chamber, and boom! He'll be here. Then we can all go home. We can all go home, Jacqueline.''

The old woman looked skeptical. "I can go back?''

"Yes, yes! I've come to rescue you!''

"But not Clayton.''

"No, I can't rescue Clayton.''

Jacqueline set her jaw and considered. "I would like to see Terra Firma. I would like to see Chelsea and Cin.''

"Yes, they're waiting for you, waiting at Terra Firma. *With Doc and Paul.'' Yes, that was where Doc was. He wasn't here on Earth at all, he was back at* Terra Firma. *"We can all go riding.'' She and Chelsea and Jacqueline and Paul—and this time she would keep up with them, because she wasn't troubled by the palsy anymore—*

"Tana?''

The voice filtered through to Tana, but she did not recognize it.

"Tana, can you hear me?''

Tana tried to speak, but her jaw didn't want to work. Besides, her tongue was so dry and parched . . .

"Come on, Tana, wake up. I can see you trying. Wake up. You have to wake up and tell me what kind of seizure this is.''

Seizure. Yes, she'd had a seizure. She was—she was—on the hillside—on the traveling mat—

"Nooooooo!''

It was a muted cry, half sob, half moan, and her mouth was so dry that her voice cracked and broke. "It's all right,'' said another voice—Nathan's. "It's all right, Tana, you're all right. Doc's here.''

Doc?

"Not that I'm much help,'' the first speaker snorted. "I don't know what happened to you, except your head hit a rock when you fell and you've got a nasty lump on it. But I don't think it's a concussion—it's on the back of your skull, and your pupils are evenly dilated, which is a good sign. Probably hurts like hell, though.''

Tana was conscious then of a dull throbbing in her head. That was not usual for the aftermath of a seizure, but the rest of it was: her leaden body, her cotton mouth. ''Water,'' she whispered.

''I'll get it,'' Nathan said, and she heard him move away from the bed, heard the sound of water pouring into a glass. Then the other person was lifting her shoulders, raising her up to drink— Liza Hanson, that was who it was. Doc Hanson.

Tana forced her eyes open enough to see the glass and managed to gulp down enough water to lubricate her throat, although she spilled a good deal in the process. She was always so clumsy after a seizure, she absolutely hated it. Clumsy and weak. ''Thank you,'' she whispered, and sank gratefully back down on the pillow.

Even that small effort had cost her, and Tana closed her eyes a moment, trying to focus. She was in a bed, in a house. Nathan's? Opening her eyes, she looked around the room and guessed that it was so. Nathan hovered close by, looking very worried. The old doctor had pulled up a chair to the bed and was studying Tana intently. She, of course, did not look worried in the least—as a matter of fact, she looked a bit impatient.

''Nathan says you've had these seizures before,'' Doc Hanson said.

''Yes.'' Tana's voice was soft, but as she worked her jaw around, it became more limber and she more articulate. ''It's— all right. I'll be all right. Just—weak for a while. Stiff. I know what to do.''

''Good, because I've really never had to deal with any seizure disorders,'' Doc Hanson replied. ''What is it, epilepsy?''

''No.'' Tana tried to smile. ''Something very rare. Genetic defect.'' It was partially true. ''I'll be okay.''

The doctor arched a fine gray eyebrow, but she slid her chair back and rose to leave. Tana thought she must have been a pretty woman in her younger days; she was still petite, and her salt-and-pepper hair was cut short around an oval face with even features. It had seen too much care, though, that face; there were deep lines around the mouth and eyes that suggested an age her quick and precise movements belied.

''I'll go back to town, then,'' Doc Hanson announced. ''Keep an eye on her, Nathan; if she starts to exhibit any strange behavior or slurred or nonsensical speech, let me know.

"At least stay for breakfast," Nathan urged as he walked the doctor to the door of the bedroom. "After I dragged you all the way out here before dawn—"

The doctor waved him off. "That's why I'm so highly paid, Nathan," she said dryly. "Just have that boy of yours run me over to Mim Fiora's place in the pedal car; while I'm out this way, I think I'll stop in and see how the twins are doing."

When they had gone out the door, Tana felt a strange loneliness rush in on her. There was daylight filtering into the room through the skylight Nathan had rigged from a scarred piece of plastic he'd found in one of the nearby ruins. What time was it? Early morning? Late? Or had Doc Hanson sat by her bedside through an entire day? Where was Paul? Did he not know where she was? Surely he would have known to look for her in Nathan's house if he'd come after her. The answer, of course, was that he hadn't been able to come. Something was wrong. Something was still wrong.

An invisible hand clutched tightly at Tana's heart. No, no, you can't let it happen again, she admonished herself. No panic, no anxiety. You have to get well. You have to fight off the effects of the seizure so you won't be in such terrible shape when Paul finds you. And he will find you.

He has to.

Nathan came back into the room and sat down where Doc Hanson had been. "Are you really all right?" he asked earnestly.

"I will be," she repeated. "I just need rest. Then exercise. What time is it?"

He glanced at the spot of sunlight streaming from the skylight onto the floor. "Still early morning. I took that, uh, chrono thing off your wrist. Didn't want Marjean or Doc to notice it."

"I'll need your help to get up," she told him. "Not for a little while—my head hurts quite a bit—but I have to start limbering up my joints. Maybe—help me sit up a little in bed."

He slid one strong arm behind her shoulders and lifted her carefully, pushing the pillow up against the headboard. Tana's head swam, but after she had rested a moment, that subsided and she tried bending her right arm. It felt like dead weight, for her muscles were terribly fatigued, but Nathan noticed her effort and took hold of the arm, manipulating it gently. "Like this?" he asked.

"Yes, thank you."

Marjean appeared in the doorway. "Oh, I'm so glad you're

awake. You had us terribly worried. Are you all right? Is there something I can get you?"

Tana nearly said coffee, when she remembered they didn't have such a thing on Earth. "Tea," she said, for she had discovered they made an herbal brew that they called tea. "And maybe some bread."

Marjean vanished toward the kitchen.

"More water?" Nathan asked.

"Please."

He put the glass to her lips, and she drank with more grace this time.

"If you're sure you'll be all right," he said as he set the glass aside, "I really do need to get back into the fields today. Marjean will stay with you; you just ask her for anything you need." He reached under the mattress and pulled out the traveling mat. "This will be right here when you need it, along with your chronometer. I, uh—" He smiled sheepishly. "I didn't know what to say about your hair when the pins came out and it fell down. I, uh, told Marjean maybe you'd had ringworm or something and had to shave one side of your head and it was just starting to grow back."

Tana laughed in spite of herself. "That's as good a story as any," she told him. "I think I'll stick with that."

His smile softened. "You look better when you laugh."

Immediately her smile faded.

"He'll come for you, won't he?" Nathan asked her. "Your husband."

"Of course," she stated, but she could hear the hollow ring to her own voice.

Nathan rose from the chair. "If Marjean gets too nosy, you just tell her to mind her own business," he instructed.

Tana gave him a wry smile. "If I told her the truth, would she believe me?"

"Oh, yes, ma'am," he replied without hesitation. "I think she's rather suspicious right now."

"But you don't want me to tell her?"

"I'd really rather you didn't."

"Why?" she asked. "Would she disagree with you about limiting contact with other worlds?"

Nathan rubbed the back of his neck. "If she did disagree," he told Tana, "I think I'd have heard about it by now."

Would you? Tana wondered. There are so many things husbands and wives don't say to each other . . . not directly, anyway. But you're right; with a look, with a veiled comment, she would have let you know if she disagreed. It's like that with Paul and me. Even when we don't say what we mean, we let each other know . . .

As Nathan went out, Tana felt the loneliness crushing in on her again. No matter where she ventured in the universe, no matter where she went on business, as a guest speaker, as a representative of the Dynasty, she was never out of touch with her emotional "storage batteries"—Paul, her father, Dak, and of course her dog. I should have brought Doc, she chastised herself. No matter what Nathan said, I should have brought him. It was stupid not to bring him—worse than stupid, it was arrogant. What made me think I could do as well without him as with him? What made me think I could handle anything that was thrown at me without any help? Vanity, vanity, all is vanity—

Marjean whisked in with bread and tea on a tray. "Here we are!" she sang out. Her cheerfulness was almost unbearable; it made Tana want to weep with frustration and self-pity, but she preferred it to the emptiness of the room. Though Marjean's one-sided conversation seemed hopelessly trivial, still Tana was glad to let the woman chatter on amiably while she ate. The sound of her voice helped fill the void that seemed suddenly oppressive, the void caused by the absence of Doc's consciousness.

When Tana had finished the last of the tea and sagged back against the pillow again, Marjean took the tray from her, but then she hesitated. The executive in Tana recognized the gesture, and she waited to hear what was on her hostess's mind.

"I just want you to know," Marjean blurted finally, "that we don't mind having you here. As long as it takes for you to recover. As long as it takes for someone to come after you. Just consider our house your house." She gave a hollow laugh. "Gracious, if old Granny Thornton could take Derek Lujan into her house and nurse him for almost a year before she found out who he was, you know Nathan and I don't mind having you stay with us."

A chill ran up Tana's spine. For as long as it took . . . "Thank you," she said, a little coldly, "but my husband will be coming for me soon." He must come for me. I can't allow myself to think that I might be here for weeks or months or . . . longer . . .

"Your husband—is that Paul?" Marjean asked.

"Yes."

The older woman nodded. "You called out for him earlier. Yes, I'm sure he will come for you. But just in case he . . . takes a little longer than you expect . . . I don't want you to worry about your welcome here. I don't know how folks are in West Flats or wherever you come from, but these are good people in Camp Crusoe. If someone needs . . . something, a place to live, or food to eat, or care of any kind—we see that it gets done." Marjean laughed. "Oh, we'll ask you to pitch in with the chores, be sure of that! But don't worry about making it on your own, because we all make it together. It's the only way we know how to live."

Tears smarted in Tana's eyes. The woman only meant to be comforting and assuring, but it wasn't what Tana wanted to hear right now: that if she was stranded, she had a home. She didn't want to hear about what would happen if she couldn't get back. "Thank you," she whispered. "I need to rest now."

Marjean flashed her a wistful smile and left the room.

For long moments Tana lay with her eyes closed and her chest trembling, dangerously close to sobbing aloud. I must stay calm, she told herself. I must not panic. Only, God, what will I do if Paul doesn't come for me? What will I do if I have to go on in this place without Paul? Without his strength and support? Without all the understanding and trust we have built between us? Without his unpretentiousness and his sharp, inquisitive mind, and those blue, blue eyes . . .

No doubt it had stolen over her gradually, this fascination with the young scientist she had hoped would invent P-TUP. There were so many things to love about him, Tana was sure the feeling must have grown from some philosophical kinship, from the great respect she had for his ethics and the admiration she had for his intellect, but it was his eyes that finally arrested her. Arrested? The blue of them struck her with such force one day that her mouth nearly dropped open. She was forever grateful that he was the one talking at that moment, for had it been she, Tana knew she would have stopped speechless. For days afterward Tana tried to reason herself out of the biological response she felt—he couldn't be sexy, how could Paul be sexy? He was so ordinary-looking, his face too round, his hair thinning away to nothing in the front—how could a man like that be sexy?

But every time she looked in his eyes, logic fled and Tana felt herself caught like a beetle in a silken web. Finally she gave up trying to make it seem rational and let herself be swept away by

the delicious feelings that coursed through her whenever she was
with him. But maddeningly, as the weeks went on, it became
clear that the fascination was one-way. She had nearly despaired
of sparking some response in him, when her father had casually
invited Paul out to *Terra Firma* to ride with her. Now there, she
had thought, there, away from the office in a more relaxed and
rustic setting, there he will notice that I am more than just a
junior executive in the IDP. I'll see to it that he notices.

*Tana showed up wearing her tightest denim pants and her
most provocative Western shirt, with a deeply V-ed neck and
fringe where it called attention to her womanly curves. But if
Paul noticed, he gave no sign of it. When Dak came out of the
old riding stable, however, leading three saddled horses, his
eyes grew wide. He glanced incredulously at Paul as though to
say, For this guy? Fortunately, at sixteen Dak had acquired some
discretion. "I'm not going with you," he hastened to say. "I'm
going out to the southwest pasture to check on the Appaloosas;
Uncle Paris has a buyer coming in on Monday."*

*Bless you, Dak, Tana projected at him, as though he were her
faithful Dalmatian Jas. Bless you, bless you, bless you . . .*

*"Well, maybe we could come with you," Paul suggested. "I've
never seen an Appaloosa."*

*Caught, Dak shrugged helplessly. "They're just spotted
horses. Uh . . . I don't know if Tana can ride that far . . ."*

Not and be back by sundown, she thought bitterly.

*"Oh! Well, maybe we'll just go partway with you," Paul
amended, with an inquiring glance back at Tana to see if that
was acceptable.*

*Tana forced a smile. "I'll let you know when I'm tired," she
assured him.*

*So they set out across the rolling hills toward the southwest,
with Jas ranging joyously in front of them. Paul was an experienced rider, his body moving in casual rhythm with his mount.
He and Dak talked horses and tack and places they had ridden.
At first Tana joined in the conversation, too, but in less than an
hour's time it became apparent that Paul was much more interested in Dakota's knowledge of ranching than in Tana's tales of
showing horses before she got sick. The wind blew dust in her
eyes, and she smudged her makeup. Her mount chafed for a
livelier pace.*

*Finally realizing that she was getting more depressed by the
minute, Tana reined in her horse and turned to the others. "I'm*

going to head back,'' she said, pretending it was only the dust that had made her eyes water and her throat choke up. ''I didn't sleep well last night, and I'm a little achier than usual.'' I'd only slow you down. ''You guys go ahead.'' At least let me see you ride, really ride, the way I used to. Let me enjoy the sight of you working as one with the horse. ''And take Jas along, will you? She needs a good run.'' The last thing I want is a solicitous dog following me around, whimpering and asking what's wrong with me.

Paul hesitated, feeling a guest's responsibility not to abandon the party too soon. But Tana turned it around for him, made it all right. ''Sorry to be such a lousy hostess,'' she apologized with her most charming smile. ''I'm just not up to it.''

''Oh, don't worry about it,'' Paul responded quickly. ''Your brother's good company.''

But Tana did worry about it all the way back to the stable. Her throat ached and her eyes stung as she realized it was never going to happen between her and Paul. Briefly she allowed herself to run, urging her mount up to the speed with which Paul and Dakota had headed away. For a moment she knew again the exhilaration of that oneness with the horse, of being an extension of this powerful beast as it galloped over the prairie, hooves cutting into the turf. But then she could feel the quivering sensation begin in her joints, and she knew she had to slow down or risk bringing on a seizure. By the time she reached the stable yard, both she and the horse had cooled down and were breathing normally. No wrangler came forward to assist her—they all knew better. She could take care of her own mount, and she'd by heaven do it herself. Even if it took her twice as long as it took anyone else.

So she was still in the tack room in the back part of the stable when she heard Paul and Dak come in with their horses. Their laughter came through the thin plank walls of the intentionally rustic building as they brushed and curried their horses, and she could hear the clink of metal bits and the creak of leather saddles as they carried their tack back toward where she still struggled to hang hers.

Quickly Tana blotted the tears that had been trickling down her cheeks and hoped that if she stayed in the shadows, neither would notice the red in her eyes. All her biocontrol skills came into play as she quieted her ragged breathing, calmed her quaking muscles, and disguised the outward signs of her sorrow.

Only Paul came in, a saddle in each hand and both bridles

thrown over one shoulder. "Oh, hi," he greeted, startled to find her there. His hair, already thinning in front, was windblown and his shirt was stained with sweat; the smell of horses lingered on him, and Tana's heart thudded in spite of her.

She managed a smile. "Hi."

"Your brother's a good kid," he informed her as he hoisted one saddle up and hooked it into its place on the wall. "I like him."

She was sitting on a rail in the center of the small room, saddle propped beside her, waiting for enough strength to seep back into her limbs to put the saddle away. "I like him, too," she agreed.

Paul hoisted the other saddle to its place. "I hope you don't mind us taking off like that, but it's been a long time since I've had a chance to ride." He arched his back, then drew the bridles from his shoulder. "I'm afraid I'm going to have really stiff muscles in the morning."

Her smile held only a trace of irony. "I know what that's like."

It was a moment before he realized what she meant; then he laughed. Not an embarrassed laugh but an oh-I-get-it laugh. "I guess you do."

With a great sigh she forced herself to her feet and tugged the saddle up from the rail. The hard part was that she would continue to work with Paul on the P-TUP project she had garnered for him. Seeing him day after day, appreciating him so much, knowing he deserved someone who'd be less trouble to him. Would she ever stop feeling like this? Would she, in time, reach a point where the blue of his eyes didn't seem to suck the very breath from her lungs?

Suddenly the weight of the saddle left her arms as Paul casually caught it up and hung it for her. Without asking, without calling attention to it, just the way Dak would have done. Like a brother, she thought miserably, sinking back down onto the rail. Nice thought, but I already have two.

The room was shadowy, its only light filtering in from the stable. Paul turned away from the wall, wiping his sweaty palms on his shirt, then hesitated, looking at her. "You okay?" he asked.

It must be written all over my face, she realized. All the disappointment, all the pain . . . "Just a little depressed," she answered, giving him a lopsided smile that was the best she could manage under the circumstances. "I get that way some-times. No big deal."

But he hesitated, never beyond the reach of another person's pain. "Anything I can do?" he asked.

Tana gave a half laugh. "Yeah, you can kiss me," she suggested.

The idea obviously came as a total surprise. But to his credit, Paul hesitated no more than a second. Then, bending to where she sat perched on the rail, he took her by the shoulders and did as she requested. There was no reluctance in his kiss or even much awkwardness, considering the circumstances. But neither was there much in the way of feeling. She had asked, and al-though he did not understand why, he was willing to oblige. How very Paul.

"Thanks," she said when it was over. "I needed that." Then, to spare him more than to save face, she slipped off the rail and left.

The same aching loneliness engulfed her now as she lay on the lumpy straw mattress in Nathan's house, awash in her need for him. With no desire to go back to her empty apartment after that ride, she had stayed over at her parents' house while Paul went back to Argo alone. That night she had wept a thousand tears for the man she was sure would never be hers. Yet three months later they had stood in the verdant yard of her aunt Helsi's gracious mansion and pledged to join their lives as one. All her agony of despair had been for nothing; no doubt all the fear and isolation she felt right now would prove to be just as unnecessary. Paul would come for her, if not today, then to-morrow.

But the panic still clutched at her heart and would not be banished.

They were playing a game of keepaway, and her brother Wy-oming kept getting between Tana and the ball. He was three years older and much taller than Tana, and his smile was ma-licious as he kept blocking her way. "Wyoming, cut it out!" she protested. "Wyoming, let me have it!"

"Keepaway, keepaway!" he chanted.

"Wy, I have to get it back!" she cried, and then she saw that it was not a ball really but a recorder with a traveling mat suspended from a tripod. "Wy, Paul's looking for me, and he can't find me if you keep getting between me and the 'corder."

"You can't go back," Wyoming told her. "You have to stay. No one leaves Earth, no one." And then he wasn't Wy anymore but Derek Lujan, with the dazzling smile and the light brown wavy hair. "Relax, Jacqueline. You're going to be here for a long time."

"No, I can't!" Tana felt her chest tighten and knew she must relax or she would have a seizure. *"Derek, be reasonable,"* she said as calmly as she could. *"We can't keep this place a secret forever. Sooner or later someone's going to find out. So just stand aside and let us go home, all right? Let us all go home."*

A wicked smile twisted his lips. "But not everyone wants to go. Right, Nathan?" He turned and looked behind him, where Nathan stood, looking very cautious.

"Nathan doesn't have to come," Tana assured them. *"But he can't stop the rest of us from going, either. That's not his prerogative."*

"How else can we keep Earth pure?" Nathan asked sorrowfully. *"How else do we keep out those evil influences that Coconino died to save us from?"*

"Another man died for that," Tana told him. *"Nathan, I know you idolize Coconino, I know you respect his people and his decision, but you can't make the decision to keep everyone trapped on this planet!"*

"But I can," Lujan said. *"Watch me!"* He picked up the recorder and smashed it against the ground—

"Tana!" Nathan was shaking her arm gently. "Tana, are you all right?"

Tana awoke with a start. "Yes," she mumbled. "Yes—is it night already?" She looked around the darkening room.

"I'm afraid so," he replied, straightening up in the shadows. "Marjean said you slept most of the day. We're about to have supper; do you want to try coming into the other room with us?"

The dream clung to her like gossamer, and Tana brushed at her sleep-numbed face with a clumsy hand. "Yes," she said. "Yes, I need to get up and move around."

He slipped a strong arm behind her shoulders as she struggled to sit up. "Easy, now. No need to rush; they won't start without us."

"No sign of Paul?" she asked stupidly, knowing full well that would have been the first news out of his mouth.

"Not yet. Give him time; he probably knows you aren't going anywhere."

Tana struggled to get her legs over the edge of the bed; her joints felt on fire as she forced them to bend. Finally she got both feet on the cool adobe floor. For a moment she just sat there panting.

"Nathan?" she said at last. "I've changed my mind. I can't keep quiet about this place. People here deserve the right to choose whether or not they stay here for the rest of their lives."

There was a long pause. Nathan continued to support her as she sat on the edge of the bed. "Before you came, they didn't have a choice," he said quietly.

"But now they do."

She could feel his gaze on her, but for once Tana could not look her opponent in the eye.

"And do they have a choice," he asked her then, "as to whether or not their home is invaded by people from your world?"

Paul rubbed a hand across his bleary eyes and stared at the readout.

"Hey, take a break, boss," Todd suggested gently. "You'll go cross-eyed looking at those lurp scratchings."

"I'm fine," Paul snapped.

At his tone, Jaria looked up from her workstation. Her eyes met Todd's, and then she hopped down off her stool and came over to where Paul sat. "Paul."

He did not look up. "What?"

"You've been up for forty hours straight. If the problem jumped out and bit you, you wouldn't see it because you're too tired. Go to bed."

"No."

Jaria stood back and folded her arms across her chest. "Are you saying that Todd and I aren't capable of finding the problem?"

"The more minds working on this, the better."

"Then call in the rest of your team!" she challenged. "Everyone knows there's something wrong; they've been tiptoeing around the outer lab all day. Call them in and put fresh minds to work. And put yours to bed."

For a moment Paul was silent, running yet another test against the data on the display, watching the results materialize.

"All right, call them in," he said finally. "I'll brief them."

Jaria headed for the door.

"Buy you a cup of coffee?" Todd ventured.

At that Paul sighed and leaned back from the display. "Yeah, I think I'd better. Can you bring it into my office?" Food and drink were forbidden anywhere near the lab equipment.

Todd scurried for the door as Paul rose and stretched awkwardly. It was not the first time he'd worked through the night on a project—far from it. In his enthusiastic youth he had been known to go for two and even three days on coffee and adrenaline, but that had always been because the work was so exciting. He'd never worked under this kind of pressure before, where there was more than an experiment at stake.

Drawing a deep breath, he forced his weary body back toward his office. It was the same office he'd had when he had taken the P-TUP assignment fourteen years ago. "I'm used to it," he had explained to Tana when he had declined more spacious quarters down the hall. "And I like being where I can see everything that's going on in the lab."

The truth was, he hardly ever looked up from his desk when he was working. It was mostly literature searching he did in here, and administrivia. When he was speed-reading files and documents, he was so focused on the display that a celophant could lumber past his window and he wouldn't notice.

What sixth sense had it been, then, that had told him to look up one Monday morning to see Tana gazing sadly in his direction?

It had startled him, for he hadn't realized it was regular working hours yet. He'd come in nearly four hours early because he was so fascinated by the new topic he was exploring that he couldn't sleep. The long walk from his apartment to the institute through the muddy gray dawn of New Sydney's summer had only served to generate more questions in his mind as it wrestled with all the new information he was accumulating. What kind of genetic defect was it that allowed a person to contract Gamaean palsy? Why could the virus be transmitted from a plant host to a human but not from one human to another? How had Tana happened to acquire the pernicious infection?

And why had she wanted him to kiss her?

It was not as though Paul had never run into that reaction in a woman before. It usually surprised him, because he didn't think of himself as attractive, but he'd been just sixteen the first time he had looked up from a centrifugal force experiment to find a young lady watching him with moon eyes and asking if he wouldn't like to come over and see a new holoflick at her house. But when Tana had asked him to kiss her, it was very different. In that moment it had struck him that she was not really the sparkling, self-confident young executive she usually seemed to be. Everything she did, everything she was, had been affected by this disease she had. Here, where she could shine in her work, it was one thing, but what about away from this place? What kind of social life did she have? How isolated and lonely did her disability make her feel?

Were people afraid to touch her? Was that why she wanted to be kissed? In this day and age, if a person did not wear a bio-meter that clearly displayed a healthy green color, many people would not risk bodily contact of any kind. Had Tana experienced that kind of rejection? Or did she feel her illness made her un-attractive to men? Was that the reassurance she had really been looking for in the stable yesterday? He could certainly put her fears to rest on that score; though he was not particularly selec-tive, he did know beauty when he saw it, and Tana was quite beautiful. But surely she knew that . . .

That was where his mind had been when he had looked up and seen her standing out in the lab, gazing at him through the transparent upper half of his office wall. His heart jumped when he saw her there; she looked startled, too, and started to turn away. But he flagged her eagerly into his office. "Have a chair," he invited when she and her dog had made their careful way through the door. "I've just been reading about your disease."

Hours had melted away as they talked. He asked every ques-tion that popped into his inquisitive mind: How had she gotten the disease? How pronounced was her case? Was she the patient in Dr. Winanga's paper? Even when the questions grew very personal, she answered without reluctance. Lunchtime came, and they got meals from the wall vendor to bring back to his office while they continued to talk. By evening he knew the full story of the two recessive genes she had inherited that made her susceptible to the Gamaean virus, and how sucking on a blade of grass had probably transmitted the microbe to her system, and how it had taken three months to figure out why she had trouble getting out of bed in the mornings, and the way her mother had cried when they found out. He was genuinely sur-prised when Monti Winthrop showed up in his doorway on his way home. "Are you two still at it?" the handsome CEO had asked. "You don't have to finish P-TUP in two weeks, you know," he had joked. "You can take two months."

They had wound up getting supper together—take-out food, since there were few restaurants that would allow Tana's dog inside—and going back to his apartment to talk some more. Or was it her apartment? His, because he hadn't yet thought to feel self-conscious about inviting a woman of Tana's stringent religious beliefs up to his apartment. Curiosity about the disease faded into the background as they talked about her childhood and his. They compared brothers—he had four, she only two—and parents—hers had married in their late twenties and signed an open-ended contract, while his mother had married first at nineteen, renewed the five-year contract twice, then opted to raise her five boys alone. She talked about her frustration with other people's reaction to her disease; he talked about the trouble he kept getting into because his curiosity prompted him to ask questions other people really didn't want to answer.

Finally she'd had to tell him she needed to get some sleep; her infected body simply could not keep the hours normal people kept. So he'd walked her to the roof lot where she'd left her flivver, and they had stood there in the cool, humid night gazing at each other and saying nothing. The significance of what had transpired that day swept over him and left him finally speechless. He stood near her but not touching her, his arms locked across his chest, and as he looked down into her open face, he knew that his whole life had been changed. Every nerve in his body ached with desire for her, but he held back. Slowly he leaned over and let his lips settle on hers, and the fire in him became a roaring blaze, but still only their lips touched. Then she got in her flivver and flew away.

For a long time he stood on the roof, amazed by the realization that he could no longer conceive of a life without Tana.

Without Tana . . .

"Paul?"

He looked up now, startled to find Todd in the doorway with two steaming cups of coffee. "Oh, good. Come on in."

"I thought maybe you were asleep sitting up," Todd told him. "I didn't want to wake you."

"No, I'm fine," Paul lied, sipping at the hot stimulant. "Just thinking. Let's go over it again; there must be something we've missed, some part we haven't checked . . ."

The message was waiting when Delhi woke up. She returned the call, although she knew the young man would be asleep. It was much better to call him from home, where Teeg would not automatically log the contact. To her surprise he was awake, waiting for her call.

"Something's gone wrong in Dr. Rutgers's lab," Jarl told her. "Rumor has it that Chang and Dr. Rutgers haven't been out of there in four days, and yesterday the rest of the team got called in, and they're working around the clock trying to fix something."

"Paul's team always works like that when they're close to a breakthrough," Delhi scoffed. "What makes you think something's gone wrong?"

"It's in their faces," he replied. "And they've been ordering parts and equipment like crazy. They've asked us to machine duplicates of a dozen things we've customized for them. It's like they're trying to rebuild the whole thing from scratch."

Delhi grunted. Jarl tended to be emotional, but it did sound as though something wasn't going according to plan in the lab. Fine timing, with Tana delayed in returning from her business trip—

"Thank you, Jarl," Delhi said. "I'll make a transfer into your account. Let me know if you find out any more about the situation."

As soon as she had disconnected, Delhi called the institute. "Teeg, has Tana returned yet?"

"Ms. Winthrop is not expected in today," the computer told her. "Would you like to speak with her secretary?"

Delhi's eyes opened wide. "What? Yes!" Gerta's smooth voice came on. "Gerta, what are you doing there at this hour?" Delhi demanded.

"I was expecting Tana in," Gerta replied, "and I thought I'd better brief her on all the changes we had to make in her calendar. But Paul said she won't be in today, either, and I'd better clear her calendar for tomorrow as well. I don't know what to think."

"Neither do I," Delhi gritted, "but I'm going to find out. I'll be there in twenty minutes."

CHAPTER THIRTEEN

Tana clutched the back of the chair, took a deep breath, and forced her reluctant knees to bend. She exhaled slowly with a gentle hiss until finally she was crouched on her heels; there she paused, panting, before taking another deep breath and beginning to rise. A burning sensation warmed her knees. This is not fire but warmth, she told herself. It is the warmth that washes away the stiffness. I am not pushing myself upward with my knees but being drawn upward on an invisible string, like a puppet. The string runs through my spine and lifts me gently upright, almost floating . . .

The routine was old and well rehearsed, the mental patter a conditioning that she had shared with other palsy victims from the time she was seventeen. That was twenty years ago. Back then it had been a great challenge, mind over body, the indomitable spirit overcoming Saint Paul's "thorn in the flesh." Then it became drudgery, this dragging her reluctant muscles through contractions they did not want to perform. But the alternative was unthinkable. A floater chair or a walking harness for the rest of her life? Never!

Still, I am so tired of this, she thought. I am so tired, and I just want to rest. I want Paul here to comfort me, to rub me down, to help me into a hot bath, to kiss me and love me and—

"Doing better today?"

Tana looked up to see Nathan standing in the doorway.

"Yes, thank you," she replied, feeling the strain between them. "It's an exercise in patience for me as much as performance, though. It takes such a long time to come back from a seizure."

"I suppose you have medicines and special equipment back where you come from," he said.

"No, not really," she told him. "Pain relievers might mask some of the stiffness, but then I'd be in danger of overexerting, so I don't use them. As for equipment—" She patted the sturdy wooden chair. "This serves very well. My body has to do all the work. Although horseback riding is wonderful, subtle exercise therapy. If I were home, I'd be wanting to ride today." She managed a lopsided smile. "Maybe we could locate this Tala your Coconino used to ride on."

Nathan smiled back, shaking his head. "Tala's been dead for centuries. Coconino found his bones. And the People say he was one of a kind, that there are no others like him."

"Too bad." Tana eased herself onto the wooden chair, clasped her arms around one knee, and pulled it gently to her chest. "Besides the exercise value, riding is good mental therapy. Just getting out of the house, feeling the wind in your face, seeing the vistas."

Nathan moved out of the doorway and into the room, leaning his tall, lanky frame up against the wall. "I could take you for a ride in one of the vehicles," he suggested.

"I've kept you from your work too long already," Tana demurred. "I'll be fine. I'll walk around the yard a bit today."

Still Nathan lingered in the room, watching her manipulate her joints and muscles. The strain of effort showed on her face, and perspiration glistened on her face and neck.

"Have you ever been camping?" he asked suddenly.

Tana lost her grip on her left leg, and it clumped ungracefully to the floor. "As a matter of fact, that's how I got this disease," she told Nathan, renewing her hold on her knee and pulling it once more to her chest. "My uncle Alex was judging a horse show on Gamaea, and Aunt Minnie took a bunch of the cousins along to go camping in the badlands there. The palsy virus had just been discovered a few years before, and they didn't know exactly how a person got it. It seemed to be regionalized on the eastern continent, so it never occurred to anyone there might be danger to us on the western one." She released her leg carefully and began to roll her shoulders. "Anyway, I haven't done much camping since then. My joints get too stiff sleeping on the ground, even on a cushion. But Dak takes the kids camping— they love it. Especially at Roundup."

There was a hesitation, then Nathan said, "What if I rigged a cot for you with a regular straw tick on it, just like the one on this bed? Do you think you could stand one night of roughing it?"

Tana stopped her exercises and studied him. "What do you have in mind?"

Nathan rubbed at his long chin. "Well, it's July," he began. "It's the Moon When the Summer Rains Begin, and the saguaro fruit are ripe. The People will have come up from the southern village to harvest them."

Tana felt a tingle of excitement. "Come where? Camp Crusoe?"

He shook his head. "No, it's a half day's drive from here, down along Tonto Creek. But it's a lot closer than trying to get to their village. I thought . . . you might like to meet some of them. See how they live. Listen to their stories."

Her heart thudded at the prospect. "I don't dare go too far from here," she objected. "Paul will be coming, and—"

"Marjean can tell him where we are," Nathan replied. "I can leave a map of sorts. He can pick you up from anywhere, can't he? As long as you have that traveling mat?"

It was true; a map, even a rough one, would allow Paul to send a recorder to spot her location and make the contact there. But she wanted to be here when he came.

"Not this trip, I think," Tana said finally. "He must be having trouble with the equipment, and I don't want to make him do two or three jumps."

"So you'll just sit here and wait," Nathan said in a voice tinged with bitterness. "Today, and tomorrow, and the day after that for as long as it takes; just put life on hold and wait—"

"Nathan, please!" she snapped. "I'm sick, and I'm scared, and all I want is to go home the fastest way possible."

"And make decisions that affect the lives of people you've never met." Nathan straightened up. "At least Coconino walked in our camp and looked in our faces before he cut us off from the stars. But I guess he was made of a little different stuff."

Tana heard him go, though her eyes were squeezed shut and her mind was caught in its litany: Breathe deeply—relax—stay calm—don't let the toxins flood your system again—breathe deeply—relax—stay calm— Finally her heart rate slowed, and she opened her eyes and looked around the room. A pitcher and basin stood on a washstand near her bed. They were not as striking as the set she had seen in Nathan's bedroom, but the very rustic nature of them touched her. She thought of the slick stamped and molded goods that littered the gift shops of Gamaea and Pololla's "primitive" areas. That was showy trash; this was useful art.

"Say-ayka-pee says . . ." How often had she heard that around Nathan's table? Say-ayka-pee seemed the font of all wisdom, Coconino the epitome of human bravery. She was not sure she would have wanted to encounter the intense, fiery Coconino just now, and since they always referred to him in the past tense, she assumed he was dead. But Say-ayka-pee . . . His insights intrigued her, and the gentle humor in his observations enchanted her. Would Say-ayka-pee be at this harvesting? No, his village was in the north, and Nathan had said the southern village came to harvest the saguaro fruit. But to meet the people who had engendered him, to glimpse their way of life—

—before she altered it radically.

I can't help it! she thought miserably. What's done is done. I have opened the door to this world, and it cannot be shut up again. What am I to do? Withhold the invention of P-TUP? Trash Paul's life's work? I can't. I can only postpone. I can only try to direct the course that history takes in reintegrating Earth. Even then it will be like trying to direct the course of a storm; I have so little real control.

But at least, she thought, I can bother to learn who the people are who will be caught in the path of this storm. It's why I came a second time, isn't it? To find out who they are. I thought I came to find out what they wanted, but it's not true. I came to find out who they are, to have some idea of what will happen to them when their world is—invaded. That's the word Nathan used, and he's right. They will be invaded.

It's the same issue I've always faced with P-TUP, Tana realized. I was concerned about the invasion of worlds I know—"unauthorized intrusion." I did not think about the invasion of this world. It needs safeguards as much as the others—more so, because they have been isolated for so long. Their protection should be of as much concern to me as the protection of sovereign planets and nations elsewhere.

And to know how to protect them, I must know who they are.

Tana struggled to her feet and made her way laboriously out to the yard, where Nathan was mending the quail hutch. He stopped as she drew near and waited for her to speak.

"Can we be back by nightfall?" she asked.

"No," he replied. "Evening is for storytelling; evening is when you will learn the most. We'll start back first thing in the morning; we'll be home by noon."

Noon—midday—Tana looked at her chronometer, trying to figure out what time that would be on Paul's schedule, and discovered it didn't matter. It was a day, and that was that. One day.

She forced a wry smile. "If they tell stories the way you do," she told Nathan, "maybe it will keep me distracted for a while."

Paul woke with a start and grabbed for his chrono, which was lying on the floor beside the cot. Jaria had dragged the cot over from Medical and set it up in his office when it had become obvious that he was not going to leave the premises. Finally, when he had begun to see what he wanted in the data instead of what was there, he had surrendered and sacked out on the makeshift bed.

That was six hours ago. A quick look out the transparent wall told him that little progress had been made. Struggling to his feet, Paul staggered toward the door.

Nikolai came on the run when he saw Paul. "Shh," the little blond man cautioned, pointing to a corner of the lab where Todd was curled up asleep. "He just dropped off about half an hour ago. We've replaced maybe forty percent of the components now, with no results. The custom orders won't be ready for three, four days, I'm afraid. But there are still plenty of standard components we haven't checked—"

Paul cut him off with a wave of the hand. "What's Shony doing?" he asked, pointing to where the thin young redhead was kneeling beside the P-TUP apparatus, his face close to the Merthacon generator.

"Trying to smell if there's any difference in the emissions," Nikolai replied. "My nose isn't that sensitive, but Shony claims he can smell something when the generator is functioning, and he's checking to see if the odor has changed. Sounds crazy, but—"

Smelling the generator . . . "No, no," Paul disagreed. "It's not crazy at all. Tana always says Doc can smell when a warp connection is in place—Jaria!" Paul snapped suddenly. "Call my brother-in-law and have him get Doc to the warp terminal. His nose is more sensitive than any of ours. And have Dak send along one of those headsets he uses to communicate with implanted dogs. I need to know what Doc is smelling."

What Nathan called a truck was the most ungainly vehicle Tana had ever seen. It bore some resemblance to ancient petroleum- or pellet-powered vehicles in that it had four wheels, a passenger compartment, and windows, but it was nothing like the relics she had seen in the Interplanetary Museum of Art or any history files. The metal shell was rusted and scarred, shaped like a hump in the front where driver and passenger rode; behind it was a wooden platform that extended over the rear wheels and was drilled through in several places around the edges. There was no glass in the windows, and the wheels were not of rubber but of some molded material. It was, Nathan had confided, Lila Gonzales's pride and joy, brought with her from the Mountain when she had come to marry Sonder Tgersa.

As the two of them bounced and lurched across the uneven ground, Tana almost wished that they could travel at the slower speed of the pedal car, but Nathan had explained that they needed to climb through some mountain passes that would take hours in the pedal car but that the truck could cruise up at nearly forty miles an hour. So Tana clutched the grab bar in the cab and focused on her relaxation exercises, telling herself the sooner they got there, the sooner she could get back to Camp Crusoe where Paul expected to find her.

It was late afternoon when the saguaro forest came into view. Tana caught her breath. She had seen holographic re-creations of the giant cactus, but only on a desk display. It could not prepare her for the sight of several acres of the monolithic plants with their multiple branches, adorned as they were with bright red fruit on the very tip of each limb. As they drew nearer, she saw that the green flesh of some was blemished by brown patches and that here and there an arm had been broken off. Once they had to drive far up an incline to avoid the remains of a fallen sentinel, its thirty-foot length broken and decaying in the desert sun.

Tana squinted at it as they drove past. The photosensitive lenses she had put in her eyes before she had left Argo made it difficult to discern fine detail in this bright sunlight, but she could see the skeletal structure of the dead plant. Woody rods ran the length of the trunk, with the interior being a spongy pith that, when the plant was alive, probably held a good deal of moisture. Vertical ridges still showed here and there where decay had not obliterated the outer skin, and from them protruded the requisite thorns of the genus.

"Are you telling me," Tana said to Nathan as they passed between two forty-foot giants, "that the People actually get that fruit down from the top of these things? How?"

"Like that," he said, pointing up the slope to a knot of people who had stopped to stare at their approach. "See those long sticks? Those are actually saguaro ribs, so they're just as tall as the plants. The harvesters reach up with the sticks and knock the fruit off the top. Then, of course, there are the cooperative saguaro." He pointed to a nearby specimen whose arms curved downward. "You see, they soak up water through their root systems and store it in the trunks and limbs. Occasionally during heavy rains they absorb so much water, the arms begin to sag under their own weight." The tip of one limb curved back upward just three feet from the ground, but there was no fruit on it. "The kids harvest those," Nathan told her.

Now a collection of brush shelters appeared down the hillside from the saguaro forest, near the stream they had been following. More people gathered outside the dome-shaped dwellings, watching the approaching vehicle. Nathan stopped the truck a hundred yards off and climbed out. *"Chee-eeyah,"* he called out.

"Chee-eeyah," replied an old woman. She was stockily built, wearing a loose dress of undecorated cotton, her gray hair caught in braids. *"Es Nay-tahn?"*

Tana was surprised at the glow on Nathan's face as he shouted something incomprehensible back to the woman. She clapped her hands in delight, then turned to the others gathered around her and sent them scurrying off in all directions. Nathan was grinning like an idiot as he came around to Tana's side of the truck. "We're in luck," he told her. "It's Eyes Like a Deer, an old friend of mine. She is a lady of great distinction among the People, and when I told her I brought a Witch Woman with me, she commanded a feast in your honor."

"A Witch Woman!" Tana exclaimed as Nathan helped her out of the vehicle. "Isn't that a character from one of their legends?"

"There was a Witch Woman with Coconino," Nathan explained, "but they used to call almost any woman from the Mountain a Witch Woman. Mostly they were health techs or crafters who came to teach the People new skills, so of course the People thought they had great magic."

"I hope they don't expect me to do magic," Tana grumbled, wincing as her knees flexed to take back the burden of her weight. "At this moment, just walking from here to their camp will be a miracle."

"I'll carry you if you like," Nathan offered, "but I can't bring the truck any closer. They dislike machines; they consider them out of harmony with the Mother Earth."

"I'll walk," Tana replied. "Just lend me your arm for support so I don't stumble and fall into a bed of cactus. And go very slowly."

Tana had plenty of time to observe the camp as they approached. It consisted of half a dozen brush domes and an equal number of ramadas—roofs supported by poles. Large ceramic kettles simmered over three fires, and a sweet, pungent aroma filled the air. "They're cooking down the fruit," Nathan explained. "They extract the seeds for grinding into flour, and the juice and pulp are used for a variety of things. Some of it becomes a syrup, some a kind of candy, and some is mixed with nuts and dried meat to make pemmican, which is good traveling food. If we're feasting tonight, you'll probably get to try some of everything."

Most of the people in the camp were elderly, Tana noticed. No doubt the younger adults were out harvesting the fruit. The men wore cotton loincloths; the women, either loose dresses or simple skirts with no blouses. The young children, when they were not hiding behind their elders, appeared to wear no clothing at all. Practical, Tana thought, even as it tickled at her prudish nature.

Eyes Like a Deer came forward to meet them, smiling shyly at Tana. She exchanged words with Nathan, who then translated for Tana. "Eyes Like a Deer says that you are welcome in the camp of the People. She has never met a Witch Woman before, and she feels that the Mother Earth has given her yet another honor which she does not deserve." Then Nathan added, "Eyes Like a Deer is a direct descendant of Father Nakha-a, who established their village two centuries ago. She was also a—a Chosen Companion, which—" Nathan hesitated. "Well, I'll explain that later. She is the widow of Touched a Bear, who organized the bear hunts, a very dangerous and important job. And she had the honor of knowing Coconino and his wife Ironwood Blossom when they came to visit the southern village many years ago. Not many of the People still live who knew Coconino."

"Tell her I am honored to make the acquaintance of so illustrious a lady," Tana replied. "Say that I am flattered that they take time from the harvest to make a feast for me and that I hope it does not cause them any hardship."

Nathan gave her a sideways glance. "You're very perceptive," he observed before translating her message to their hostess.

They were offered a place to sit in the shade of a ramada far from the cook fires. It was still extremely warm, but after the oppressive heat and constant jostling of the truck, Tana was relieved to take a seat on the firm ground. A mat of woven yucca leaves had been spread, and Nathan fetched a pillow from the bedding he'd brought in the truck for Tana to use as a cushion. They were given cool water from the stream and cold cakes of spicy corn bread. Tana's mouth burned from the unaccustomed seasoning, and she learned after the first bite to surreptitiously extract the bits of green pepper from the bread before she ate it.

Eyes Like a Deer sat with them, and with Nathan translating, they carried on a conversation of sorts. Tana learned that only six families came every year to harvest the saguaro fruit, always the same six, with the skills and the privilege being handed down from one generation to the next. Eyes Like a Deer's grand-daughter, Yellow Mushroom, who had just celebrated her wom-anhood ceremony, was learning all the recipes for cooking the saguaro fruit and would someday preside over that part of the harvest, as her grandmother did today.

"I also learned my skills from my parents," Tana told her. "From my father especially."

"And what do you do?" Eyes Like a Deer asked.

Tana hesitated. "I encourage other people to do well," she said finally.

"Ah." Eyes Like a Deer nodded wisely. "That is powerful magic indeed."

Soon the rest of the harvesters began filtering back into camp, carrying large baskets heaped with red fruits. Many of the fruits had burst open to reveal thousands of tiny black seeds. Nathan brought Tana one to examine; she could hardly believe that such a giant cactus grew from so tiny a seed. Then he cut a piece for her to taste, carefully peeling off the thorny skin and offering the red flesh on the point of his knife. It was pulpy and sweet, and the seeds crunched pleasantly.

The People approached the encampment with subdued voices, giving dignified nods to the two strangers. Some greeted Na-than, though most did not. They moved quickly off to the river to wash, and there was no small amount of horseplay, Tana noted, even among the adults. They seemed to be a happy peo-ple, content in their community. As they came back from bath-ing, they settled under the ramadas, talking together, watching the strangers.

"I thought you were well known here," Tana commented to Nathan.

"No, not in the southern village," he replied. "At least not to these families. I spent an extended time in the northern village, and some of the people I knew there have moved south, but I've really only been to the southern village a few times. Eyes Like a Deer knows me because her daughter is married to my *moh-eh-ehtah*, my spirit brother; he's the one I've gone to the southern village to visit."

"Spirit brother?" Tana was curious.

"Say-ayka-pee's son," Nathan explained. "He was five or six when I went to live with them, and he really was like a kid brother to me."

"Why did he move south?" Tana wanted to know.

Nathan shrugged. "Adventure, at first. Journeying to a strange land, making his way across the bosom of the Mother Earth, meeting a people he had not known all his life. Then he met New Flowers, and they married, and—I don't know. I think basically the place got under his skin. It's a different kind of village than the northern one. The climate is milder there, and the wisdom of Father Nakha-a seems to give the place a different atmosphere."

"Different from the wisdom of Say-ayka-pee?"

Nathan considered that. "Not so different these days," he admitted. "But once it was very different. When I first met Say-ayka-pee, he was . . . like a *shee-moh-ohtah*, a caged spirit. Over the years he has grown more mellow." Nathan pointed to a teenage girl who was dragging a hot stone from the fire with a stick. "That is his granddaughter, Star That Sings."

"She's a very pretty girl," Tana observed. "Say-ayka-pee must be very proud of her."

"He's never seen her," Nathan replied. "His son Howling Coyote, the girl's father, has been living in the southern village for many years." There was an unmistakable note of sadness in his voice.

Tana studied him, wondering what had caused that. "Does it hurt you to see them migrating away from Say-ayka-pee's village?" she asked gently.

Nathan plucked a dried stem of grass and began to break it idly into small pieces. "It's what Say-ayka-pee wants, I think," he told her. "He speaks highly of the southern village. Only—only I'm afraid that one day I'll go north to visit and the whole village will be gone; just those empty houses will be left crumbling on the hillside. And that will make me sad, because then

I will know that Say-ayka-pee walks no more among the People.''

Just then Eyes Like a Deer stood up in the center of the gathering and began to speak. Nathan translated as she welcomed the strangers, recognizing Nathan's prior friendship to the People and the exalted status of his companion, the Witch Woman. Tana was sure there was something Nathan did not translate for her, something about himself, and she distinctly heard Coconino's name, but interrupting to ask was out of the question.

Then Eyes Like a Deer began to chant. It was a haunting sound, thin and eerie, like the wind playing through the terrabaum trees on Juno. As Nathan translated her words, it was a prayer to the Mother Earth thanking her for her great bounty and most particularly for the saguaro fruit. A tingling ran down Tana's spine. It was the first time on this planet that she had encountered any manifestation of a religion. This worship of nature was a far cry from her own monotheistic beliefs, but the prayer touched her. Eyes Like a Deer was acknowledging that their blessings were a gift not of their own making, and that was a sentiment that struck home deeply for Tana.

Eyes Like a Deer went on to thank the Mother Earth for Coconino, the Earth Saver, who had restored the great saguaro to them. Tana could see in their faces the respect in which they held their hero. It was on Nathan's face as well. She wondered what the People would think if they knew that she had torn the fabric of the protection Coconino had brought them.

Then the feasting began. Eyes Like a Deer returned to sit with the honored guests, along with an old man called Three Feathers and his son, Red Hands. They laughed and made small talk as they ate, but as the soft desert night settled gently over them, Nathan turned to the old man and asked a question.

In the gathering darkness Tana could see Three Feathers's broad smile, a flash of white teeth in his rich brown face. ''I've asked him to tell a story,'' Nathan whispered to her. ''The story of how Coconino returned the saguaro to us.''

Not to them, Tana noted, but to us.

''It is known that Coconino made many adventurous journeys,'' Three Feathers began. ''He made the journey to seek Tala, the one-horned antelope. He made the journey up to the Sky Ship in order to destroy it. He also made a journey to the Mountain, which none of the People has made before or since.''

Around them, people listened with rapt attention. The old man's voice was not powerful, but it was sonorous, and Tana soon was caught in the illusion that she actually heard the story in his tones and not in the soft words of Nathan translating beside her.

"It was on that journey that Coconino had a dream," Three Feathers went on. "He dreamed that he saw the Grandfather standing on the side of a hill, waiting for him. So in the morning he rose and climbed on Tala's back, and together they flew to the hillside he had seen in his dream. There Coconino found the Grandfather. He was a great and very old saguaro, bigger around than a man could stretch his arms to encircle, if a man dared try such a thing." There was gentle laughter; those who harvested the saguaro fruit had a great respect for the spiky thorns of that cactus.

"The Grandfather was the last of his kind. Alone on that hillside he had waited patiently while one by one his relatives died around him. Even his children succumbed to cold and drought and rushing streams. But the Grandfather held fast; he was waiting." Tana could picture the lonely sentinel, beleaguered but strong, withstanding the elements and the sorrow of seeing his species die. Such was the power of the story that it did not seem the least bit strange to her that a plant should have feelings.

"At last he was rewarded," Three Feathers told them. "Out of the skies, riding the great kachina called Tala, came Coconino. He was a fiery young man in those days, full of pride and the spirit of the Mother Earth. With a stick in his hand he swooped down from the air and struck the bright red fruit from the top of the Grandfather. Then he landed and picked up the fruit, cradling it gently, for he knew what a great treasure it was. Carefully he tucked it away in his pouch. When he returned to the Valley of the People, he offered the fruit with its many seeds to his mother, Two Moons. From those seeds came all of the cactus that you see here today."

It was nearly dark now, and Tana looked around at the shadows of the towering giants. They seemed an army of silent watchers, proud and solemn. We are here, they seemed to say. We are here because of Coconino. We are here because of his care and foresight. We are here because he did what had to be done to rescue our kind.

More stories followed. There was the story of the Survivors and how the People had first come to be at the beginning of This Time. There was the story of how Coconino found Tala and how he and his Witch Woman brought that strange winged antelope back to the village. There was the story of a woman called the Mother and how the coming of the Others had stricken her like a blow, but she would not die until Coconino had vanquished them. There was the story of when Coconino came again after seven generations and, finding himself torn from his Witch Woman, how he cried out his grief on a cliff top for two days and a night and still could not banish her from his heart.

The story struck too close to home for Tana. "Please," she whispered, her voice thick. "Ask them to tell something else, something uplifting."

So they told her how the Mother Earth loved Coconino and gave him courage and wisdom. They told how Coconino had tricked the evil Lujan and kept more Others from coming. "Not that we mind the ones we have," they assured her politely, "for they are no more troublesome than the Men-on-the-Mountain were of old, but we are glad they are few. It has taken the Mother Earth some time to teach even these few how to behave."

And they called Coconino by a name of honor, as they called their ancestors the Survivors by names of honor. As Alfonso was He Who Had Faith, Coconino was the Earth Saver.

The night was well advanced now, and Tana discovered she had no more strength to keep her head upright. Nathan went to the truck to get her cot, and Tana watched as two of the women banked the cook fires and tended their pots of fruit juice once more in the darkness. Above her the sky was now littered with stars, undoubtedly the same stars she saw from Juno, but in different patterns. As she stretched out on a mat and waited for Nathan, they seemed to Tana a veritable ocean of twinkling lights. Crickets chirped all around her, and in the distance a whippoorwill called. To Tana it seemed to say "Earth Saver. Earth Saver."

"Did you ever meet him?" Tana asked Nathan when he returned.

"Who?"

"Coconino," she replied. "You must have. When you lived with Say-ayka-pee."

There was a brief silence. "Yes," Nathan said briefly. "I knew him."

"What was he like?"

Again he was a moment in answering, working at assembling the cot. "Very much like the stories paint him. Strong. Fiery. Proud." Nathan tossed the straw tick onto the taut fabric stretched across its wooden frame. "But . . . wounded. It tore a great hole in him when he was snatched away from his own time. From his Witch Woman. I didn't understand that at first; Ironwood Blossom explained it to me. The cost to him of saving the Mother Earth from the Others—from us—was very high. It did not blunt him, but it—it tempered him. It very definitely tempered him.''

He patted the tick, and Tana struggled onto it. Her joints still protested, but they were not as stiff as they had been that morning. Slowly, steadily, her strength and agility were returning.

As soon as she was settled, he stretched out on the ground beside her. The rough ramada over their heads provided an eerie blot of darkness against the brilliant heavens. "Didn't it ever bother you," she asked Nathan, "that he thought of you and your people as the enemy?''

There was a rustling sound as Nathan settled himself into a more comfortable position. "He never thought of me as the enemy," he told her. "Lujan was the enemy—Lujan and the mentality he represented. Take what you can, no matter who you take it from; take, take, take, and never think about giving back. That's what nearly destroyed the Earth, you know: people only thought about what made their own lives easier, what brought them power and wealth. If that left the Earth and her other creatures a little poorer, what did they care?''

"It's still true," Tana admitted regretfully. "I see it every day.''

"And here," Nathan added. "It didn't die with Lujan. That's what Coconino hates. It's the attitude, not the people.''

The straw tick was lumpy, and Tana felt a little aching in her back, but she was tired and well fed and knew she would soon be asleep anyway. "Still," she sighed, "it must have been very intimidating for you the first time you went to the northern village with Say-ayka-pee, knowing that Coconino was there, knowing what he thought of your kind.''

There was a soft laugh from Nathan. "No," he whispered gently, "I had no fear of Coconino when I went north.''

Tana's brain was beginning to fuzz as sleep approached. "Why not?''

A distant coyote barked a laughing bark. It was an eerie, mocking sound, and Tana was glad she was not alone in this place.

"Because it was Coconino who invited me," Nathan said finally. "The People often have more than one name, depending on who they are talking to or about, and it has suited Coconino well to have more than one. That's why, in Camp Crusoe, he calls himself 'Keeps His Own Counsel'—*Say-ayka-pee*. Say-ayka-pee is Coconino.''

Doc whined softly in distress. Todd stood staring helplessly at his mentor, not knowing what to say. The rest of the team clustered near the door, speaking in whispers.

Paul sat on the dais of Chamber Five, turning the tiny duo-decahedron over and over in his palm.

Jaria came and squatted down near him. "Look, Paul. Tana's father works for the Pax Circumfra, doesn't he? Can't he get them to suspend the embargo for this? It's an emergency!''

Paul simply shook his head. "Monti doesn't have that kind of influence,'' he said softly.

"Well, damn!'' Jaria swore, springing back to her feet and beginning to pace. "There must be someplace else we can get one. Kalopis may be the only place they're manufactured, but it can't be the only place they're used. Who else has got one?''

"The Transportation Guild,'' Todd volunteered. "But there's some kind of snag there—they won't even tell us what it is. They just won't sell us the part. Unless—get this—unless Tana asks for it. Figure that one out.''

"Politics,'' Jaria muttered.

Paul continued to finger the small jumble of crystals and electronics in his palm. Fractured. Somewhere deep inside it had fractured from the strain, and without it his entire elaborate construction was useless. Without it, Tana . . . Tana . . .

"We can send a ship for her,'' Todd said urgently. "We've got permission, we've even done a press release; all we have to do is follow through. Six weeks, maybe? She'll be fine, Paul. The people there will take good care of her.''

Six weeks of fighting down panic. Six weeks trying to hold off a seizure, without Doc there to help her. Six weeks—or ten—or twelve.

Jaria put a hand on his shoulder. "It's not your fault.''

Fault? No. Failure. It was his failure. When they'd blown the altphase deconnector, he'd replaced this krystalager as well; routine, to replace one when replacing the other. And of course he'd ordered backups of both parts. But he hadn't waited. He hadn't waited to make sure they were on hand before he had sent Tana off. He just assumed they would come before he ever needed them. He'd been unaware of any embargo against the manufacturer, unaware of any problem with the Transportation Guild. Buried in his work, immersed in his research—

A chime sounded, followed by a sharp voice from the computer. "Paul, it's Delhi. Let me in."

Every person in the room froze except Paul. He continued to turn the krystalager over and over in his hand.

"Paul, I know something's going on, and I demand to know what it is. Open the door."

Jaria swore. "Just what we need."

"Wrong approach," Todd muttered. "It's Paul's lab. She has no right to—"

"Let her in," Paul said quietly.

Both Todd and Jaria turned to stare at him.

"Let her in," Paul repeated.

Jaria recovered first. Moving to a workstation, she keyed in the sequence that would release the door lock. Delhi heaved the heavy door open and marched into the lab. She took one look at the mournful Dalmatian in the room, then went straight up to Paul and stood in front of him. "Where's Tana?" she demanded.

Paul lifted his eyes to hers. His fringe of hair was uncombed, and he had not shaved in three days. His lab coat was soiled, and there was a heavy odor of perspiration about him. But his face was stony, his gaze unflinching. "This is P-TUP," he said with a wave of his hand toward the elaborate equipment. "Three days ago I put Tana on Earth. Now she's stranded there." He held up the krystalager. "The place that manufactures these is under embargo; the Transportation Guild has these but won't sell one to us."

Everyone waited for the explosion, knowing how she would rant and rave at the stupidity of sending Tana, the recklessness of the research team, the insult of having kept all this from her for days. They watched Delhi's face as she and Paul stared at each other, eyes locked, and the seconds dragged by like hours.

Finally she spoke. "Can we build one?"

"No one here has the skills," Paul said simply.

"Is there nowhere else we can get one?"

"The computer's doing a second search right now, in outlying industries. It's not very likely."

Still they only faced each other, the gaze of each as steady as the other's. Then Delhi chose her course of action. "Teeg," she barked. "Tell Gerta to clear Tana's calendar for a week. Then get me Woflgang Montag of the Transportation Guild.'' To Paul she said, ''He's the slimiest member of the Guild; if there's something behind their refusal, he'll be the one to know.'' She turned away now and headed for Paul's office. ''I'll assume without the dog Tana probably had a seizure. When I'm through with Montag, I'll alert her doctor to stand by. I'll use your office.''

Even as she spoke, she thumbed the door shut behind her, leaving the members of Paul's team to gape after her in wonder and relief.

''You intended for me not to know he was alive, didn't you?'' Tana asked Nathan as they jounced over the rough track back toward Camp Crusoe.

''He prefers anonymity,'' Nathan replied. ''I try to grant him as much as I can.''

''Short of lying to me. You were very careful not to lie to me,'' she observed.

''Coconino wouldn't want me to lie.'' Suddenly Nathan grinned. ''Although he would approve of my having tricked you. He has a very droll sense of humor.''

''I wish I could meet him,'' Tana said.

But Nathan shook his head. ''Let him be. He's an old man now; he wants only to be left in peace. You've met the People now; you've gotten a taste of who they are and how they live. What more do you want?''

I want to meet him, Tana thought. The one who rode a flying antelope and destroyed a spacecraft. The one who saved his people and marooned mine. The one who connived with Derek Lujan, then tricked him and defeated him. The one who passed through a time warp and finally had to take his enemy's life. The one who taught you, Nathan, to respect him so deeply. I want to meet that man. I want to know the Earth Saver.

''Tell me what kind of man he is, then,'' she badgered.

''I've told you!'' he protested. ''A good man. A wounded one. A wise one. A man who loved his children and his wives and put service to the People and the Mother Earth above his own desires.''

''I have a hard time with it,'' Tana admitted. ''The idea that he tricked Lujan and destroyed the *Homeward Bound*. Coming from a primitive culture like that, how could he possibly have planned such a deception? How could he have known that an electrical charge from Tala would damage the spacecraft? Honestly, Nathan, don't you think that last part at least was accidental?"

"Not for a minute," Nathan replied certainly. "You don't know the whole story. It wasn't the first time Coconino and Tala had attacked a piece of advanced technology and destroyed it. When the probe from the *Homeward Bound* was discovered, the Men-on-the-Mountain constructed a beacon in one of their towers, figuring a spacecraft was probably nearby. But Coconino didn't want them to speak to the sky; he didn't want the Others to hear them and come. So he and Tala flew at the tower, and the sparks from Tala's horn started a fire in the beacon that burned it to the ground. He knew what Tala's horn could do to machines, and he knew how to make Tala excited enough to use it."

"And did he know what he was doing to my ancestors?" she asked.

Nathan sighed. "He knew. That's why he sent the young hunters to steal all our weapons, so we wouldn't attack the People out of vengeance. We did, anyway." The road was improving; they were passing between cultivated fields now. "Coconino never expected to live after he destroyed the Sky Ship. He believes the time warp was the Mother Earth's way of saving him."

Tana studied the weatherworn farmer beside her. "Is that what you believe?"

Nathan turned his head to look at her. "I believe," he said softly, "Coconino was a man worth saving."

They bounced along in silence for a while, waving occasionally to people in the fields. The rickety bridge across the river came into view before Tana spoke again. "I have a friend named Jull. She's a minister in my religion, but she has an unusual saying. She says no good deed goes unpunished." Tana gave a wry smile. "Her unique sense of humor. But when I think of Coconino being torn away from his own time, from his family and his friends—when I think of my own good intentions in coming here and of all the problems I've created—she's right. Every time you act on your conscience, it costs you."

"Not every time," he contradicted. "And besides, think what the cost would be if you didn't."

They crossed the bridge to the settlement side of the river, and Tana's thoughts drifted away from Coconino as she began to wonder what they would find when they returned to Nathan's farm. Would Paul have been there? Would he be waiting? Would there be any kind of message that he had gotten through? Would he be angry with her for having left the farmhouse? Would he think it cavalier of her to have wandered off while he drove himself to distraction trying to reach her?

It caught her by surprise when Nathan stopped the truck and started to get out. "What's the matter?" she asked anxiously. "Why are we stopping?"

"Something I want to show you," he explained, coming around to her side. "It's up a little hill; here, let me carry you. I know how tired you are."

"I'll walk," she insisted. "I need to walk to build up my strength. We'll just go slowly."

So they made their way up the small hill with her leaning heavily on Nathan's arm.

As soon as she saw the stone markers, she knew where they were. She had seen monuments of innumerable styles and materials in her travels throughout the galaxy, but she had no trouble recognizing the simple gravestones. The names were familiar to her, some from the people she had met here: Tsorks. Mason. Martin. Tgersa. And then there were names she knew from the crew roster of the *Homeward Bound*: Mike Thornton. Cyd Ryan. Karen Reichert. Terry Johanneson.

On the side that faced the settlement, just below the crest of the hill, were the markers she had wanted to see. Rita Zleboton, chief engineer. Jacqueline Winthrop, chief medical officer. Clayton Winthrop, captain. Tears sprang to Tana's eyes.

"Clayton's not really buried here," Nathan told her. "They never found his body. But after Jacqueline died, it didn't seem right that her marker should be here alone, so they put one up for him, too. One story says that was her request; another says it was Chief Zleboton's idea. Personally, I wouldn't be surprised if a lot of people thought of it. Now they're all here, except the two who didn't make it off the *Homeward Bound* before it crashed. And Lujan. No one cared to have Lujan's name here."

Slowly Tana forced her knees to bend until she knelt on the prickly dried grass and weeds that covered the hill. She ran her fingers across the stone with Jacqueline's name, a rough stone chiseled with crude tools, but the best the residents could do at the time. Putting her hand on the ground beside Clayton's marker, she could almost feel the emptiness of the earth. "I'm sorry, Chelsea," she whispered. "I'm sorry I couldn't find your father, but you seemed reconciled to that. But she's here, Chelsea. I did what you wanted me to; I looked where you said, and here she is. I found her for you, Chelsea. I found your mother."

CHAPTER FOURTEEN

Phoenix looked out over the sea of faces—brown faces, beautiful faces. Some were narrow; most were round. Some had eyes with a pronounced slant; others were hardly tilted at all. The noses were large, the brows strong, and the cheekbones high. Until her thirtieth year she had never seen such a face. Now they were as familiar to her as the shape of her own hands. They all looked toward her expectantly as she approached the ceremonial fire.

She hated speeches.

Fire Keeper added a log that was handed to him by a young boy of ten. The boy was Juan's grandson. You have grandchildren, my *compadre*, she thought. Half a dozen grandchildren and more on the way. Your sons are fine men. Would you had lived to see this day.

Flint was looking at her reproachfully. Flint always looked at her reproachfully. Flint had a grandchild, too, a little girl born last fall to his oldest daughter. She had been born with two fingers webbed together, but Phoenix had told them that only meant she would love the water when she was older. So they called her Loves the Water, and everyone was happy.

At the very edge of the crowd stood a beautiful, portly woman with gently graying hair and a new cotton shawl her husband had bartered from the Others. The woman's eyes burned with undisguised hatred as she looked at Phoenix. Castle Rock. You think I stole your son from you, Phoenix thought. But I did not make the decision to banish him from the village—your friend Moon with No Shadow suggested that, before she resigned from my Council. But you will always hold me responsible, won't you? Go ahead; it doesn't matter anymore. Tell your grandchild that the evil She Who Saves drove his father from the village.

At least you have a grandchild to tell.

And where are my progeny? Where is my beautiful daughter Sky Dancer? Where is her child?

There was no mourning as Phoenix buried the sedated child in the deep shadows of the forest. Three of the People watched over her shoulder as she scraped a hole near the base of an ancient alligator juniper, using the shoulder bone of a mule deer, but none of them wept. Back in her wickiup, Phoenix knew that Sky Dancer cried out her heart in genuine grief; this child, the child of the brother she loved, would never be hers to hold, to teach, to sing to. Even if Phoenix managed to save it somehow, he would never be a part of her life.

Weep, my daughter, Phoenix thought as she laid the tiny bundle in the dirt and placed a basket over it. Weep for your lost child and your lost love. In your great love for them you have put them both away from you. Would that they knew the depth of your sacrifice! And now you send me away from you as well. Who is there to console you?

Gently Phoenix began to push the dirt back over the basket. Nakha-a will have to take care of you now, my daughter, she thought. Pray Mother Earth that Krista's medicine works, because Nakha-a is all that you have left. I wish I could stay to see him recover, to charge him with your care—but he will know. Nakha-a doesn't need to be told.

A foot planted itself firmly in the soft soil Phoenix had scraped into the grave. Nina tamped it down carefully, pointedly. "The evil is gone," she said. "Now my son will recover."

And he would, Phoenix knew. Then Nina would proclaim the rightness of what they had done and how her decision had saved Nakha-a for the People. But what would her son say to her? How would the gentle young man receive the news that his mother had urged the death of his sister's son?

"That," Phoenix said coldly, "is Coconino's grandchild."

"Coconino was not a god," Nina replied flatly. "He made mistakes. One of them was in getting a son on some Witch Woman. We did not need him; why did he come?"

What would you say, Phoenix wondered, if you knew that Witch Woman is the very one who has saved your own son's life? But she dared not say that, not until Krista was gone. So instead she said, "You didn't know about him, did you? You didn't know there was a third child of Coconino."

"The Mother Earth did not acknowledge him," Nina said

stubbornly. "Even my son did not know about him until he came here. She tried to protect us from his evil, from the evil he got on his half sister and the sickness he brought to my son."

"Ah, but you said the child caused Nakha-a's sickness, not Michael," Phoenix goaded. "You can't have it both ways. Which is it?"

"They are one evil," Nina sneered. She stomped meaningfully on the dirt, and Phoenix's heart thudded in fear that she would crush the child through the sturdy wicker basket.

"Perhaps there is another explanation," Phoenix said, rising and moving away from the grave to lure Nina as well. "Perhaps the Mother Earth did not tell you because she was protecting Michael from your fear, from your jealousy. What did you do, Nina, when you found out you were not the only mother of a son of Coconino? What did you do when you discovered that your son was not the only inheritor of Coconino's blood?"

"My son is the only true son of Coconino!" Nina shouted.

"Is that what Nakha-a said?" Phoenix challenged. "Did Nakha-a reject his brother?"

"Nakha-a believes evil of no one," Nina replied bitterly. "He would welcome the bear into our village if it were not for the alarm it caused the People."

"And so he welcomed Michael, and called him brother, and sought his company," Phoenix guessed. "Perhaps even his counsel. And where did that leave you? You who can no longer hear the voice of the Mother Earth!"

"I hear well enough!" Nina cried. "And she tells me now it is time for you to go."

Yes, Phoenix thought now, looking out over the faces of the northern People. It is time for me to go. There is a time when it is better to leave than to continue causing dissension.

"You who are of the People," she began. "Long ago I came to you from the Mountain. You were a happy people with good leaders, and you made me welcome among you. It was a good thing you did, and I have never forgotten. But when Coconino was taken from us, bad times came. The People wept, and our hearts have been sore for many years. Some of the People went to another place in search of healing; we chose to remain here."

Was it a mistake? she wondered for the thousandth time. At least Michael found us here, which he might not have done if we had all gone from the place where Karen Reichert knew we lived. And someday, someday Coconino will find the People here. He has to. He just has to.

"Through these years," she continued, "I have been as a cloud to you, shielding you from the burning wrath of the Others. But their wrath has cooled, and the cloud is no longer necessary. It is time for that cloud to be swept away by the wind. The bad times have gone from us; the good times are upon us once more. Let us rejoice and be happy, for we are the Children of the Mother Earth."

Smiles began to appear among the looks of concern. They needed joy in their lives, deserved it. It was something Phoenix knew she could never give them.

"Tomorrow I leave on a journey from which I will not return. Those of you who like may come with me, for I go to the Well, but there I will bid you farewell. The Mother Earth has called me to go down to her there, and I go gladly. As the seed must be buried for the young plant to grow, so must She Who Saves go down to the bosom of the Mother Earth so that the People can flourish. You are strong and healthy; let the harvest be bountiful."

There was a murmur of voices as she left the fire, but no one contradicted her, no one tried to stop her. *Of course not,* came the voice, sighing in the treetops in the canyon below. *I won't let them.*

I don't want to die! Phoenix protested. Can't you understand that? I don't want to die.

Be at peace, said the voice. *I will keep you.*

As you kept the infant with no name? Phoenix wanted to know. Asleep but not dead?

She had found Krista in Nakha-a's wickiup. "He's breathing much easier," Krista told her, "and his fever has come down. I think he'll make it."

"Good," Phoenix said shortly. "There's not much daylight left; you'll have to hurry if you want to reach the truck and find that old roadbed before dark." She picked up Krista's satchel of medical supplies and ducked out the door. Krista followed her.

"Witch Woman," came a gentle voice in the dusk.

The start showed on Krista's face. No doubt she had not been called that in twenty years. "Witch Woman," Sky Dancer called again from outside her wickiup.

Nina darted out of the cluster of people waiting near Nakha-a's wickiup. "Sky Dancer, you should not be up," she scolded, reaching out to her.

Sky Dancer struck her hard across the face. *"Don't touch me,"* she hissed. *"For as long as you live, I forbid you ever to touch me again."*

Nina drew back, pain written for only an instant across her lean face. Then the hardness came back into it, and she lifted her chin. *"Someday,"* she told Sky Dancer, *"you will see that I was right."*

But Sky Dancer ignored her, turning again to Krista. She took a few careful steps toward the blond woman, exhausted from her physical and emotional ordeal. Nakha-a's young wife, Tender Corn, slipped quietly into place beside her, sliding a supporting arm around Sky Dancer's waist, walking with her to where Krista and Phoenix stood. *"Witch Woman, I thank you,"* Sky Dancer said in her broken English. *"And I say, your son, he is good man. What they say here, no listen—he good. Best. This not his . . ."*

Phoenix did not stay to hear if her daughter found the right word to fill that blank, slipping away between the wickiups. No doubt Krista understood Sky Dancer's intent; the mother knew what kind of son she had. When, several minutes later, Sky Dancer and Tender Corn walked with the blond woman to the edge of the village, Phoenix was waiting. A knot of people followed the departing doctor, including Nina.

Phoenix looked at Nina one last time and knew an overwhelming sadness. *Where have you gone?* she pleaded silently with the woman who had once been her closest ally. *You were so quiet and unassuming, so gentle and full of wisdom. Where have you gone? If we had stayed together all these years instead of tearing the tribe apart, would this have happened to you? Is it because you were forced to lead on your own, and without the Voice of the Mother Earth, that you became so fearful and superstitious? You are like a bobcat that hears enemies in every rustling leaf.*

"Here," Phoenix said, handing Krista her pack. *"It looks like Nina's arranged an escort for you. I need to hang around here till dark. I'll try to catch up with you later. I'd like a ride north to the old highway, but if I miss you, have a safe journey."*

Nina did not understand the words, but she recognized the tone of leave-taking and the gesture of returning Krista's pack. *"You will go, too,"* she told Phoenix.

Phoenix balked. "I would like to stay with Sky Dancer until morning."

"You will go, too," Nina told her firmly. "I will care for Sky Dancer."

A worried looked passed between mother and daughter. "It's all right," Phoenix said quietly. "I will take the Witch Woman back to her Machine That Crawls, then, Nina, you will not need to send a guide."

"Cloud Kicker will go with you," Nina announced, seemingly determined to contradict everything Phoenix said. "I would not have two Witch Women tramping through the forest alone with night coming on."

Phoenix ground her teeth at the insult, but there was little she could do.

"Aren't you going back for the baby?" Krista asked softly as they started down the trail.

"They aren't giving me a choice," she replied.

"But—"

"It's my problem; I'll deal with it," Phoenix gritted.

After that Krista was silent.

By the time they reached the truck, the sun had slipped behind the western mountains and Krista was exhausted. Their silent escort stood watching solemnly as both women climbed into the vehicle. "I'll drive you out of sight," Krista said, "and drop you off. Do you think you can make it back up to the village in time?"

"No."

Krista stared dumbly at her companion.

"You want me to drive?" Phoenix asked. "You look done in."

"But—"

"It would be dawn before I made it back up there in the dark," Phoenix told her. "That's if I could do it without being caught, which I doubt. Nina is suspicious of me; she'll have her minions watching for my return, I'm sure."

Tears spilled down Krista's cheeks and glistened in the golden blaze of sunset. "Then the baby—"

"Is in the bottom of your medical pack," Phoenix told her. "I got him while Sky Dancer was keeping you and everyone else distracted. I suspected that when it was time for me to go, Nina would watch me like a hawk, so it was safer for you to carry him."

Krista trembled. "I told you I wouldn't—"

"I meant to catch up with you," Phoenix assured her, *"but I did what I had to do. I knew in the end you would, too. Now come on, Grandma. Move over and let me drive."*

Phoenix did not return immediately to her adobe house but stood instead on the path in front of it, gazing off to the south. It was here she had stood when Nina had first told her that there was a child of Coconino to be born to a woman of the Others. How that moment had changed the course of her life! Even with all the heartache raising a child had caused, Phoenix had never regretted her decision to bring that child into the community of the People.

How young we were then! she thought. I was just thirty-one, and Nina was—what? Seventeen? Eighteen? That's— She did the math quickly. Thirteen years. Thirteen years between us. Back then I was her provider, and she prophesied to the People that yes, Coconino would come again. I wish I could remember her that way. I wish I could remember that sweet young innocent, so blessed by the Mother Earth that all the hardships of this place she saw as mere inconveniences. She had Coconino's child, she had the voice of the Mother Earth—what more could she want?

But she didn't know when to let go, Phoenix realized. When the gift of prophecy turned out to be Nakha-a's and not that of the mother who carried him, Nina did not want to let it go. She wanted to hang on to that treasure, the feeling that all wisdom was given to her. She did not want to admit that it had only been lent her for a time, until Nakha-a could take command of it himself. And she did not want to let go of him. Even in that short time I spent in the southern village, I could see that she was hanging on to her grown son, trying to manipulate him, trying to keep for her own the gift the Mother Earth had only lent her. He was an extraordinary son, indeed, to keep her negative influence at bay without demeaning her in front of the People. No doubt his life is easier now that she is gone.

Suddenly tears smarted in Phoenix's eyes. It had still hurt, though—hurt even now—when word had filtered back through a chance encounter of trading parties from both north and south at the Camp of the Others that Nina had gone to the bosom of the Mother Earth. Did you find any comfort there? Phoenix wondered. Did she give you back the gift of knowledge she had taken from you? Did you see at last that it was time to let go?

As it is time for me to let go now.

But I can do it without dying! Mother Earth, I have seen what needs to be done. Let me go to the southern village and live with Sky Dancer. Those among them who knew me as She Who Saves have mostly gone to your bosom. I could live there without making ripples on the pond.

You told the People you go gladly, the voice chided her.

It is necessary for them to think so.

You told Coconino in your letter that you go gladly.

It is necessary for him to think so, too. When he comes again, it will be as a young man; he needs to get on with his life. Let him believe that I lived a full and happy life and came to your bosom with a grateful heart. That much of it is true.

If you only went to the south, the People would follow you there, the voice told her. *Michael would follow you. Do you want that?*

No.

Be at peace, child. Rest. Your service is ended. I will put no more heavy burdens upon you.

"She Who Saves."

The voice startled her from her reverie. She turned toward the speaker, hoping her tears would not show in the moonlight. "Yes, Gray Fox?"

The old man was the picture of sober dignity, his lined face framed by flowing gray hair. He wore a headband decorated with the Council emblems and a breechclout of woven yucca fibers. Phoenix tried to imagine Falling Star having grown to such an age. Would he have been as dignified as his father? Would his shoulders have grown as stooped, his eyes clouded with cataracts? Or would that sly sparkle have always been there, telling her that this was all just a mask, that he really did not take himself so seriously at all?

My *compadre*, will you be waiting for me on the other side? The other side . . .

Phoenix was sure she heard laughter. Or was it only the gurgling of the creek far below?

"Something is not clear to us," Gray Fox said carefully, "and so we have come to ask. When you have led us to the Well and have gone down into it, who will lead us back?"

Who, indeed? It was not a simple question of finding the way home, of course—any one of the hunters would show them that. They were asking who would now set the direction for the People and guide them on their Way. Phoenix looked over the cluster of faces at the old man's elbow, stretching back along the path toward the Elvira, the ceremonial fire. In her unabashed exercise of leadership here, she had groomed no one to succeed her. She hadn't known how; unlike the Mother or Two Moons, her predecessors, she was not a teacher. She had instructed young hunters, yes, but with no great measure of patience. Anyway, that was nothing like the kind of questioning and sharing required to prepare another for the role of leadership.

I never knew what I was doing in the first place, Phoenix thought. How could I teach someone else to do what I didn't know how to do? What I never felt I was doing well?

So who did that leave them now? It was not as though she hadn't thought about it. Flint might do it, but he was too easily swayed by the opinions of others. Corn Hair could do it best, but she was old and frail, and the strain would kill her. Besides, it should be no one from the old days, no one who remembered living in the Valley of the People. A new vision was needed for this new era in the life of the People.

There was only one person she knew of who met all the requirements. Someone who would be open and fair yet who had the courage of his own convictions. Someone who could do what was right no matter what it cost personally. Someone who could teach, as she had never been able to. Someone young and charismatic, to whom the People looked with respect.

"Who will lead you back?" she echoed. "One who knows the way. Michael will lead you."

Across the crowd she saw the young man's jaw drop in shock.

"Phoenix."

The voice outside her door rasped with controlled anger. No, it was not anger, she knew, although he masked it as such. It was terror. The young man outside her door was terrified.

"Come in, Michael," she called tiredly.

He ducked through the doorway and dropped to his knees on the ground before her. But there was no humility in that kneeling. As his father might have done, Michael assumed a stance of defiance, knees spread wide apart, hands resting on his thighs. Those thighs had grown more muscular in the past five years as he had filled out and as he had made his living tramping across the harsh high desert, but still it seemed to her that he was not as heavily muscled as Coconino had been. Or have I twisted that image all out of proportion? she wondered. Patiently she waited for him to speak.

"Don't do this to me," he said finally.

"To you?" Her eyebrow arched cynically. "Do you think all this has been orchestrated around you?"

"I think you're so busy thinking about yourself, you haven't considered what you've just done to me!" he snapped.

Phoenix smiled in spite of herself, a bitter smile. "Is that what you think? You think that I want out and you're the most convenient person to stick with the job? Well, I hate to disillusion you, Michael, but the sun does not rise and set on your well-being, or mine, either. I'm not doing this for either one of us. I'm doing it for the People."

"You're doing this to fulfill your dream!" he accused. "Your dream of Coconino coming back. You can't have him, so you're setting me up as a substitute. *Don't do it*, Phoenix. It's a mistake."

"It won't be the first one I've made," she replied. "But I haven't backed away from any of them before. Don't expect me to start on your account."

Even as she saw the conflicting emotions working behind his face, Phoenix wondered, Why do I say such things? Why do I keep trying to hurt the people I care most about? Why can't I speak to him gently, with understanding, and tell him that I know how frightened he is? Why can't I just tell him what I really feel—that I'm as scared as he is?

Anguish shone through his eyes and crept into his belligerent stance. That was like Coconino, like the haunted young hunter who had carried the pain of the Mother Earth in his very body when the Others had first touched down. "I am not my father!" Michael cried in despair.

The truth of it lanced through Phoenix. "No one is," she whispered.

Not even the nameless child she carried on her back as she struggled through the heat of the low desert and the rugged terrain of mountain passes. As she gazed into its tiny brown face, she had wondered: How much of Coconino is in you? Because your parents are both his children, did you inherit more of him than even they did? Will your nose have the same forceful cut, your voice the same timbre? Will the smoothness of your mother's features and the wide expanse of your father's brow give place to the strong lines and commanding visage that were Coconino's?

No, logic cried at her. This child is more white than red. But her heart said, This is where Coconino lives. The genes of the

People are dominant, and this child has more chance to inherit Coconino's genes than any other child could have. If only it will live to prove me right. If only I can keep it alive.

Krista had rigged a few bottles for her, filling them with a glucose solution and capping them with the fingers from a rubber glove. But the supply would last no more than two days; Phoenix had much farther to go than that. Following the riverbeds was her only hope of finding her way back, but many of them were dry now in the summer's heat. Phoenix prayed the rains would come soon and set those dry arroyos to rushing with precious water.

She traveled long into that first morning, until heat and fatigue dictated that she stop. The child slept blissfully, wrapped securely in its cotton burial blanket. Exhaustion drove Phoenix quickly into a deep sleep. It was late afternoon when the hungry cries of the child woke her again.

She fed it, then looked around for something to fill her own empty belly. Finding nothing close at hand that did not need to be cooked, she ate sparingly of her traveling food and pushed on. Through the night she traveled on, a bright moon lighting her path. When she stopped to feed the baby near dawn, a fat rabbit came out to sun itself and fell under her throwing club. When, late in the morning, she was forced to rest again, she took time to build a fire pit and left the rabbit roasting while she slept. By sundown she was on the trail again.

But the bottles of glucose ran out, and there was nothing but water to feed the hungry child. She found some late berries as she made her way through a mountain pass and crushed them for their juice, but that seemed to irritate the child's stomach, and it cried pitifully as she struggled on. By the fourth day she was desperate, and when she spotted hoof marks at the water's edge, a strange plan occurred to her.

With no few misgivings, she fastened the child's pack to a tree branch, far out of the reach of predatory animals. She could not do what she needed to save the child if she could not move stealthily through the rocky mountain reaches. The tracks led her far away from her river path, as she knew they would, to the high, jagged cliffs above.

On a cliff top a family of bighorn sheep had escaped the summer's heat and was munching calmly on the few blades of grass that survived on the stony ground. Phoenix studied the animals carefully, knowing it was late in the season for a ewe to be lactating, but it seemed the Mother Earth had smiled on her bizarre plan. Of the three ewes in this group, one's udders were more prominent, swollen with milk. Phoenix eyed the ram cautiously; he was an ugly fellow and quite capable of causing her serious harm. I could kill him, Phoenix thought—*just bring him down with an arrow.*

But that seemed such a waste, since there was no way to carry the meat. After so many years among the People, the thought of killing an animal and leaving it to rot offended her. She could kill the ewe, as well, for the lamb was surely old enough to be weaned, though it must have been born late and looked rather weak. However, death seemed poor repayment for the gift she sought from the ewe.

So carefully, patiently, Phoenix laid a snare. Making a loop of the thin yucca twine she always carried, she concealed it in the dust and ran its length behind a large stone outcropping. Then she gathered a pile of fist-sized rocks and dirt clods and sat down out of sight, the end of the rope in her hands.

With careful aim she tossed one rock into the brush on the far side of the sheep. The ram's head jerked up, and he tested the breeze, but smelling nothing, he went back to grazing. A few moments later Phoenix threw another rock; this time two of the ewes looked up as well. They seemed nervous now and started edging away from the sound, nearer to where Phoenix was concealed.

Phoenix waited even longer before throwing another missile. The ram was genuinely disturbed now. He left off eating and warily began to pick his way across the cliff top toward the waiting snare. *Mother Earth, help me,* Phoenix prayed. *If you won't do it for me, do it for Coconino's grandchild. Do it for the offspring of your favorite son.*

Slowly the sheep approached, the ram in the lead, the ewe with her lamb following. Phoenix closed her eyes and listened, heart pounding, for the tiny rustling sounds of their approach. She counted the clickings of the insects in the brush; she named the birds from their occasional cries. And she waited for the sheep.

They stopped, maddeningly, a few feet away from her snare. The ewe began to graze again; the ram studied the area carefully, tested the breeze, and caught a whiff of something. *No, please,* Phoenix begged, *don't run. Just walk slowly, just a little farther. Wander a little as you crop the high desert grass and do not—*

Suddenly a coyote sprang out of the scrub not far away. The ewes bolted and ran. The ram turned to face this enemy, pawing the ground and warning the coyote not to come too near. But behind the ram three other coyotes sprang up, and the ewes turned their headlong flight, swinging back toward Phoenix. Trapped between the rock outcropping, the single coyote, and the rest of his pack, they milled about momentarily, then broke and ran in the direction of least resistance.

It was the lamb the coyotes were after, of course, and they bounded quickly to cut off its escape. The panicked mother turned back to defend her child, but it was too late. The coyotes had it down. Even the ram backed off now. The ewe emitted one bleating sound of distress, then turned and—

—stepped directly into the snare. Phoenix yanked with all her might, catching the animal's right rear foot. Off its feet it came, and Phoenix knew she must act quickly or the ewe with its precious milk would be next on the coyote's menu. Rising up with her stone and dirt clods, she began to pelt the coyotes, shouting furiously at them. They were startled at this assault, hesitated, then grabbed their prey and dragged it off a hundred yards before setting once more to their grisly meal.

In a flash Phoenix was on top of the snared ewe. She suffered no small number of bruises and cuts as she wrestled to tie it securely. Then she went back behind the outcropping for her pack and the four glass bottles it contained. She filled only two of them, for she did not know how long the milk would keep in the summer heat, but she knew it would not be long. Then she released her unwilling wet nurse and watched it bound away after its comrades.

Returning to where she had left the child, Phoenix was relieved to find it safe in its elevated hiding place. The great owls that could have been a serious threat did not come out until nightfall, but a large hawk might have been as deadly. As she sat in the shade of the tree and gave the child its first nourishment in days, Phoenix reflected in stupefied amazement on the sequence of events that had secured the milk. *Mother Earth, you must love this child as much as I do,* she thought. *Only with your help could it have been done.*

The child drank greedily, collapsing the makeshift nipple with frustrating frequency, but eventually it had its fill and promptly fell asleep. Phoenix wedged the remaining container of milk into the shallow stream, where the running water would keep it reasonably cool, then curled up around the child and slept herself.

When she awoke, she fed the child once more, then started

back on her way. Regardless of the favor the Mother Earth had shown so far, Phoenix knew it was highly unlikely that she could find another bighorn ewe lactating this late in the season and even less likely that she could accomplish the absurd feat of snaring it again. But a statement had been made; though she had heard no voice, Phoenix felt sure that the Mother Earth had spoken her approval of the child by providing the milk. Mother Earth, do not withdraw your hand, Phoenix prayed. Act again. Open my eyes to the food you will provide.

Toward the end of the next day she found a beehive whose occupants were absent. The honey made a superb glucose solution, and after filling two of the empty bottles with sticky honeycomb and cramming her own mouth with the same, she set off again.

But she knew this supply would not last her for the entire trip back to the northern village. Furthermore, by not taking time to hunt or cook regularly, she herself was growing fatigued. Her ribs ached where the ewe had kicked her, and the moon was waning, forcing her to travel more in the day's heat.

This is my beloved's grandchild, she told herself as she trudged onward. I will bring him to the People, as I brought his unborn mother. Coconino's seed belongs to the People.

But what would happen when she got there? How would she explain having brought an infant back with her? Would Michael guess whose it was? Would others? And would their reaction be any different than Nina's had been?

In her house on the island cliffside, Phoenix looked now at Michael, his face so like Coconino's, and knew how impossible it would have been to keep him ignorant. The child, as it grew, would have borne the imprint of his grandfather as well, perhaps more so. Everyone would have known. And what would Michael have done? He suffered still for the love he had borne for his half sister and for the weakness of succumbing to incest. How much worse would it be if he knew there had been a child, knew how Sky Dancer had suffered for its birth?

Her own face softened as she looked across at him. "You don't have to be Coconino," she said more gently. "You only need to be Michael. Michael has a strong heart and a wise one. Michael has a love for the People that is greater than his love for himself. Michael represents a new generation, a new relationship to the Others. Michael is what the People need."

Her praise was more devastating to the young man than any blow could have been. He let his head drop forward, his shoulders sagging under the burden she had laid upon them. He lifted one arm and wiped it across his face, as though he could somehow wipe away the stamp of his father, a stamp more on his soul than on his visage. But he could be rid of neither one.

"All right, I'll do it, then," he said abruptly, lifting his head again. "But only if you stay. I'll take over the leadership, I'll accept the responsibility, but you stay! Just be here. Just—just don't do this thing! Don't do this."

Tears sprang unwanted to her eyes. "Michael, you still don't understand," she whispered. "It has to be this way. For the Mother Earth. For the People. For the Others. For you. And for me. I've waited so long for Coconino, and now—now if he came—" She could not say it. Now if he came, he'd still be twenty, and I'm an old woman, and if he rejected me for a younger bride, as he would have to, I couldn't stand it. I would rather be dead. "But Michael, in spite of all that, in spite of hearing the voice of the Mother Earth as clearly as I hear you now, *I don't want to do it!* I don't want to die. But you can't argue with her, Michael. The service she requires, you cannot shrug off; the life she wants, she will take."

For a moment Michael only stared at her in amazement and wonder as it finally came home to him that she truly did not want to give up her life. Then, suddenly, his arms were around her, clutching her fiercely, and Phoenix surprised herself by breaking down in tears. His arms were powerful, like Coconino's, and it felt so good just to be held and comforted. It was a long time since she had allowed anyone to comfort her. She had been too determined to be her own strength.

"I just wish I could do something," Michael gritted at last. "I feel so helpless, and I don't—I don't understand why this has to be. Once—" His voice caught. He stopped and started again. "Once, when I was fifteen, I was supposed to play in a racquets tournament. But my two uncles, Jonathan and Eric—they were my age, you know. My two uncles decided they'd have a better chance of winning if I didn't play. So they and a couple of their friends caught me down at the courts and—and they pinned me against a wall and took a stick and just—broke my right arm." His voice was ragged with the memory of that violence, that intentional maiming by his grandfather's two sons. "And I knew it was coming," he said hoarsely, "but I couldn't believe it— and I couldn't stop it. All I could do was live through it." He stroked her thick braids. "I feel that way now. I know I can't stop you, but—I don't know how I can stand by and watch. I don't know how I can do that.''

Phoenix was startled by the story; she had never heard it before. How must Dick McKay have felt when he learned his own sons had done malicious harm to his beloved grandson? ''What did you do to your uncles afterward?'' Phoenix wanted to know.

''The only thing I could do,'' Michael replied. ''I played in the tournament left-handed and beat the shit out of them.''

A laugh escaped Phoenix, just as Michael had intended that it should. It felt good to laugh, too. She had laughed so little in the past few months. ''I don't think I can beat the shit out of the Mother Earth,'' she said. ''In the end she'll have her way.'' As she had with belligerent humankind, forcing them out into space centuries before. As she had with the nameless child, the grandson of her favorite son. ''All I want is to live through it with a little grace and dignity. Help me do that, Michael. Help me live through it as I ought to, as a credit to the People and to Coconino, who made me one of them.''

Michael drew back and took her lined and narrow face in his hands. ''I can't help you do it,'' he told her sincerely, ''because I think it's wrong. But—'' He sighed. ''I won't interfere. And if the People are stupid enough to want to follow a nitwit novice like me, I will lead them back from the Well.''

''They will follow,'' she promised. ''Now go home to your Chosen Companion, say good night to your children, and pack your traveling gear. I want to leave early tomorrow; no point in keeping the People away from their work any longer than necessary.''

With a sigh he let go of her and turned toward the door.

''And Michael, what I said before about not going to the southern village—I meant it. Don't let any of the People go there. Let them trade with the Others but not with the southern village.''

''Why?'' he asked in curiosity.

Phoenix hesitated. ''I really can't say,'' she replied. ''Only there's no good to come from it. Promise me, Michael.''

Now it was his turn to hesitate. ''I don't think I can promise that,'' he said finally. ''But I will promise you this: I'll allow it only if the Mother Earth tells me I should.''

Perhaps he was jesting, for as yet he had not heard the Voice of the Mother Earth. But Phoenix took him at his word. ''That's good enough,'' she said.

CHAPTER FIFTEEN

Shanna trudged diligently behind her grandmother, gathering the uprooted weeds Marjean had loosened with her cultivator. The garden plot was not large, for those crops which might have taken up a fair portion of it—corn, potatoes, winter squash— were grown in greater quantities in the community fields. Even beans and turnips were grown in large plots maintained by one or two families for community use. The Johannesons' garden contained only those things which they preferred to pick and serve the same day, such as tomatoes, summer squash, and a few sweet peas. Half the garden was fallow at the moment—the radishes, lettuce, and spinach that had been there would not survive in this heat. When the summer rains had peaked, they would be planted again for a fall harvest.

Tana watched them from a hillock north of the farmyard. Marjean moved relentlessly on her knees, hacking, tugging, crawling on. Shanna stooped and plucked the weeds with gloved hands—everything here had stickers!—shook the dirt from their roots, then deposited them in the basket she carried. At the end of a row she would toss the contents of the basket out onto the unwatered desert ground, where the weeds would wither without being able to reroot themselves in the cultivated soil of the garden.

With a heavy sigh Tana turned and struggled up the hill, determined to travel a little farther while it was still early morning, before the heat of the day drove her back into Nathan's ingeniously but only moderately cooled house. Humidity increased as the rainy season—late this year, Nathan had told her— threatened to arrive any day. The evaporative principle that made the chimney system work did not function well in high humidity. The Crusoans responded to the sultry heat by rising before dawn and working until late morning, then sleeping through the hottest part of the day, to rise again in late afternoon and work until long after the fiery sun had set over the western mountains. It suited Tana; fighting the aftereffects of her seizure, she was always exhausted by midday.

It was two days since they had returned from the saguaro fruit harvest. It had not been a pleasant return for Tana; her emotions were in turmoil from her visit to Winthrop Hill, and coming back to the farm to find no sign of or word from Paul had sent her sliding into a deep depression. Afraid for her health, afraid for her husband, afraid for her future, she had retreated into the small bedroom provided for her and had indulged in the luxury of weeping herself to sleep. Too like Jacqueline, she thought, stranded here without her husband, not ever knowing what really happened to him. But I have no work to throw myself into as she did; there is nothing to keep me from brooding on my sorrows day after day after endless day . . .

When she had risen toward evening and joined Nathan's family at table, she knew she had suffered a setback in her recovery, but there was no help for that. In the cooler evening air she began her exercises again, both physical and mental. *Paul is fine, it's only P-TUP that is in trouble, and he will fix that. He will come for me, and I must get myself into better shape before he comes. I must not let him see me like this, it would hurt him to see me like this. So I will coax my reluctant joints into moving, stretch my wearied muscles gently, and think how grand it will be to see him again, to go home to* Terra Firma . . .

She had slept and risen and exercised and rested and watched the sky for any trace of a recorder, but none had come. Napping through the heat of the day, she had dreamed Paul walked into the room and then felt her heart twist when she woke enough to realize it wasn't true. When she had slipped back into light slumber, she had dreamed Coconino came to visit Nathan, but he was not the old man Nathan had described. He was young and haughty, with jet-black hair and smooth, coppery skin, and he demanded of Nathan why he harbored a woman of the Others, one who endangered the Earth. In her dream Nathan had defended her strongly to the young man, promising that Tana would not betray them, that Tana would protect their culture and their way of life, no matter what the cost. "Will she pay my cost?" Coconino had demanded. "Will she lose the one person she loves more than any other?"

Tana had awakened on the verge of tears again. Dear God,

don't let it be, she prayed. I want to help these people, I want to do what is right for them, but I don't want to give up Paul. I can't lose him, I can't, he's my strength, he's my other self . . .

Forcing herself out of bed, she had struggled to the limit of her returning strength to climb the rugged swell of ground that lay between the farmstead and the place where she had arrived via P-TUP. Spreading her traveling mat on the ground, she had stood upon it and waited, hoping— But of course nothing had happened. The sun sank behind the western mountains, and she knew she must return to the house before darkness made the short trip even more dangerous for her. There was nothing she could do from this end. She would have to wait for Paul to come for her.

Now she struggled once more to gain the hilltop that separated the farm from that place. She did not intend to go down to it again; there was no point in that. This morning she intended to use the small rise for her vantage point in looking over Camp Crusoe. For as long as it took Paul to find her—and he would find her if he had to go ahead and hire a ship to make the voyage—she needed to make her way in this place.

But how? What could she do to contribute in this society? How could she ever be more than an invalid here? They had no executives. There were no scholars or planners or other intelligentsia per se—everyone also did manual work. Even the doctor, the most highly educated citizen in the village, walked from place to place, carried her own bag, lifted patients, moved supplies. As people grew older and their strength began to wane, there were family members or apprentices to help them with the more difficult physical tasks. But young and old, everyone did physical labor.

There must be something, Tana thought as she plodded slowly up the hillock. There must be something that my frail body will not prevent me from doing. Who keeps track of the stored foodstuffs? Who signs out common equipment to those who need it? I could be a quartermaster of sorts. I could track all those administrative details no one likes to bother with.

But who bothers with them now? Would I be inventing a job where none is needed? Would I be taking away work that some other person—perhaps also with physical limitations—is already doing?

Cresting the hill, Tana turned and looked back down at sturdy Marjean laboring in the garden, her pint-sized helper sweating along beside her. I will never belong here, Tana realized. If something should happen—and it won't, it can't—but if a ship doesn't get here for years or even decades, I will always be an alien among them. Someone who thinks differently, someone who does not know their ways and their traditions. The tag of outsider will stay with me forever. Even old Doc Hanson, who has lived and worked in this village for over forty years, is still thought of as being ''from the Mountain.''

The irony struck her. She would be to the Crusoans as they themselves were to the People. ''Others,'' the primitives called them still. People from another place. People with a different way of thinking. People who did not understand the simplest truths . . .

But truth is so different from one culture to the next, even from one person to the next, Tana thought. For Coconino, needing to protect the Earth from invaders was truth. For Claire Ryan, to learn more, to venture forth, that was truth. Which was right? Or was there one truth that encompassed them both? Tana had always thought Clayton Winthrop's philosophy, etched in a monument on *Terra Firma*, ran deep in her: THERE IS ONLY ONE ROAD WORTH TRAVELING: THAT WHICH VENTURES FORTH. And yet the need to protect this place, these people, from her own aggressive society tugged at her . . .

Turning from the farmstead, Tana gazed down upon the point of her arrival in this world. It was an unimpressive piece of ground, hard-baked and bleached by the unforgiving sun, tufted with scraggly weeds, pernicious desert broom, and the various species of pervasive succulents. How odd, Tana thought, to call them succulents when they thrived in this arid climate, but of course it was their ability to store moisture in their pulpy pads and stalks that allowed the cacti to survive. Like the People— and the Crusoans, for that matter. It was their ability to draw and store sustenance from the reluctant land that allowed them to flourish.

That and the favor of the Mother Earth . . .

Tana laughed at herself and shook her head, turning to start back down the hill toward the garden. It was a picturesque manner of speaking, certainly, and it did reflect her own belief that there was something beyond human ingenuity that entered into the equation. But she knew very well that when the People spoke of the Mother Earth, it was not the planet Earth and its elements and compounds they meant. It was their ecosystem, their interdependence with creation, and service to the Mother Earth was not service to a lump of rock but rather . . . She pondered. A spirit of stewardship, of responsibility toward all the gifts one had been given. The gift of the land was one, surely, but there were others: the gift of family, the gift of friends, the gift of appreciation for beauty, the gift of creativity. When the People spoke of their love for and duty to the Mother Earth, it was a response to all these gifts they meant. Not to love a child was an offense to the Mother Earth; not to enjoy the sunset was a crime as well. Both were as much a taboo as wiping out a living species or poisoning the land.

Perhaps that was why she was drawn so strongly to their point of view. Though they expressed it differently, it reflected her own guiding ethic, one engendered by her religion and her up-bringing in the rural traditions of *Terra Firma*. Yet how could she reconcile it with Clayton's mandate to go forth, to go forward, to explore, to challenge . . . ?

Ah, well, she sighed as she approached the gardeners. It may be out of my hands now. If Paul has to send a ship for me, the word will be out. Maybe that's God's reprieve for me, His way of saving me as Coconino believes the Mother Earth saved him. I'm really too tired to struggle with the issue.

Marjean looked up as Tana stopped at the edge of the garden to watch them. "Looks like you're doing better today," Marjean called to her.

"A little," Tana replied, and hoped that was true. At the moment she felt exhausted, and she wanted to go back inside to get out of the broiling sun. She tugged the wide-brimmed hat from her head and fanned herself with it. Perhaps she would stop by the pump in the backyard and soak her neckerchief before going inside to pour a glass of tepid water to drink. Ah, for a chilled glass of water.

Thirsty? came the inquisitive thought, a touch so familiar on her mind that Tana did not think twice about it. Yes, thirsty. Nothing here seems to quench my thirst, though, not even the tea they brew. I miss cold drinks so much—

Come home! came the mind-voice again, fraught with excitement, so powerful that Tana jumped when she felt it.

"What is it?" Marjean asked anxiously.

But Tana had no more thought for Marjean and Shanna. "Doc!" she shrieked as she turned back toward the hillock with all the speed her clumsy body could manage. "Doc!"

An instant later the huge Dalmatian bounded into view, his thoughts an ecstatic jumble. *Down,* she warned instinctively, knowing that in his exuberance he could easily knock her off her feet. "Oh, Doc, am I glad to see you!" she cried as she knelt and threw her arms around his heavy neck. Doc twisted and squirmed, turning circles in her embrace, rubbing against her and threatening to tumble her into the prickly foliage. He yapped a happy yelp, licked her face unexpectedly, and then yelped again.

"Tana!"

The cry was breathless as a lean figure crested the hill at a dead run. In the blazing sunlight his white lab coat gleamed, an alien thing in this place, but even at this distance Tana knew it was not Paul.

"Todd!" she shouted back, and struggled back to her feet as the young man came flying down the hill that had taken her so long to traverse. "Todd, here!" Instinctively she began to take steps toward him, but before she had gone even two he was there. She flung her arms around his neck and felt the reckless pressure of his embrace nearly cutting off her breath. For a long moment they clung to each other, each desperately needing to know the other was real. Finally Tana released him, and even as she pulled gently away, she could feel his reluctance to let her go.

I know, Todd. You may think I don't, but I do.

"Where's Paul? Is he all right?" Tana demanded.

"Fine, he's back at the lab," Todd replied. "Worked himself to the point of exhaustion trying to get you back, but other than that he's fine. And you? Are you okay, Chief?"

"Reasonably," she hedged. "I did have a seizure, but I'm recuperating . . ." Her voice trailed off as she remembered Marjean and Shanna. Turning, she found them gaping at the strangers: Todd, with his half-shaved head and pronounced Oriental features; Doc, frisking and yapping, with his glistening white coat and shining black spots catching the sun.

"Marjean, this is a friend of mine, Todd," Tana tried to explain. "Paul sent him for me. Um . . ."

Marjean forced a smile. "Pleased to meet you," she said uncertainly.

"I'll be going now," Tana said, thinking that perhaps the best course was to say as little as possible. "I do want to thank you for taking such good care of me. You've been more than kind."

"Nonsense," Marjean scoffed, recovering enough to assert her opinion. "Only did what was decent, what anyone else in Camp Crusoe would have done. Don't think twice about it."

Todd's arms was still around Tana. "We need to get you back," he urged. "The boss is awfully worried. He's going to attempt a pickup every fifteen minutes until he's got us."

Again Tana turned to her hostess and the little girl whose round eyes kept moving from the man to the dog and back again. "I'm sorry to leave so abruptly," she apologized. "Tell Nathan good-bye for me and tell him . . . tell him . . ."

Marjean's smile was understanding. "He'll know."

"No, tell him I'll do everything I can," Tana insisted. "I don't know how much of it will be out of my hands now, but tell him I'll try. I'll try my best."

"I know you will," Marjean said softly.

"We need to go," Todd repeated. "Here, let me carry you." Without waiting for permission, he scooped her up and started back up the hill.

Her mind a turmoil, Tana let herself slump in Todd's amazingly strong arms. But when they were halfway up the hill, she twisted around and called back to Marjean one last time. "Tell him," she called, "that I'm not Coconino, but I'll do what I can."

The lab was crowded with people awaiting her return. They were familiar faces, but Tana did not think back to them until much later. She did notice Delhi standing near Chamber Five, and that registered as curious, but she could spare no thought for that now. The only person she wanted to see was the one who strode across the room from his workstation, lab coat streaming, boots clomping loudly on the hard flooring. Tana opened her mouth to speak, but no words would form; all she could do was cling to him and sob in relief.

"She's okay, boss," she heard Todd telling Paul. "She's had a seizure, but she's okay."

Paul said nothing. From long habit his embrace was gentle, but she could feel the desperation in it. After a moment he drew a ragged breath, then scooped her up in his arms and carried her to Chamber Three, which was a more or less conventional warp terminal. Doc slipped in beside them.

"Jaria," Paul said, his voice husky. "Send us home." Then there was the familiar stomach-quivering sensation of cross-dimensional travel, and the room full of faces was left far behind.

The old primitive was lean but not gaunt; like Three Feathers, his gray hair was long and braided, but he was not Three Feath-

ers. Tana knew who he was. *"I have come to plead for our world,"* Say-ayka-pee said.

"I told Nathan I would do what I could," Tana said.

"That was while you were here," the old primitive replied. *"Now you are far away, and you will forget us. We will be only one of many concerns to you."*

"No, that's not true!" she protested. *"You are of great concern to me, and I will not forget you."*

"Your children, your brother, you worry about them," he told her. *"Your company, your Dynasty, your church, they demand your attention. How will you care for them all? How will you manage to give them each a piece of yourself and have any left over for us?"*

"Because I must," she insisted. *"Because you have been given into my charge. Because I can't not care for you all and still be myself—"*

Tana struggled against the covers and woke herself, finding the sheets sticky with sweat. For a moment she imagined herself still in Nathan's house, but there was the comfortable touch of Doc's mind as he slept in his corner and the comfortable presence of Paul beside her, still sleeping a slumber of exhaustion. She was home, on Juno. She was back with her family, and her heart rejoiced.

For a long time she lay there dozing, alternately giving thanks for her return and reveling in the many familiar sensations of the place. Downstairs she could hear Bertha clattering in the kitchen, and the smell of roasting meat drifted up to her. From outside came the constant yapping of dogs and the occasional whinny of a horse. There were voices, too: hands calling out to each other, although she could not distinguish what they said. Down the hall Derbe was running one of his interminable nature studies, and Lystra was chastising him sourly: "Will you keep it down? You're going to wake Mother and Dad!"

Precious Lystra, Tana thought. I didn't expect her to cry when I came home, but why didn't I expect her to cry? I should have. I need to spend some time with her when I get up. We need to just talk and be together.

If we can stay civil, that is.

The air pressure in the house changed as the front door opened and heavy boots stomped in from outside. Dakota's voice rumbled, and Bertha's twanged in reply. Tana could just imagine the conversation: Are they still sleeping? Yes, and you keep your voice down. And use the bathroom on this end of the house—that old plumbing creaks like a rusty gate in a high wind.

I should get up, Tana thought. I should get up and go downstairs and talk to Dak, let Paul keep sleeping. He's in worse shape than I am, I think.

Then she drifted off to sleep again.

They ate and slept and made love and talked and slept again. It was just before daylight the next morning when Tana forced her reluctant body out of its cozy nest with any intention of staying up. With Doc padding quietly beside her, she made her way down to the living room to start her stretching exercises. Paul was still sleeping, as was the rest of the family, and Bertha was not due for another hour at least. Doc went to the door, paused slightly as the computer recognized him and slid open a panel, then went outside to check the grounds and relieve himself. Tana opened the drapes and looked out onto the darkened farmyard as she began her stretches, coaxing her muscles and joints into greater flexibility.

How different it was from Earth! And yet how similar. The ground cover in front of the house was kept green by an underground irrigation system, while the flora at Camp Crusoe waxed and waned with the rains and the runoff in the streams. Yet in both places it was real vegetation growing from the fertile soil, nurtured by natural sunlight. This ground cover was decorative, meant to be soothing to eye and spirit as well as providing a soft, fragrant place for the children to play. But to the south, just beyond a screen of cultivated trees, lay pastureland whose prairie grass was functional: it fed the horses, it kept the ground from eroding, it held precious moisture in the soil. Earth vegetation was like that, supplying harvest and habitat for innumerable creatures.

Like the Crusoans and the primitives . . .

What happens now? Tana wondered as she bent and reached for the toes of her left foot. The muscles in her back protested, relaxed, stretched out. What do I do with P-TUP? How do I break the news of my journey to the other Winthrops? Do I keep quiet? Do I stage a victory celebration?

Then she remembered Delhi. Paul had told her during one of their waking periods that Delhi had contrived to get the replacement part they needed to make P-TUP functional again. Delhi knew the whole story, more or less, so keeping it quiet was no longer an option. It was only a matter of how to control the news.

"Luke," Tana called softly, and a computer panel in the wall sprang to life. "What time is it on Argo?"

"Half past eight in the morning," the computer replied.

Delhi should be in by now. Tana knew she ought to check in, see what kind of fires had sprung up while she was absent. Still, she wanted to talk to Paul more about what had happened before she spoke to anyone else. "Luke: send a message to Delhi at the office, voice only. Record: Delhi, this is Tana. I'm feeling much better this morning; Paul is still sleeping, but I think we'll both be in around lunchtime. I'll want to confer with Gerta briefly, but then I need to meet with you. Let me know if you have time constraints; I'll work around your schedule. You're my first priority today. Luke: end record and send."

The computer panel faded back into darkness, and Tana continued her exercises. Doc wandered by the window, nose to the ground, thinking wistfully of Derbe, whose scent was here in the grass. Down the hall Tana heard Darian chime music as the computer woke Dak. He would have a couple hours of chores out of the way before returning to the house to tear into Bertha's monumental breakfast. The sky was beginning to lighten outside the window; Tana thought briefly of going out into the yard to watch the sunrise. That is what Say-ayka-pee would do, she thought.

Suddenly the computer panel returned to life. "Incoming message," it reported. "From Delhi Striker."

Tana's heart skipped as she wondered what was so urgent that it could not wait until she got in to work. Delhi rarely called Tana at home. Quieting her pulse, Tana rose and crossed to the computer panel, aware that she was still rather rumpled and without makeup, but if Delhi thought it important enough to call, she would not be giving any thought to Tana's appearance. "Luke: put the call through."

Almost instantly Delhi's image appeared on the panel; Tana had never bothered to install holographic capabilities in this room. "Yes, Delhi, what is it?"

Delhi glared back at her—or was that just a trick of the flat screen?—with cold and fiery eyes. "Your color looks better today," the older woman observed. "You were quite the mess when you came back from your little excursion."

The hair on the back of Tana's neck began to prickle. "I'm recovering nicely, thank you."

"Did Paul tell you what the delay was?" Delhi asked curtly.

Tana took a careful breath and exhaled slowly before answering. "Yes. I understand you are the one who procured the needed part. Thank you."

Delhi's face was dark was disapproval. "You don't know what I had to trade for it."

Again Tana focused on her breathing, forcing her tightening muscles to relax. "Come to the point, Delhi," she said quietly.

"I've sold P-TUP."

Tana's heart lurched against her rib cage. "You've done *what*?!"

Outside Doc began to bark furiously as her rage flooded over him; he charged back to the house, banging his head against a door panel that was slow in responding to his presence. He continued to bark furiously until it recognized him and slid out of the way. Upstairs she heard Paul's feet hit the floor; down the hallway Dak's door flew open.

Calm yourself! her mental training commanded, and Tana turned her back on Delhi's image while she expanded her lungs, drew in a great draught of air, then expelled the breath with a great rush. I am in control, she told herself, filling her lungs again, willing her heart to slow its pounding. I am in control, and this woman will *not* rob me of it! Rage is nonproductive. Cool reasoning is the answer, and careful speech.

This time she exhaled more slowly. Turning, she faced Delhi again. "You don't have the authority," she replied calmly.

"You know that," Delhi told her, "and I know that, but Wolfgang Montag doesn't, and he's going to be furious when he finds out. So you'd better be prepared to back me up or have the institute face charges of poor-faith bargaining."

She thinks she has something over me, Tana realized suddenly. Somehow, she thinks she's gotten control of the institute away from me. What is it? Has she talked to Zim? Not likely, or I'd be having this conversation with him and not Delhi. Has she gone to the board with accusations of some sort? Not formally; there hasn't been time for her to do that. But evidently she is prepared to do one or the other of those things, and she is confident that she cannot lose.

Oh, no, Delhi. Over the years we have tussled, you and I, but you have never come up against me in a real battle. You won't win.

Doc had stopped his barking when Tana had turned back to face Delhi. Now Tana could hear Paul on the stairs, and she was aware of Dak in the room behind her, poised, ready to intervene. She laughed softly. "This precludes, of course, your being fired on the spot for inappropriate business dealings," she said with a smile.

"You won't do that," Delhi said flatly.

"You're right, I won't," Tana agreed. "I'll fight Montag and the whole Transportation Guild on your behalf before I'll sacrifice someone of your caliber. There is undoubtedly another way out of this. We'll talk about it when I get in."

But Delhi was not through. "One more thing," she said. "I'm calling a meeting of the board of directors for a week from Thursday. I find your conduct in traveling to Earth unconscionable. You are the CEO and too valuable a person to risk in this manner. I am charging that your reckless use of insufficiently tested equipment for purely personal reasons is grounds for dismissal."

Behind her she could sense the two men holding their breath, but Tana only smiled at her self-declared adversary. "A week from Thursday? That's just in time for Roundup, isn't it? Excellent planning. We could have the meeting here at *Terra Firma* and get everyone in person for a change. What a lovely idea, Delhi! I'll make arrangements here for a meeting room—you will come in the flesh, won't you? I haven't looked at the guest list, but I'm assuming Sasarmi and his family are going to be here." Tana beamed as Delhi's face grew flushed with ill-concealed anger. "Well, those are details we can iron out later. I'll be in in a couple of hours—Junoan hours, that is. See you then." With a wave of her hand she broke the connection.

For a moment Tana stood quietly, staring at the blank panel, her thoughts racing. Delhi had undoubtedly gotten to several of the directors already, or she wouldn't be so sure of herself. Which ones? She'd have to find out, assess the damage. And Montag! What kind of legal battle would there be now that he believed he had purchased the rights to P-TUP?

Tana turned quickly, too quickly for her infected joints. She lost her balance and saw both Dak and Paul leap for her, but she recovered herself and held up a hand to keep them back. Both knew enough not to persist when she had decided she needed no help.

"Paul," Tana said decisively, "file the patents on P-TUP. There's no point in stalling any longer."

Paul did not hesitate. "Luke: patch me through to Jezebel," he instructed the computer. "Jezebel: open File 573, code

Lambda Beta Three Omicron. Enact filing sequence specified.''
Then he crossed to the panel and keyed in his personal code.

"I see you were prepared," Tana commented dryly. "Dak,
when you go down to the stable, would you ask one of the hands
to saddle Sugarfoot for me. I think a horseback ride will do me
worlds of good.'' She patted Doc, who continued to hover nervously at her side. "Paul, will you join me?"

"Sure." He came to her then and touched her gently, as
though asking permission. Gratefully she slipped into his arms,
glad for this fountain of strength she had had to do without for
too long.

Dak took a deep breath and blew it out, running a hand through
his uncombed hair. As always, he could not fathom why his sister
persisted in this cutthroat game of corporate politics. He had
hoped that, having achieved her goal in reaching Earth, she would
give it up, but not in the face of Delhi's challenge. Tana had never
backed down from a challenge in her life, and she was not likely
to start now. With a sigh he turned back toward his bedroom.
"Welcome home," he commented wryly.

Doc eyed the sturdy desert stallion in the far corner of the
corral, then turned wistful eyes to Tana. *Play?* he inquired hopefully.

No, Tana told him. *Stay with me.* "Well, Dak, is your stallion
doing his job?" she asked her brother, turning from the railing
to where Dak had opened a utility panel in the side of the stable
and was keying switches to activate feeding and watering systems for the stabled horses, kennel cleaning and rotating exercise run systems for the dogs, and power charging of the
equipment he anticipated they would need this day. He could
have done it all from the computer in his office, of course, but
like Uncle Paris he never set the day's program until he had
personally inspected each of the animal enclosures to know that
conditions there were what they ought to be. Every now and
then a surprise litter of puppies or a horse gone lame required
an adjustment.

"He's doing his job magnificently," Dak replied with a wide
grin. "Three mares pregnant, and tissue samples from the foals
promise some very interesting results. I don't know." He
scratched his clean-shaven chin. "I keep toying with the idea of
doing an *in vitro* fertilization and making the coat a little shorter,
but I'm afraid we'll go too far in that direction. I think I'll just

wait for these foals, breed them back into the existing stock, and see how those animals do in desert conditions.''

What patience it took, Tana thought, to wait for nature to produce the horse he wanted. But Dak never seemed to be in a hurry for anything. Like the People.

"Dak," Tana said suddenly, "do you remember we talked about the *Celux nobilis*? You told me the progenitors of that species could fly. Could you make a crossbreed that would fly again?''

Dak's eyebrows shot up. "I don't know. I'd have to study it awhile.'' She could see the quick mind working behind his handsome face. "They're an awfully bulky animal as they exist now; we'd have to slim them down, as well as enlarging and strengthening the wings. I wouldn't attempt it on my own, but Sihrmon could probably handle it. DNA is DNA, whether in horses or dogs or *Celux nobilis*.'' He shot her an inquiring glance. "Are you serious about this?''

Tana sighed. "I don't know. Probably not. Let me think about it.'' With all she was taking away from the People, she had wanted somehow to give something back.

Just then Paul came out of the riding stable with their two mounts, followed closely by a short ranch hand with two more saddled horses. "Are you joining us?'' Tana asked her brother.

"No, Mouse and I are going to ride out to look in on the pintos,'' Dak responded. "I've got five or six foals I want to check on, and there's a report of pirrarah moving south from the river. We'll plant a few sonic sticks to discourage them from bothering the livestock.'' The carnivorous pirrarah was possessed of wicked talons, a razor-sharp beak, and a particularly nasty disposition. It could tear apart a full-grown dog in minutes and only stutter over a half-grown horse.

Paul was chatting amiably with the ranch hand as they approached. She appeared to be scarcely older than Lystra, although more solidly built; probably an Omniversity student, Tana realized, on intersession.

" 'Mouse'?'' she asked Paul as the girl rode away with Dak.

"Andy's niece,'' Paul replied. He grinned. "Looks a little like Bertha, doesn't she?''

"Except there isn't as much of her,'' Tana commented. "Do people really call her Mouse? To her face?''

Paul shrugged. "From what I can tell, she prefers it. But you can ask her yourself. She's a very forthright person.''

"Being Bertha's granddaughter, I have no doubt of it.'' Tana sighed. "Unfortunately, I haven't the time to delve into the psyches of Dak's seasonal help. Let me ask you a question." She lifted herself carefully into the saddle, feeling the strain in elbows, knees, and hips, and grunted with satisfaction when she succeeded on the first try. "If P-TUP were in the hands of the Transportation Guild, is there any physical way to keep it from functioning? Is there any way to block it, to shield against it?"

Paul hesitated before swinging easily into his saddle. Even then he sat for a moment, brow wrinkled in concentration, holding his eager mount in check. "You might be able to shield a specific area," he admitted. "Using warp crystals in a disruptive pattern. You could certainly prevent someone from being picked up that way by confusing the grab coordinates. But not on a planetary scale, if that's what you're getting at." He clucked to his horse, and the two of them headed southeast with Doc ranging happily ahead.

"I don't think there's any hope of keeping Earth's habitable condition a secret," she told him. "If Delhi's taking it to the board of directors, it will spill out and be on the news indexes in a matter of days. So the first thing I have to do is get Earth declared a protected area." She frowned. "They aren't prepared for the invasion of advanced technology, and we have to give them time to adjust. There's no central government to represent them, and by the time the Pax Circumfra solicited a delegation . . . No, it has to be something we do for them. Maybe as a . . . a living anthropological site or . . . a museum. That's it. I'll call Wyoming at the Omniversity; maybe they'll petition to have it declared a historical site, for research only."

"That would make it illegal to tamper with Earth," Paul pointed out, "but not impossible."

"It's a start." Her brow furrowed as she continued to ponder. "Maybe we could ring the Earth with satellites which would at least detect the arrival of any spacecraft. That would deter interference by people using vessel-housed warp to reach the Earth."

"Costly," Paul commented. "I don't know if the Omniversity would go for that. And then there's still P-TUP. Although . . ." His voice trailed off. "You know, you might . . ."

"What?" Tana prompted.

Paul took an audible breath, hesitated, then spoke. "You might be able to use satellites to detect if P-TUP had been used," he ventured. "I've never given that aspect much thought, but the warp field undoubtedly creates some kind of disturbance which could be monitored. Provided you could filter out all the noise: use of other kinds of warp terminals, industrial usage of the crystals, variations in patterns, etc. Much easier on Earth, of course, than on other planets—less noise. All the same, it might take years to invent a reliable detector.''

Tana thought of the fourteen years they had spent developing P-TUP. Would it take any less time to protect against it? ''I haven't got years,'' she sighed. ''I've got days. Once the board meets and the word is out— Even if I can get out of the sale to Montag, I'll have to sell P-TUP to someone or the board will remove me and install a CEO who will. Even if I could convince the board to keep quiet about my trip to Earth, there are leaks— there are so many leaks! You know the Dillon story. Once news of a plague-free Earth is out, some enterprising Terraphile, or art collector, or simple merchandiser is going to try exploiting the Earth for personal profit. I have to make that illegal at the very least, and preferably unprofitable. But I need time to do that, time I don't have. Look how long it has taken me to get the minimal legislation that now exists to protect the Inhabited Worlds.'' Tana gnawed at her lip in frustration, and Doc stopped his explorations to look back at her with an inquiring bark.

''Tana.'' Paul's voice was gentle but firm. ''Maybe you'd better let this one rest for a while. I know you're concerned about protecting the Earth, but maybe you should concentrate on protecting your job first. You can be much more effective in controlling the use of P-TUP with the power and resources of the institute behind you.''

The image of the old primitive in her dream rose up to haunt her. ''But if I rest, who'll save the Earth?'' she demanded.

''Save the Earth?'' Paul cocked one eyebrow. ''That's rather grandiose, isn't it?'' he chided.

Grandiose, yes, and presumptuous—Jull would make it into a theological dickering point. But she only meant who would intervene to stop the invasion of Earth by returning humans—

Suddenly, Tana's eyes went vacant and her jaw slacked.

Paul watched her curiously. Usually she was the one chiding him about ''going away'' mentally while they were together, always involved in his work. But it was plain from Tana's expression that she had been struck by an idea that totally consumed her thoughts. Her horse plodded along calmly and her body swayed instinctively with its rhythm, but Tana's mind was not on the ride. ''What?'' he prompted finally.

"If we really want to save the Earth," she said slowly, "maybe we should turn to someone with experience."

"Experience?" Paul reigned in his horse. Tana was never shy about going after experts in a given field, seeking knowledge and information from the minds of those who used it regularly. It was one of the things that made her a good CEO. But an expert in saving planets? "Who?" he asked.

Tana reigned in, too. "Paul, I have to go back to Earth," she said flatly.

At that he stiffened. "Over my dead body!" he protested. "I won't put you at risk again!"

Tana knew how he felt—she could still feel the desperation in his embrace when he'd finally gotten her back. But this was too important; she couldn't back away from it. "I'll take Doc with me this time," she promised. "I'll take Todd, too, if that will make you feel any better. But I have to go back and find him."

"Find him?" It made no sense to Paul, but then, he didn't care about the sense of it. He only cared that she wanted to go back there, back to that place where he'd almost lost her. It was insane; it was unthinkable. Go back there? Why? What could justify his ever letting her make the trip again? To find someone? "Find who?" he demanded.

But she had that look in her eye, that crusading look she had. It was the one that had sold him on the P-TUP project the instant she had proposed it. "The old Earth Saver," she replied. "Think about it. He did it once before; now if we're going to do it again—I have to go back there, Paul. I have to find Coconino."

CHAPTER SIXTEEN

Coconino sat in the shade in front of his house on the west canyon wall. He was carefully fletching a new set of arrows with the pinion feathers of a brown hawk. His son-in-law had brought down the hawk for him; Coconino no longer tried for birds in flight. For deer and javelina and bighorn he could still outhunt any other man in the village, mostly because he was so crafty in sneaking up on them, but his eye was no longer as keen as it needed to be for smaller, quicker game. When they flushed a hare or a quail, Coconino always smiled and let the younger men shoot, preferring to rest on his laurels rather than make a fool of himself.

Still, he had managed somehow to lose three good arrows so far this summer, which was why he was making this new set. Six was the proper number to carry in one's quiver: as many as the fingers of one hand, plus one more to signify bounty. That was *moh-ohnak*.

He was just finishing the last arrow when he heard the excited voices of children scurrying down the path from the western rim. They had been out with their clubs and snares, boys and girls alike, trying for hares in the meadow near the forest. He smiled at their exuberant clamor, glad that he was through with his work, for they would undoubtedly want to tell him of their success or lack of same. "Grandfather! Grandfather!" they called, though only four of them were his own grandchildren. "Grandfather, come and see!"

Coconino rose slowly, wincing only a little from the pain in his knees. Years of running had taken their toll, but that was all right. He could still walk wherever he wanted to go; he was in less of a hurry these days. And he could still sling a mule deer carcass over his shoulders and carry it into the village. Well, perhaps he could not carry it from the canyon floor up to the island butte houses, but that was what a good travois was for.

"Grandfather, Grandfather!" the children shouted as they drew near him. "Grandfather, come and see; there is a Witch Woman coming to our village, and she is asking for you!"

Blood roared in his ears, and for a moment his vision darkened. His mind was filled with the image of long ebony hair, of an oval face with high cheekbones and dark flashing eyes. A Witch Woman! Ah, Phoenix, my love, my *moh-ohyanta*, the companion of my soul—

But reason returned, and his vision cleared; it could not be Phoenix. Phoenix had gone to the bosom of the Mother Earth, and her death was recorded in the stories of the People. This must be some other Witch Woman, perhaps one of the Others, rather than one from the Mountain. It might even be some daughter of Nay-than, his spirit son. "A Witch Woman!" he called back to the children. "*Aiie*, this is a good day, then. Let me come with you and see this Witch Woman who comes in search of Coconino."

Together they climbed the steep path back to the canyon rim. The youngest one, six-year-old Jumps in the Leaves, was only just starting down; Coconino scooped him up and carried him under one arm the last few steps. Then, as he saw the figure approaching in the distance, he put the boy down. The hair on the back of his neck prickled just slightly, and he gestured to one of the older boys. "Laughing Tortoise, take the other children back into the village. Tell Fire Keeper to light the Elvira and bid my Council await me there. This is a Witch Woman indeed."

There was a slight hesitation from the children, who wanted to be in on the excitement, but although Coconino could be a great tease, they knew from his tone that this was not a time to test his resolve or his patience. Quietly they turned and started back down the trail, wondering what Coconino saw in this Witch Woman that prompted him to call upon the strength of the Elvira, the ceremonial fire.

Slowly Coconino walked out to meet the Witch Woman. She was slightly built, although taller than most women of the People. Her hair was a soft golden color, like the tassels of ripe corn, and strangely arranged; one side bristled like a roadrunner's crest, the other side was gathered in a flowing tail. Her clothes did not distinguish her from any other woman of the Others he had met, but she walked slowly and with great dignity.

At her side padded an animal the likes of which Coconino had never seen before. It was the size and general configuration of a coyote, but its ears flopped over rather than standing up, and it had the most remarkable coat. Glistening white, it was speckled thickly with jet-black spots. This strange kachina was also bulkier than a coyote, and it wore a strip of leather around its neck. This, Coconino decided, was how the woman put her mark upon it, as a woman of the People might mark a pot she had molded or a basket she had woven with a special design. He did not doubt for a moment that the beast was hers, and its obedience a thing of her creation.

A feeling of resignation washed over Coconino. For forty summers he had dreaded this day. Now that it had come, he discovered he did not fear it. It was like standing on the bank of the creek after a summer storm; the violence of thunder and rain were gone, and there was only the dark swirling water carrying out its inexorable mission of creation and destruction. He advanced to within a few paces of the Witch Woman. "Welcome," he said in the tongue of the Others. "I have been expecting you."

Tana gazed up into the face of the sturdy primitive. He was not at all what she had pictured. Though his face was lined and his eyebrows graying, there was no sense of frailty or even the ancientness she had imagined. Instead, the deep lines seemed to enhance the rugged character of his face, adding drama and strength. His stone-gray hair fell thick and loose to his shoulders, bound by a muslin headband embroidered in black and red. His loincloth was also muslin, and around his neck hung a talisman of silver and turquoise.

He was only about Paul's height, she guessed, which was short of six feet, but his regal bearing made him seem much taller. Combined with broader shoulders and muscular limbs, it gave the impression of latent power that Tana associated with Uncle Paris. In his solemn countenance there was no trace of anger or hostility—or of compromise. Her heart raced at the sight of him. She did not have to ask who he was.

"You are Coconino," she said.

"I am." His eyes were dark and steady.

"You are called by your people the Earth Saver."

He gave a sober nod. "The Mother Earth once chose me to serve her in that way."

His voice was deep and richly accented, sending a quiver through the pit of Tana's stomach. "She chose wisely."

To that Coconino did not reply.

"I am Tana Winthrop," Tana went on. "I come from . . . a great distance."

"You come from the stars," he said.

Tana drew a deep breath. Nathan had exaggerated neither the magnificence nor the perceptiveness of this man. "Yes, I come from the stars," she agreed. "I came to learn what had happened to my ancestors, the ones who came in a Sky Ship many generations ago. I learned—" Tana hesitated. What had she learned? "I learned," she said finally, "that they should not have come."

Sadness tinged the magnificent countenance of Coconino. "That is true," he said softly. "But they did come. And so have you."

Tana drew an arm across her forehead to clear away the sweat that had beaded there. Even in this northern, more temperate climate, the heat was powerful. A breeze slipped along the cleft of the canyon and eddied around them, cooling her face, swirling Coconino's hair. "So have I," she echoed. "That, too, was a mistake, one I would like to undo. But I don't know how. That is why I have come to you, Coconino. I have come to seek the wisdom of the Earth Saver."

At that Coconino stiffened and turned away. Voices drifted up from the canyon, voices of children shouting the news as they scurried across the canyon floor, splashed through the shallow stream, and climbed the steep slope to the island butte. They were innocent, these children, innocent of the threat to their world, innocent of the violence that had been done once before to preserve it. A litany ran through Coconino's mind, a chanting of names from one of the Stories of the People: *And there by the water did She Who Saves find them, brave men of the People struck down by the fireshooters. Juan, the friend of Coconino; Falling Star, his brother-in-law; Always Hungry and Runs Like a Fox; and youngest among them, Broken Arrow, who had not yet courted a wife.*

Because of me, Coconino thought. Because I angered the Others, my friends died young. I did not think it young then; I thought it would be my last day, as well. But I have lived to see three times the twenty summers I had seen then, and I know how young we were. I know how costly it was to the People to stop the Others from coming. My friends were cut down, our valley home lost, and eventually the People divided. And it cost me Phoenix, a woman of greater strength and courage than even

I knew. Perhaps it cost her most of all, for she carried the burden of their safety, Phoenix who walked in both worlds and could belong to neither.

He turned back to the golden-haired Witch Woman, whose strength, he suspected, was also far greater than it appeared. "If you have come for wisdom," he told her, "I fear you must go away empty-handed. I have none to give."

Then he turned and started slowly back toward the canyon rim.

Tana's heart crashed against her ribs, and Doc gave a sharp warning bark. "Wait!" she cried.

Coconino stopped, more startled by the noise from the dog than by the tone of her voice.

"Please," Tana pleaded. "I've come so far; please don't walk away. Talk to me, at least. Listen to my story and tell me yours. Tell me what you did the first time and why. Perhaps in what you say there will be some kernel of truth that will help me know what to do now."

Coconino eyed her carefully, eyed the beast beside her. "My son Nakha-a was a wiser man than I," he said. "The People of the southern village love to quote his proverbs. One of them says, No one grows poorer by listening to what another person has to say. I will trade stories with you, Tah-nah-win-trup." A smile stole across his lips. "I am a very good storyteller."

He led her down the steep path to his adobe house, steadying her with a strong hand on her arm when it seemed she might lose her balance. "I'm not very strong," she apologized.

"Your knees hurt you as well," he commented.

"Yes," she admitted.

He grunted. "Mine, too."

At last they stood in the shade on the narrow ledge before his house. Tana clung to the mud wall of the cavelike structure and tried not to think about the drop, which was less than a yard away. Doc peered over the edge. *Trees,* he told her, testing the breeze. *Water. Thirsty. Drink?*

"My dog is thirsty," Tana said to her host. "Could he have a drink of water?"

Coconino saw that she was fearful of the height but did not speak of it. It pleased him that her only request was not for herself but for the animal with her. "Come into my house," he said. "We will all have water."

The house was one of four clustered wall to wall in this pocket in the limestone cliff. Tana had thought she heard sounds from another of the dwellings; now, inside, she could hear a soft female voice and the irritable fussing of a child. As she lowered herself gingerly onto the mat Coconino indicated, she wondered how many families lived in the baked mud chambers here and across the way, in the other groups of similar dwellings she had seen.

Coconino set a bowl of water before Doc; the dog sniffed it cautiously, then began to lap it up noisily. *Good,* was his only comment. As Tana took the bowl she was offered, she realized she had not brought any pills with her to counteract the bacteria in the water, but there was nothing else to drink in this place, and it would have been extremely rude to refuse Coconino's hospitality. So she smiled and sipped at the cool liquid, promising herself she would take one of the pills as soon as she got home.

Coconino then poured water for himself, but before joining her, he crossed to the door and called out to someone, presumably next door. There was a reply and a brief conversation; then he crawled to a mat near Tana's and sat down. "That is my daughter-in-law, Two Hands," he told her. "She will bring us something to eat." He drank briefly from his bowl, then set it down. "How did you come to this place?" he asked. "In another Sky Ship?"

"No," Tana told him. "I came . . ." Good grief, how do I explain warp travel to him? she wondered.

"In a Magic Place That Bends Space?" he asked.

Tana's eyebrows flew up. "Yes," she agreed. "Yes, that is how I came."

Coconino nodded gravely. "That is how I came to this place as well."

Tana was confused until she remembered the time warp that had brought Coconino and Derek Lujan to this century from another. "You came by accident," she replied. "I came intentionally. But now I would like to keep others from coming the same way."

To that Coconino only shook his head. "They will come," he said sadly. "No matter what you do, they will come. Even if you should destroy this Magic Place and every one like it, they would still come. I tried once to keep them out; it cannot be done."

"But you succeeded," she protested. "You succeeded for two centuries."

Coconino did not understand the word century, but he understood her intent. "Phoenix told me it could not be done," he said. "And yet she stood by my side as I destroyed the Sky Ship, risked her life with mine because—because she, too, was a child of the Mother Earth, and we did what we had to do. Only . . ."

"Only what?" Tana prompted.

He gave a great sigh. "Only now I do not think it was the right thing."

Tana nearly dropped the small bowl in her hand. "What do you mean?"

Coconino stretched his arms, and Doc lifted his head at the movement, watching this strange man carefully. Coconino saw it and continued his stretch more slowly, his muscles flexing subtly beneath his copper skin. Then he returned his attention to Tana. "When the Others first came," he told her, "I felt the pain of their presence, felt the violation of the Mother Earth within my own body. I thought that to die would be better than to live with this pain. Then, when the Magic Place That Bends Time cast me up here, the pain was gone, and I thought I had won. Even when I learned what had happened to me and all that I had lost, I thought I had won something because I could no longer feel the pain of the Mother Earth.

"But the Others were not gone," he pointed out. "Lujan was not gone. And in the years that followed I learned that there are many kinds of pain. The pain of being thought a god when I am too much a man. The pain of losing my firstborn child. The pain of . . . of watching a child make a mistake and knowing I cannot stop him, for the knowledge will not be his until he learns it himself."

Tana was moved by the depth of truth in his observations, particularly the last one. *How well I know that pain!* Tana thought.

Then Coconino grinned unexpectedly. "The pain of knowing the arrogant young fool in the stories of the southern village is really me." He leaned forward in the filtered light of the chamber's interior. "You wanted to hear my story, Witch Woman. Let me tell you a good one.

"Once, when Coconino was a boy and the bow of his manhood ceremony was still green wood curing by the fire, his mother sent him out to collect sotol for supper. Now, Coconino was a very proud boy and thought that task beneath him. To make matters worse, he saw his friends Juan and Digging Squirrel setting out to snare rabbits. 'Oh, that is a pastime for children,' said Coconino, who wanted his friends to feel as unhappy as he did. 'Are you men or boys? Why don't you take your throwing sticks after rabbits?' He said this because he was better with a throwing stick than his friends, and he wanted to show them up.

"But the other boys knew what he was up to. 'Why don't you take a throwing stick and come with us,' they said. 'We can get more rabbits with our snares than you can with your throwing stick.' That pricked the pride of Coconino; he threw down the basket, which was half full of sotol stalks, and ran back to his wickiup for his throwing stick. There his mother stopped him. 'Where are you going?' she asked. 'To hunt rabbits,' he replied. 'And what of the sotol I asked you to gather?' she asked.

"Coconino stamped his foot. 'That is for children,' he sneered. 'If it is such a simple task,' she replied, 'do it before you go hunting.' 'I will!' cried Coconino. 'I will bring you a full basket of sotol *and* a rabbit for supper.'

"Now Coconino had a task before him, indeed. To make things worse, he could not find the basket he had dropped. By the time he found it, a herd of javelina had been there; they had eaten the sotol and chewed on the basket as well. So Coconino left the basket and went to find his friends. They already had a fine fat rabbit, and when Coconino took up his club to stalk his prey, it began to rain. No rabbits would come out in the rain, so Coconino had to return to the village with no rabbit and no basket of sotol. There would be empty bellies in his wickiup, he knew, for he had promised to bring the food for supper and had not done so.

"But as he came to his mother's wickiup in the rain, Coconino smelled the smell of good food cooking. There he found that his mother had a whole pot of sotol steaming near the fire, and a fat quail roasting. 'What is this?' he asked.

" 'You said gathering food was for children,' his mother replied, 'and so I sent your sister to see what she could find. She brought me a whole basket of sotol, and she managed to snare a quail as well. See what a fine hunter she is, who has not yet seen her sixth summer!'

" 'She is not a hunter!' protested Coconino. But his mother said, 'A hunter is one who brings back food for his family. Where is your food, mighty hunter?' And at that Coconino was ashamed, for he knew he had set more store by the actions of his hand than by the result of them."

Coconino stopped and drank again from the small bowl of

water. "That is a story like the ones my old uncle Three-Legged Coyote told to the People in the southern village," he explained. "How angry I was when I first heard them told around the fire, with people I did not know laughing at my foolishness! How disrespectful, I thought, for I wanted to be remembered as a great hero, as a brave and skillful hunter, as the Earth Saver. But now, as you see—" White teeth flashed in his dark face as he grinned. "—I tell old Three-Legged Coyote's stories myself."

"To make a point," Tana guessed.

"Yes." He sighed once more and set his bowl down. "What a glorious deed I did to tear the Sky Ship from its place! How clever I was, and how daring! But what did it accomplish?"

"It kept Earth protected for a time," Tana repeated.

"For a time, yes," he admitted. "It also brought great sorrow to your ancestors and to the People. My friend Juan did not live to see his sons grown. Here in the north, where we fled the wrath of the Others, many died before we learned how to change the way we farmed and to find new plants to replace those that would not grow here. And my Witch Woman . . ." His shoulders sagged. "My Witch Woman ended her days by going alone into the depths of the Well, there to wait for the day we shall be together again." He fingered the pendant that hung on a thong around his neck.

Doc whimpered softly. Tana could feel Coconino's sorrow and wanted to touch him, but she dared not. Instead she leaned forward urgently. "We must work together, you and I," she said sincerely. "We must find a way now to protect the Earth without using violence, without causing the harm that was caused the first time. If I did not already know it from Nathan, your story would be enough to tell me that you are a man of great insight. Help me, Coconino. Help me find a way to keep your world safe."

But the old man shook his head, looking suddenly tired and worn. "I have had enough of noble causes," he said. "You are young, and your heart yearns after what is good for your people and mine. You must be the Earth Saver now."

Just then the room darkened slightly as a small form blocked the sunlight in the doorway. Doc pricked up his ears hopefully. A child stood there with a shallow basket in its hands, and from outside came the encouraging voice of a woman.

Love shone in Coconino's face. *"Chiquilla,"* he called gently, motioning to the child, *"acercas."* The girl stepped carefully into the room, staring with wonder at the strange woman and the stranger animal. She gave both a wide berth as she approached her grandfather. Like the other children Tana had seen, this one wore no clothing. Her black hair streamed long and loose past dimpled shoulders, and her belly was rounded in the contours of childhood. Tana guessed her to be three or four.

Coconino reached out for the child, taking her basket in one hand and settling her on his knee with the other. "This is my granddaughter Tse-wayah—I think you call this Mourning Dove. She has brought us something to eat. Would you like some?" He offered the basket to Tana.

"Thank you," she said, taking a thin cake from the basket. Its color and aroma were like the corn bread she had been served by the People of the southern village, but this was much flatter and she could detect no green bits in it. Nibbling carefully at the cake, she also found it of a more leathery texture.

"Will the animal eat as well?" Coconino asked.

Tana glanced at Doc. The cake would probably be better for him than many other foods her host might offer, but it was still not a good idea to augment his regular diet. "This is not the time for him to eat," she replied. She watched the little girl staring at Doc and could not suppress a smile. "But he likes to have little girls scratch his neck."

"Does he!" Coconino whispered to the child on his lap, who proceeded to cling to him all the harder. "He likes children, this animal of yours?" Coconino asked.

"Very much," Tana replied. "His name is Doc, and he is a dog."

"What is his magic?"

Tana was surprised at the question, although she knew she shouldn't have been. Eyes Like a Deer had asked her what her magic was; no doubt Coconino assumed a Witch Woman's dog must also have magic. "He has no special magic," she answered. "He is only an animal, very much like your coyote or fox, except that he likes people."

"Then that is his magic," Coconino decided. He spoke again to the little girl, who looked at her grandfather with round dark eyes, then looked again at the dog. Doc's tail switched in anticipation. Mourning Dove drew back again, but she could not take her eyes off him. For his part, Doc put on such a pitiful expression that Tana was hard-pressed not to laugh. His eyes flicked toward Tana.

May I go to her? he pleaded.

No, Tana thought back sternly. *You must wait for her to come to you.*

Soon the little girl climbed out of her grandfather's lap, although she stood hanging on to his shoulder for a moment. Then she began to step carefully closer to the dog, her hands behind her back. Doc's tail started to wag. Finally she reached out her short brown fingers to touch his speckled coat, and Doc pushed his muzzle up against her bare stomach.

Mourning Dove jumped back. *"Fria!"* she exclaimed.

Coconino chuckled. "She says his nose is cold," he translated. At a gentle instruction from him, the little girl reached out again and began to scratch Doc's neck.

"This is interesting magic," Coconino told Tana, "for a kachina such as this to like people."

"What is a kachina?" Tana asked.

"It is a spirit thing," Coconino explained. "An animal, or a person, or perhaps both in one body. Kachinas have great magic, either good or bad."

"Doc's magic is good," Tana assured him. Mourning Dove had squatted down on the floor beside Doc now and was stroking his short, shiny fur.

"So was the magic of Tala," Coconino replied. "But he did not like people—except me." His lips strayed into a smile as he remembered. "He was my brother. He let me ride upon his back as our ancestors once rode upon the backs of horses."

Tana was surprised that Coconino knew of horses but not dogs. Nathan had told her that neither had survived the Evacuation. "Was that Tala's magic?" she asked, "that he carried you on his back?"

Again Coconino broke into a grin. "No, that was his—how do you say—good taste? Yes, that was his good taste." Tana could see in the grin that Coconino was in truth making fun of himself. "His magic was in three parts: first, that he could change color, like the changing lizard. Second, he could fly, and oh! what magic that was!" Coconino drew a deep breath and closed his eyes, as though he could feel again the rush of wind past his face, the rhythmic pulse of wings beating the air. "I tell you, Witch Woman, to ride upon the back of Tala as he flew is a feeling I have never known before or since."

"And the third part of his magic?" Tana prompted.

"His horn." Coconino came back from his reverie to look her in the eye. "Tala could shoot lightning from his horn. It was he who destroyed the Sky Ship, not me. The lightning from his horn burned it so that it would no longer fly.''

It was the same story Tana had heard from Nathan: electricity from the horn of the *Celux nobilis* had damaged the controls on the *Homeward Bound*, causing its orbit to decay so that it crashed somewhere over an ocean. The Crusoans had watched its blip fade from their instrument panels in the command center and had known they were finally, irrevocably stranded.

''And did you command Tala to do this?'' she asked, remembering her discussion with Nathan.

''One did not command Tala to do anything,'' Coconino replied dryly. ''One asked, and if he was willing, Tala might do it. He often did things for me because I was his friend, but in the end he only did what seemed good to him, and the Mother Earth made him able to do it.''

''Then it was the Mother Earth's doing that the Sky Ship was torn from the sky,'' Tana persisted. ''It was not your mistake at all.''

But Coconino shook his head. ''She made it possible for Tala and I to do what we did, but she did not tell us that was what we should do. She only said the Others were not welcome here. It was for me to find a way to stop them.''

Tana grunted. ''My god is behaving much the same way with me,'' she admitted.

Coconino's eyebrows flew up. ''You serve a god?'' he asked in surprise. ''I did not know the Others served any kind of god.''

''*I* do,'' she replied too quickly, ''a very old and ancient one.'' Then she thought to amend her statement. ''Everyone serves some kind of god,'' she said. ''For some it is a god of pleasure, for others a god of greed. For many it is their own convenience. Even those who say they have no god have some yardstick by which to measure their actions and their lives; that yardstick is their god.''

''And what kind of god is yours?'' Coconino asked.

Tana hesitated. ''The kind who says that you are my brother and I must treat you fairly. The kind who says Mourning Dove is my child and I must take care that the world she lives in will be a good one. The kind who will not let me walk away from the Earth and not care about what happens because of what I have done by coming here.''

Coconino nodded sagely. ''That is a good kind of god,'' he said. ''Perhaps it is the Mother Earth whispering to you through the Magic Place That Bends Space.''

A sly smile stole across Tana's face as she regarded the old primitive. "Perhaps the Mother Earth is only one voice that my god uses to speak to his children."

He chuckled. "Perhaps that is so."

Suddenly a giggle erupted from Mourning Dove. Tana looked over to see Doc licking the chubby little face. The girl rubbed at it with her hands, then impulsively she threw her arms around the dog's neck and hugged him.

"I met another of your granddaughters," Tana told Coconino as they watched the pair. "One who lives with the southern people."

She thought she saw a flicker of sadness cross Coconino's smiling face. After a moment he said, "I have many grandchildren in the southern village. Most of them I have never seen." Then his eyes twinkled. "But I am sure they are all very handsome, like me."

Tana smiled back. "The one I met certainly was. And the rascals who greeted me above, how many of those were your grandchildren?"

He shrugged. "Four or five—I lose count. They all call me *Ababba*, 'Grandfather,' so what does it matter? They are all mine, one way or another."

Mourning Dove had now decided Doc was a resilient plaything, and she proceeded to climb on top of him. Accustomed to the antics of Tana's children, the Dalmatian rolled onto his side and spilled her off. She laughed out loud and climbed right back on.

"What will happen to your grandchildren," Tana asked Coconino, "when more people begin to come from the stars?"

Coconino reached into the basket Mourning Dove had brought and picked up a tortilla. He rolled it up, bit off the end, and then said, "I thought your god told you to solve that problem."

At this sly response Tana laughed in spite of herself. "He told me to ask you," she came back.

"Then he gave you bad advice," he responded, still chewing. "I have no ideas at all."

"Perhaps you should ask the Mother Earth."

At that Coconino stopped chewing and stared down at the rolled tortilla in his hand. "I stopped asking the Mother Earth for things long ago," he said softly. "I only give thanks for what I have and try to be content."

"But you are not."

Longing burned in the old eyes. ''Sometimes I am more content than others.''

What is it he wants? Tana wondered. If it is something I can give him . . . ''I can return Tala to you,'' she replied impulsively. ''Not the same Tala you knew but others like him: kachinas that fly and shoot lightning from their horns.'' If only Dak would take an interest in the project, she was sure it could be done.

But Coconino shook his head. ''Tala came to me—to the People—at the Mother Earth's bidding, because he was needed. If he is needed again, he will come to us again; if he is not, why should we ask him to come? He was my brother, Witch Woman, but I do not wish him to walk at my side as this animal does with you.'' He nodded toward Doc, who was trying to catch Mourning Dove's long hair in his teeth. ''A kachina that loves people—perhaps he is what we need now.''

Tana glanced at her wrist chrono and knew she needed to return to the rendezvous soon. The climb up the steep path would take her more time than she liked to think about. But she hated to give up on Coconino, hated even more the thought that she must come up with a solution alone. ''There is an empty place inside you, Coconino,'' she said, watching for his reaction. ''I can feel it. It is a place that longs to be filled. Is it not the place that seeks to serve?''

''No!'' he said sharply; then more gently, ''No, it is not anything so noble, Witch Woman. It is a desire for something which has been denied me; after so many years, I should know that it can never be filled.''

There was such pain in his voice that Tana could not press him further. She glanced at her chrono again, wishing she had more time, then surrendered to the inevitable. ''Very well,'' she sighed. ''I must go now, back to—to the Magic Place That Bends Space. Back to my own world.'' Doc disentangled himself from his playmate and scurried to her side as she struggled to rise. Using him as a brace, she hauled herself up, although she still needed to stoop over in the low-ceilinged room. ''I wish, Coconino, that you would change your mind. I still think you have great wisdom to offer.''

''I have only what the Mother Earth gives me,'' he demurred. ''And she has been—silent—for many years.''

Tana took one last look at the man seated cross-legged on the floor, a man whose wisdom had come from painful experience. You are not so poor as you claim, she thought. You are only afraid of being wrong. I understand that; I understand it very well. But we must try, Coconino. We must always try.

She turned and started stiffly toward the door.

"Witch Woman."

The tone in Coconino's voice sent a chill down her spine. She turned back to him. "Yes?"

A strange fire burned in his dark eyes, and for a moment Tana glimpsed the younger man who had battled a spacecraft and won. Then, "I will do what I can," Coconino said evenly. "I do not know yet what that is, but I—I will ask of the Mother Earth, and I will listen carefully for her answer. Come back tomorrow and we will talk again."

Her heart pounded, but with a sweet flush of joy that did not threaten the chemical balance in her bloodstream. "Thank you," she breathed.

"But you must do something for me."

The hair on the back of her neck prickled suddenly. There was a condition, then, on his change of heart. She tried to read his face in the dim light, but he had turned it toward the bowl of water in his hand. "What is that?" she asked.

"Your Magic Place That Bends Space," he said. "It can also bend Time, can it not?"

Joy fled like a shadow before the sun, and a cold finger of anxiety slipped along her spine. "That used to happen sometimes," she admitted carefully, "but not anymore."

"But it can be made to happen."

Goose bumps sprang up across her arms, though the day was still uncomfortably warm. She remembered Paul's failed tests, the trouble with the time-stabilizing algorithm, the polyzig that disappeared. "Yes, it can still happen." She would be no less than honest with this man.

"Good." He turned his face toward her now, and it was a hard, uncompromising face. "You must use it to send me back to the Time That Was. You must send me back to Phoenix."

CHAPTER SEVENTEEN

Paul and Tana sat in his office looking grim. Doc whined at Tana's feet; she shushed him and tried to pull herself out of the dismal mood she was slipping into so that he wouldn't persist in his whimpering. "Well, let's tackle the easy question first," Tana suggested. "Is it possible to send him back?"

Paul's eyebrows shot up. "That's the easy question?"

"Is it *theoretically* possible?" she qualified.

"Theoretically, yes," he replied. "The natural tendency of fifth-dimensional travel is to condense time, to send the traveler forward—as your friend Coconino seems to have been sent. To execute successful 5-D travel, we have to fight that tendency. We have to bend time back the other way. In theory, we should be able to bend it far enough so that a person arrives at his destination before he left."

"Then why hasn't it been done before?"

Paul slumped farther into his chair. "I'd like to think it's because we're smarter than that," he groused. "Unfortunately, it probably has more to do with the fact that once a traveler goes back in time, we have no way to retrieve him. Even P-TUP can't lock on to a traveling mat that's in the past—or the future. Only the now."

Tana sighed deeply. "That is a rather effective deterrent. For most people, that is. But Coconino doesn't want to be retrieved. For him, going back is going home. Nathan always seemed so . . . protective of him. Now I know why. Paul, if you could have seen his face when he asked me to send him back . . ." She sighed again. "He lost so much, protecting his world the first time." Tana ran a hand through the short half of her hair and felt her scalp still gritty and sweaty from her visit to the desert village. Here in the climate-controlled institute her strength was returning, but the heaviness of that other place still weighed on her.

"Okay," she said, pushing on, "that was the easy question. Now the somewhat harder question: Can you do it?"

A scowl wrote itself across Paul's ruddy face. "I don't like it, Tana."

"I didn't ask if you liked it," she prodded gently—oh, gently, for she knew that look. "I asked if you could do it. Can you make the P-TUP equipment send Coconino back two hundred years?"

"I don't know." He was uncharacteristically short.

"But you have an idea how it might be done."

His arms were folded across his chest and his brow was furrowed, but behind his intense blue eyes his mind was working. Tana could almost see the synapses sparking as his thoughts raced, darting from one possibility to the next, testing principles, questioning givens, bending physical laws until they broke. It was a long moment before he spoke. "I have an idea," he admitted grudgingly. "It's not like I've never thought about it before."

Tana was sure he had. Paul's was a questioning mind, and nothing was sacred in the realm of physics or anywhere else. If it had occurred to Coconino that time could bend both ways, it had most certainly occurred to Paul.

"Now the really tough question." Tana took a deep breath and straightened herself in her chair. "Should we?"

"From a safety standpoint, no," he answered immediately. "I can't send a recorder ahead to test the environment, find out what he's warping into. I can't be sure of the destination coordinates. I'd have to send him to a point I believed was six inches off the ground just to make sure it wasn't inadvertently six inches under it. I might be sending him into the middle of a tree that used to grow on that spot. Two hundred years! Do you know how land features can change in that amount of time? And I have no way to test the system, no way to get feedback on the accuracy of my calculations. Will he arrive two hundred years ago, or one hundred ninety-nine, or two hundred four? I don't like it, Tana. I don't like it at all."

"Neither do I," she admitted, "and for different reasons."

Paul cocked an eyebrow, and a trace of levity lightened his dark expression. "You're afraid he'll kill his own grandfather? Institute the paradox that unravels the universe?"

"Something like that." Tana flexed her elbows and rotated

her shoulders a few times, feeling the stiffness of resting too long. "When Nathan and I got back from the saguaro harvest, I badgered him to tell me more about Coconino, but all he would tell me were the legends. How the People fled to the north after he disappeared. How She Who Saves never broke faith with his eventual return. The legends, he said, differ slightly from the northern to the southern village, but the basic story is the same: This woman Phoenix, whom the northerners call She Who Saves, waited for Coconino all her life, but she waited in vain. She finally cast herself into a lake with the whole village as witnesses, to wait there until Coconino came again. And he didn't come until forty years ago. How can we send him back without changing that? As I see it, there are two options: One, the change will have a ripple effect which carries forward to our time and affects conditions on Earth. Two—what we try won't work, and he won't get back to her at all."

"Then why are we debating this?" Paul asked, rising to pace to the transparent half wall and back. "Either it creates a disaster or it's a failure. Why attempt it?"

"Because that's his price." Tana ran her fingers through her hair again; she wanted to go home and wash it, wash all of this away. "And because I'm scared to death I can't carry this off alone, Paul." Even as she said it, she knew how true it was. "I've wracked my brain for some scenario which, if not foolproof, will at least give these unique Terran cultures a chance to retain their integrity. Nothing has the ring of victory to it." She let her head rest on one hand, her elbow propped on the arm of her chair. "Have you read any histories, Paul, of what was done to Native Americans in the nineteenth and twentieth centuries? A sad story which has repeated itself far too often throughout history. Invaders decide that native culture is perverse, or at the very least not worth saving. In the name of progress or civilization or God, the natives are seduced or forced into changing."

"Sometimes change is necessary," Paul said softly.

"To adapt to a changing environment, yes, and they did that when the rest of us fled Earth in the Evacuation. But why does their environment have to change now?" Tana flared. Doc raised his head and gave a short bark. *What's wrong?*

Nothing, she thought at him, and forced herself to be calmer.

"They should be allowed to change at their own pace," Tana continued. "And to control how much foreign influence comes into their world. But Paul, I don't know how to insure that. If

Coconino has something, anything, to contribute to that effort, I'll take it. Of all the people—'' She broke off, recognizing the rising level of toxins in her bloodstream. ''Of all the people on Earth,'' she went on with more control, ''I think he has the best chance of helping me. Nathan, Doc Hanson, Tavaria Mason— it's like they're all frozen, waiting for something to happen to them. They can't get past the shock of the concept well enough to deal with it. But Coconino—'' She gave him a lopsided smile. ''Coconino's been through this before. He took action once, and now he's had forty years to watch the results and think about it. And because he's wondered if he did the right thing, he's also wondered what else he could have done. He's got a perspective on this that you and I could never have.''

Paul heaved a sigh. ''I want to say, 'What can he do?' But I would have said that the first time, and he managed to be very effective then.''

''Anyway, when I talk to him tomorrow,'' Tana went on, ''I want to at least be able to negotiate with him. If there is something he can do, if there is some way he can help, I want to know if I can pay his price.''

There was a pregnant pause before Paul spoke. ''Tomorrow?'' Warning edged his voice.

Tana lifted her head and saw the hardness written in his eyes— hardness that covered fear. ''I have to meet him tomorrow to hear his plan.''

''Send someone else,'' Paul said flatly.

''You know I can't do that.''

Paul grasped the arms of her chair, leaning over her. ''How many more times are you going to ask me to send you back there?''

She looked up into his vivid blue eyes and knew what it cost him. Knew what she had cost him and knew he would never see the end of payment for the kind of wife he had taken, for she was a Winthrop of the truest kind. Yet he was an adventurer, too, in another way. He journeyed to the edge of his science and stared out across the void—

The answer struck her like a shaft, and she seized his arms. ''Don't send me this time,'' she urged him. ''Because you'll never feel right as long as you only send me. Come with me, Paul. Come with me to meet Coconino.''

* * *

It was not often that Coconino came to the top of the island butte that housed most of the village in its limestone caves. To him it was a lonely and painful place, lifted up away from the community of the People, standing exposed on the rounded pinnacle of this mountain. It was here he had come forty years ago to chant out his grief for all that he had lost: his family, his friends, the way of life he had known. He had laid them to rest here and tried to go on about the business of living. But one ghost remained. There was one for whom he had never danced the Dance of Grief, one spirit he could never put away; she haunted him still.

Lifting his face to the wind, Coconino turned slowly in a circle, looking beyond the canyon rim on both sides, looking far beyond its cleft running north and south, searching the skies where rain-laden clouds scudded toward the village. His face was as rugged as the canyon itself, and his hair was streaked gray like the chalky streaks in the cliff walls. He wore no ceremonial shirt or moccasins, carried no staff or implement of any kind. His only adornment was the ancient phoenix medallion that was ever around his neck, as much a part of him as the lines in his face and the weariness in his bones. He had only himself and the need within him.

Where are you? he asked, but without rancor. His rancor had run out years ago. Now even his apathy had run dry. He was filled with a yearning, hungering for something he had known as a youth but had lived without for too long. It was something that had fled him on the night he had buried his first child, a child dead before it had lived, and he had demanded *Why?* In that rebellion he had blocked out the warmth and the presence that had been his companion as long as he could remember, the presence he knew still existed but he could not feel. Now he longed to have it back, longed as a recalcitrant child longs for home and parents.

Where are you? he pleaded.

And the moist breath of breeze on his cheek was warm and comforting. *Where I have always been,* came the answer. *In your heart.*

The presence filtered through to him gently as dawn seeping slowly back after a long winter night. *So close?* he wondered. *So close all this time, and I could not feel you?*

Down in the canyon that same breeze rustled through the trees like soft laughter. *So close as to be at the center of your being. But that center was wounded; you sealed off the hurt places, holding the pain away from you. You held me away from you, too.*

Coconino drew a great breath and felt the sun laying on his skin like a blanket. *I have missed you, Mother Earth,* he sighed inwardly as a great tear slipped down his cheek. *I have served you because I knew it was right, served the People because they are your children, but I have missed your voice in my heart's ear and the sense of your presence flowing in and around me.*

A bird called from the far canyon rim. *I know, my son. I have missed you, too. But that is past now. Much healing has happened in your heart since you first came to the Time That Is.*

Healing, indeed. As he thought back on his life, the sun shone brightly on it and he knew how fortunate he was. *You gave me many balms,* he acknowledged. *My Hummingbird, who was as light and colorful as her namesake; my Ironwood Blossom, whose patience and strength were as deep and far-reaching as the Great Canyon. How my battered spirit needed them both! And when they were both gone, you gave me Jumping Moon to make me whole again.*

Thunder rumbled softly in the distance. *Not quite whole.*

No, not quite whole, he admitted. *But by then I had learned to live with that one piece of me missing. Like a finger or a toe that has been gone so long, one cannot remember what it was like to have ten. There were so many joys to fill my days: my children, my grandchildren, and all the little ones of this village. Teaching them to stalk the Great Antelope, telling them stories around the Elvira. Happiness coursed like water through the canyon of my life. Even a leaky vessel like me can hold much water for a time.*

From somewhere below him came a cry of delight; the children had spotted Many Ripe Squash and Snapping Turtle coming back from First Canyon with a basket full of something. Mesquite beans, Coconino supposed; it was too soon for corn or squash, let alone the black walnuts that grew in and around this place. The children would be disappointed that the men had brought no better treat than the starchy seeds of the mesquite tree. But the disappointments of children were fleeting, for some new adventure lay always just around the bend in the stream.

Insects creaked in the brush near Coconino. *They are going away.*

The clouds were rolling in faster now. Yes, Coconino thought, *they are all going away: this handful of children, their parents— even the old ones. There are hardly enough of us to bring in the harvest. I will tell them tonight. I will tell them it is time for our two villages to be one. When the corn is in, we will take all that we have and go to the south to join the People of that place. It is* moh-ohnak.

A noisy jay chattered from deep within the canyon. *And what of Coconino? Will Coconino also leave this place and go to see his children there?*

Coconino toed the dirt with his bare foot. *Yes, I would leave this place*, he replied. *And I would see my children, but not those in the southern village. I would go back to where I came from, Mother Earth. I would see the children of my Chosen Companions, those who were born and buried before I took my first wife. I would see my Witch Woman again. Mother Earth, I would be whole before I die.*

The breeze died away to nothing, and a great stillness lay about him. *It is* moh-ohnak.

But a heaviness lay on Coconino like the heaviness of the impending storm in the air. *Yet I have one task to do before I go. She came, the half-haired woman of the Others, and begged my help. I do not know what help I can give her. Speak to me, Mother. Tell me what thing I can do, what word I can say, that will make some difference this time. Tell me how I can protect you and the People without harming the Others. I will cause no more pain.*

The first flecks of rain tickled Coconino's chest and arms, prickling coolness on his flesh that seemed to come from nowhere. *How did you protect me from Nathan?*

From Nathan? Coconino laughed. *You did not need protecting from Nathan.*

Why not? He is of the Others.

Yes, but he is my spirit son, Coconino protested. *He came to me like a thirsty babe and sucked up every drop of your milk I offered.*

A raindrop kissed his cheek. *Even so.*

Coconino was puzzled. *What has that to do with the half-haired Witch Woman? Am I to call on Nathan as well? He is an old man like me now, though the Others do not seem to age as quickly as the People. This Witch Woman is young and, I think, very powerful. What can two old men do that she cannot?*

The breeze stirred again, warm and moist, and more drops began to spatter the dusty ground. *You do not need Nathan for this*, they laughed. *Sit down, Coconino, and hear what I have to say.*

* * *

Tana steeled herself and sat down at her dressing table to wait for Wyoming to take her call. She picked up her brush and made a pass at her hair, wondering what smart remark her older brother would make about this new hairstyle, about the drug-induced darker tone of her skin that had protected her in Earth's desert sun. Maybe he wouldn't be in. Maybe he'd be busy and not able to take the call. Maybe he'd decide he didn't want to talk to her today.

But the computer chimed softly, and the display on her dressing table glowed with the scholarly image of Wyoming Jensen. How it had hurt Monti when his oldest son had rejected the Dynasty name and had chosen to use his mother's name instead. But then, that was exactly what Wy had intended. Looking at his closed, impassive face now, at the blond hair going white at the temples, she thought what a mockery this mask of self-possession was. Inside was the hot Winthrop temper and a burning hurt that she had never been able to understand. What did we do to you? she wondered. What did we ever do to you?

"Well, well, well, if it isn't the chief executive officer of the IDP," Wy greeted her with the touch of sarcasm that always tinged his voice. "How are you, Montana?"

"Fine, thank you," she replied with intentional gentleness. "How are you, Wy?"

"Busy." He leaned forward in his chair, a huge black upholstered chair behind a massive simulated-wood desk. An antique globe of Argo sat on one corner, and an assortment of light pens, input pads, and other interacting tools were scattered about, managing to make the desk look cluttered. A coffee mug and the remains of his lunch added to the effect. "Where's the brilliant research scientist?"

"In his office, working," Tana replied, and thought, You can't have it both ways. If you want to scorn the world of business which has given the Wynthrop Dynasty its wealth, if you want to laud academics and scholarship as the most noble of all pursuits, fine, but then you can't criticize Paul for being brilliant. He's everything you want your professors to be, everything you'd like to think you are, but you're not. The truth is, Wy, when you took the associate chair in first-wave colonial history, you became an administrator just like me.

"Working?" Wy raised his eyebrows in mock surprise. "You mean he hasn't perfected P-TUP yet? I thought he'd have dusted his hands of that project long ago and been on to even greater invasion techniques."

Tana knew it was hopeless to try to explain to Wy all the work she had done to make sure P-TUP was not abused, how she was even now trying to keep it out of questionable hands until appropriate restrictions were in place. He would ignore her every defense. Besides, he was right. That was why she needed him now.

"Wy, who's the chair of pre-Evacuation history?" she blurted out.

This time his surprise was genuine. "Pre-Evac? Sung Kaipau, I think. Yes, Sung Kaipau; she took over from Dr. Radimorton last year when he retired. Why?"

Now Tana hesitated. "Can you secure this link?"

Immediately his guard went up, and with it the level of his sarcasm. "What, cloak and dagger stuff? Proprietary information? Trade secrets?" A sneer twisted his otherwise handsome face. "Better be careful, little sister; I'm not cleared for Winthrop confidential information."

"Just shut up and secure the link," she flared. From his corner Doc whined and Tana knew she was treading dangerously. *Help me, Doc*, she pleaded silently. *Help me be calm and careful. I need all the help I can get to deal with Wy because, God knows why, I still love him. He's my brother, and I don't want things to be like this between us.*

Doc did not understand half of what she said, but he rose and padded over to her chair, leaning against her thigh. His undemanding touch was a comfort, and Tana stroked his fur with her left hand, feeling the soothing effect of that simple action.

"All right," Wy said in a moment, "we're secured. No records being made, no one but you and me and fourteen light-years of uncaring space. Now, what's the big deal?"

"Wy, I've been to Earth."

He was silent for a long moment. Then, "Congratulations," he managed to say.

"Wy, there's no plague there, there never was. The reports were fabricated to keep people away. The *Homeward Bound*— the crew survived, Wy. Their descendants have a little settlement in a river valley, and there are—there are some survivors from the Evacuation. At least two groups, two cultures. Seven hundred years, Wy. They've been on their own for seven hundred years."

It was still a moment before he could find something to say.

"Well, I guess we need a new chair in history then, don't we? Post-Evacuation Terran survival."

Ignoring his glibness, she went on. "Besides the people, Wy, think what is there to be investigated. Cities, artifacts, the remains of Terran civilization. It's all there, Wy, touched by time and the elements but not by human destruction. Mount Olympus is still there. Berlin is still there. Houston Control is still there."

He was plainly stunned, clearly intrigued with the possibilities. But he was Wyoming. "You don't need history, you need archaeology," he grumbled. "You never could tell the difference. What are you proposing, to donate Earth to the Omniversity on behalf of the Winthrop Dynasty?"

"Earth is not mine to donate," she said evenly. "I can't lay claim to it and wouldn't if I could. But there are others who won't feel that way. There was a reason, Wy, for giving out that report of plague two hundred fifteen years ago. The Terrans were trying to protect themselves from invasion. That's what will happen. Any business that thinks it can turn some kind of profit, any country that thinks they can gain an advantage, will be off to Earth to take what they can while the picking is good. I've met these people, Wy. They deserve better than that."

"Well, I'm glad they meet your criteria," he sneered. "So what do you want the Omniversity to do? Get there first?"

"I want them to declare Earth a protectorate," she replied. "Claim it as a research area, not to be visited without authorization, not to be looted or invaded or interfered with in any way. It'll be a gold mine for you, Wy, for history and archaeology, and anthropology, too. There's a Stone Age culture surviving, and a strange hybrid with just a smattering of technology left from before the Evacuation. And the crew. And the strangest story you'll ever hear, about a *Celux nobilis* that flies, and a time warp, and a man whose madness transcended two centuries. We can't lose it, Wy. We can't afford to lose it."

Slowly it was sinking through to him, seeping past all his resistance to anything she proposed, anything that began with the Dynasty, anything connected with her lifelong dream of fulfilling Chelsea Winthrop's intention for the institute. He was a historian, after all, fascinated with the lessons of the past, possessed of a scholar's curiosity about the unknown. "That would be the thing to do, wouldn't it?" he admitted. "Have it set aside so no one could obscure the physical evidence or influence the anthropological flow."

"Can you help?" she asked eagerly.

But Wyoming shook his head sadly as he leaned back in his chair. "It won't work," he told her.

Of course not. Nothing she proposed ever would. "Why not?"

He sighed heavily, and genuine regret showed in his face and voice. "Because we have no more right to declare Earth an Omniversity protectorate than the Wynthrop Dynasty does to claim it as family property. Less, probably. After all, Winthrops did lead the expedition that apparently has settled it. We could try, but the lawyers would throw it out. There's no precedent for that kind of claim, and governments and businesses alike would fight us tooth and nail. We could go up against one or two opponents but not the number that would jump into the fray if we tried something as far-reaching as this. Hell, the Pax Circumfra would probably disallow it, and you know how few things they can agree on. I'm sorry, Tana." He leaned forward across the desk again. "I really am. If I can catch the chair in a good mood, I'll see if it wants to bring it up to the history council, but I'm afraid all we'll really be able to do is make noise about the situation. It doesn't sound like that's what you want."

"No." Tana slumped dejectedly at her dressing table. "No, the last thing I want to do is call attention to the situation while Earth is still so vulnerable."

"Try Dad," Wy suggested.

She shook her head. "He's a lackey. They've got him warping around the universe looking for a new headquarters, talking leases with the various governments, doing all the negotiating and legwork. They don't let him speak to policy." She gave her brother a wry smile. "After all, he's a businessman, not a politician."

Wyoming snorted. "Thank God for small favors."

All the anxiety had drained out of Tana, along with the hope. "I don't suppose you're coming to Roundup," she said.

He glared at her from the display. "And do what? Chat with Zim about multinational contracts or the level of consumption of frivolous consumer goods? No thanks."

A small tear slipped out of the corner of her eye. "You used to love Roundup," she whispered.

"I used to want to be a dog trainer, too," he snapped. "I haven't the patience for either one anymore." But seeing the tear glisten on her cheek, he softened his voice a little. "People change, Tana. I grew up."

Did you? Or are you still the hurt little boy, trying to get back at us for imagined injuries? "And we'll continue to change," she said with resolution. "And grow. Maybe someday you'll find all these insufferable family connections are not as odious as you thought they were." Behind her, she heard Paul enter from his office. "It's late here, Wy. I appreciate your listening to my problem. I'm sorry you couldn't do anything."

"So am I." He raised his hand to cut off the connection. "Good-bye, Tana." Then his image disappeared from the display.

For a long moment Tana just sat there, fighting back tears, concentrating on bringing her heart rate and breathing under control. Paul came up behind her and began to massage her shoulders gently. "Hasn't changed a whit, has he?" Paul observed.

"It will catch up with him," she replied with a confidence she did not feel. "They say as you get older, family gets to be more important to you. Someday he'll regret all the years he spent trying to shut us out." She sighed. "I just wish I knew what I'd done to him to earn his unflagging disrespect."

"Oh, that's simple," Paul answered quickly. "You weren't perfect."

A laugh erupted that was dangerously close to a sob. "Well, excuse me, no one is."

"Including Wyoming," Paul agreed. "Which is a large part of the problem. He can't meet his own standards of perfection."

Tana snorted. "But does *he* know that."

"All too well," Paul replied. "You see, he wanted—no, he expected—to be the perfect brother, but perfect brothers don't let bad things happen to their little sisters."

Tana looked up in surprise. "He never let anything happen to me."

"But you got sick," Paul explained. "In spite of everything he did right, you got sick, and he can't fix it. He can't fix it, he can't tell you how to make it better, and he can't deal with that failing in himself."

Tana shook her head. "I don't think you understand Wy as well as you think."

"Sure I do." He stopped massaging her shoulders and grinned at her in the mirror. "You Winthrops are always trying to save someone or something. I even see it in our kids. Look at Lystra. Now, there's a future crusader if I ever saw one."

Looking up at his round face, Tana smiled thinly. "Sometimes I wonder if she can stop being disgusted with the universe long enough to find something worth crusading for.''

He leaned over, slipping his arms around her. "Oh, she will,'' he assured her. "But what that finally is and how she goes about it, you and I can't control. Any more than we can change Wy.''

Tana sighed. "Life doesn't get less complicated as we go along, does it?''

"No, but we learn little tricks to cope with it,'' he said, straightening up and drawing her to her feet. "How about a nice soak before bed?''

"Mm, sounds heavenly,'' she breathed. "Luke: open the tub.''

Coconino heard the audible gasp from his companion as the Others suddenly appeared in the meadow. Though the younger man knew they would come by Magic, he was still startled by their abrupt arrival. *"Aiiee!"* he exclaimed. "There are three of them.''

Indeed there were three: the half-haired woman, the kachina she called Doc, and a man whose hair did not begin at his forchcad but nearer the top of his head. This was something Coconino had seen on the Mountain as a youth and from time to time among the Others in the river valley, but for young Hoot Owl, who had visited the Camp of the Others only twice in his life, the man's lack of hair was more unusual than the way the woman wore hers.

The trio approached across the meadow, with Doc ranging ahead, sniffing the ground and testing the wind. "Is that some kind of coyote?'' Hoot Owl asked incredulously.

"It is a dog,'' Coconino replied with careful aplomb.

"What is a dog?''

Coconino hesitated. "That is a word from the language of the Others. It means a piebald coyote.''

"Oh.'' Hoot Owl nodded solemnly at this sagacious answer. "And why does the man cut away the hair from his head?''

"I do not know,'' Coconino admitted. "But do not speak of it in his presence. My experience has been that when you comment on this strange practice, men of the Others become very offended.''

"I will say nothing,'' Hoot Owl avowed. "You must do all the speaking. I cannot twist my tongue around their strange words.''

Coconino greeted their guests now. "Good day, Witch Woman. Good day, Doc."

"Good day," Tana replied. "Coconino, this is my husband, Paul."

"Good day, Paul," Coconino greeted. "This is my stepson, Hoot Owl."

"Good day, Hoot Owl," Tana said. Hoot Owl only nodded politely.

"Will you come to my house?" Coconino invited.

"Thank you, no," Tana replied. "It is very difficult for me to climb down to your village and back again."

"Then come into the shade," Coconino suggested, pointing toward the nearby forest.

It was still only midmorning, but the day was already blistering hot and Tana was grateful for the cooler temperature beneath the towering oaks and firs. "How is your granddaughter?" she asked as they settled themselves on the ground near the base of a fragrant juniper.

"She is well," Coconino told her. "She talks all the time about the kachina who likes little girls; it makes her mother tired. She wants us to name the new baby Coyote with Spots."

Tana laughed. "She is a precious little girl."

"Yes," Coconino agreed. "I will be sorry to leave her."

At that Tana's expression saddened. "I wish you would not leave her, Coconino."

"I must," he replied simply. "It is *moh-ohnak*."

"Have you thought of something to do, then?" Tana asked him. "To save your world from mine?"

"I spoke with the Mother Earth," he responded, "and she told me."

"What did she say?"

But Coconino looked away toward the east, where a hawk circled over the canyon, occasionally dipping down out of sight below the rim. "It was good advice," he hedged. "If she had only told me this as a young man, I might never have had to leave my Witch Woman in the first place. But then—" He turned back to his guests with a slight smile. "Young men tend to hear what they want, no?"

"Young women, too," Tana agreed.

"Will you send me back to her, then?" Coconino asked.

Paul and Tana exchanged a look. "We're not sure we can," Paul explained. "It has never been done before. I think I know how, but I have no way to test my theory. Once something is sent back in time, there is no way to check on it to see if it arrived where it was supposed to. Or when it was supposed to. And there is no way to ever get it back."

"I do not want to come back," Coconino said simply.

"But I don't know exactly where I am sending you," Paul repeated. "I might send you someplace dangerous by mistake. A place where you can't breathe. A place where you fall and break your neck. And I will never even know what I have done."

"When I loose an arrow from my bow," Coconino told him, "I am responsible for where it strikes. But if I loose a bird from my hands, I am not responsible for what danger it flies into. I am a bird, *hombre*, not an arrow. I ask you only to set me free."

Paul shook his head. "How can you be a bird," he asked softly, "when the bow is in my hand?"

Coconino smiled broadly. "Because I am as insistent as a noisy crow, and I will squawk and squawk until you set me free. Please." The smile softened. "I would fly back to the woman I loved long ago. Only point me as near as you can, and I will trust Mother Earth for the rest."

"That's another problem," Tana interrupted. "Even if we manage to get you back there, *you can't change things*. The stories your people tell say that She Who Saves died in the Well. If that is what happened, you can't stop that."

Now Coconino's face darkened. "I cannot believe she would cast her life away. I have never believed that. The People tell many stories of me that are not true. Why could not this telling be false as well?"

"And if Coconino had come among them again, as an old man, would the stories not say so?"

Her challenge stopped him. "That is so," he admitted soberly. "If I had—but they did not expect an old man, they expected a young one. When I go back, I will tell them I am Say-ayka-pee; they need never know I am Coconino."

That thought had occurred to Tana. "Might work," she muttered. "But if Phoenix is going down into that Well—"

"Perhaps it was another who was also called She Who Saves," Coconino interrupted. "The People tell stories of a game they say I learned on the Mountain; I learned no game there, and I think the stories must be of my son Michael, who came from the Mountain. Things change in the telling; perhaps this was so with She Who Saves."

Tana pointed to the medallion on his chest. "Your spirit son,

Nathan, told me that this was hers and that she left it by the Well to mark her place. Is that not true?''

Coconino looked down at the blue-green bird stone. ''Perhaps she gave it to another,'' he said stubbornly.

''Many perhaps, my friend.''

Coconino scowled fiercely at the medallion, then looked away to the south. He rubbed his fingers lightly over the turquoise stone. ''If I come to her,'' he said finally, ''and find her intent on the Well, then—then I will only stand to bid her farewell,'' he promised. Then his voice dropped. ''And join her.''

''Coconino.'' Tana's voice was thick with emotion. ''Choose life. Stay here with your family. I have spoken with my brother; I believe I can return Tala to you. Not Tala himself, but others of his kind.''

''I have seen Tala's resting place,'' Coconino replied, ''and felt his dead bones with my hands. I know he is gone, as my wives are gone, as my Teresa is gone, as all my old friends are gone. That is the way of the Mother Earth: birth and death, birth and death. But in my heart, Witch Woman, my Phoenix has never died. She is there like a live coal that I cannot rub out no matter how it burns me. Send me back to her, Witch Woman. Send me back so that the circle of my life is complete.''

Tana would have objected further, but Paul reached out and touched her arm. His eyes brimmed with moisture, and he shook his head slightly. ''Let it go, Tana. It's like Wyoming; you won't change anything by talking at him.''

With a sigh Tana let her shoulders droop. On the ground beside her Doc whimpered and put his head in her lap. She stroked his head idly. ''All right,'' she said finally. ''We will do what we can. But I am afraid we will only send you to disappointment and death.''

''You may be afraid, but I am not,'' he assured her. ''The Mother Earth will care for me.'' A sly smile glided slowly over his weathered features. ''After all, am I not her favorite son?''

CHAPTER EIGHTEEN

"But why here?" Flint asked in surprise when Phoenix stopped at the foot of a featureless ridge. Behind and in front of them the land looked the same: rolling, chalky desert tufted with grass and cactus and small shrubs. "It can be no more than an hour's walk to the Well from here, and there is still enough daylight. Here there is no water. Why not go on?"

"We carry enough water," Phoenix said flatly, motioning to Michael to carry her message back to those who trailed behind. "Many with us are unaccustomed to travel, and they are weary. We will stay here tonight."

Indeed, it had taken them four days to come the distance she and her hunting companions could do in two, because so many of the People had chosen to accompany her on this journey. It was both flattering and frustrating. Witnesses she wanted, and much pomp and ceremony, but she had not expected so many older people to come, so many women with small children in tow. Her first reaction when she had seen the company making ready was to object, but Flint had stilled her. "We are one People," he told her. "Our joys and our sorrows are one; do not try to shut out those who want to share in this grieving."

Or rejoicing, Phoenix thought privately as she dropped her small pack to the ground. Trudging resolutely along, unused to so much walking but determined to pay any price for the privilege of watching her die, Castle Rock had trailed last in a group of forty-odd people in Phoenix's entourage. That was over half the population of the village.

Phoenix sipped sparingly at her water, waiting for the travelers to settle down a bit, to arrange themselves in the inevitable circle. Then she took her bow and slipped back up the ridge to see what game might not have abandoned the area as they came tramping through. It was not that she particularly wanted to add some meat to the cook pots one last time; it was more that she did not want to talk to anyone. Even those who did not question with their voices questioned with their eyes. *Why? Why do you leave us, She Who Saves? Why does the Mother Earth call you, and what does that mean for us? Have we displeased her? Is Coconino not coming for a long time?*

It was not easy to escape unnoticed, for there were no tall trees here and hardly any mesquite or paloverde. There was nothing to hide behind until a rolling swell of ground lay between her and the encampment. Then she stopped and shook her arms, trying to relieve the tension knotted in her shoulders.

Peace, came the voiceless voice.

You be at peace, she thought angrily. You are not the one who has been told to leave the People, to go away into the Well and not come back.

It will not be hard, the voice promised. *I will be with you.*

But it would be hard, Phoenix knew. Tomorrow morning she would rise before dawn, dress in her ribbon shirt, and bid the People leave their things behind as they traveled the last short distance to the Well. There on its western rim, facing the rising sun, she would make her final farewell, strip off her finery, and descend alone to the lake at the bottom of the sinkhole. Before the morning was old it would be done; Michael would lead the People back here to their camp, and they would begin the return trip to homes and fields that wanted their attention.

"Let them go quickly, that's all I ask," she growled to the empty air. "No point in lingering when it's clear I'm gone." Seven minutes—Michael knew that. Seven minutes was as long as a person could survive without air. She would have him drive a stake into the ground and mark where its shadow fell so they would know when sufficient time had passed. Telling Breeze had brought his drum as well, to measure out the time. They would know when it was over. They would know when to go home.

"I hate this!" she barked at the growing twilight. "It scares the hell out of me, and I hate it! But if it must be done for the sake of the People, I will do it. If it must be done . . ."

If it must be done. How many times had that phrase driven her to do what she did not want to do, what she did not believe she could? Milking a bighorn sheep—ha! The idea was so impossible, it was laughable! Yet she had done it. And going on, mile after weary mile, with a newborn child strapped to her back and not enough food for either one of them—she had done that, too. Over a mountain pass so steep that it took her a whole day to climb. Down again to a lake where, weary as she was, she nearly stepped on a diamondback rattlesnake that sunned itself on the concrete remains of an ancient dam.

Somewhere she lost the trail and could not find the river she needed to follow through even more high country. Instead, she wound up switchbacking along an old highway to the top of a wall of cliffs, where she got caught in an early rainstorm and sat shivering through the night, unable to find dry wood to make a fire. But she collected enough water to slake her thirst and keep the infant hydrated and to fill her canteen. The next day she headed due west and by midafternoon had found the river she sought.

Her head reeled as she sat in the shade of an ironwood tree and stared stupidly at the trail ahead. How much farther to the northern village? Three days? Five? She looked down at the infant in the pack, which she had shrugged off while she rested. He had given up crying hours ago, too weak now even to protest his fate. He would not live another three days without proper food. In the end she would have to bury the tiny body in a foreign place, another victim of senseless fear. It would be an ache she'd carry alone in the northern village, for who would know what she had done? Buried her foster daughter's child. Failed her daughter. Been defeated by Nina. Lost Coconino's grandson.

What was it that had caught her eye? The sun glinting off something metallic? A flash of motion like a Flying Machine near the horizon? Or was it truly a sign from the Mother Earth? Whatever it was, Phoenix suddenly realized that she could not be far from the Camp of the Others. She had skirted it on her way south, slipping through under cover of darkness so she need not face any strangers, need not find out how Coral Snake fared in that place, cut off from the People and the only way of life he had ever known. But now it spelled salvation for the infant: not only food but medical care. That was, if Jacqueline Winthrop still lived.

Picking herself up and hoisting her pack once more, Phoenix had forced herself into a trot, pushing on up the trail while the sun climbed relentlessly toward the western horizon.

The figure that rose from a chair on the dome's porch was small and frail but not bent. The white hair had grown thin, so that pink scalp showed through even in the fading light, but the

*gleam in the blue eyes was as sharp as ever, the set of the wrin-
kled mouth one that Phoenix knew. "Dr. Winthrop," Phoenix
rasped, her voice rough with exhaustion.*

*"You look like death," Jacqueline informed her. "Must feel
like it, too; you didn't try to sneak up on me this time."*

*Phoenix managed a thin smile. "Didn't want to give you a
heart attack. I need your services."*

*There was the slightest pause, as though that thought had
surprised the elderly doctor. "Sick?" she asked, concern thinly
veiled in her voice.*

*"Not me," Phoenix replied. "Tired and hungry, yes, but—
it's the baby." She wavered on her feet, struggling to unsling
the pack. "He's . . . not been fed. For a long time. Mother dead,
and I'm not equipped to provide—"*

"Rita!" Jacqueline snapped. "I need your help!"

*The dome door slid open, and the substantial form of Rita
Zleboton filled it, a dark shape in a darkening night. "What is
it?"*

*"We need to get this woman and this baby to the Infirmary,
stat. And they both need food. Give us a hand with the first,
then see Mike Thornton about the second."*

*Somehow Phoenix managed to slide out of the pack and sur-
render it to Jacqueline, who headed purposefully down the path
toward her Infirmary. "I can walk," Phoenix protested as Rita
approached her.*

*"You'd better, because I can't carry you," Rita responded as
she put an arm around the wavering woman. "I'm old, you
know. Not as old as Jacqueline, but that's not saying much."*

*It was not far to their destination. "Phoenix, isn't it?" Rita
asked as they stumbled into the brightly lit dome. Jacqueline
already had the baby out of its wrappings and on an examining
table. "Well, I'm glad to see you again. Sorry I missed you on
your last visit, but you came and went so fast, I didn't hear
about it till you were long gone." She helped Phoenix into a
chair. "Do you intend to make a habit of bringing stray children
to us?"*

*"That's not a stray!" Phoenix flared. "That's—that's—" Tell
them it was Coconino's grandchild? Tell them its mother was
Karen Reichert's blood daughter? It seemed unwise. "That one's
my responsibility. Mine. I just need help for him because—
because his mother can't feed him—and neither can I . . ."
Her voice failed.*

"Rita, get her some water," Jacqueline directed.

"Drank at the stream," Phoenix croaked.

"Then get her some food. But first hand me that packet of saline there. When was the last time this child ate anything?"

Phoenix couldn't remember. *"I made a glucose solution— honey and water—but that ran out—yesterday? I think. Or the day before."* She felt dizzy. *"Before that he had . . . sheep's milk. For a day or so. That was—ten days? I don't know. And before that—"*

"Before that he was sucking his nutrients through an umbilical cord," Jacqueline surmised, deftly setting up the saline drip. *"This child's no more than two weeks old. Mother die in childbirth?"*

"Right after," Phoenix improvised.

"Tough little bugger," Jacqueline observed as she scanned the child with assorted instruments. *"Dehydrated, a trifle anemic, but that appears to be all. No doubt he's hungry as sin—sheep's milk?"* Her voice faded in Phoenix's ear as sleep overtook her. *"Where in the world did you get sheep's milk?"*

When Phoenix awoke, Rita had returned. Seeing her stir, the big woman brought a tray laden with foods Phoenix had not seen in twenty years. Wheat bread, apple butter, goat's cheese, and a large wedge of peach pie. With them was a small brown bottle, which she sniffed suspiciously. *"Beer,"* she confirmed, and sipped it carefully. It was warm and not as smooth as the brew Jack Parsons used to make on the Mountain, but it would wash the bread and cheese down nicely. *"I shouldn't drink this, tired as I am, and on an empty stomach."*

"Drink it," came Jacqueline's voice from somewhere beyond Rita. *"It's high-calorie, and you're not going anywhere."*

"How's the baby?" Phoenix called back, trying to peer around Rita.

"Consuming nourishment like a black hole," Jacqueline replied, and when Rita moved aside, Phoenix could see that a young woman had joined them, a plump teenage girl who looked to be no more than sixteen or seventeen. Her hair was a dusty blond color, long and pulled back from her face. Like most of the inhabitants of Camp Crusoe, she wore loose cotton trousers and a loose cotton shirt. The shirt was pulled up now, and Sky Dancer's baby nursed hungrily at the girl's breast. His dark skin and darker hair were a sharp contrast to the fair-complected girl in her light-colored clothing.

"Hi," the girl greeted brightly. *"I'm Lana."*

"Lana has a little girl at home," Jacqueline elaborated. *"The first actual third-generation Crusoan. She was good enough to get out of bed in the middle of the night to help feed your orphan."*

Orphan. The word rang harshly on Phoenix's ear. He was not an orphan; he was hers. She was his grandmother, not by blood but in spirit. Spirit counted much among the People. No one would contest her claim to the child.

"Oh, I don't mind," Lana was saying. *"Darla had me awake, anyway, and I've got lots of milk."*

"She's our second volunteer," Jacqueline added. *"Cyd Ryan was over here earlier, while you were asleep. She's just about to wean her youngest, so she had milk to spare, too."*

"How late is it?" Phoenix asked, through a mouthful of bread.

"Too late for old ladies like me," Rita grumbled as she moved toward the door. *"Everything's under control here. I think I'll go home to bed."*

"It's after midnight," Jacqueline told Phoenix. *"I've checked your little boy out thoroughly; he'll be just fine as long as he gets enough to eat. But don't plan on taking him anywhere for a while. He's got some catching up to do."* She rose slowly from the chair where she'd been sitting, and Phoenix saw again the frailness she'd noticed on the porch, a frailness that had never been part of Jacqueline Winthrop. *"Lana, when that monster is through gorging, just tuck him into that drawer I laid out on the floor—it's a fine bed for one so tiny. I'll see you in the morning."* She paused by Phoenix's chair. *"You, too,"* she added pointedly.

As though I would go anywhere, Phoenix thought. She finished her food quickly and the beer, too, and felt the gentle wash of sleep lapping at her. But there was something she had meant to ask earlier, something she had forgotten to do . . . What was it? She needed to check . . . something . . .

Coral Snake. A chill slipped through her as she remembered. Coral Snake would be curious about any child she brought, wondering who its parents were. With his sinister, dark-minded view of Michael and Sky Dancer, he might well guess what had occurred. Phoenix did not want that. Bad enough Coconino's children had had to struggle with Coral Snake for an enemy; there was no need to expose this hapless grandchild to it as well.

"When was your baby born?" Phoenix asked Lana by way of opening a conversation.

"Three months ago," Lana replied, beaming. "She seems so big now compared to this one."

Phoenix made herself smile and nod, but her mind was elsewhere. "I was here last fall," she said. "I brought some traders. There was a young man with us . . . who stayed."

"Coral Snake." Lana wrinkled her nose. "I know it wasn't easy for him, trying to learn a new language and new customs, but . . . He just struck me as sort of—obnoxious, you know? Pushy and—well, awfully full of himself. Like he was going to learn how to be just like one of us in six weeks' time." A giggle escaped her. "I know I shouldn't laugh, but it was so funny when he would try to say something to one of the girls here and the words came out all backward. Then he'd get so angry because they laughed at him instead of being impressed."

Phoenix smiled in spite of herself. She could picture the arrogant young man's chagrin when he could not manipulate people here the way he had manipulated his friends in the village. "Is he still here?" she asked, for something in Lana's phrasing suggested that the boy was no longer around.

"No, he left last spring," Lana told her. "As soon as that other boy—what was his name? Michael. As soon as Michael went through here headed north, Coral Snake took off in the other direction. I gather they don't get along well."

"No," Phoenix agreed quietly.

"Anyway, Coral Snake announced he was going to the Mountain to find a Witch Woman to marry." The young girl sighed. "I hope he has better luck there than he did here."

Phoenix breathed a sigh of relief. That was one less thing to worry about, then. With so many concerns for the child's welfare, she was glad to have even one set aside. Sleep sucked at her now like an undertow, but she fought it off until the child had finished nursing and his provider had gone home for the night. Then she curled herself around the drawer where the infant lay and let herself drift. The Mother Earth must be watching over you, indeed, grandchild of Coconino, she thought. You cheat one danger after another. What a tale you will have to tell your children of this incredible journey! Not that you will remember any of it. But I will tell you of it.

What I can tell you of it. Because I can't let Michael know too much. I must think of some other story to tell him. Something less painful . . .

* * *

"Second thoughts?"

Phoenix had heard Michael coming, knew it was he long before he spoke. She had given up any pretense of hunting and seated herself on a rock, watching the sun slip silently behind the distant spires of the Red Rock Country. The People should be resting by their cook fires now, finishing their evening meal. Soon they would turn to finding a patch of ground for their sleeping mats that was free of cactus and did not have too many rocks. She had hoped to wait until they were settled for sleep before returning to the camp; apparently Michael was not going to let her do that.

"Not second thoughts," she replied. "Just the first ones over again."

He sauntered nearer and took up a stance too cocky for one of the People. His skin glistened with perspiration in the fast-fading light, and he was beautiful. Damn you, Michael, you are beautiful, she thought. Just like your father. Seeing you there in the shadows, I could believe it was him . . .

"You know," he began, "if you really wanted to—"

"Stop, Michael, just stop," she snapped. "You agreed to go along with this; can you please just do it with your mouth shut?"

There was a ringing silence between them like the harsh silence following the clash of swords. Phoenix regretted her tone, as she had so often regretted it with Coconino, but she didn't know what else she could have done. She was tired of arguing with the young man. She wanted these last hours between them to be free of conflict.

"You gave Gray Fox a letter for my father," Michael said after a moment.

"I tried to give it to you; you threw it back at me," she reminded him.

He ignored the comment. "I looked at it," he told her. "You told him the Mother Earth called you and you were glad to go."

"I lied."

"Why?"

She looked up at him, dark eyes meeting dark eyes. "If someone came to you twenty years from now and said, 'By the way, Sky Dancer fell off a cliff and broke her neck after you left,' how would you feel?" He flinched visibly. "So how do you think Coconino will feel when he comes back if he believes I fought the Mother Earth over this final decision and lost? Let him believe I was glad to rest, Michael. In many ways I am. I am glad to be free of the responsibility. I just don't want him to think . . .'' She touched the turquoise medallion that hung from her neck. ''I just don't want him to think I gave up waiting for him. Tell him that, will you? If you're here when he shows up. Tell him that was my only regret in doing what I do, that I had to give up waiting for him.''

The cockiness melted out of Michael's stance; he dropped wearily to the ground, squatting near her, watching the glow that had been sunset evaporate from the horizon. After a moment he asked, ''Is that what happened to Sky Dancer?''

''Of course not,'' Phoenix scoffed. ''She's fine. She needed another life, that's all, and she found it there in the southern village. Let it be.''

Stars began to appear overhead, dim flecks of light that eased into being, one here, one there. Phoenix tilted her head back and tried to count them: five, six, seven—oh, there was another by the first; had she counted that one? Six, seven, eight—a dozen—more, and brighter now—

''Does she hate me?''

''Not as long as you stay where you are.''

Michael gave a great sigh that trembled slightly. ''Last night I was thinking maybe I'll just go home. Back to the Mountain, visit my mother.'' Phoenix stiffened, but he went on as though he hadn't noticed. ''It seemed like the easy way out, just walk away from all the responsibility, all the hard decisions, but I knew I couldn't. I love the children, and Swan, and—and all of them. Flint. Muddy Hands. Old Cactus Flower and even Castle Rock, bitter as she is. I have a dozen mothers here and a dozen grandmothers, and all the children are my little brothers and sisters.'' He scratched his chest absentmindedly. ''Life on the Mountain would be just as complicated, anyway.''

Phoenix let her breath out slowly in silent relief.

''*Someday* I'd like to go back,'' he went on. ''Maybe when my children are older—I'd like them to meet their other grandmother, and Ababba, and their aunts. But it would just be to visit.'' He turned his shadowed face toward her with half a smile. ''I am of the People,'' he said softly. Then he added, ''But I may have to build a racquets court somehow, and teach Purple Thistle and Many Sneezes how to play.''

Phoenix smiled, too. ''I hope you do,'' she told him.

He rose to his feet, tall and lithe, with no trace of the adolescence that had lingered on him when he had first come to the northern village. ''I should go back to camp,'' he said. ''Dancing Leaves asked me to eat at their fire. The way Fat Badger eats, if I don't get back soon, the food will be all gone." He paused. "Are you coming?"

"Soon," she promised.

Still he lingered, reluctant to leave her. Phoenix returned to counting the stars—dozens of them now, and the sky growing ever darker. A new moon was slipping up from the eastern horizon, a mere sliver of light, like a sliver of hope in a darkening world. Finally Michael turned and went back toward the camp alone.

You take care of him, Mother Earth, she chided. He needs taking care of.

I took care of his child, did I not?

Oh, yes. Saved it from death by starvation. Brought it safely to where there was medical attention for it. But then—

Phoenix watched over Jacqueline's shoulder as she examined the child again in the morning, wondering at the temerity of this hero who had cheated death twice now: once at Nina's hands, once from starvation. How charmed is your life, little hero? she wondered. Will it extend to your father when we get back? Will it keep him from knowing who you really are?

"You're sure he's all right?" Phoenix asked anxiously.

"Remarkably well, all things considered," Jacqueline replied. The baby squalled its protest at being examined before breakfast. "Lungs are fine, that's for sure."

"There's something I didn't tell you last night," Phoenix confessed. "He's a child of incest."

Jacqueline glanced up at her, studying her face. After a moment she turned back to her instruments. "No trace of physical defect," she responded. "Or any mental retardation. Incest doesn't guarantee aberration, you know; it just increases the likelihood." She picked the child up and cradled him in her arms, jiggling him and crooning softly. "Father and daughter?" she guessed.

"Half brother and sister," Phoenix told her. "And the mother isn't really dead; but the rest of the People . . ."

"Rejected him," she surmised. "So you took him."

There was a barb in the comment that Phoenix did not miss. "I rescued him!" she flared. "I had to smuggle him out of the camp so they wouldn't kill him. I'm not in the habit of stealing babies."

The eyes Jacqueline raised to hers were hard. "Oh?"

That burned even worse. "Karen Reichert rejected her child!"

Phoenix snapped. "She wouldn't feed it, wouldn't hold it, wouldn't even look at it. That's not my fault. Yes, I was thrilled to have Sky Dancer, but I would never have taken her away from a mother who wanted her."

"If you'd left Karen here," Jacqueline said levelly, "where there was adequate care for her during delivery—"

"The child belonged to the People!" Phoenix insisted. "Just as this one does. Karen was willing to come with me; you heard her."

"Karen was willing to avoid conflict," Jacqueline shot back. "If you'd left her—"

The Infirmary door slid open, and Jacqueline broke off abruptly as Lana came in. "Good morning, Dr. Winthrop," the girl sang. "Good morning . . . uh . . ."

"Phoenix," Phoenix supplied. "Good morning."

"Sounds like he's hungry!" Lana commented, taking the child from Jacqueline. "Come here, little guy; we'll take care of that." She took the wailing infant off to a chair in the corner, where his screams were quickly quieted.

Jacqueline turned back to the examining table, picking up her instruments. "Did you ever wonder what happened to Karen after you brought her back here?" she asked softly.

"I tried not to," Phoenix said candidly. "Was she—did she suffer injury from the childbirth?"

"Not physical injury, no." Jacqueline moved to a bank of cupboards to stow the instruments. "But she never had another child. Hysterical contraception, you might call it. Her mind just wouldn't let her body go through that again."

"Well, you'll pardon me if I haven't much sympathy," Phoenix gritted. "She didn't do very well by the one child she had."

"She did all right by Mike Thornton's kids after their mother died," Jacqueline replied. She nodded toward the nursing girl. "Lana's the oldest of three. They all call Karen 'Mom.'"

"Very touching. I'm happy for her." Phoenix folded her arms across her chest. "When can I take the baby on to the northern village?"

For a moment she thought the older woman hadn't heard her. Jacqueline continued to put things away, until the last instrument was in its place and the cupboard door was closed. "Give him at least two more days to recover," she said finally. "I'll rig up some bottles like the ones you had, two of milk, the rest glucose. Milk won't keep long in this heat; I can spare you a couple of coldpacks, but that's it. Is there a wet nurse waiting?"

"There are always three or four women nursing," Phoenix *assured her, trying to think of someone beside Swan. The irony was too heavy: Michael's child nursing at Swan's breast, and neither of them aware of its parentage.*

"Medically speaking, I know he'll survive the trip," Jacqueline *said, her back toward Phoenix.* "But humanly speaking, I ask you not to do this."

The request cut at Phoenix, for she knew how just it was. But this was Sky Dancer's baby, and she had promised to save it. "I have to take him," *she whispered.* "He is Of the People."

And he is Coconino's grandson, she added silently. And mine.

Once more the door slid open, and behind Phoenix a familiar voice called out, "Oh, there you are."

Phoenix spun around, startled as a rabbit caught in a snare. But the speaker was not looking at her; she was looking at Lana. Off to the side with Jacqueline, Phoenix had not even been noticed.

She stared at the newcomer. Karen Reichert had put on weight in the past twenty years, a good twenty or thirty pounds, but it had the effect of making her look healthier and more content. Her face with its delicate bones seemed to glow as she greeted her stepdaughter, and there was no trace of the worry or the apathy that had always warred across her visage when she had lived in Phoenix's house among the People. One could imagine she was a proud grandmother, looking down at her own grandson—

—her own grandson!

Phoenix gasped, and at the sound Karen turned. As soon as she saw the primitive woman, Karen blanched and her eyes took on a haunted look. I know that look, Phoenix thought. That is the look in the eyes of a deer when it knows the hunter will send a shaft to its heart.

"Hello, Karen," she said gently. *I am no hunter today.*

Karen swallowed. "Hello," *she managed.*

"Don't worry, I'm just passing through," Phoenix *assured her.*

"I—I—needed to talk to Lana," Karen *explained, waving a hand vaguely at the girl.* "I'll just—I'll see her later." *She turned for the door.*

"Oh, no, Mom, don't go!" Lana *protested.* "Come here and look at this little fellow. Look how sweet! He's almost as dark as Darla, isn't he? Only his hair isn't curly like hers." *She*

detached the baby from her breast and held him up for her stepmother to see.

Torn back by the small, sweet voice, Karen stopped her intended flight and turned to look at the child. Immediately the fear faded from her eyes and face, and she knelt beside them for a closer look. "Oh, isn't he precious!" she breathed. "Look how bright his eyes are! And his fingers are so tiny. Were Darla's ever this tiny?"

"They grow so fast," Lana agreed, laying him on her shoulder and patting his back. "Dr. Winthrop, I was wondering, if you don't mind, could I just take him home for today and feed him there so I don't have to keep running back to the Infirmary? I mean, who's going to watch him here, anyway?"

I am, Phoenix wanted to shout. But she kept silent.

"From a medical viewpoint there's no reason you shouldn't." Jacqueline told her. "But that's up to his guardian angel here."

Now a new fear wrote itself on Karen's face as Phoenix's connection to the child made her guess at the truth. *Is he—?* her eyes pleaded. *Is he in your keeping because he is Sky Dancer's child?*

No, Phoenix wanted to shout. *No, he's an orphan and no part of you. His tribe rejected him just as you rejected Sky Dancer. He's mine now because I want him. Because his mother is my daughter, not yours. Because he has only one grandfather, and that is Coconino.*

But again she kept silent. She turned her back on them, on the pleading eyes and the unspoken question. When she thought logically about it . . . "It's probably best if you do," she forced herself to say. "Silly to make you run over here all the time." *It's only that I want him near me, where I can watch over him, protect him, love him . . .*

"Take him to Cyd Ryan at least once today," Jacqueline cautioned as Lana and Karen started for the door with the baby. "I don't want you shortchanging Darla."

"All right," Lana promised. Then to Phoenix she said, "You can come, too, if you like."

From the corner of her eye Phoenix saw Karen stiffen. *I am not a thief!* she wanted to shout. *I did not rob you!* And yet she knew she had. The theft had occurred long before Sky Dancer was born. Perhaps it had occurred the night she had sent Coconino to Karen, using the hapless woman in their plot to destroy the Homeward Bound. "No, thank you," Phoenix declined po-

litely. "You'll have your hands full with two babies. I'll just stay out of the way."

Then Karen and her stepdaughter went out, taking Coconino's grandchild with them.

When the door had closed, Phoenix was silent for a long time, face toward the wall. *Mother Earth, why did you send her here? she raged. Why did you let that woman intrude upon my mission? Why did you show me the joy in her face when she saw the child—and the terror when she saw me? I never meant to hurt her, I only meant . . .*

I only meant to have Coconino's child, in whatever way, at whatever cost. But Karen is the one who bore the cost, and what has her compensation been?

Finally Phoenix heard Jacqueline stir behind her. "Well, I'm going to the commissary for some breakfast," the older woman announced. "Want to come along?"

Phoenix drew a deep breath and tried to square her shoulders. "If it's all right with you," she managed to say, "I'll just take some bread and cheese and be on my way."

Jacqueline did not move. Then, "Phoenix," she began softly.

But Phoenix turned to cut her off, tears streaming down her face. "The People believe there is a balance to life," she said, her voice catching. "Something added here, something subtracted there. For every day of scorching sun, a day of cooling rain. For every crop that fails, one that is bountiful. And when a person is given a great gift by the Mother Earth, eventually there's a price to be paid." She picked up her bow and pack from where they rested against the wall. "Sky Dancer was my gift," she told Jacqueline. "I've just been called to account."

"Not by me!" Jacqueline said.

"No," Phoenix said. "By the Mother Earth.

It's all about letting go, isn't it? Phoenix thought as she drew near to the camp now. When I find something of value, I try so desperately to hang on to it, but sometimes when you love, you need to let go. Sometimes what is best for the one you love is to let go and let someone else carry the burden. So with children, who must shoulder their own burdens; so with the babe, whose life could not be among the People; so with the People tomorrow morning . . .

They had not, she saw, gone off to bed yet but were gathered around a small fire, kept burning for its cheer and not its warmth on a night that was balmy and clear. Overhead the sky was ablaze with stars that laughed at the tiny fire, silent laughter that was echoed in the audible calls of night birds.

Purple Thistle was telling a story. "And then Coconino mounted up on the back of Tala, and they flew around the village once, twice, three times. The first time Tala's coat was as red as the Red Rocks, the second time it was blue as the sky, and the third time it was black as night. Wherever their shadow passed, the corn grew half again as tall and the rabbits ran in terror from the fields and did not disturb the grain again. Then they came down to the earth, and where Tala's feet landed, four mesquite trees sprang up, one by each hoof, to shade great Coconino from the blazing sun."

Nonsense, Phoenix thought. Drivel. Coconino would have loved it.

"Then Coconino said to the People," Purple Thistle went on, " 'Behold! See that my word is true! Have I not brought you Tala, as I said? I will make the rains to fall upon your fields and the squash to grow fat on the vine. While I walk among you, you shall lack for nothing. It is the gift of the Mother Earth.' "

She caught Michael's eyes across the fire. He looked totally disgusted with this blatant fabrication, but Phoenix laid a warning finger across her lips. Let them invent stories to celebrate the greatness that had been theirs, for Coconino represented to them all that was good in the People. Few here had actually known him: those on her Council, a handful of others, and that was all. The life of the People was strenuous, and they seldom lived much past their fourth decade. They needed these stories to connect them, to pass along their enriched memories to succeeding generations.

Besides, Coconino always wanted to be a hero in the stories of the People.

Not me, she thought, turning away from the gathering. I never asked to be She Who Saves. I did what I had to do, because it had to be done. I moved the People north to protect them when Tony Hanson took retribution into his own hands. I led them for years, keeping them safe for Coconino's return. I saved Sky Dancer's baby even though that meant giving it up. In none of those things did I seek glory for myself; I was only as strong as the circumstances demanded I be.

And as clever, sighed the night breeze.

Phoenix suppressed a smile as she sought out her own sleeping place. Not as clever as you, though, Mother Earth. And whomever else I have bluffed or buffaloed or plainly deceived, I can never do that to you. I know it now.

A cricket chirped a chuckling chirp. *You grow wiser, Witch Woman.*

Just in time, Phoenix thought wickedly.

Peace. I will care for you. Come to my bosom, as the child came to Lana's breast, for sustenance and warmth and comfort.

Phoenix found a spot far from the fire and knelt to check the ground carefully for anything that might disturb her sleep. She had stayed away from the Camp of the Others, though for the past several years traders had gone every fall and sometimes again in the spring. None of the People ever remarked on a child there with copper skin and black hair, but why should they? The skin tones of the Others ranged from Rita Zleboton's lava black, to warm browns and muted yellows, on up to Jacqueline Winthrop's pinkish pale. The child would never stand out among so many. Even Coral Snake, if he returned there, would probably not think to ask where one more child had come from.

Stretching herself out on the ground, Phoenix breathed deeply of the sweet fragrance of the grass and the soil. Is this what it smells like from the grave? she wondered. When I laid Sky Dancer's baby in a shallow grave to fool Nina, when I placed the basket over its head to protect it, is this what he smelled? I wish I could have asked him . . .

CHAPTER NINETEEN

"Gerta, have we heard from all the directors?" Tana asked her secretary.

On the display, Gerta's image showed no sign of the fact that Tana had her working on at least six projects simultaneously, not to mention screening all her calls and mail and acting as a receptionist for three other executives. She simply glanced at one of the many displays built into her workstation and reported, "All but Rhodesia Winthrop; I have a call in to her now to see what's what there. It looks like eight directors are attending Roundup with their families, one coming alone, but in the flesh. That's Conti."

Tana shook her head, tapping her fingers lightly on her transparent desk. "He's got five kids. I don't care about the ex-wives, but I want the five kids at Roundup. Call Marseille and have her check into it. If it's the cost, I'll foot the transportation bill; if it's anything else and there's something we can do, we'll do it. Do we know where Jordan is?"

"Still connected to the Patent Bureau. Do you want me to break in?"

"No!" Tana exclaimed quickly. "No, I need him to push Paul's patent through. I'll go with just Lu; I can't stall around anymore. Get Montag for me and bring Lu into the conversation."

When she had disconnected, Tana leaned back in her chair and took a deep breath. It had been only a week since she and Paul had visited Coconino, but it had been the most frantic week of her life. The plan Coconino had presented to them was remarkable and testified to a depth of understanding that surprised even her, but it seemed somehow too simple. For all its brilliance and beauty, Tana didn't know if it would work. Unwilling to risk failure, she had continued to work on schemes of her own that, she hoped, would complement his plan, buying the time and the commitment it needed to be effective.

Where was her call? Doc whined as Tana fretted, so she leaned over to stroke his chin and found that action as soothing to herself as to Doc. "Good dog," she crooned. "You'd rather be at home, too, wouldn't you?" Then, on impulse, she asked him mentally, *Are there many puppies at home?*

He cocked his head and looked at her quizzically. *Puppies?*

Yes. Are there many? At home, with Dakota?

Many puppies, he agreed, and then he turned and tested the air in the room. *Not here.*

No, not here, Tana smiled at his confusion. *We will see them later.*

Suddenly something caught his attention. *Someone comes,* he informed her. *A no-smell person.*

Tana straightened up as the computer chimed softly. "Your call with Wolfgang Montag and Lu Parnette is ready."

"Go ahead," Tana instructed, calling Doc to attention at her side.

Montag's huge desk appeared in space across from Tana's with the slick shipper seated behind it. At her right Lu Parnette appeared in a chair that looked as though it were part of Tana's office. Flanked by quiet lawyer and regal Dalmatian, Tana gave the briefest of smiles. "Mr. Montag."

"Ms. Winthrop." He did not stand up to greet her today, nor did he call her by her first name. The look on his face was smug, the look of someone who had the upper hand in a bargain. Tana itched to disillusion him.

"I understand," Tana began, "that my CFO agreed to sell you P-TUP."

"Terms and conditions to be negotiated, but yes," he agreed with glinting eyes. "I have her witnessed agreement to sell."

"You have Troaxian stock, Mr. Montag," she informed him. "Delhi Striker has no authority to sell without my approval, and it doesn't matter how many Guild justices witnessed it."

Eyes flashed, and he half rose behind his impressive desk. "That was a good-faith bargain," he hissed. "You try to back out on this and I'll sue you—"

"And lose," she finished for him. "You will sue me and lose, Mr. Montag, because Jordan Zleboton assures me that's what will happen. The Dynasty structure is ironclad and allows me to override any agreement, any time, for any reason. But do sit down. As it happens, I am willing to honor that agreement with certain stipulations."

Montag hesitated, glaring at her, weighing in his mind the validity of her assertion. Jordan's reputation was well known in Transportation Guild circles. As for Tana herself . . . He sat down. "I'm listening."

Tana gave him a cool smile. "Good. Now, I found it unusual when we spoke several weeks ago that you would have an interest in acquiring a patent for new warp technology. Transuniversal is in the shipping business; you buy warp terminals, not warp technology. But my chief of information resources tells me that you have recently made an offer on a small manufacturing plant. Is it your intention, Mr. Montag, to manufacture P-TUP yourself?"

His eyes gleamed as he mistook her intention. "A share in the profits, is that it? Yes, I intend to manufacture it, and because there is no competition for it, the profits will be astronomical. But you know very well I can't bring you in on the deal. If I bring in outside investors, my company becomes subject to a number of unfavorable restrictions. However, there are ways around every obstacle. If you would like to see a royalty arrangement—"

"No, I'd like to see your ethics take a turn for the better," she replied smoothly. "If you bring P-TUP onto the market suddenly, existing manufacturers of warp equipment will have to either sink millions into developing similar technology or face the prospect of going out of business in the next ten years. Your colleagues in the shipping business will have to either buy the product you manufacture or face a similar fate. This creates chaos in the industry, Mr. Montag. I dislike chaos. It's bad for business, and it's very, very hard on individuals.

"Now, let's pretend for a moment," she continued, "that you are an ethical man. A taxing stretch of the imagination, I grant you, but bear with me. If you were an ethical man, you could do two things. One, you could go to your colleagues in the Transportation Guild and tell them what you have done: purchased a new warp technology which will profoundly affect your industry in the coming decades. They will gasp; they will be amazed; they will begin to invest in research along similar lines; and they will make plans to meet the challenge of change. Two, you could tell these fine colleagues of yours that you are going to bury the patent for five years to allow them a chance to carry out their preparations."

"Five years!" Montag barked.

"Why, you'd be a hero!" Tana said sweetly. "Your status in the Guild would be higher than the Guildmaster's. You'd be the savior of your industry. And in five years you would still have the only P-TUP patent in existence and the opportunity to make more money than you can spend in one lifetime. Think about it, Mr. Montag. Five years of honor and adulation, and at the end you have the P-TUP patents, or five years of litigation, and at the end you will have no patent—only a very large legal bill."

There was murder in his eyes, but all Wolfgang Montag could do was ball his hands into impotent holographic fists. "Three years," he gritted, "and you halt all research on further P-TUP devices."

"This is not negotiable, Mr. Montag," she told him coolly. "Ms. Parnette has a contract prepared. The terms and conditions in it are the only ones to which I will agree. Lu?"

Lu straightened up in her chair. "I'd like to send this document for your eyes only, Mr. Montag. Will you give me a secured address?"

Montag glared at the lawyer, then punched a code into the keypad on his desk. The code appeared in the air over his head. Lu tapped it into her wristpad without comment.

"I'll study the contract and get back to you," he grumbled as the code dissolved in a shower of colored sparkles around him.

"You'll sign the contract and return it," Tana stated. "Or you'll be holding so much fairy dust in your hand. Good day, Mr. Montag." A wave of her hand dispelled both his and Lu's images from the room.

Doc's tail thumped against the floor. *Good?* he asked.

Great! she exulted, blowing out a noisy breath. *Let's go tell Paul.*

Tana and Paul had seen little of each other during the past week, and when they had, they'd both been tense and worried. While she courted directors and diplomats and plotted her strategy against Montag, Paul chiseled away at the problem of sending Coconino back in time. To complicate matters, he had elected not to bring any of his team in on this project. "I don't want them to know," he'd said simply. "I don't want anyone to know."

Narrowing the date Coconino wanted had been a problem in itself. It was in "the Moon of the Shallow Rivers" that Phoenix had gone down to the Well, or so legend said. And according to Coconino's recollection of the letter she had left behind for him, it was twenty-five years after the loss of the *Homeward Bound*. The year was easy enough to calculate, but Tana had had to go back to Nathan to find out that the Moon of the Shallow Rivers translated to month Six, Argoan Standard. As for the day within that month—"I do not know," Coconino had confessed. "Send me to the day of the new moon; that would be an auspicious day for a ceremony."

Paul had grumbled about being able to get within a year of the right date, let alone a day.

Again Tana had voiced her caution that Coconino must not try to interfere with what legend said had happened to She Who Saves. "Then set me in the Well some days before the new moon," he replied. "I will wait for her there to say good-bye if that is all. The walls are very steep and jagged, and there are many shelves cut into them. I can stay out of sight of the People up above; they will not know I am there. Only to Phoenix will I reveal myself."

That's the problem, Tana thought now as she approached the lab. If she sees him, what will she do? How will that change things?

Or did she see him the first time? Is all this worry for naught because it has already happened?

We will never know. Whatever occurs, whatever does or doesn't change, we will never know.

The lab was strangely quiet when she entered. Gone to lunch? she wondered. All in their offices working furiously? Even Todd was nowhere to be seen.

Paul sat alone in his office, visible through the transparent half wall. He looked tired—worse than tired, she thought. He looked . . . gray. There was none of the intense concentration that characterized his thinking, no casual slouch to his body while he played with ideas. She stopped in his doorway, watching him gaze numbly at his display, his brows slightly knit, one hand cupped over his chin.

"Penny for your thoughts?" she ventured.

He lifted clear blue eyes to her, but even they seemed dull today. "Do you know what a penny is?" he asked.

Tana shrugged. "Something you give someone for their thoughts."

"An ancient form of coinage," he told her. "It fluctuated in value over several centuries, decreasing steadily until the universal monetary system was established in the twenty-second century.''

"Then I guess I can't really offer you a penny," she said. "Share your thoughts anyway?''

"The truth?'' His hand dropped to his lap, and he stared at the figures on his display. "I've been thinking of resigning''

For a moment she stood in the doorway as the implications rolled over her. The institute without Paul? It had been before, it could be again. But Paul without the institute? What would he do? Another lab somewhere? No early retirement, certainly. For Paul, research was like breathing; his scientific curiosity could not be shut off without killing the man. Yet his statement did not take her totally by surprise. His work had laid heavy demands on his emotions lately; this last project was the worst.

Slowly Tana came into the room, moved around his desk, and settled herself on the edge of it like a schoolgirl. Her hand reached out to stroke his thinning hair. "I'm tired, too," she whispered.

But Paul took her hand, kissed it, and shook his head. "It's not just tired, Tana," he said. "It's—it's no fun anymore." Sorrow tinged his voice. "For all the years I've worked here, I always enjoyed what I did. There were days, sure, when I'd rather have gone riding, but I never dreaded coming in to work. This past week, Tana, I have dreaded work. It's an odd feeling, and I hate it.''

"It will be over soon," she assured him.

"Will it?'' He turned questioning eyes to her. "Coconino vanishes, and I don't know if I've fulfilled his dream or killed him; will that ever go away? The technology I've devoted my life to creating now threatens not only his world but every other world; will that ever go away? I've always worked in research, Tana, but I've never been very close to the application until the past few years. At first it was heady, but now I'm not sure I like it. It's like a composer hearing his work done badly; you're not sure you want anyone to play it ever again.''

"No one has played your work badly," she told him. "Not yet. And even if they did, is that any reason to stop creating?'' She slipped off the desk and settled herself in his lap. "Paul, if you're not having fun anymore, I agree you should find something else to do. But it doesn't have to be outside the institute. What you need is a new project. Leave P-TUP in Todd's hands— he's perfectly capable of handling things from here on out. Set your sights on something new. Push the envelope. You'll never be happy doing anything else.''

A small smile tugged at the corner of his mouth. "Why do I think you have a project in mind?''

She grinned back at him. "Because you know me so well. Just finish up the time warp problem, and then we clear the books. As soon as Roundup is over, we start with a fresh screen.'' Her look turned sly. "Or would you like to go to work for Wolfgang Montag?''

A wry laugh escaped him. "What did he say when you threw those conditions at him?''

Tana shrugged. "What could he say except uncle? I expect I'll have the signed document back tomorrow.''

"Just in time for your board meeting Thursday.''

"I don't know about you,'' she said, "but I'm looking forward to the weekend, when all this is behind us.''

Just then the computer chimed, and Gerta's voice came through. "Tana, I'm sorry to interrupt, but Zim is calling. What shall I tell him?''

Tana felt Paul's arm tighten around her. It occurred to her to say she was necking with her husband in the lab and would call him back, but of course she didn't. "Ask if I can call him back in fifteen minutes,'' she told Gerta. "I suspect I'll want to be comfortably seated in my own office when I talk to him.''

Zimbabwe Goetz was an impressive figure, nearly seven feet tall with a well-muscled, angular frame. He was darker than the ancestor for whom he was named, Zimbabwe Zleboton, although not as dark as the old judge, Zachery. His eyes were a soft brown flecked with green, and he wore his tightly curling hair closely clipped. The square jaw and the high forehead gave his head a rectangular shape.

Tana was surprised when his full image appeared in the space in front of her desk. Their infrequent conversations were usually held on small desktop displays, not using life-size holographics. Apparently he thought this conversation important enough to warrant such a medium.

"Hello, Tana.'' He towered over her, his robes richly done in green and gold. The stiffened shoulders were less winglike than the ones Wolfgang Montag wore, but then, they didn't need to be as severe. Zim's size didn't require augmentation.

Tana rose gracefully from her chair and came around the desk. "Hello, Zim,'' she greeted. "I still haven't seen your name on the accommodations list for Roundup. You really should come in the flesh.''

"I may yet," he conceded. "It depends on a number of things. I'm sure Helsi will find a place for me if I decide to come.''

Tana's aunt Helsi had been coordinating Roundup for two decades, and Tana had no doubt the woman would find accommodations for the CEO of the entire Winthrop Dynasty should he choose to grace that event with his corporeal presence. It would also flatter Helsi no end. "Fresh Junoan air and unfiltered sunlight," Tana tempted.

"And the constant Junoan wind laden with hay dust," he pointed out. Zim was city born and raised, and although he claimed he could ride a horse, no one had ever seen him do it. "Have a chair, Tana," he invited. "I don't mean to keep you standing.''

Instead of going back behind her desk, however, Tana instructed Doc to push her chair out to one side. It was poor etiquette to face Zim across a desk. He also drew up a chair away from other furniture, and the two of them sat face to face, she leaning back into the supporting upholstery, he leaning forward with long legs crossed and hands clasped and resting on his knee.

"I hear you've sold a patent you haven't filed yet," he began.

On the attack already! But then, Tana expected nothing less of Zim. "It's been filed," she contradicted. "Jordan's getting the final approval as we speak. The sale contract hasn't been signed yet.''

"But the agreement predated the filing," he pressed.

"Yes, it did." One never lied to Zim. "In my absence, Delhi found herself in a difficult position. She made the agreement as the least of many evils and with full disclosure to the buyer regarding the filing status. I support her decision.''

"That's good of you," he commented, "since it was your absence which put her in that difficult position to begin with.''

Only long training in controlling her reactions kept Tana from flushing red. This was exactly the point Delhi would try to make at the board meeting. "It was the Pax embargo on trade with Kalopis that put Delhi in an untenable position," she disagreed. "Research always has risks, Zim; there's no getting around that. What happened to me was no different than being on a one-terminal asteroid when a cylinder of warp crystals fails. It's just that the replacement part was a bit more costly.''

"It looks to me as though it's not through costing us," he

replied. "I know you and Delhi have had your differences over the years, but outside the boardroom you've always presented a united front. Now, these are serous allegations she is making. If the board supports her and recommends your removal as CEO . . ."

"Then I'll tender my resignation without protest," Tana finished. "I'm not looking for a power struggle, Zim. I have much more important concerns at the moment."

His eyebrows shot up. "More important than losing the institute?"

A small smile played at her lips. "Lose it? What is there to lose? The institute has accomplished its. goal, Zim. Chelsea Winthrop set it on course, and I took it across the finish line. It's not a question of winning or losing the institute but of creating it anew." Tana shook her head. "A good many things stand to be lost in that meeting Thursday, but the institute is not one of them."

Zim leaned his tall frame back in the chair. "You always did have a unique perspective, Tana," he told her. For a moment he studied her with his deceptively mild eyes. As a man who held the reigns to one of the most prestigious and powerful dynasties in the universe, he found this woman who valued other things more than prestige and power quite intriguing. Finally he said, "Let me hear the story from your point of view. Because if the board calls for your resignation and I accept it, you can't just slide over to another Winthrop company. You know that."

"I know, Zim." Tana shifted in her chair, wishing it had not already been a long day. "Only let me get something to drink before we get started. This may take a while."

There were nearly five hundred members of the Winthrop clan now, and each year over two hundred of them returned to the family estate on Juno for Roundup. As with all family reunions, there was a lot of food, a lot of laughter, and a lot of remembering. Elders cooed over how youngsters had grown, youngsters played with the puppies and rode the horses, and ranch hands grumbled under their breath at the general state of chaos that existed for four days. Dozens of activities were planned: a venkball tournament, a horse show, light painting and roller surfing and croquet and other games without number. But mostly people clustered in groups of five or six and traded stories. "Did I tell you about the time Monti asked his elementary graphics instructor if 3-D was an optical illusion?" "Someone told me that Great-great-great-grandma Verde Winthrop served briefly as minister of agriculture under the Troaxians.'' ''I understand Sydney's daughter, Genoa, is taking her family to that new colony they've opened up in the Korianne system.''

Tana always enjoyed the warmth and mayhem of Roundup, for she reveled in her extended family, in its history and the values it represented. Normally she put on her denim pants and Western shirt and disappeared into the masses of relatives, just another niece or cousin or something twice removed.

But this year Roundup was her tool, and she set out to wield it with maximum efficiency. Beginning Thursday morning, she camped out by the warp terminal at *Terra Firma* and greeted the arriving guests, sizing up their mood, their receptivity, and counting the children in each family. By noon all nine of her board of directors had arrived, and she was pleased to note that while some of them were obviously uncomfortable with her, none of them was openly hostile. Whatever Delhi had said to them individually, they had not closed themselves off from her. Not yet. Gratefully she retired to her bedroom for a hot soak and a quick nap before setting the final phase of Coconino's plan in motion.

Dak was in the living room when she came downstairs, gazing out the window toward the riding stable and smiling to himself. He was freshly showered and smelled of some pungent male cosmetic, rolling up the sleeves on a casual open-weave tunic. Doc sniffed curiously, straining his nose in Dak's direction, but he knew better than to leave Tana's side without permission. ''And which female cousin are you trying to bedazzle this year?'' Tana asked drily.

Dak turned from the window with a grin that belied his deprecating shrug. ''None of them,'' he protested. ''I like to be clean once a day; is that all right?''

But his biometer glinted subtly in the hollow of his neck above his left collarbone, a deep, healthy green. The cut of his tunic made it just barely visible should any female be inquisitive. Tana tried to peer around his broad shoulders to see what or whom he had been watching out the window, but all she could see was Lystra and Mouse patiently leading a pair of ponies around the yard with assorted Winthrop younglings on their backs. ''If I didn't know better,'' Tana teased, ''I'd think Wanda had decided to come.''

Immediately his smile faded, and Tana knew it had been a

stupid thing to say. Why keep pointing out the woman's faults? She tried to apologize. "I only meant—"

"You've been kind of busy the past few weeks," he interrupted, his voice level. "I guess you haven't heard much gossip."

"Gossip?" Frantically Tana tried to recall something the children might have said, some comment of Bertha's that she might have overheard.

"Wanda and I had a little set-to the other day," Dak told her calmly, still rolling his sleeves. "The long and the short of it is, I don't think we'll be seeing each other anymore."

Tana's jaw dropped. "Oh." She didn't know what to say. In many ways she thought it was the best thing that could happen to her brother, but after so many years— "Oh, Dak, I'm sorry. I—I didn't—"

"I'm not," he said flatly, rescuing her. "It was my choice. She just went too far with her—her snobbery and said one too many uncalled-for things, and I had enough. I don't need that. I don't need her." Clear blue eyes stared unseeing out the window for a moment; then he turned and grinned down at his sister. "Don't worry. I've fallen off horses before; it never takes me long to get back in the saddle." He arranged the tucks his belt formed in the tunic. "There is a dance tonight, isn't there?"

"I don't know," she had to admit. "I haven't really gotten past tonight's board meeting. Is the portable ready?"

"Parked it myself," he assured her. "Just past the knoll, like you specified. Controls are all active, furniture's in place—all the comforts of home." Then he noticed her business robes. "You aren't going to supper dressed like that, are you?"

"I'm having supper with Paul at the lab," she told him. "I have some things yet to do, and I don't really want to be available before the meeting, anyway. I'll see you later."

"Tana." He stopped her and gave her a sturdy hug. "Don't worry. Things are going to go great tonight."

"I hope so," she murmured. "For Earth's sake, I hope so."

Monticello Winthrop was waiting for his daughter when she arrived back at *Terra Firma* twenty minutes before the meeting was to start. There was no mistaking the concern in his eyes as he greeted her, but he smiled that roguish Winthrop smile. "You look radiant," he told her, observing the emerald-green robes that clung to her slender form and caught the light with each step she took.

"Thank you," she said. "I feel like yesterday's lunch. How's the search for a new headquarters going?"

He made a deprecating noise. "The DeBanians want too much money; the Loki will lease, but they won't sell. Personally, I haven't seen a site yet I'm excited about. It'll keep me out of mischief for another year or two, at least."

"Have you got that much time?" she asked frankly.

"More than you have," he said gently. "Tana, I've talked to every one of the directors. Marseille and Jonathan are the hard cases, of course; Conti and Dublin and Chattanooga are solidly in your corner. As for the others—"

But she stilled her father with a finger on his lips. "Dad, this is not about me," she said. "This is about basic rights of self-determination, and protecting the defenseless, and respecting what we don't understand. You always taught me that a Winthrop was a cut above other citizens; tonight we're going to find out if that's true."

Monti said nothing, but she read the doubt in his face, in the grim set of his mouth. Human nature was human nature, after all. Look at Delhi and Jordan and the others who served the institute without caring about the purpose for which it was founded. The workings of the machine were more important to them than the task it was designed to do.

"Where's Paul?" Monti asked, seeing that Tana and Doc had arrived alone.

"He'll be along later," Tana assured him. "I'm afraid I'm running late myself. Walk with me to the portable?"

Monti smiled again and gave his daughter his arm. She took it gratefully as they left the hangar and started across the bare dirt yard toward a stretch of grassy ground that rolled away to the north of Uncle Paris's house.

An ancient butterleaf tree grew at the top of a knoll. Every Winthrop who ever set foot on *Terra Firma* had come to that tree at some point. It was not impressive for its height or for the patchy shade its spreading branches offered, but it was a *tree*, after all, in a prairie where few grew naturally. So it was under this tree over two hundred years before that Cincinnati Winthrop had erected a slab of Junoan marble with an inscription in plain block letters: THERE IS ONLY ONE ROAD WORTH TRAVELING: THAT WHICH VENTURES FORTH. —CLAYTON WINTHROP.

Tana had asked Dak to set the portable just beyond that knoll so that the directors coming to the meeting would have to pass by the monument and be reminded of their spacefaring ancestors. Though she was late, Tana could not resist pausing herself to run her fingers across its wind-scoured surface. She thought of that other marker on another small hill, crude by comparison to this fine stone. But the sentiment that had erected it had been the same. "What would you think," she asked her father, "if I told you that on Earth there is a knoll very like this one on which there is a stone marker that bears the name Jacqueline Winthrop?"

Monti looked down at her with a measuring eye. Unlike Dak, he had not been apprised of Tana's recent misadventures. "I'd say that a lot of rumors I've been hearing lately are true," he responded.

A smile spread slowly across her face. "Many of them are, Dad. There is such a knoll. They call it Winthrop Hill, and it is covered with stone markers. I've been there."

Monti took a deep breath and let it out carefully. "I always knew you'd do it," he said softly. "I didn't think it would cost you this much."

"I can afford it," she said bluntly. "I don't want the Terrans to have to pay as well, though. That's what this is all about tonight, Dad."

"Anything I can do?" he asked.

"Yes," she replied quickly. "See Dak; he knows the plan and he could use your help. And Dad?" She slipped her arms around his neck. "Say a prayer for me, will you? I'm going to need it."

Then Tana turned and walked on toward the portable alone, with Doc padding quietly ahead.

The room grew quiet as Tana walked in. As Dak had promised, the portable building had been suitably appointed to serve as a conference room, right down to the upholstered chair that floated on air jets, ready for her use at the head of the table. Tana paused in the doorway to look at her directors, to take in their faces, their attitudes, their relative positions. They were all seated and waiting, including Delhi. Tana moved to her place and activated the official recorder. "Thank you all for coming," she began. "Zim has requested to view this meeting, so no remarks about the Marauders losing to the Belt Jockeys last week."

There was a spattering of soft laughter; the Marauders were Zim's favorite venkball team. Tension in the room eased slightly.

"I didn't call this meeting," Tana went on. "Delhi did. So at this point I'm going to turn it over to her. Delhi?"

Delhi looked surprised. Had she expected Tana to take the offensive, to speak out before Delhi had a chance, to make her fight for the floor? No, that is what you would have done, Cousin, Tana thought. My instincts tell me that would be wrong. You say your piece, make your accusations, state your case. Then I will speak. Then.

Her surprise quickly banished, Delhi rose from her place. Like Tana, she had opted for business attire, a chic tailored suit in charcoal black. She cut a stylish but no-nonsense figure as she addressed the board. "Not many months ago," Delhi started out, "our esteemed CEO sat at a board meeting and told you P-TUP was five years away. Shortly afterward I learned that was a blatant and purposeful misrepresentation. The very day that she told us this, a working prototype was being tested by Dr. Rutgers in his laboratory."

Tana smiled blandly, leaning back in her chair and watching Delhi perform. Her eyes did not stray from the tiny woman, yet she saw the reactions on all their faces. Some were shocked; some had foreknowledge; one or two were excited by the prospect. So far it was just as Tana had imagined it would be.

Delhi went on. "Needless to say, I was outraged at this bald-faced deception. But Tana claimed it was for reasons of security, for fear that even one of us here would leak the information. So I agreed to keep silent for a time, although I thought her temerity in not making at least her CFO aware of the progress exhibited extremely poor judgment. Knowing now what she planned to do, I understand why she tried so hard to keep me ignorant in the matter."

Still Tana smiled, gray eyes mild as she observed her opponent. She had a flare for drama, did Delhi; her timing here was impeccable. Everyone waited for the bomb to drop.

Delhi drew her face into a dour expression that resembled, Tana thought, a pout. "Two weeks ago," Delhi said sourly, "Tana stepped into the unpatented, partially tested, unregistered P-TUP terminal in Dr. Rutgers's lab and had herself warped—to Earth."

There was a general indrawing of breath from around the table. Oh, well played, Tana thought. Highly charged words, selective truth, a denunciatory tone.

"While she was there, the test equipment failed," Delhi pushed on. "She was left stranded in an unknown situation, while on this end a talented and dedicated staff worked frantically around the clock to find a way to rescue her. But was I apprised? No. Were any of the senior executives apprised? No. In accordance with Tana's directions, the staff was not allowed to convey this information. For five days the institute was without its CEO: no one at the helm, no provisions made for delegation of authority, critical business lost in the shuffle. When I finally forced my way into the lab, the staff had encountered an unsolvable difficulty: they needed a piece of equipment which could no longer be legally purchased from the suppliers, and Tana had alienated the one person who could resell that item from his own warp equipment."

Tana told herself it was amusing, this slanted picture Delhi drew. Rather like a silhouette painting in the Interplanetary Museum of Art in which a man appeared to be plunging a dagger into a woman's throat—until the lights came up within the work and revealed that the silhouetted dagger was actually a colorful scarf clutched in his hand and the couple were not struggling but dancing. Go ahead, Delhi, she thought. Paint your silhouette. I can easily bring up the lights.

"Fortunately, I was able to reason with that person," Delhi was saying, "and obtain the needed item. It came at a high price, however; I was forced to make a sales agreement for the P-TUP patent without the proper leverage to obtain optimum compensation and without the time to approach other possible buyers. Had Tana not withheld the filing of patents connected with the P-TUP project, no covert sale could have been forced. Had our purchasing department had even so much as an equipment list from the P-TUP project, the needed item would have been at hand. Had she not recklessly exposed herself to danger, we would now be receiving offers from half a dozen major manufacturers instead of dickering with just one over a sale which is a foregone conclusion."

Delhi squared her shoulders. "Because of her irresponsible behavior and because she continually puts her personal wants and desires ahead of the best interest of the institute, I therefore urge you to demand her resignation as CEO."

Delhi sat down. Still Tana did not take her eyes from her older cousin or allow her smile to fade. Instead she waited patiently for a full minute, letting her directors begin to shift uneasily as they looked expectantly toward her for her response.

Finally Tana leaned forward in her chair and rested her arms on the table. "Half a dozen manufacturers?" she repeated. "You are modest, Cousin. Not just Filamont and Nikosa and Blue Space but the Unified Military, the Twenty Systems Military, the Sunanto Nations Defense Council . . . And don't forget the Darian Free Alliance, the Meta Zed Liberation Army, and other covert groups who would all be anxious to have the exclusive rights to P-TUP. Just think what they could do with it, ladies and gentlemen." She let that hang just a moment. "Just think what they could do," she echoed softly.

She turned to look directly at Conti, perhaps her best supporter on the board. He was her own age, descended through the Zleboton branch, an agile, energetic man with a notorious social conscience. "Of course," she added, "the increased profits from such a sale would no doubt allow the Winthrop Dynasty to step into the various areas of devastation and help with repairs. They might also offset the economic chaos which is sure to follow the news that conventional warp is obsolete. By the time we finished, we might actually be ahead of the game monetarily—provided we all work for the Dynasty and don't have children and in-laws working in the transportation industry. Having to support three or four extra people whose jobs have disappeared in the turmoil might tip the balance in the other direction."

Drawing a small, slender cylinder from the folds of her robes, Tana slipped it into a port on the conference table. "Speculation. We shall never know now." Her eyes turned to Minsk, a matronly woman who was Monti's first cousin and a financial analyst on call to a number of Winthrop enterprises. "Fortunately, we had a bit of leverage left in dealing with Transuniversal on this sale," she said dryly. "Enough to come up with this. Jethro: show File One."

Around the table displays sprang to life as the signed contract with Wolfgang Montag appeared for each director's review. Eyebrows flew up as the final sale price glittered attractively at the bottom of the file. "Not a bad sum of money, as you can see," Tana commented. "Enough to bring us out of the red and into the black for the past five years—and possibly the next five. Plus, Mr. Montag has graciously agreed to keep P-TUP off the market for those five years, allowing the transportation industry time to adjust." She gave an artful smile aimed at the twin pillars of her opposition, Jonathan and Marseille. "Those of you who know Mr. Montag know what a fine humanitarian he is.

"I also expect," she continued, leaning back, "that five years will buy us enough time to complete the institute's next project.

I have given Dr. Rutgers a new assignment, to commence after an extended vacation which rumor has it he will spend with his wife and children in some remote and peaceful location.'' They were all smiling now, if only a little. No admirer of her politics Jonathan might be, but he was a family man from the word go. Eight of his eleven grown children had come back for Roundup this year. "I have asked him to find a way to block P-TUP transmission," Tana told them, "so that no nation or company or group of people need fear that their environs will be breached without their knowledge and permission. The proper use of P-TUP, Cousins, is in exploration, in venturing into the unknown, not in violating the privileges of others.''

Now she leaned forward again, her gray eyes sharp, her voice earnest. "I have always been concerned with the possible abuse of P-TUP," she said frankly. "But during my recent travels I have discovered reasons to be doubly concerned. Yes, Cousins, I have been to Earth.'' She met each pair of eyes in turn as she spoke: doubtful Jonathan's, dour Marseille's, delighted Conti's, cautious Dublin's. "I had a research waiver from the Transportation Guild; my visit was legal. Jethro: File Two.'' She waited while the displays refreshed with another document. "Earth is not a plague planet; here is a copy of the viroanalysis and biodetection report conducted before any living thing made a test voyage to Earth. Copies were duly filed and verified with the Transportation Guild as a condition of the waiver.'' Filed *after* my visit, she thought privately, but they don't need to know that. It was Lu Parnette's careful wording of the application that allowed for that loophole.

She gave them only a moment to glance at the file. "I have been to Earth, and yes, Cousins, our ancestor Clayton Winthrop was right—Earth is not dead. Chelsea and Zachery were right: the crew of the *Homeward Bound* did survive, marooned in that place by Derek Lujan. I went there to find them, and I will not apologize for that.''

"You did not need to go yourself!'' Delhi interrupted, her face flushed with anger. "You endangered yourself recklessly using equipment that was only in the initial testing stage!''

"And would we have struggled less to bring someone else back?'' Tana pulled a face. "Did you see on the news that a traveler to the Cyrus system was killed when a tube of crystals shattered unexpectedly? Do you suppose that sixty-year-old warp terminal was not fully tested? They're called accidents, Delhi, because that is what they are.'' Again she turned to meet the eyes of each of her directors. "Do any of you honestly think Dr. Paul Rutgers would let any human being—let alone his wife—step into a warp terminal chamber unless he felt it had been fully tested?"

"Why not send his assistant instead of you?" Delhi persisted.

"He did," Tana snapped. "Mr. Chang was the first person to travel via P-TUP." Only to Aunt Shelby's, of course, but they needn't know that, either. "Some research institutes are founded to cure diseases. They don't apologize when that is accomplished. The IDP was established to find and rescue survivors of the *Homeward Bound*. I will not apologize for having found them." Now her expression softened. "But I have learned, dear Cousins, that they do not need rescue. Or at least, they didn't until I came."

Her strength was ebbing rapidly. At her feet Doc shifted restlessly, pricking up his ears. Good, Tana thought. Almost ready.

"There are three civilizations surviving on Earth," Tana told her directors, and saw Dublin's mouth drop open. "One is a settlement peopled by descendants of the *Homeward Bound*. It has been growing and evolving for two hundred sixteen years. They are a clever and resourceful people, proud of what they have built. Two other cultures predate this one by some five hundred years. One is a technological culture which Captain Clayton Winthrop found at the mountain installation which was his destination. He was not privileged to see the other; Derek Lujan saw to that."

Doc got to his feet. *Lie down,* Tana commanded. *Be still, be patient.* He balked but finally lay back down.

"I was so privileged," Tana said. "They call themselves the People. They are primitive, what we call Stone Age. They are untutored in math and science but wise in the ways of nature, and they have built their culture on harmony with the Mother Earth. Each of these three cultures exists in a balance, a balance with each other and with the world they know. If we change their world—if we open the door and let all of our universe come rushing in—what will happen to their balance?"

Heavyset Dublin Winthrop shifted in his chair, a man in his late sixties who had spent twenty-five years as curator of the Interplanetary Museum of Art before retiring two years earlier. That he was excited at the prospect of contact with Earth was obvious. "It seems to me," he told her, "that your sales agreement has effectively stoppered the P-TUP hole. What have they to fear from us?"

"Contamination," Tana replied. "Vessel-housed warp travel is still a viable method for reaching Earth, and with no defenses and no central government in place, how long do you think it will take for fortune hunters to find it? For tourists and thrill seekers to pay to explore it? You know we have a poor track record with aboriginal cultures, Dub. Without appropriate safeguards, why should we do better today than we did a thousand years ago?"

"I don't see that that's our problem," Marseille interjected. She was a woman Delhi's age, a close cousin to Zim, and a formidable presence in her own right. Tana was sure Marseille was the channel through which information flowed to Zim. "It is not up to us to protect nation from nation—that's the job of the Pax Circumfra. Let them deal with it."

"And who moves the Pax," Tana challenged, "except people like you and I who believe in what it does? Who will talk to the ambassadors? Who will present the case of Earth? Who will push it through? We in this room have the power to make it happen. We can talk to other family members until we have the whole Dynasty with us. We can talk to diplomats and legislators from our own worlds and try to sway them in the right direction. If we unite in this cause, there is no end to the good we may do."

"The *right* direction?" Delhi parroted. "The *good* we may do? And how do we know it is right and good? Are we to believe you? You, who have this obsession with Terra and things Terran?"

Doc was on his feet with a short bark, but Tana silenced him. "If you have not believed me in the past, it is doubtful you will now," she told Delhi. "But there is someone else with me tonight I think you will believe. Jethro: disassemble the walls."

Suddenly the ceiling of the portable folded back to reveal the deep black of the Junoan night, with stars partly obscured by high, thin clouds. Then silently the walls folded in on themselves and lay down flat around the portable, leaving their conference room as only a raised platform at the foot of the knoll. There, on the side of that small hill, sat forty-odd squirming children. "Hi, Mom!" called Derbe. Tana waved at her son.

"Grandpa!" cried a little girl, and came running to clamber up into Dublin's lap. "Dad, Dad, over here!" called Conti's group of five. "Hey, Mom, can I come sit with you?" asked another.

"Yes, come, children!" Tana invited. "We have a very special guest at our meeting tonight, and I wanted all of you to come and be with your parents and grandparents while he talks to us. Come, Delaware. Come, Kyle.''

A large half-moon shone down from a clear patch of sky, illuminating the knoll. Dakota and Monti stood just down from its crest, where they had built a moderate bonfire. Tana left the platform of the portable even as a half dozen children scrambled onto it and, with Doc guiding her over the uneven ground, went to join her brother and father just as Paul came out of the shadows near the butterleaf tree. ''Is he ready?'' she asked Paul when he drew near.

''Oh, yes,'' Paul agreed heartily. ''The question is, are they?''

Tana turned to the crowd of children and adults. ''My cousins, my family,'' she called out. ''I present to you a native Terran, a wise man of the People. I present to you Coconino.''

CHAPTER TWENTY

Coconino rose up from the ground where he had been sitting and stretched his hands toward the sky. Long ribbons streamed from the sleeves of his ceremonial shirt, fluttering in the evening breeze, and his voice rang out:

> "Hear me, O Mother Earth!
> "Distant though I am from you,
> "I am still your son."

Now his arms moved to encompass the land around him.

> "Hear me, O Aunt,
> "Sister of my Mother.
> "Welcome me
> "As you welcome your own children,
> "And know that I honor you
> "As I honor my own Mother."

Again his arms reached heavenward.

> "Hear me, O Father Sky,
> "For you cover both our worlds.
> "If we have one father,
> "We must be one people."

Absolute silence followed his chant. Slowly Coconino lowered his arms and stepped forward into the firelight.

Rugged contours and lines of age made his face bold and powerful as he stood before them. His shirt was richly embroidered with geometric designs, and the firelight danced on the pendant hanging from his neck. Tiny beads of bone and wood adorned the fringe of his calf-high moccasins, making a dry rattling sound as he walked. But more than the clothes he wore, more than the shadows that played across his form, it was his presence that arrested the assemblage. His stately bearing, the utter confidence in his face, kept even the smallest children quiet.

Slowly Coconino surveyed his audience, turning his whole body as he took them all in, wide-eyed youngsters and stunned adults. A small smile crept over his lips, and there was a twinkle in his dark eyes. *"Chee-eeyah,"* he said, his voice as rich and resonant in speech as it had been in song. "I bring greetings to you, Children of the Stars. I am Coconino, a Child of the Mother Earth." He winked at a six-year-old who sat near the fire. "Not a very young child," he confided, "but a child no less."

Now his chest swelled with pride. "I am Of the People," he told them. "As we say in my language, *del pueblo.* Among them I am known as a hunter and a storyteller. I hunt not with fire-shooters such as you have but with a bow and arrows and a good sturdy throwing stick. Tonight, though, I did not bring my bow or my throwing stick, for I do not wish to hunt the animals of your world."

Near Tana a childish voice asked, "Grandma, is he an Indian?"

Coconino turned to the little one. "In the Before Times," he responded, "the ancestors of the People were sometimes called Indians. But I am not my ancestors, just as you are not yours. We have our own way, the Way of the People, which we follow. We have learned this way over many generations, as the Mother Earth has taught it to us. We teach it to our children, and they to their children. Tonight I have come to share with you some of the Stories of the People, so that you might understand this Way that we follow."

Now he came around the fire and seated himself in front of it. Once again he chanted, this time in a strange and guttural language, and it seemed to those watching that he prayed. Then he turned his attention back to his listeners. "This is a story of how we came to be," he began. "Long ago, at the beginning of the Time That Is, the People stood on the edge of the world . . ."

It was the silence that woke Phoenix. Night creatures were settling down to rest, and those which rose with the daylight had not begun to stir. It was time. Her heart thudded as she rose from her sleeping place and turned to face the east. "Hear me, O Mother Earth!" she cried. "Bring forth your sun to shine upon the People, to light their paths and nurture their crops. Grant us once more the blessing we call day."

Behind her she heard the soft rustlings of the People as they woke.

"Guard our footsteps," she prayed, "that we may tread always with reverence upon your bosom and treat our fellow creatures with respect. Give us wisdom to know your will, and courage to do it." Especially courage, she thought. Especially courage.

There was the barest hint of gray in the east, and the sound of people rising from their sleeping places. Sure of her audience now, Phoenix raised her last petition. "Walk with me, your daughter, on this last of my days among the People. As you have made my life rich among them, so let my passing from them be rich in their memories."

She turned to face the shadowy figures behind her. "Leave your things here," she commanded, "and do not pause for food. We go to the Well."

Tana listened, as caught up in Coconino's tale as were those around her. She had heard the story of the Survivors from Nathan, but this telling was different. "When she had frightened away those who had hurt her, the Mother Earth sought to wash herself clean with many floods. Rain fell from the skies as a river pours from the edge of a cliff." Coconino's voice was almost musical in its accent, and his phrasing was so poetic that the tale spun out in nearly hypnotic fashion. "On staggered Alfonso, with Ernestina close by his side. 'This is madness!' cried Chico over the storm, but he, too, followed in the steps of Alfonso, though no one could see where those steps led."

Tana felt herself drawn into the lives of that ragged band as they fought their way through a deluge to arrive at the brink of a cliff. Survivors, she thought. Like the Crusoans. Like Chelsea and Zachery during the Troaxian Occupation. Like me, with my palsy. Faced with adversity, we struggle and survive.

". . . but Chico was filled with scorn," Coconino was saying. " 'If you climb over the cliff on a rope,' said he, 'you will die.' Alfonso told him, 'If the Mother Earth seeks my life, there is nowhere I can hide. But if she smiles on me, there will be shelter here, just above the raging waters of the river.' So Juan and Ernestina held the rope while Alfonso climbed over the edge and disappeared from their sight.''

A good story to tell, Tana realized. A story of faith versus cynicism, a story of believing in a just leader. Coconino had chosen well. She nestled back into Paul's arms where they sat on the hillside and glanced back toward the platform of the portable. Some of the directors had come down to sit with their children; others had children on the dais with them. Even Delhi had little Kyle on her lap. That is good, Tana thought. I want them to forget their grown-up concerns about money and business and politics. I want them to see with the eyes of children.

Delhi watched the proceedings through narrowed eyes, seething at this blatant manipulation. Couldn't they see what she was doing? Couldn't they see how she was preying on their emotions, using their families to get their sympathy? It was unprofessional and unforgivable. If they fell for such a cheap trick, she was going to go over their heads to Zim.

On her lap five-year-old Kyle looked up at his grandmother's pinched-up face. Her lap was as hard and rigid as that look, and it did not make for comfortable sitting. Kyle was not much for sitting still, anyway. He was a boy's boy, resisting all attempts by his parents and grandparents to pamper and spoil him. No amount of threatening kept him out of trees and mud holes; no amount of scolding kept him from going back again in his new clothes. Right now he found the old storyteller fascinating, and his grandmother preoccupied. He squirmed himself off her lap and sat down on the edge of the platform near her feet, craning his neck for a better look at the man on the knoll. So angry was Delhi that she hardly noticed that he had moved.

''. . . and there they found the Village of the Ancients, just as Alfonso had told them. It was sheltered and dry, and as each little one climbed down the rope to safety in that village, they felt the blessing of the Mother Earth. The storm might howl outside the stone houses, but they were safe in her bosom, where they could rest at last.''

Rest, Tana thought. How I could use some rest myself! Some place away from the storm that scourges my life. She looked up as Lystra slid over next to her, leaning her head on Tana's shoulder. Derbe, too, had come and was tucked in on Paul's right side. Tana felt a sweet peacefulness settle over her.

"Do you live in a stone house?" asked a curious ten-year-old.

Coconino turned with respectful attention to the child. "Yes, I live in a house made of stone and mud," he answered. "It is—how do you say this?" His arms folded in demonstration. "Held as a mother holds her child."

"Cradled," Lystra piped up.

"Yes, cradled," Coconino said, and smiled at her. "My house is cradled in the bosom of the Mother Earth. But I did not always live in such a house. When I was young as you are, the People lived in wickiups. Wickiups are rounded houses made of sticks and grass. The floor is a circle, as all of life is a circle. For the People in that time it was *moh-ohnak* to live in a wickiup. The People of the southern village still live in such houses. But when I was a young man, a great change took place in my village, one which caused us to leave the Valley of the People where I grew up and go to another place. Like the Survivors, we came to a Village of the Ancients, and there we have lived in stone houses ever since. It is not a bad way to live, but I look forward to a time when I can live in a wickiup again."

He singled out a boy near him, a curly-haired child of eight who watched with closed mouth but wide eyes. Leaning toward him, he asked, "Have you noticed that sometimes when you are looking for something very hard, you find something else which you did not expect to find?"

"I found a pinmouse today," the boy offered innocently. "And I was looking for a flower."

"There, you see?" Coconino nodded sagely. "That is how we found the Village of the Ancients which is now my home. We were looking for something else. We were looking for a great kachina called Tala."

Dakota's ears pricked up at the mention of Tala. Beside him, Mouse perked up, too. "Is that that animal your sister was telling you about?" she whispered. "The one that sounds like a flying celux?"

"Yes," he whispered back. "I've been thinking a little about it. Remind me next week, I want to go into Newamerica City and talk with Sihrmon, get his reaction to the idea. You might like to come along if you're taking a class in genetic engineering next term."

"No thanks," the girl grumbled. "Last time I went into town with you, you lost your girlfriend."

Dak's eyes flashed uncharacteristically. "That wasn't your

fault,'' he said sharply, upset that she might feel any blame for the incident. He wanted to add that he was no worse off for it, either, but Mouse would never believe that. She knew the pain he had gone through in breaking off his relationship with Wanda. The night after it had happened, he'd sought her out to apologize for Wanda's behavior when they had encountered her unexpectedly at lunch; then he had wound up apologizing for his own when he found himself weeping in her comforting arms. But Mouse seemed to take it all in stride. Nothing he'd seen ever ruffled the girl. If a flying celux landed in front of them, she'd want to check its forelegs to make sure it hadn't injured a foot in landing.

''. . . then suddenly great wings sprang forth from Tala's sides! He raced across the meadow and flung himself into the sky, soaring higher and higher toward the burning sun. And as he flew, the color of him began to change, to grow lighter as the sky was light . . .''

Changing color— It had to be a celux, Dak thought. Now, if it had interbred with a native Earth species . . . What was native to Earth, anyway, that might have a compatible chromosome pattern? He'd ask the computer when he got back to his room. Maybe he'd skip the dance later and . . .

Dak looked down at Mouse, who was watching the storyteller with an open, guileless face. A stranger might mistake her for one of the children clustered around, but he knew her to be a young woman of few illusions, wise in the ways of both animals and people. A strange and delicious feeling of warmth wrapped him around.

Tomorrow, he decided. He'd work on the celux problem tomorrow.

''Whose kid is that?'' Mouse asked abruptly.

''Hm?'' Drawn back from his mental wanderings, Dak looked where she pointed and saw Kyle Striker inching closer and closer to Coconino's knee.

Kyle had been drawn by the magical voice to the very front of the crowd, almost close enough to touch the old man's sleeve ribbons as he gestured. The boy studied the storyteller's shadowy face with its large nose and high cheekbones and sharp jaw, watching with fascination the way the lips moved and shaped words that fell like music on Kyle's ear. All thoughts of his big cousin who had brought him here or his grandma Delhi whom he had come to see were lost when the old man spoke. When

Coconino finished his tale of the flying beast, the silence was empty and profound. In the vacuum Kyle's voice was louder than he intended as he asked, "Can I ride Tala?"

Coconino smiled down at him, a smile that was crinkled eyes and the gentle curving of a strong mouth. Kyle felt warm inside, as though the sunshine Coconino had spoken of was in his chest. "No, little one," the old man said with just a trace of sorrow. "Tala has gone to the bosom of the Mother Earth, and there are none like him. You must search for your own kachina, the one that speaks to your heart."

More than anything at that moment, Kyle wanted to search as Coconino had searched, but he wasn't quite sure of his object. "What's a kachina?" he asked sincerely.

"A kachina is a powerful spirit," the storyteller replied with an expansive gesture of his arms. "Sometimes it appears as an animal, sometimes as a person. It can be a good spirit, or an evil one, or a little of both. But it is always unusual."

Kyle's hand shot out and touched the medallion hanging from the old man's neck. "Is that a kachina?" he wanted to know.

A tender look filled Coconino's eyes as he touched the talisman resting on his chest. "Yes," he said softly, "that is a powerful kachina." Then he raised his eyes and his voice so that all the others could hear. "This bird stone that I wear is a phoenix, and the phoenix is a powerful kachina. Stories older than those of the People say that this phoenix was a magical bird that was burned up in its nest but would not die. It rose from the ashes to live again. I will tell you the story of a woman whose name was Phoenix."

Now the storyteller hesitated, and for a moment Kyle was afraid he would change his mind. But then Coconino squared his shoulders and lifted one arm so that the ribbons of his sleeve waved and fluttered. "Once there was a woman who lived on the Mountain," he began.

The sun was still no more than a promise as Phoenix and her band set off toward the east. "You should have let them eat first" was Michael's only comment as he fell into place beside her. "They'll grow tired."

Phoenix herself felt strangely invigorated, every nerve in her body tingling. "They can rest soon enough," she said, setting a brisk pace. "We can all rest soon enough."

A shadowy form was waiting on a hill. Phoenix's blood turned suddenly to ice, and the hair stood up on the back of her neck.

Coconino? her heart cried. But no, this figure wore the trappings of a Man-on-the-Mountain: trousers and shirt, with a duffel of some kind slung over one shoulder. "Friend of yours?" she asked Michael.

Michael's eyes strained in the darkness. "I didn't have any friends on the Mountain," he told her. "Besides, he doesn't stand like a Man-on-the-Mountain; his stance is like one of the—" Suddenly his voice broke off, and he swore in English, there being no profanity in the language of the People.

Phoenix made the connection at the same time. There was only one of the People who had gone to live on the Mountain. "Coral Snake," she hissed.

"She was a strong woman," Coconino told his listeners, "but there was great sadness in her heart because the Mother Earth would give her no children. When her husband saw that no children were born, he thought she was worthless and sent her away. This was a great sorrow for her to bear, for she loved her husband very much."

The dangling ribbons on his sleeve captured Kyle's attention. He put out one finger to touch them and make them dance even more. The old man smiled at him.

"But instead of weeping her life away," Coconino went on, "the woman left the Mountain to seek a new life. She came to the Valley of the People, hoping to wash away her sadness among them."

"Good morning," called Coral Snake as they drew near. His voice had the mocking quality Phoenix remembered well; how he had tormented Sky Dancer with it, and Michael in his turn. So cocksure, looking down on everyone else, but all a mask, she had to remind herself. All that posturing and taunting was a mask for the pain in his soul, a soul that could not understand why he was not loved as the children of Coconino were and why, if the Mother Earth cared about the People, she did not speak to him.

Michael had no such charity in his heart for the man who had tried to maim him and rape Sky Dancer. "It is not a good morning," Michael told the intruder, "and you have made it worse."

Coral Snake grinned broadly and fell into step beside them as they marched on. "Then I'm glad I have come."

"What do you want, Coral Snake?" Phoenix asked wearily.

"I don't know," he replied, blue eyes pale in the growing dawn. His hair had been cropped short in the style of the Men-on-the-Mountain, and his face showed now that his heritage was more of the Mountain or the Others than of the People. "I was on my way from the Mountain back to the Camp of the Others when I saw the light of many camp fires last night. This morning I came to see what it was, and I found you."

"You have no place here," Michael told him harshly. "You are no longer of the People."

"I am of three peoples," Coral Snake replied easily. "I have left my seed among the People, and now, like your father Coconino, I have left it on the Mountain as well."

Michael's shoulders tensed, and his face grew hard. Coral Snake laughed. "Yes, Michael, I, too, have known the pleasures of a Witch Woman."

"At that time," Coconino told them, "it was the custom of the Men-on-the-Mountain to send Teachers to the People. So this woman came as a Witch Woman, one who brought magic to the People. But no one knew what her magic was, not even the Witch Woman herself. And there was much bitterness in her heart, so that the People did not know what to think of her. How could she teach the People anything?"

The fringe of the storyteller's moccasin lay in a neat row along his leather footwear. Kyle saw that polished beads had been knotted at the end of the leather strips. All the strips were exactly the same length, and all the beads were tied in the same position. He began to count them with his finger as he listened to the sonorous voice.

"Among the People there was a proud young man," continued Coconino, "who had dreamed that one day he would marry a Witch Woman. But when this Witch Woman came to the People, the young man was greatly embarrassed because she was not what he expected. She was not round and beautiful, as he had hoped, or quiet and gentle, as he thought all Witch Women must be. Instead, she was tall and skinny with a sharp tongue. It seemed to him that she was no Witch Woman at all."

"Do you know, Michael," Coral Snake goaded, "that when you showed up in our village, people thought Coconino was a god indeed to have won the heart of a Witch Woman on her own Mountain and blessed her with his seed?" He chuckled. "If only they knew, Michael. It is no great feat to lure a Witch

Woman to your bed. They are curious about men, and they have no modesty.''

Michael flushed deeply at the slur on his own mother, but he could say nothing. It was true. Except for the rare occurrence of the custom of Choosing, adolescents of the People were all chaste until their wedding day. But young people on the Mountain experimented rather freely with sexual pleasures, as he had reason enough to know. ''Why are you here?'' he gritted at this unwelcome intruder.

Coral Snake shrugged. ''I told you, I don't know,'' he replied. ''But it seems the Mother Earth has brought me. Do you go to the Camp of the Others to make a Choosing?''

Michael's right arm flexed, but Phoenix stopped him with a simple lifting of her hand. ''Do not touch him, Michael,'' she commanded. ''It is beneath you.'' Then she turned to Coral Snake. ''We go to the Well,'' she told him. ''And if you will keep that snake tongue still in your head, I will explain why.''

When Kyle looked up from counting the beads, he discovered he was directly in front of the old storyteller, looking up into that fascinating face with its dark, luminous eyes and prominent nose. He watched the firelight playing on the medallion as Coconino gestured, and it seemed to him that the phoenix bird was flapping its wings.

''One day the Witch Woman demanded that the young hunter take her along on a journey,'' Coconino was saying. '' 'Before I take you on a long journey,' the hunter said, 'I will take you on a short one. I will take you to the Well.' And so they set off running from the village to a lake which is called the Well. Now, the hunter thought that if the short journey was hard, the Witch Woman would not want to go on a longer journey. So he set a pace which he thought would make her want to turn back. But she did not ask to turn back. Though she did not have a hunter's ways and know how to run long distances, still she would not give up. Finally the young hunter felt guilty and stopped so she could rest.''

Staring at the medallion, Kyle imagined it was the Witch Woman. Its hard stone eye became her determined one; the thrust of its stone wings spoke of her strength. As the firelight lent it motion, he watched the kachina dive and struggle and soar in the darkness.

At the back of the crowd, seated on the platform of the portable, Delhi straightened up in consternation. Was that *Kyle* up there, practically crawling into the storyteller's lap? Glancing around at the other mesmerized listeners, she discovered the boy was nowhere to be seen here. It must be he. Quietly she slipped from the dais and began to circle the group to rescue her lost youngling.

"But when she had rested a little," Coconino was saying, "the Witch Woman asked to go on. So on they went, farther and farther, though she was at the end of her strength. The hunter began to regret his attempt to discourage the Witch Woman, for he saw how strong her heart was. He began to encourage her, to do what he could to make the journey easier now, so that she would succeed in it. They had to rest often, but always she asked to go on, until at last they came to the Well."

And there it was. Coming upon it from the west, it was not until they crested the hill that Phoenix discovered that what had appeared to be only a few scattered boulders on a rock outcropping was actually the lip of the limestone sinkhole called the Well. The sides fell away sharply, leaving a ragged stone wall where only moss and lichens could grow. At the bottom, however, was a spring-fed lake around whose lip lush grasses and a few desert trees were growing. A stone shelf circled partway around the lake, making a beach of sorts for those who descended to its cooling waters. Algae lay undisturbed on the surface, which was still black in the dim light of dawn.

As Phoenix stood on the rim above, looking down at its placid depths, she remembered the first time she had stood here gazing down. Then she had been giddy with exhaustion, seeing only water to quench her throat, cool shade, a place to swim, and the end of her grueling journey. Now she saw the end of a metaphorical journey, the end of her service to the People, the end of her long wait for Coconino's return. The peacefulness below called to her, beckoned her, but the walls were steep and forbidding and threatened her resolve.

Do not be afraid, came the silent voice from the limestone at her feet. *I will go with you. It will be all right.*

It's only for a swim, Phoenix told herself. Just a cool, refreshing swim. Like the one I took while Coconino sat on the shelf and watched . . .

"There she cast herself into its cooling water," the storyteller continued, "and let the heat and the tiredness wash away from her. When she came forth from the Well, more than the weariness of her body had been washed away. Some of the bitterness and anger which had clung to her soul for so long was gone as well. It was like laying down a great burden; she seemed to float up from its loss, and she knew that this struggle had made her heart stronger still. The young hunter was humbled by her, and he gave her a new name that day. He called her Phoenix.''

Phoenix turned to the People. ''In this place,'' she said, ''the woman called Debbie McKay died and a new woman was born. Coconino was witness to the birthing, and he gave the new woman a name. On this spot, here above the Well, he prayed to the Mother Earth and bestowed upon the woman a name from the Before Times, a name of great power. He called her Phoenix.''

At last the dancing medallion came to rest as the old man sat still in the firelight. Kyle reached out to touch it again, half expecting it to jump out of his grasp and soar off into the night. But it was only a stone, after all. He wrapped his fingers around it. ''Did she change into a bird and fly into the sky?'' he asked sincerely.

Now the old man reached out and eased Kyle into his lap. Neither of them saw the small dark woman hovering just off to one side. ''No, she did not fly away,'' Coconino told the boy. ''She learned to be a hunter, like her companion. She followed the Way of the People and was a true daughter of the Mother Earth. And . . . and she taught the young hunter many things. She taught him that when you do not get what you want, it is often because the Mother Earth has given you something better. She taught him that beautiful things are easy to love, but love that is not easy is often stronger. And she taught him that the strength it takes to draw a bow or run long distances is nothing compared to the strength it takes to keep living when your heart wants to break.''

Something glittered on the old storyteller's face. Kyle reached up to touch it and discovered that it was a tear.

Phoenix drew a deep breath and touched the turquoise medallion that hung from her neck. A tear glistened in her eye as she recalled the day Coconino had given her her name. She had laughed at him because he had mispronounced it: Fo-ee-nix, he had said, a name from the Before Times. It had taken her a moment to connect it with the name of one of the Dead Cities, and then she had laughed. But she had stopped laughing when she realized how close to the truth he was.

"Phoenix," she repeated. "The bird that rose from the ashes of its nest." Barren, divorced, bitter as hemlock. But Coconino had stirred those ashes, and slowly, painfully, up she had risen. "I am that woman," she told the People. "It was here at the Well that I received my new life and my new name from Coconino and the Mother Earth. It is here I shall return them."

"Did the hunter marry Phoenix?" asked a girl nearby.

Coconino's smile was sad. "No, he did not," he replied. "Before he could, the Mother Earth took him away from her. And so she had to begin her life yet again. From the ashes of her nest she rose up to lead the People, people that were not hers but his, people that she loved for his sake more than her own. This she did for twenty-five years, keeping them safe from many dangers, until at last the Mother Earth called her to rest."

Now Phoenix stripped off her ribbon shirt and cast it aside. She wore only her cotton loincloth, her knife, and the medallion. Pausing, she rubbed her thumb across the polished turquoise of the pendant. Must I? she asked the silent voice.

You must, it told her. *You do not wear it because it represents what you are; you wear it because it was once Coconino's and it represents your waiting. Your waiting is over now. It is time to let go.*

With resolution Phoenix removed the talisman. Her eyes went first to Michael—ah, sweet face! Coconino's face, but not quite. There was more Mountain blood in it, as there was in the face of Coral Snake beside him. The symbol would not speak to Michael of his father and of the waiting he must carry on. To him, to the rest of the People, it would speak only of her. Very well, then. Let it be so.

From the nearby ground Phoenix picked up a rock twice the size of her fist and set it on a boulder at the very edge of the Well. Around this rock she draped the phoenix medallion so that it hung down the side of the boulder. "This is my place," she announced. "Remember that it was here I descended to the Mother Earth, where I will wait, as I have always waited, for the return of Coconino."

The moon had sailed clear of the high, thin clouds and was on its way to the western horizon. Coconino stood up, lifting

Kyle in his arms, and he looked out over the crowd once more. "I must leave you now," he said, "and return to my Mother. It is very strange for me to be parted from her for so long, although . . ." He cocked his head as though listening. "This place has a voice, too, which is very sweet. You should listen to it; it will tell you many things."

Kyle cocked his head, too, and listened intently.

"Do you hear what she says?" Coconino asked the boy.

"A little," Kyle answered, puzzled. It was not a voice exactly, but it was not just the pinmice creaking, either.

"What does it tell you?" Coconino asked.

"I can't tell," the child admitted. "But it's saying nice things."

"That is enough for now," Coconino told him. "Someday perhaps the meaning will be clear to you, but for now you have learned to listen, and that is enough."

Impulsively Kyle hugged the man. "Do you have to go?"

The storyteller set him down and squatted in front of him. "Yes, little brother, I must go."

"Can I come to visit you?" the boy pleaded.

White teeth glittered in the darkness as a smile broke across Coconino's face. "Come and visit my grandchildren," he said. "They are near your age, and you would be great friends. They can teach you new games, and how to hunt for rabbits and wood-chucks, and where the juiciest berries grow in spring."

"And will you tell us more stories?"

Now the smile slipped away from the storyteller's face, and Kyle wondered what had made him so sad. "Another storyteller will do that," Coconino told him. "When I get home, I am going on a long journey, and I do not expect to come back."

Kyle's lips trembled, and his throat felt tight. He wanted to hear more stories, to sit in the old man's lap and listen to his voice. Somehow it did not seem that hearing another storyteller would be the same. "Won't I ever see you again?" he pleaded.

For a long moment the two of them looked at each other, the bond formed in a few short hours already strong enough to hurt when it was broken. Then Coconino took the medallion from around his neck. "Where I am going, I cannot take this," he said. "Will you keep it for me?"

Kyle's eyes grew round, and his mouth dropped open.

The old man slipped the leather thong over Kyle's head and straightened the phoenix on his chest. "Every time you see this, you must think of me," he said, "and of the People, and of our mother, the Earth. Remember that I called you little brother and asked you to be a friend to my grandchildren.''

As Coconino stood up again, Kyle turned around to show off his medallion and was delighted to see his grandmother standing right there. ''Grandma!'' he cried. ''Look what the storyteller gave me!''

Grandma Delhi knelt down beside him to inspect the phoenix, and Kyle was glad she wasn't wearing her sour look anymore. But he didn't understand why there was a teardrop trickling down her cheek, too.

Phoenix took the coil of rope she had brought and fastened it around the same boulder where her medallion now hung. Then she paused and took one last look at them: old friends she had known for years and old adversaries as well. Castle Rock hovered near her son, who remained disdainful of her. Let her in, Coral Snake, Phoenix thought. What harm she did to you, she did from love and ignorance—don't hold her responsible for that. It tore the heart from her when you were banished; let that be punishment enough. It is time for healing among the People.

But to Michael she said, ''Don't go south. Trade with the Others but don't stay long. The Way of the People is fragile; it wouldn't take much to throw it out of balance. Keep the balance, Michael, until your father comes again. And when he does—''

Tell him I love him still! her heart screamed. Tell him every time I see his face in yours, my heart breaks all over again. Tell him that was why I couldn't stay.

''When he does, he will lift this burden from your shoulders,'' she finished. ''Coconino will lead the People then.''

Turning her back, she took the rope firmly in both hands and began to climb down the jagged rock face into the Well.

The ceiling of the portable slipped back into place, and they were sealed off again from the firelight and the children and the twinkling stars. Tana sat silently in her chair, knowing there was more to do and wondering where she would get the strength to do it. The story of a woman left to carry a burden she did not desire had struck close to home. I chose this, Tana told herself; and yet, like Phoenix, I had no choice. It needed to be done, and who else was there?

Finally, hearing the restless rustlings of her directors, Tana drew a deep breath and spoke. ''Tonight you have glimpsed Coconino's world, the world of Earth. There are two other cultures, each with a lore as unique as this one. They have adapted to each other; they have found a balance which the rest of the universe would do well to emulate.''

Doc had settled himself at her feet, but now he lifted his head. *People,* came his thought.

Yes, Tana replied, *the children are leaving.* She went on with her speech. ''You came here to determine whether or not to request my removal as CEO. I tell you, that is a small matter and of less consequence to me than you might imagine. Settle it and settle it quickly; then take on a more important issue. Will we wash our hands of Earth and say it is not our business what happens to them now? Or will we use every influence we have, collectively and as individuals, to see that appropriate precautions are taken—''

Suddenly Doc came to his feet with a growl. Then the door to the portable flew open, and Zimbabwe Goetz walked in. ''Thank you, Tana,'' he said brusquely. ''As head of the Winthrop Dynasty I am taking over this meeting. Executive officers are excused; I will speak with the board of directors alone.''

Tana's heart crashed against her ribs even as she silenced her growling dog. She had not expected Zim to come in person, though she knew he had witnessed the whole affair via the flat-view camera mounted on the portable. Doc whined and rubbed against her leg. *You hurt,* he complained.

Tana heeded his warning and slowed her pounding heart. It's all over, anyway, she told herself. Coconino has done all that can be done; he doesn't need me to interpret it. It is up to the directors now. I may as well go home.

Carefully she got to her feet, feeling a great weakness in her limbs. She looked across the table and saw the look of shock on Delhi's face; Zim's sudden appearance had thrown her for a loop, too. Good, Tana thought with grim satisfaction. If I am to lose control of this situation, I want her control shaken as well.

Still somewhat stupefied, Delhi rose and looked around the table, at Tana making her way slowly toward the door and tall Zim taking her place at the head of the table. She seemed to waver, unsure exactly how she ought to behave just then. Then decision snapped into Delhi's eyes. She lifted her chin, turned on her heel, and marched to the door. There she stood until Tana arrived. Then Delhi opened the door, waited for Tana to exit with Doc, and followed them out.

The night air was cool and fresh. Tana breathed deeply and wished she had asked Dakota to leave a sled or some sort of vehicle nearby for her. There were only a few children left, mostly older ones, clustered in small groups and murmuring together. Tana looked around for Paul, but of course he was gone; he would be taking Coconino back. Dak was gone, too, and her father—shepherding children back to their parents, most likely. She gritted her teeth and began the long walk over the knoll toward home.

Delhi fell into step beside her. "Did you know he was coming?" Delhi asked evenly.

"No, that part was completely unplanned," Tana confessed. "I expected he would wait for the vote and then address us by holo."

Delhi gave a soft grunt. "Do you know how many times I've seen Zim in the flesh?"

"No."

"Once," Delhi said. "That's tonight."

Well, at least I got his attention, Tana thought wryly. The ground was sloping upward now, and she struggled against the incline. But somehow I thought . . . I thought . . .

"Are you all right?"

Delhi's voice sounded distant in Tana's ears. She looked down into her tiny cousin's worried face and realized she was weaving badly. "I—think I'd better sit down," Tana said, feeling the trembling in her arms and legs.

Doc! she shouted mentally. *Get Dakota. Get Dakota now.* Doc gave a sharp bark and charged off over the hill.

"Let me help you," Delhi urged, taking Tana's arms and easing her down onto the ground. "You look like death."

"I'll be all right," Tana told her between deep breaths. "I think I caught it in time. Doc will bring someone."

Delhi sat down on the ground beside her and was silent for some time. Grateful for that silence, Tana focused on her breathing, willing her pulse to slow and the quivering of her limbs to stop.

"That was artfully done," Delhi said finally. "The bonfire, the children—very artfully done."

No point in taking offense. "It was Coconino's idea," Tana told her. "I asked him how we could save the Earth. He said, 'Let me talk to the children. In the end, that is how it must be done. We must teach the children to love the Earth.' "

"Hmph." Delhi clasped her arms around her knees and stared up at the stars.

But we haven't truly saved it, Tana thought sadly. The Pax

might adopt a resolution in the next five years, but how will it be enforced? And if Paul's attempt to find a way to block P-TUP takes more than five years . . .

After a moment Delhi spoke again. "What do you suppose Zim is saying in there?"

Tana leaned back braced on her arms, feeling the stiffness in her shoulders and elbows and trying to ignore it. She, too, looked at the stars, automatically seeking out the constellation of Bessie the Cow. Bessie was standing on her head at this hour, the bright red star of her left eye winking down at Tana. "One of two things, I imagine," she responded. "Either that he believes in the institute's profitability and that although we've accomplished the purpose for which it was set up, we'll now find some new purpose and continue on as we have. We'll do research in dimensional physics, patent what we invent, and sell the technology."

"With you as CEO."

"Maybe." Tana's shoulders began to tingle a warning; she leaned forward again and clasped her hands around her knees, looking back at the portable. She wondered how the directors felt, having Zim take over like this. It had to be intimidating—Zim was intimidating. "I gave him my letter of resignation with the date blank and told him he could fill it in whenever he wanted it."

Delhi snorted softly. "No one could ever fault you for lack of nerve."

Shadows moved across the window of the portable. Someone was pacing. Zim?

"What's the other thing he might be saying?" Delhi prompted.

Tana could feel Doc at the edge of her consciousness now, excited, worried, impatient with Dakota, who could not keep up. *Be calm,* she soothed him. *I am all right.* "That he's going to endow the institute heavily and give it to the Pax Circumfra."

Delhi turned to Tana in the starlight. "What makes me think you gave him that idea?" she asked.

Tana did her best to grin. "Because you know me so well," she replied. "The profit motive is not necessary to drive research. People like Paul explore because it excites them. All they need is proper funding to lubricate their way. The Winthrop Dynasty will have a much better feeling about the institute if they endow it and give it away. Then they'll have put their money where their altruistic mouth is, and there won't be any temptation to let baser considerations have sway."

There was a chattering in the darkness, the nightly serenade of Juno's lictals. The finger-sized insects beat their wings against their body shells, sending unknown messages to each other across the prairie. Coupled with the creaking of the pinmice, it had a strangely soothing effect.

"He'll never buy it," Delhi said simply. "And buy is the operative word. I've known Zim longer than you have; he's a profit man from the word go. That sale you hammered out with Trans-universal makes a tidy profit, enough to remind them how lucrative breakthrough technology can be. And the project you've given Paul next? Think about it. It boils down to defense technology, and everyone will want it. Zim's not going to let go of that."

Tana sighed as Doc came panting over the hill, closely followed by Dak. "Tana, are you all right?" her brother demanded.

"Yes, I'm under control now," Tana told him. "Sorry I frightened you, but I started for home and got the sudden feeling I wasn't going to make it." She rubbed Doc's broad chest and patted his sides, soothing the agitated animal. "Delhi's been keeping me company."

"We've been resting," Delhi put in. "And talking. A very enlightening conversation." She stood up now. "What you did tonight, Tana, bringing that storyteller here, was blatant manipulation and I know it. But—" She brushed dry grass from her skirt and tugged her jacket down into place. "—you were right. The Winthrop Dynasty has always been special because we put people first, not just employees but all of humanity. If we want to retain that distinction, we can't rest on past accomplishments." She looked down at the blond woman seated on the grass, her dog and her brother protectively close. "Jedediah has a cousin in the foreign service of Darius IV; I'll be contacting him to see what influence we can swing with their ambassador to the Pax. And I will see what other members of my close family can do as well."

"Thank you," Tana said sincerely.

"And now, since you seem well cared for," Delhi concluded, "I think I'll go back. I'd like to tell Kyle a bedtime story myself. One about the country on Earth which was home to my mother's people."

They watched her march away over the knoll. Dak smiled at Tana. "I think you've won," he said.

"A single battle," she replied. "Earth is not safe yet."

CHAPTER TWENTY-ONE

The sun was peeking over the eastern horizon now as the People stood on the rim of the Well, looking down at their leader. To the People, She Who Saves was an old woman at fifty-five, and they were amazed at the agility with which she had lowered herself down the steep side. Yet there she stood on the rock shelf below, gazing out over the water, seeming not even to breathe hard.

Coral Snake shook his head. "That old man-woman," he said softly. "I would never have believed she would do this. Not if I had not seen it with my own eyes."

"She has not done it yet," Michael grumbled. He looked down at the stake in his hand, the one he had promised to drive in the ground to measure by its shadow how long the People should wait. "But she will."

"If that is what comes of hearing the Voice of the Mother Earth," commented Coral Snake, "I hope I shall never hear it."

An ache was rising in Michael's chest as he watched the sinewy woman at the water's edge. "I hope I shall," he whispered. "For all the good it will do. I haven't her courage. If she only knew what kind of leader she leaves the People to . . ." His voice trailed off as the memory of his liaison with Sky Dancer rose before him. Did Phoenix know? She had to! Never in the five years that had followed had she said a word to him about it: no questions, no recriminations. But she had to know.

Is that why you've done this to me? he wondered. Is this my punishment, to have to take up your burden among the People? It would be fitting and just. Only you don't have to die to do it. You could just go away, go to be with Sky Dancer in the south, and I would understand.

Or is this part of your punishment, too?

Below him, Phoenix looked up at the band collected on the rim. The two young men stood out from the others, bonded in spite of their enmity by their youth, their mixed heritage, and the notoriety of their fathers. They were two phases of the same moon, both showing light and shadow, but how different they were! Even in silhouette Coral Snake looked sly and faithless, yet the dress of the Mountain had an odd effect upon him. It weakened him. His image on the rim was that of a jay: noxious but ineffectual.

Michael, on the other hand—Phoenix caught her breath. As he leaned forward, one foot braced on a rock, the contours of his well-muscled body masked only by a breechclout, there was power and dignity in every inch of him. Yet even in that stance that spoke so of his father, he was not his father. He did not have the self-assurance that drove Coconino.

The smug, egotistical, frustrating self-assurance, Phoenix thought. Or the vision.

Yet I will use him, came the voiceless voice at her feet. *He is my son as well.*

"Take heart, Michael," Phoenix whispered from the depths of the Well. "If she can use me, she can use anyone."

As though he had heard her, Michael turned away and set his stake to drive it into the ground. Sharp cracks split the air as he struck it with a rock, and the echoes came back from the far side of the Well. Telling Breeze began to beat the drum, and Flint's voice raised a chant of waiting. The sun was beginning to send its golden shafts down the wall behind Phoenix, and she knew that soon the lake would lose its shrouding of shadows. Quickly now, no time to waste.

Sitting on the edge of the rock shelf, Phoenix slipped her legs into the cool, dark water.

Nathan stopped short when he saw the spotted creature bounding down the road toward him. Though he'd met the dog several times as Tana came and went with her questions and her puzzles, the animal still made him nervous. It was so *big*. And solid. And powerful.

Doc yipped a happy greeting, lowering his chest almost to the ground while his hindquarters remained elevated and he wagged his tail in glee. "Where's your mistress, Doc?" Nathan asked, looking up the road past the hound. It was dusk; Tana preferred to come at dusk, not only for the cooler temperature but because the dwindling light hid a multitude of offworld sins: her strange hairstyle, her strange clothing, her strange animals. A bulky shape moved up over a rise in the land now, the size of a small tractor but with the lumbering gait of a beast.

"Good evening, Nathan," came Tana's voice from that hulking form. "Please don't let the horse frighten you; she's very gentle."

Nathan waited, heart pounding, as Tana approached. His brain told him that there was nothing to fear, that he trusted her, that she had some reason for bringing this monster here. But his knees were a little unsure of that.

"Help me down, please," she asked, turning the horse sideways in front of him and swinging one leg over its neck. Not knowing what else to do, he caught her by the waist as she slid to the ground. She was so light and supple; the horse was so huge and foreign. The size of a Great Antelope, Nathan thought. But no one has ever tamed a Great Antelope.

"Is she that unsettling?" Tana asked her friend frankly.

"Yes," Nathan replied with equal candor.

"I'm sorry not to forewarn you," she apologized, "but I've overtired myself these past few days, and I just can't make the long walks on your planet that I need to make. It was either this or a motorized sled; I suppose both would be equally disruptive, but riding is better to me. Therapeutic."

Nathan looked at her now in the twilight and thought she looked no more tired and worn than when he'd seen her last, but she was adept at hiding her fatigue and the ravages of her illness. "How did it go yesterday?" he asked.

She smiled and leaned against the horse, rubbing its neck. "Very well," she admitted. "Coconino touched their hearts, even the most stubborn of them. My board of directors voted to act in concert and as individuals to pressure for a protected status for Earth."

Nathan knew that was important to her, and he couldn't tell her how little difference he believed it would make. "And your position with the institute?" he asked.

"The board voted to retain me as CEO," she told him, "and Zim elected not to interfere. But he let me know in no uncertain terms that he still has my letter of resignation and he'll feel free to date it whenever he sees fit to remove me."

"Then he did not want to give the institute to your Pax Circumfra," Nathan deduced.

"No." Tana shook her head sadly. "Not this time. But Paul's

lab will be submitting an outrageous budget, and there won't be any sign of profit until he makes some kind of breakthrough, which may take years." Her mouth twitched in a wry smile. "Zim may change his mind down the road."

"And Coconino?"

Tana laid a hand on the farmer's arm. "You know what he asked of me in exchange for his help."

Nathan was silent.

"Paul is ready to try. I'm going to get Coconino now; I want you to come with me."

"I won't try to talk him out of it," Nathan warned her. "It's his decision; I know how much he wants this."

"I won't try to talk him out of it, either," Tana replied. "I just thought you would like to say good-bye."

Nathan blinked back tears. "Yes," he said, his voice husky. "Yes, I would like that. Thank you."

Phoenix slipped off the rock ledge and into the water, hardly noticing its coolness in this warm weather. Though it had been years since she'd swum, her body remembered. Strong arms propelled her through the darkened pool, legs fluttering behind. The sun was reaching the rock ledge now and would soon be creeping out over the water. She struck out purposefully for the center of the lake.

Above her, the drum beat out its steady cadence and the voices of the People joined in song, but Phoenix heard another voice. It was her own as she lay exhausted on the rim above, gazing down at this pond that Coconino had told her she could not reach because they had no rope. She had wanted nothing, nothing more than to descend to it and immerse her tired body. "I want to drown myself in that lake," she had moaned. "My whole body, top to bottom, wants to be in that water."

And her protector—arrogant, opinionated, single-minded, *nineteen*—he had squatted on the ground beside her and instructed her as he might a small child: "Someday perhaps you *will* drown yourself in it," he had told her, "but while you are with me, you will take no such chance with your life."

You're not here, Coconino, she thought as she paused to tread water in the middle. Who will protect me now?

Coconino waited at the appointed place, alone this time. That evening he had bid farewell to his stepson and daughter-in-law, his grandchildren, and all his friends. "When the harvest is in," he had told them again, "load it on travois and go south. It is time for reuniting what has been separated."

"But why will you not come with us?" his daughter-in-law had pleaded.

"I, too, am bound for a reunion," he had replied, "but it is not to be had in the south. Only, as you pass the Sacred Well of She Who Saves, say a special prayer to the Mother Earth that the long wait of the Witch Woman there may be ended."

But as he had walked away from them, their murmurings had reached his ears. "He is Coconino," the People had said. "Though he goes away, he will come again."

Now there was a flash of shadow as a small, round object appeared in the air near Coconino. It hovered there no more than two heartbeats, then it was gone again. A moment later Tana appeared in the darkness, mounted on the back of an enormous creature, with Doc at their feet and Nathan seated behind.

The creature did not frighten Coconino much, for had he not ridden on the back of winged Tala? Had not his Witch Woman ridden behind, as Nathan rode now? He smiled to see his old friend with his new one, glad for one last conversation with his spirit son. "*Chee-eeyah*, Nathan," he greeted, "*Chee-eeyah*, Tah-nah. Is that a horse?"

"It is," Tana replied, urging the animal forward off the large traveling mat that had been constructed for them. "How do you know of horses, Coconino?"

"I read about them," he replied. "In books."

Tana's jaw dropped. "You *read*?" She remembered now that Nathan had told a story in which he had said that "the magic of books was open to him," but somehow she had never connected that with Coconino reading for himself. A talking book, perhaps, or a holographic recording, but reading? The thought of Coconino with a book was just too incongruous.

"I did once," he demurred. "A Witch Woman taught me when I was a boy. But I have had no books for many years. I do not know if I could still do it."

Nathan clambered awkwardly to the ground from the horse's back, then turned to help Tana dismount. "What kinds of books did you read?" Tana asked, curious.

"Great adventures," Coconino replied quickly. "About people called Greeks and others called Israelites, and of course about the ancestors of the People." His heart tightened as he remembered some of those stories: Custer, and Crazy Horse, and Wounded Knee. "Those were the last books I read. They tore my heart."

"There were bad times for the ancestors of the People," Tana agreed, "when the Europeans came to this place. But for all the bad they brought, the Europeans brought one very great gift which your ancestors loved and cherished. They brought the horse."

"Yes," Coconino agreed, admiring the beautiful creature with Tana, "I have read that my ancestors loved this animal dearly and measured their wealth by the number of ponies they owned." It was a very patient beast, he noted, waiting calmly while they talked. Tala had never been so calm with strangers around.

"I would like to give ponies back to the People," Tana told him.

Coconino considered the notion, seeing the horse's gentle brown eyes and the proud arch to its neck. Tentatively he put out a hand to touch its muzzle and found it soft, as Tala's muzzle had been soft. Sliding his hand along its neck and withers, he felt the familiar warmth of animal flesh beneath a sleek coat, the pulse of life in a creature both greater and more limited than himself. "I think that would be a good gift," he said softly. "It is *moh-ohnak.*"

"I would give them one other gift as well," Tana went on. "Together you and I have postponed the time when Others can come and go as they wish upon the Earth, but I do not know that we have stopped it entirely."

"No," Coconino said simply, "I did not expect that we would."

"So I would like to give the People some of these 'piebald coyotes,' " she said, waving a hand at Doc. "They are good friends and can help to hunt game and bear burdens, but most of all they can smell when someone uses a Magic Place to come among the People. They will bark and let you know, and you will be forewarned."

"The *People* will be forewarned," Coconino corrected her gently. "I will not be here."

"No," Tana acknowledged. "It is time, then, Coconino."

Now he turned to his friend Nathan, the boy who had grown to manhood in his own house and was now an old man like himself. "Good-bye, *moh-ohahnee,* spirit son," he said, holding out his arm.

Nathan clasped the extended arm in a hunter's grip, forearm

to forearm. "Good-bye, Say-ayka-pee," he said. "I shall miss your wisdom."

Still the two men clung to each other, searching for words neither had. Tana slipped quietly to the other side of her horse, allowing them what privacy she could. "Once the Men-on-the-Mountain sent Teachers to the People," Coconino ventured. "I have been thinking it would be good if they sent young men and women once again, but not as Teachers this time. As learners. To become *moh-ohahnee-sa,* as you were to me. And the People should let their sons and daughters go, not just to become Chosen Companions but to be *compadres*, close friends, with the children of your camp and of the Mountain."

Nathan nodded. "I have long felt this to be true. I will speak to the leaders of my camp about it, and I will go to the southern village and seek out Juan, your son who is my spirit brother. I will tell him what you said."

Coconino looked slightly surprised. "You have long felt this way?" He shook his head. "That has always been your weakness, Nathan—you keep silent when wisdom is in your mouth." He turned to Tana, who was hidden by the bulk of the horse. "Tah-nah." She poked her head around its neck, a blob of shadow emerging from a greater shadow. "See that he is not too quiet," Coconino admonished her. "There is great wisdom in those who can see, not only from the Mountain but from the Valley." Then he turned back to Nathan. "My Witch Woman was such a person."

"I wish I had known her," Nathan said. Then he noticed in the pale starlight that Coconino's chest was bare. "Where is your medallion?"

Reflexively Coconino's hand went to where it should have hung. "I have left it in good keeping," he told Nathan. "If someday a young man comes to you wearing that phoenix around his neck, trust in him. He may be one who sees, not only from the Mountain and the Valley but from the stars as well."

Tana glanced at her wrist chrono. "Nathan," she called softly, "it's time. Paul will return you to your farm directly from here." She stepped away from the cluster of people and animals to spread a smaller traveling mat on the ground a few yards distant.

Reluctantly Nathan let go of Coconino's arm and stepped onto the smaller mat. "Good-bye, Say-ayka-pee," he repeated.

"Will you not bid good-bye to Coconino?" Coconino asked.

Nathan's chin came up in the moonlight. "Never," he said

firmly. "Say-ayka-pee may pass from my life, but Coconino lives forever."

Then he was gone, and only the starlight glimmered where he had been.

"Now it is time for us," Tana told Coconino, leading her horse back onto the larger traveling mat. "We'll go to the lab first; Paul has to make some adjustments in the equipment after we get there." She called Doc to her. "Do you want to sit on the horse, Coconino?"

"No, thank you," he refused politely, coming to stand beside them. "But I will hold on to his neck, I think. I have never liked this Bending of Space your Magic Place does."

"She's not going to do it," Coral Snake said, watching the swimmer in the middle of the lake. "Look! She loses her courage."

"She is waiting for something," Michael insisted, defending Phoenix and hating himself for doing it when he believed she was wrong. But it was the truth. "She will do it. She has too much pride to turn back now."

Below them, Phoenix watched the sun creeping across the surface of the water, turning the dark surface to a brilliant blue, reflecting the cloudless sky. *Are you frightened?* asked the voiceless voice, sighing up from the depths of the lake.

Some, she admitted.

Do not be afraid. I am with you.

Only tell me one thing, Phoenix protested. When you took Coconino from me, you gave me his daughter to raise, and for many years I was as happy as a widow could be. But when you gave me this son of his . . .

I did not give him to you, the voice corrected. *I gave him to the People, and the People to him. He needed them, and now that you are going, they need him as well.*

They need Coconino, Phoenix responded.

Him they cannot have.

Phoenix sighed deeply. The shadow of the Well's eastern wall was not ten yards from where she floated. She took a few strokes deeper into that shadow.

Coconino waited uncomfortably as Tana's husband and the half-haired man did things to their Machine. Had he been less uneasy, he would have noticed the tension between the two men. As it was, he knew only the queasiness of his stomach from his trip in the Magic Place and the terrible emptiness he felt when enclosed in a building such as this.

"This place has no voice," he told Tana, who waited nearby.

"It has a voice," she contradicted. "But not one you and I can hear. Only people like Paul and Todd can hear the voice that whispers in a research laboratory."

Coconino grunted, watching the two men more closely. "They do not look very happy," he commented.

Tana sighed. "Yes, I know. But that has nothing to do with hearing the voice. Paul will not tell Todd what they are doing, only how it should be done. That is very hard on Todd for two reasons: one, his mind always wants to know the why of things; two, Paul has never shut him out of anything before, and that hurts him."

"Why does he not tell?" Coconino wanted to know.

"He is afraid," Tana replied. "He does not like doing this because it is very dangerous. He is afraid it would be dangerous for Todd to know how it is done."

Coconino nodded sagely, remembering his own curiosity about the ancestors of the People and what he had learned when he had read the books on the Mountain. "Sometimes knowing can be very dangerous," he agreed. "But more often it is not knowing that creates the danger. And lack of trust between friends . . ." He shook his head. "That is very bad. Tell your husband—" But he broke off. "Tell him nothing," he said finally. "It is not my place to speak here. Perhaps your god will speak to him."

A faint smile colored Tana's mouth. "Perhaps he will."

"Does your god give you dreams?" Coconino wanted to know.

"Not to me," Tana replied. "I wish he would; things would be much clearer."

"Perhaps not." Coconino scratched his chest, feeling a phantom tickle from the medallion he no longer wore. "The Mother Earth gave me a dream last night, but I do not understand it. She showed me a cave and all manner of people coming and going in it. They were children of the stars, and yet this cave was in the bosom of the Mother Earth, and she did not mind their presence. They were respectful, and she welcomed them."

"Maybe she only meant that if we are respectful, she will welcome us all," Tana volunteered.

Coconino rubbed his chin. "No, I do not think that is what she meant. This was not a spirit cave but a real one. A place, not an idea. In my dream people came and went from this cave to the Sisters of the Mother Earth by a Magic Place . . .'' He shook his head. "There is something to it that I do not understand. Perhaps it will come to me yet."

Now Paul approached them. "I think we're ready." He wiped perspiration from his extensive brow, though it did not seem to Coconino that the room was warm. "Now, Coconino, you understand that you—"

"—cannot change what is," Coconino finished. "Yes, yes, we have agreed on that."

"And if you—when you—live among the People," Tana added, "you should not use your real name."

That made Coconino smile. "I have many names, and all of them are real. They all say something about who I am or who I was. I will find one which is suitable."

Paul shifted nervously. "Now, I know you wanted to go into the Well, but that's just too dangerous. The space between the wall and the water is so narrow, the slightest miscalculation on our part could put you inside solid rock or out over the deep water. So I'd like to put you down at the river. Just in the shallows along the edge is the safest place—no chance of a tree or cactus growing there that you could run into, and if we misjudge the surface height by a little, the water will cushion your landing."

Coconino took Paul's hand and shook it, as he had been taught to do long ago on his visit to the Mountain. "You are a good man," he pronounced. "I know you are worried, but do not be. I am a Child of the Mother Earth, and she will care for me." Then he crossed the floor to stand within the Magic Place one last time.

Paul made a helpless gesture. "I wish I could make you understand how many things could go wrong."

But a slow smile spread across Coconino's face. "It is a good day to die," he told Paul. "Have courage; the Earth is all that lasts."

With a sigh Paul turned and walked resolutely to his workstation. "Ready, Todd?" he asked.

The young man's face was sullen. "Ready, boss."

"Tah-nah," Coconino called from the chamber. "There was great peace in the cave."

Paul pulled on his programming gloves, for the last of the calculations he had refused to inscribe in any file; he carried them in his head. He would not risk their ever being duplicated. "Jezebel," he said. "Run program seven-two alpha niner."

The rainbow tubes of the warm chamber glowed and swam; Paul worked his final magic, and Coconino disappeared from their sight.

Phoenix took one last look at the People standing on the rim of the Well watching her, and suddenly her heart turned cold. How can I do this? she demanded. The surface is clear and bright, but down below the water is murky and—

Courage, counseled the voiceless voice. *I have brought you this far; I will take you to the end of your journey.*

Once I tried to bargain with you, Phoenix thought. But I could only lose, because you always know more than I do; you always have some trick that spoils all my plans. So I won't try to bargain with you now. I only beg you: see me through this.

Have I not just said I would? the voice chided.

"This is it, then," Phoenix said aloud. She took several deep breaths, hyperventilating for courage as well as oxygen, then flipped herself over and dove for the bottom.

Up on the rim, Michael saw her go. He turned and marked the shadow of the stake with a rock; then, tears trickling down his face, he began to count the drumbeats: one, two, three, four—

Paul stared at the empty chamber. Tana came and stood beside him, slipping her arm around his waist.

"Well, he's gone," Todd remarked sullenly. "Wherever."

Suddenly Paul turned to his workstation and stripped off his programming gloves. "Jezebel," he snapped, "open files two-seven alpha niner, two-six beta four, and two-niner delta three. Destroy contents, authorization my voice and this code." He tapped six digits into the keyboard.

Todd jumped. "Paul! That's your—that's everything—what are you doing?" He dashed to Paul's workstation and stared at the display as though trying to see how he could reverse the command before it was too late. "This project drove you crazy for two weeks and you just—"

Tana touched his arm. "Let it go, Todd," she said quietly. "He knows what he's done."

"But all his notes, all his—I may not know what he was doing, but I know it was something way beyond the envelope—"

"And that's where it belongs," Paul cut in. "Way beyond the

envelope.'' He turned toward his office. "I need a cup of coffee.''

Todd turned pleading eyes toward Tana, begging to understand what his mentor had just done.

"Let it go, Todd," she repeated. "He doesn't know if he's just granted Coconino's every wish or killed him. And he'll never know.''

"Can't we send a 'corder after him to find out?'' Todd asked helplessly. Except when Tana was in jeopardy, he had never seen Paul this distraught.

"No," Tana explained, tears brimming in her eyes. "Oh, Todd! I made him tamper in an area he finds ethically repugnant. He didn't want you to bear the burden with him. We've tried to send Coconino back in time.''

Todd stared after his boss, and Tana watched the emotions war across his face: shock, anger, pain, love, revulsion, worship. Finally the young man straightened himself and walked into Paul's office.

Paul was slumped in his chair, staring at the vacant display on his desk. Todd flopped into the side chair and watched him a moment. What a pair they are, Tana thought. Different backgrounds, different ages, yet with one common drive: to explore the scientific frontier, to fathom the unfathomable. No wonder Todd had been shocked when Paul had destroyed his notes. To the young physicist it was like God taking back what he'd done on the sixth day.

"So, boss," Tana heard him say finally. "Do I get to use your office while you're on vacation?''

Coconino's stomach seemed to be turning inside out, and he was falling, falling, falling—and then suddenly there was a cold sensation on his feet and the sucking feeling of something trying to pull him off balance—

Overhead, the sun shone brightly in a brilliant blue sky, and the birds chattered loudly in the relative coolness of early day. A breeze touched Coconino's cheek; he drew a deep breath of the sweet air and felt it revive him. Then he looked around. He was standing in the shallow stream that ran east of the Well, and the sucking sensation was the swiftly moving water eddying around his feet and pulling at the sand on which he stood. To the north he heard the splashing of water pouring from the outlet of the Well as it flowed into the stream, keeping the water within that lake fresh and level.

I am here! he realized. I am where they tried to send me. But am I *when* I want to be? They said it might be off by a day or a handful of days, or even a season. Have I come before my Witch Woman goes down into the Well? Or have I come too late?

Over the sound of the splashing water he heard a drumbeat. As he listened, it seemed to him that there was chanting as well, drifting down from the hill whose steep side kept the river in its place. Could it be the People stood even now upon the rim of the Well to bid their leader farewell?

Mother Earth, have you brought me so close to the time I needed to come?

You have arrived at the exact moment, sighed the mesquite trees along the bank. *Only hurry, Coconino, hurry!*

Coconino turned and slogged toward the shore.

Well below the surface, Phoenix flattened out her steep dive, heading for the eastern wall. The water was too murky to make opening her eyes useful; she groped blindly ahead of her for the jagged rock, wondering how far down her objective was. When her fingers touched the rough limestone, she concentrated her senses on the movement of the water. At first there were only the ripples she had caused herself by her passage; then those died, and she felt the gentle pull of the current. Her head was pounding now, but she followed that gentle tug deeper and to the left, searching for what she knew was there . . .

She had begun to despair when her hands found the opening, felt the strong rush of water through this passageway to the river outside. But how long was the tunnel? No time to think of that now; she forced her way into it, pulling herself along with her arms.

Do you remember how Coconino tricked you when he first brought you here? asked the voiceless voice. *He made you tired and thirsty, then showed you water at the bottom of the Well, which you had to make a difficult climb to reach. All the time he knew that the river ran just out of sight beyond the hill, but he did not tell you that. Now you have brought the People here and shown them a lake with no visible exit other than its surface, yet you knew all along that there must be a tunnel because you have seen the water coming out the other side and into the stream.*

But so has Flint, Phoenix thought. And Gray Fox and a hand-ful of others who grew to manhood in the Valley of the People.

They have been to the Well; they know that a spring flows from the hillside into the stream below.

To know two things is not always to connect them, the voice pointed out. *And you told them you came to my bosom. They believe you have come to die.*

You made me believe it, too, Phoenix thought. For a while.

The more you believed, the more they believed. Now, with the sun in their eyes and the shadow upon the water—

Just then the current got stronger and the tunnel narrower. Phoenix winced as her bare flesh scraped up against the sides. Thrusting her hands out in front of her, she felt them break free, but her head was still in the narrow tunnel. She struggled to gain enough purchase on the slippery rocks to pull herself through the constricted area. But her air was running out, and her brain began to fog. Panic set in. I must get out, she thought. I must get out, I am so close— But I must breathe. I have no air, I must breathe, I can't breathe— I can't— I—

Suddenly strong arms grasped her hands and pulled her through the strangling rock into the air. Phoenix gasped and choked as she breathed in life, ushering forth from the side of the hill as a child from the womb. Her passage had been painful, and she bore many scratches and bruises upon her body, but she was free, she was alive, and—

Someone held her upright on legs that would scarcely support her. She straightened her knees and brushed the water from her eyes so that she could see who it was. Who had guessed her treachery? Was her savior also her conqueror? After all of that, had she failed to carry off her charade?

The sun was behind him, and it took a moment before his features would come into focus. But when they did, Phoenix gasped and stared in disbelief at the face before her. It had none of the arrogance she remembered, none of the youthfulness she feared, but there was no mistaking that precious face. It was weathered and worn and wizened and wonderful, but it was Coconino's face, and Phoenix wept for joy. "Coconino!" she sobbed, gazing up at him. "Coconino, you're *old*."

His eyebrows shot up, and the corners of his mouth quirked. "You are no fledgling yourself," he observed dryly.

She gave a choking laugh. "Well, you haven't exactly caught me at my best."

"I should hope not," he agreed, eyeing her up and down. "You look like a wet coyote." Then he smiled, and it was Coconino's smile, and the sun broke across his face and dazzled her, and she wept anew.

Coconino drew her to him and held her tight, as he had dreamed of doing a thousand times. His tears mingled with the water dripping from her hair, and when he could pry her head back from his shoulder, he set his lips on hers as a younger Coconino had longed to do and had never dared. The fire that had never died burst forth in flames as their hungry souls fed on the touch of each other after so many years.

It was she who broke away first. "We have to go," she said urgently. "The People are just up on the hill; if one of them sees us, if they find out I have deceived them—"

"Yes, we must go quickly," he agreed, leading the way downstream. "It is important that they do not recognize me or guess that I have returned. But by our good fortune in finding each other today, I would say that the Mother Earth will keep us hidden from their eyes."

Phoenix sloshed through the water after him, clutching his hand, determined never to let go of him again. "All the same, I'll feel better with a few miles between us and them."

"We will go as far as the Valley of the People," he said. "There we can rest."

Rest! What a blessed word, she thought. Her limbs stung and her lungs ached, but her heart glowed as it had not done in many years. "The village isn't there anymore," she told him.

"I know." They left the water for easier footing along the bank, ducking in among the mesquite trees that lined the shore. "But the Village of the Ancients will still be there, and it holds something for us."

"Provisions," she guessed. "I was going to go south to see Sky Dancer. I thought I might find enough things that got left behind twenty-five years ago to equip me for the journey."

"That may be," he replied, "but that is not what I seek there."

"Oh?" She was studying his face, realizing he was more than the forty-five years he would own if he had not been caught in a time warp at all. What had happened, then? Where had he been, and how had he come back to her?

"All I seek in the Village of the Ancients," he explained, "is a wedding chamber, one that has awaited us too long." He stopped abruptly and took the time for one more kiss. "You made me a promise long ago that you would spend your nights with me, and I told you then I would hold you to it. The time has come.''

This time Phoenix did not argue but melted into his powerful arms.

Tana watched the two scientists a moment, feeling their way through the breach between them, closing the gap, forgiving and apologizing without ever saying anything about the wound. Is it just something about male relationships, she wondered, that I will never understand? Or does it happen across genders and I'm the only one who doesn't get it? Not that it matters. They are coming back together, my husband and his young colleague, my chief physicist and his protégé, and that is what counts.

Slowly she turned and made her way toward the laboratory door. Doc padded ahead of her, glad to feel the tension draining from the air and the sorrowful heart of his mistress lifting once more. *Home?* he suggested hopefully.

Soon, she thought back at him. *We must give Paul and Todd some time together. They need to find their balance again.*

That puzzled the Dalmatian. *Were they falling?*

They were hurt, she tried to explain. *Todd thought he was being forced out of the pack, and Paul was so busy protecting this young one that neither could see how the other was injured.*

All right now? Doc wanted to know.

Yes, all right, she agreed. *No more fighting within the pack. Pax in the pack,* she thought to herself. Then for Doc she translated, *Pax: peace.*

Peace!

Suddenly Tana stopped in her tracks. Oh, dear God, that's what Coconino meant, isn't it? she demanded of her own deity. There was peace in the cave—*pax.* The Pax, housed in a cave, on Earth! A perfect nonpolitical headquarters for the Pax Circumfra and a guaranteed protectorate for Earth! ''Teeg!'' she called out in excitement. ''Get me a comm link to my father, and get it now!''

It was late July when Phoenix and Coconino reached the sea of grass that they had to cross to reach the southern village. Rain clouds were building in the southeast as they left the last ridge of hills and waded into the waving tufts of vegetation. ''I do not like this place,'' Coconino grumbled. ''It always makes me feel there is a monster at my back.''

''I know what you mean,'' Phoenix agreed, for while her

agoraphobia was not as profound as his, she did not like to be far from the comforting presence of mountains and cliffs and trees. "But we can't go back. The southern village is the only place for us now. They'll know me, but it's quite possible that they won't recognize you. You have no relatives here except your children who have never seen you."

Coconino wondered about his old uncle Three-Legged Coyote, who had told all the embarrassing stories about him that were part of the lore of the southern village. Did Phoenix not remember he was there? But the Witch Woman charged on with her logic. "Most of the older people who knew you as a young man have died," she pointed out. "Those who did know you certainly won't expect to see you as an old man. Nina and I managed to convince them all that you would come again just as you left."

They had taken their time traveling, stopping to make snares and throwing sticks, since both had left their bows behind. Phoenix had her knife, which was ever upon her person, but Coconino had left his behind at Tana's urging, afraid to bring any implement from the future. So they had stayed for many days in the Valley of the People, provisioning themselves and planning their future and catching up on their divergent pasts.

"*Two* wives?" Phoenix had hooted when he had told her about Hummingbird and her sister, Ironwood Blossom. "But why should that surprise me when you had children here by three different women in one summer? You are greedy, Coconino."

"I had need of much comfort," he had protested, "when I was torn so cruelly from you. Even two wives could not take the place of one Witch Woman." But his expression grew soft then as he remembered the two. "I did grow to love them, though. Each differently, and neither in the way that I loved you." He chewed thoughtfully upon a gristly piece of rabbit from the stew she had prepared. "Where did you learn to cook, woman?" he complained.

"From you," she shot back.

"Oh, yes." He sighed. "I have been pampered too long. I will have to learn once more to eat tough meat and quail with feathers still on it."

She swung at him, and he caught her wrist, laughing. Then she launched herself at him and toppled him over backward on the floor of the adobe house they were occupying at the time. "Stop!" he protested through his laughter. "I am an old man; you will break my bones!"

She had lain still then, her body pressed against his, head resting on his chest. How sweet to be here once more, and this time with no reason to fear the fire all too easily kindled between them, the coming together this simple touching could lead to.

"Coconino?" she ventured softly. "Thank you for telling me. About your wives. About the fact that you loved them."

"I will not be untruthful with you," he told her, stroking her back with a callused hand. "There are things in my life I am ashamed to speak of, but loving my wives is not one of them. Nor carrying you in my heart for forty years."

Her fingers twined in his hair, coarse and tousled as it had always been. "Your wait was longer than mine," she realized, seeing the strands more gray than black now.

"But not as lonely."

No, not as lonely, she thought. But for a long time I had the hope of your return; you had no reason to think you would ever see me again.

Now, as they entered the sea of grass, Phoenix marveled once more at the impossible events that had brought him back to her when she had finally given up waiting and had brought him not as a young and beautiful boy but as a seasoned and chastened man whose years numbered more than her own. He loved her, it seemed, with no less passion but a great deal more patience.

And he is still beautiful, she thought, gazing fondly on the craggy face with its brows slightly knit in distaste at crossing this open area.

"Nakha-a will know me," Coconino said to her, leading the way in his haste to be quit of this terrain.

"Most likely," she agreed, content to follow for a change. "But he is as prudent as he is perceptive. He will not give you away." They skirted a sizable cholla. "Sky Dancer may recognize you, too," she added. "She knew Michael well, and he resembles you very closely."

"Hrmph," he grunted, eyes searching the ground at his feet for any holes or obstacles hidden by the tall grass. "And did you not say Michael visited this southern village? Will they not remember his face as well?"

"But that was a young face," Phoenix pointed out. "Yours is an old one. We could tell them you are some relative—they will never know."

Coconino grunted again. Then suddenly the darkness lifted from his face, and a twinkle came into his eye. He slowed his steps to walk beside Phoenix instead of in front of her, and he looked down at her with a curious expression. "Do you remember my old uncle, Three-Legged Coyote?"

"Of course," she replied. "It has not been so long for me as it has been for you. He lived in my village until the Mother Earth called him; that was before Sky Dancer left, so—maybe seven years ago, maybe eight." She eyed Coconino critically. "You do look a little like him," she had to admit. "Not a great deal, and you are too young, but . . ."

"Time clouds the memory," he said. "So does the Mother Earth, if she wishes. It may be enough."

Phoenix looked at the strong straight body beside her. "Is that it, then?" she asked. "Shall I learn to call you Three-Legged Coyote?"

"I may limp like one before this journey is through," he grumbled, steering around a fallen yucca. Still the strange expression lit his face, a wicked smile just beneath the surface of it. There was some private joke here that Phoenix did not understand.

"What's so funny?" she demanded finally.

The smile broke through. "Did you know my old uncle was a great storyteller?" he asked her.

"Three-Legged Coyote?" She snorted. "Not that I noticed. I wouldn't say he was a great anything. Rather nondescript, really."

"He will be a great storyteller now," Coconino assured her. "Generations from now his stories will still be told around the campfires of the southern village. They will remind people that when Coconino walked among them, he was only a man—and sometimes a very foolish one."

And suddenly Coconino threw back his head and laughed.

EPILOGUE

The dogs began to bark furiously, and Spreading Vine looked up from his work. Leaning on his hoe, he watched as two strangers appeared on a hillock beside the field, wearing strange tight-fitting garments that looked too warm for the late summer weather here in the lowlands. But they would not stay in the fields long; no, when visitors came, they always wanted to go up into the mountains to see the Village of the People, to climb to Father Nakha-a's Thinking Place, and to gaze out upon the rock formation called Coconino's Head.

Spreading Vine signaled to his daughter, Dry Leaf, who was working nearby. With a broad smile she jumped up from where she was gathering up some late yellow squash and ran lightly across the field to where she had tethered her dun-colored pony. She would ride up to the village and tell them that guests had arrived, and the People would make a feast. It was no trouble to do so, for visitors never came in lean times—Walks with Caution saw to that. Also, they never came empty-handed: a basket of fruit or bread or some other wholesome food always filled their hands. But they would not take anything away with them. "No, no," they said. "It is enough to have been here, to have listened to your stories and looked upon Coconino's Head. We take only memories with us—they are our greatest treasure."

At first it had made the People sad that these visitors would take no gifts from them, for the People were gracious and generous by nature. But then Walks with Caution had come to them and explained that what was a simple gift to them was a thing of too much pride among the Sisters of the Mother Earth. For one person to have it would set him farther above his companions than was good for him to be set, and so the People should

358

confine their hospitality to what was consumed there in the village and the mountains.

So now Spreading Vine and others who spoke the language of the Others were content to tell their guests stories about Coconino and to take them on the long climb to Father Nakha-a's Thinking Place, from which they could see the great man's profile in the folds of the earth. Spreading Vine had known Coconino when he was a boy, before his family had come to the south, and to him the likeness in the mountain ridge was remarkable. "I never saw him lying down so," he admitted to guests. "He was always striding about the village, tall and strong, meeting with his Council, teaching the young hunters. I never saw him rest on his back. Perhaps that is why the Mother Earth finally gave him this place."

"Was he a great warrior, this Earth Saver?" guests often asked.

"He was only a hunter and a storyteller," Spreading Vine would reply, for that was what was always said in the stories of Three-Legged Coyote. "But the Mother Earth used him for many great deeds, and he saved her not once but twice." Then he, too, would look out at the strong brow, the jutting nose, and feel a sense of pride rushing up from his toes to his scalp. "He was her favorite son."

Tana left her office in the depths of the Carlsbad Caverns and walked through dimly lit passageways toward the warp depot, Doc padding ahead of her. Walking was easier for her now than it had been in thirty years, thanks to a sophisticated new walking harness she had begun wearing. It was invisible to the eye, a network of tiny fibers encasing her like a body stocking and amplifying the movement of her own muscles. It would not ward off a seizure, but it made the stresses and strains of everyday living so much easier to bear. She liked the name the People had given her, though: Walks with Caution. She liked to think it was simply more metaphorical now than it had originally been.

Glancing at her wrist chrono, she was glad to see that she had gotten out in plenty of time; she could take her time strolling through the fairyland in which the Pax Circumfra had located its headquarters on Earth. The limestone and crystal formations were breathtaking, and construction had been confined to those areas already modified in pre-Evacuation building. This made for a hodgepodge of offices—one here, two there, another suite some three hundred feet below—but the very atmosphere of this

place bred the peace of which Coconino had spoken as he had
left her ten years before. Tana was glad she had taken the offer
to become the Pax's special liaison for Terran cultures. Long
before the first construction crew had arrived via the institute's
P-TUP prototype, Tana had set up the ground rules for habitation of this place and for contact with the native population.

Doc grunted as he climbed up onto the platform of the warp
chamber beside her. His muzzle was somewhat grizzled these
days, but he was only eighteen and had a good seven to ten years
left in him. Tana tried not to think about what would happen
then. Instead she turned her mind to happier thoughts—her father's retirement party this evening. When Tana had announced
her resignation as CEO of the institute eight years before, Zim
had grumped and harrumphed and looked at the weak field of
successors, then finally asked Monti if he would consider coming back.

Tired of planet hopping with the Pax, Monti had been delighted to settle back in at his old job. He did not, however, run
it as the tough-minded conservative Zim had hoped he was getting; instead, he continued to push Tana's program of ground-
breaking research regardless of the monetary expense. Prototype
warp detection monitors had been tested in Earth's orbit before
his first year was up, and before the second year was out he had
put Todd Chang in charge of a group that refined the monitors
while Paul assembled a new team to begin work on a P-TUP
blocking device. By the time Wolfgang Montag began to market
P-TUP commercially, safeguards against its abuse were available as well.

But now with Paul's project making great progress and young
Palermo Goetz groomed for the CEO-ship, Monti was retiring
once again. Paul was giving the keynote speech at the din-
ner/reception tonight, which was sure to attract a huge crowd
even from the technical personnel as well as Dynasty members.
Not only was Paul well liked by the staff at the institute, he now
held a total of seven VanKurtz Prizes, more than any other living
scientist. Even Lystra was impressed.

Lystra had her own plans, of course. As Tana arrived at *Terra
Firma* to prepare for the party, she wondered if she should call
her daughter at school and remind her. But no, Lystra never
forgot anything. Not even when she was deep in the midst of
her research, like her father. Ten years had made the girl much
less cynical but no less single-minded; she had chosen her cru-
sade, as Paul had once predicted. Lystra had decided it was up

to her to find a cure for Gamaean palsy, and so she was now pursuing doctoral research in microbiology at the Omniversity.

Well, Tana thought as she stepped out of the warp chamber in the hangar, I hope she's not too disappointed if she doesn't find the cure in my lifetime. She may be another Chelsea Winthrop, whose fate it is to set the goal and build up momentum, while to another falls the task of getting the job done.

Doc's ears pricked up as they approached the door to the outside. *Children,* he identified. *Coming here, running fast.*

Indeed, they had hardly stepped out into the late afternoon sunlight when Dakota's three oldest children came pelting across the yard from their house, the one that had belonged to Uncle Paris. "Aunt Tana, Aunt Tana!" they shrieked, as three-, six-, and eight-year-old swarmed around her. "Dad says come down to the east pasture as soon as you get home! Uncle Paul is there, too."

Behind them, Mouse came out of the house carrying the baby on her hip. "Don't you kids give away your dad's secret!" she called in a warning tone. "Now, back in the house! Every one of you has chores to do before Great-Gram comes to stay with you tonight."

Tana smiled after them as they trudged off, moaning and complaining about grass to clip, disposals to run, dish cleansers to empty and load. Winthrops they might be, and heirs to a fortune, but as long as Mouse was their mother, not a one of them would grow up pampered and spoiled.

Turning her steps toward the east, Tana soon saw what Paul and Dakota were watching. After numerous experiments with the incredibly long-gestated celux, Dak had finally produced a calf this year that gave promise of evincing characteristics of the legendary Tala. It was there in the pasture with its host mother, eating the thistly sgorf grass and frisking hither and yon. It was an ungainly looking creature, all long, thick legs and deep barrel chest, the tiny nub of its first horn protruding on the crown of its head just above the slightly telescoped eyes. To Tana, raised with horses as the ideal of beauty, this bulky, hollow-boned creature was ugly.

Both men looked up grinning as she and Doc approached. "How was work?" Paul asked.

"Still having fun," she replied. "The kids said you have some kind of secret, Dak."

Her brother's eyes sparkled. He was beginning to look his age, with fine lines creasing his eyes and mouth, but he still had that mischievous, boyish Winthrop smile. "Watch this," he gloated. Lifting two fingers to his lips, he emitted a sharp, piercing whistle.

The gawky calf jerked its head up, startled. Its eyes rolled, and it bolted across the pasture, hooves tearing up clods of dirt as it went. Tana had seen the calf playing a hundred times before; it always put on that quick burst of speed, bunched its muscles, then leapt and kicked like a frisky colt or young bovine. Sometimes it even unsheathed its awkward wings and flapped them around uselessly.

But today was different, and Tana sensed it from the first quick sprint across the pasture. The calf ran with a purpose in mind, an intent. With a snap, its leathery wings sprang forth from their hiding place and stretched out on the prairie wind. There was no frantic beating, just long powerful strokes of wings grown longer and wider than the last time Tana had watched. Her heart caught in her throat as the increased power of the calf began to tell. Then, with a powerful thrust of its muscular hindquarters, the young animal drew up its legs and soared into the sky.

Science Fiction

at its best
from
Tara K. Harper